MY Heart & OTHER BREAKABLES

Alex Barclay lives in County Cork, Ireland. She is the award-winning author of several bestselling crime novels for adults. *My Heart & Other Breakables* is her first book for 11+ readers.

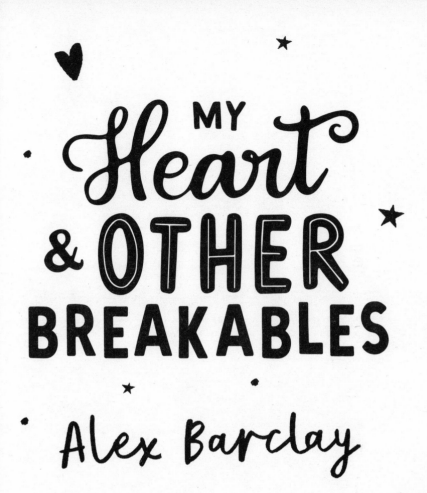

MY Heart
& OTHER
BREAKABLES

Alex Barclay

HarperCollins *Children's Books*

First published in the United Kingdom by
HarperCollins *Children's Books* in 2022
This edition published in 2023
HarperCollins *Children's Books* is a division of HarperCollins*Publishers* Ltd,
1 London Bridge Street
London SE1 9GF

www.harpercollins.co.uk

HarperCollins*Publishers*
Macken House, 39/40 Mayor Street Upper
Dublin 1, D01 C9W8 Ireland

2

ISBN 978-0-00-829520-2

Alex Barclay asserts the moral right to be identified as the author of this work

A CIP catalogue record for this title is available from the British Library

Typeset in Profile Pro 12/24

Printed and bound in the UK using 100% renewable electricity at CPI Group (UK) Ltd

**TO THE TALENTED, JOYFUL
AND BELOVED LILY CONLON**

THIS DIARY BELONGS TO

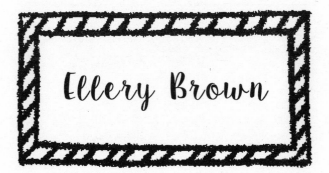

Ellery Brown

1 January (FRIDAY)

'The End' were the last two words my mother typed before she died. They were her favourite. Mine too. 'The End' meant she had finished another book. 'The End' meant she had time for me.

Except this time.

Sorry. I forgot: Dear Diary.

4 February (THURSDAY)

Dear Diary

5 February (FRIDAY)

Dear Diary

6 February (SATURDAY)

Meg tells me the Dear Diary thing is the problem. She says I have to write like I'm writing to the friend who doesn't judge. I'd love to say Meg is the friend who doesn't judge, but she respects honesty. And it's not that she's judgey – she's just real. And has lots of 'views'. Like this one on my first diary entry: 'That is literally the most depressing opening to anything I've ever read in my entire life.'

And she would know. Meg's the reader. She's super smart. She's scary too. But just to other people. She reads and reads and reads, and I know nothing, and she knows EVERYTHING. I said that to her once, and she said, 'Yeah, but you travel the world. I'm just a stay-at-home savant.'

Anyway.

'Introduce yourself to your non-judgemental friend,' she said. I'm **Ellery Brown**. I'm fifteen years old – soon to be sixteen. I have long brown hair and green eyes. I'm five feet six and a half. I am a lover of clothing. And a passionate watcher of Netflix. I have no brothers and no sisters. My grandparents are Max and Lola. They live in Rhinebeck, New York. My aunt is Auntie Elaine. She lives in hotel rooms. I was born in New York, but for the past four years I've lived with my mom in Eyeries village on the Beara Peninsula. In south-west Cork. On the Wild Atlantic Way. In Ireland.

'Don't just write a LIST OF FACTS!' says Megser when I read her my amazing introduction. 'Write about your FEELINGS. Diaries are about *FEELINGS.'* I *FEEL* that I should have given this diary to Meg.

7 February (SUNDAY)

Why I couldn't give this diary to Meg: it was a gift from my Auntie Elaine. She's my mom's sister. Mom died last November.

Why I can't write about feelings: see above.

8 February (MONDAY)

'Then don't write about feelings,' says Meg. 'Just . . . be yourself.'

SERIAL KILLERS
ARE BEING THEMSELVES.

9 February (TUESDAY)

I don't write – that's the other problem. My mom was a writer. I feel like everything I write should be **BRILLIANT**. I'm imagining my mom looking down on me going, 'Jesus (literally: she could be talking to him), has she learned ANYTHING?'

So, Mom . . . if you're up there . . . and are able to make out my writing . . . sorry in advance for any grammatical errors/disturbing revelations. One thing: I know you hate swearing, but it's going to be unavoidable at times. How I'll deal with this is not by using asterisks because they're like stars and we both love **stars** too much. And I'm not into writing loads of different symbols, so I'm using these little guys: &&&& because they kind of look like someone shaking their fist.

10 February (WEDNESDAY)

'&&&&'S SAKE!' says Meg.

'AMPERSANDS! JESUS.'

I'm confused about whether to replace 'Jesus' with

ampersands there. Because, unlike Mom, Megan is definitely not talking to Jesus. Not just because she's not dead, but because she doesn't believe in him, which I thought would be really awkward when I asked her the question: 'So, where do you think my mom is now?'

But no! Megser goes: 'Your mom is in Shakespeare & Co., Paris, hovering like a fairy in the dust motes, and if you're a customer, standing there flipping through the pages of a book, and you find a sentence that is so beautiful it's painful and you have to raise your eyes to a source that is bigger than your tiny human mind, you will catch her there, glinting. But not like a wispy kind of fairy – she is glinting like steel, like an ad for an advanced razor. Like if fairies were Avengers.'

I SWEAR TO GOD,

Megser believes in *fairies*. Anyway, that answer was pretty cool.

11 February (THURSDAY)

So, I live in a bird's nest. This drives Meg nuts when I say it. Okay . . .

it's a house, but my living arrangement is called bird nesting. It's the new divorce trend, where the kids stay in the house and the parents take turns living there, like, one week on, one week off, so the kids don't have to keep moving around. Because my family lives in America and I'm still in school here, they decided that I would stay here, and Grandpa and Lola, and Auntie Elaine would do pretty much a month here at a time.

Auntie Elaine is here now. She's so kind. She gave me you, Non-Judgemental Friend, because I think you are meant to be therapy. I think I am meant to fill you with thoughts about my mom.

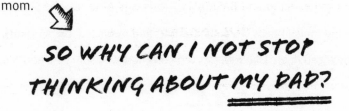

SO WHY CAN I NOT STOP THINKING ABOUT MY DAD?

Especially because it is so weird to think about someone you don't know.

LIKE, LITERALLY, I HAVE NO IDEA WHO MY DAD IS.

12 February (FRIDAY)
• ♡ • ♡ • ♡ • ♡ • ♡ •

First day of mid-term break! Megser and I go to the community school at the edge of town – Castletownbere (rhymes with 'hair'). We're in fourth year – Transition Year. TY is where you legitimately get to do the least possible academic work of your entire school life but still make a huge effort to do even less. Which is REALLY helped by how beautiful it is when you're staring out the window. The view from most of the classrooms is across the sea to Bere Island and there's this cool lighthouse on the headland and BASICALLY if this was America, the school would have been **BULLDOZED** and replaced by a luxury hotel/gated community. It's amazing it's not some celebrity's European hideaway where no one would bother them because that's not what Irish people do. And especially not Beara people. If you're a celebrity and you come to Beara, which they do (but you probably won't know until they're gone), you'll be treated EXACTLY like the regular human being you've forgotten you are. You do NOT want to come here if fame has changed you. They will cut you down with some razor-sharp Beara wit (but you probably won't realise until they're gone).

Our school is mixed. And here's what you need to know about

Beara boys. Firstly they're not called boys: they're lads.

And I'm not joking — they are almost **ALL FIT.**

But accidentally fit from hauling things around the place, like boxes or sheep. Oh, and playing football. I forgot sport. But I reject sport and all its works.

It's Gaelic football they play. But it's just called Gaelic OR football. It's like soccer, except you can run with the ball. It's big in Ireland, and HUGE down here. There's a school team, a town team, a county team – Juniors, Seniors, Under-Whatevers. And people are **OBSESSED**. Like people want to watch these games and they really care about the result. Imagine gladiators in ancient Rome. That's people's parents on the sidelines of Gaelic matches.

And whichever team wins, the supporters drive around the place honking horns and shouting out the window and scaring visitors to the area who are like, *WHAT IS THE EMERGENCY? And are these people causing it or rescuing me from it?*

The captain of the boys' football team is Silent Johnny. In Wild Guess Challenge I call him that because . . .

'Allow silence,' is what Mom used to say to me, which seemed really profound and spiritual, until I realised it was her way of getting me to shut up so she could work. Admittedly I STRUGGLE with silence, in that I rush to fill silences like a river rushes to the sea but as if only the river has been struck by a raging storm and it's all wild and splashing up over the banks but the sea is all calm and

GET OFF ME LEAVE ME ALONE.

I don't go near the calm sea that is Silent Johnny, though. Actually he's not the sea – he's the dam built to block you from hitting the sea. He's this blond, massive, muscular, chiselled dam.

He is – objectively – ridiculously hot.

13 February (SATURDAY)

Mom **LOVED** Megan. They used to talk about books. And Megser wants to be a writer. I think Megan was the daughter Mom never had. Megan says I'm the daughter her mom never had, because I like make-up and shoes and 'glamour', and Meg would rather 'stand in line at a reality star's book signing' than wear make-up/dresses/skirts/heels/anything involving sheen/

gloss/shimmer. It's not like Megser's mom goes around like that all the time either, but when Susan does go out (with the girls, once a month), she goes ALL OUT. I do her make-up. Meg is always horrified. 'And Mam sells her soul once more.' Then, when she's gone, she'll say, 'Thanks. Mam looks beautiful. She's delighted with herself. She'll have a ball now.'

SADNESS: Susan is a widow, and she isn't even forty. Megan's dad died when she was eleven. He was so shy, and so sweet, and Susan and him were *madly in love.* Susan is **AWESOME**. After Meg's dad died, she studied law at night, and became a lawyer while looking after THREE CHILDREN UNDER TWELVE. The other two are Megser's little brothers – I call them The Ferals. But not out loud. The Elder Feral is eleven, and the Younger Feral is nine. They were only small when their dad died, and they used to go everywhere with him. And then . . . I don't know what to say. But it sucks. And I think it's the widely accepted excuse for why they are little *&&&&S.*

So, my mom wrote popular fiction. 'Whatever that is,' she used to say. Her first two books were fantasy but no one really bought them. Her first popular fiction book made her a UK, Ireland, European, Commonwealth (no idea) number-one bestseller.

'Not the US, though! You'll have to leave something for the rest of us!' Lola said at the time. Auntie Elaine told me this one night when she was on her nth glass of wine. (She calls every glass of wine she's drinking her nth, which I love.)

'"Us" was not what Lola meant, of course,' said Auntie Elaine. '"ME" is what Lola means . . . always. And actually what she meant by "leave something for the rest of us!" was "I am the American success story in this family. Let ME have ME."'

Lola was a massive soap actress in the US in the seventies and eighties. Like **SUPER FAMOUS.** And then: 'My whole world – bam! Gone! Over!' Yup – she got pregnant. With my Inconvenient Mom. Followed by my Dreamwrecker Auntie Elaine. And, yes, Lola says these things out loud. And SERIOUSLY – she still worked after they were born! But there's no point saying anything because everyone just accepts that Lola is dramatic.

Lola is seventy-four and still *wildly glamorous.* Willowy, silver-blonde, yoga-fit. If she's had work done, it's also an American success story.

In the spirit of opposites attract Grandpa Max is ADORABLE. He is *totally in love* with – and terrified of – Don't-Call-Me-Grandma Lola. They're married fifty years this year. Grandpa is this big plaid-shirt-wearing cowboy kind of guy. From Montana. He's got this big head of white hair, and big hands, and a big smile for someone who's abused on an hourly basis. He's like a Labrador who keeps coming back to the owner who hits him on the nose with a folded-up newspaper.

One day, when I was about five, Lola had to go to an audition, so I got to hang out with Grandpa at the tennis club.

'Look! It's Grandma!' he said, and he pointed across the court. It was one of those machines that rapid-fires tennis balls.

Lola loves Grandpa ... in her own way. I've spent a lot of time with them. Every summer Mom would come to Ireland to write, and I would stay with Grandpa and Lola in New York.

Me and Grandpa are BEST pals. Lola introduced me to mirrors, clothing, make-up, fashion magazines, beauty salons and juices. Grandpa introduced me to mud, horses, card games, *The Hardy Boys/Nancy Drew Mysteries*, *Murder She Wrote*, *Quincy* and *Columbo*. Or as I used to call them: 'faded television shows'. I said that to Grandpa once when I was about nine: **'WHY ARE DETECTIVE SHOWS ALL FADED?'** and he loved it so much he told all his friends. MOST of those shows are ancient. *Columbo* is definitely the most famous ... He's this dishevelled-looking detective in a trench coat who always lures the killer into a false sense of security by acting all confused, while sneakily pumping them for info, and then – BAM – just when they think he's about to wander off and be harmless some place else, he says: 'ONE MORE THING . . .' Which really means: you'll never wear shoes with laces in them

EVER AGAIN.

xoxo

14 February (SUNDAY)
• ♡ • ♡ • ♡ • ♡ • ♡ •

Does NOBODY get that if they hate Valentine's Day they're actually NOT being different? EVERYONE hates Valentine's Day. The lads all go: 'I don't want to be told I have to be romantic on a particular date.' No – you just don't want to BE romantic. On any date. Even on an actual date.

I Love Valentine's day.

What's wrong with someone sending you something nice and telling you they like you? That's all. I'm not OBSESSED – it's not like my mom had to send me Valentine's cards so I wouldn't throw myself off a cliff.

4.30 p.m. update

Auntie Elaine sent me a Valentine's card and – PARADOXICALLY –
I WANT TO THROW MYSELF OFF A CLIFF.

'What makes you think it's from Elaine?' says Meg. We're sitting on my stairs.

'Well, who ELSE could it be from?' I say.

'Duuuuh, OBVIOUSLY Oscar,' she says. And flashes a last-minute smile.

'Whuttt?' I say. Oscar is from our year. He is short, skinny, has brown hair, freckles, glasses, and looks like he's from a BBC adaptation of a Charles Dickens novel during which I would call Meg, get no answer, check the TV listings and know why.

Oscar often can be seen clutching books . . . which should really make him Megser's type, but nooo. So no. Megser does NOT approve. And I know that shouldn't matter, but it DOES.

'If I ever get married, the guy is going to have to ask *you* for my hand,' I say to Megser.

'If it's Oscar,' she says, 'I'd give him my own hand. Severed. To scare him off.'

'You're just used to Oscar,' I say . 'You've known him since you were five years old. He's like another annoying brother.' I didn't mean to say *another*.

'It doesn't matter what I think about him,' says Megser. 'YOU like him. He sent YOU the Valentine's card. This should be EXCITING.'

'Except you don't APPROVE!'

'OHMYGOD,' says Megser. 'Don't EVER need anyone to approve of ANYTHING.'

'But it's YOU!'

'I don't CARE!'

We talk like this sometimes. It sounds worse than it is.

'GIRLS!' said Auntie Elaine, coming out into the hall. 'Are

you fighting?'

See?

'We do not fight,' we both said at the same time.

Then Megser just asks her straight out: 'Auntie Elaine – did you send Ellery the Valentine's card?'

'What? No!' says Auntie Elaine. 'Why would I do that? That would imply I don't have faith in Ellery LEGITIMATELY having an admirer.'

'GRANDPA got you to do it,' I say just to give her an out.

'There is no way Grandpa would do that,' says Auntie Elaine. 'For exactly the same reason I didn't.'

'LOLA then,' I say.

And we both kind of **LOCK EYES.**

And Auntie Elaine goes: 'I know grief can change people but . . .'

'It's from Oscar,' says Megser.

And Auntie Elaine side eyes her. 'The fake guy?'

'He is NOT FAKE!' I'm saying. 'And WHY do you think that?'

'You know the way there are ghostwriters?' she says. 'I think Oscar is a ghostREADER. I mean, he looks the part. But . . . if he read that much, shouldn't he be a bit . . . sharper?'

And I'm just shaking my head, which is what I do when

Megser is **_VICIOUS._**

'The truth can be vicious,' says Megser, because she knows that about me.

'Okay – you have FORCED MY HAND!' I say. And then I go upstairs, and I bring down the letter Oscar sent me after Mom died, which was SO kind, and beautiful, and thoughtful and even though he made me promise to NEVER, EVER tell anyone about it, I hand it to them and make THEM promise to never, ever tell anyone about it, and unlike me to actually STICK to their promise. (I would never have done this if it wasn't to DEFEND OSCAR'S HONOUR in the eyes of two of the most important people in my world, who/whom I trust one hundred per cent/in who/whom I have one hundred per cent trust.)

THE LETTER:

When someone is lost to you, grief will find them, carrying them to you in a memory like a pearl from an ocean floor. You may not see this for the gift it is. But to honour grief, to honour love, is to take each memory in the shell of you, and let the beauty of then shine through the tears of now.

Oscar. . .

'Gosh,' says Auntie Elaine. 'That was beautiful. And very mature for sixteen. Sorry, Megser – that's a bright kid.'

'Okay . . . okay,' says Megsers. 'FINE.'

She won't say sorry, though. Because Megser is the WORLD'S WORST APOLOGISER even when she feels she should be apologising. I think it's because she is so used to being right. Seriously. Megser is hardly ever wrong. And that's why I can hardly ever make a decision without her.

Anyway, when Auntie Elaine is gone, Megser asks me how could I be so sad when it's SAINT ELLERY'S DAY.

'Just,' I say, 'you know when people feel sorry for you?'

'UNDER NO CIRCUMSTANCES.'

'Your dad died – you DO know. Everyone's looking at you like you might BREAK. Or, like, they're running ahead of you with one of those blue pharmacy rolls of cotton wool, and they're unfurling it like a red carpet, but they're wrapping it all around you too, and it's getting in your eyes, and your throat, and up your nose.'

'People who love you can be AWFUL,' she says.

15 February (MONDAY)

* ★ * ★ * ★ * ★ * ★ * ★ * ★ *

THINGS I AM GRATEFUL FOR:

1. My family
2. Megser
3. ALL my friends
4. My horses in Rhinebeck: Lumbo and Twister
5. Stars (the ones in the sky)
6. Netflix and All its Works

7. *Terrors* (my current sub-obsession of Netflix): a drama about high-school kids with special powers who are all about doing great things in the world, until . . . the special powers malfunction, and the kids slowly turn evil. It's not just the show, though, it's . . .

8. HUNTER THREAT (You've got to LOVE American names. Especially American actor names)

9. Clothing and All Its Works (minus: cold-shoulder tops, Capri pants, nude bodycon outerwear, sneakers encrusted with anything, peek-a-boo anything, asymmetrical anything, tops with random slogans just because they're in French. And Ellery says NO to: crushing velvet, boiling wool, dropping waists, dipping hems.
So MAYBE: Clothing and SOME of Its Works).

10. Burritos

Hunter Threat is the Oscar of *Terrors* – the quiet nerd/book clutcher who says meaningful things that Meg pays close attention to, but I don't, because:

⭐ **HIS EYES:** the colour of Head & Shoulders shampoo (I knowww, but they ARE!)

⭐ **HIS HAIR:** like a day at the beach (in that it is the colour of sand and shaped like the ice-cream part of an ice-cream cone, but not exactly because that would be weird)

⭐ **HIS CHEEKBONES:** like ROBOTS'

⭐ **HIS MOUTH:** like the ones you draw yourself, but using a ruler – because you can't draw, so both lips are the exact same size and shaped like a roof on top of an upside-down roof with angles that are completely perfect and unrealistic but not in his case.

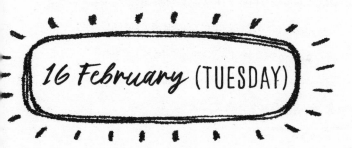

16 February (TUESDAY)

It's **PANCAKE TUESDAY,** which is one of my

TOP FIVE DAYS OF THE YEAR.

- **PANCAKE TIP #1:** avoid the first pancake. It is the temperature trial. It is the butter trial. No one gets either of these right first time.

- **PANCAKE TIP #2:** do NOT avoid ANY OTHER PANCAKE.

Mom was the source of these tips. She'd always eat the first pancake and say: 'Taking the hit, Ellery, taking the hit.' And then: 'There is NO END to a mother's love.'

And I know I'm not supposed to think this but it kind of feels like there IS. Because she's GONE. Sometimes I just sit here and try to sense her presence around me. And I don't know if the feeling I get in my heart is Mom loving me so hard to let me know she's not gone and that she's actually everywhere now. Or if what I'm feeling is just how much I love her.

2 a.m. update ᶻ ᶻ ᶻ ᶻ

When I was small Mom always read me stories. And obviously she would also make stories up too. And you know when you're small and you think everyone else's life is the same as yours? When I started school I couldn't understand how other kids had either no stories in their lives or only bedtime stories. I had breakfast stories, lunchtime stories, dinnertime stories, dentist's-waiting-room stories, stuck-in-traffic stories, make-them-up-silently-and-keep-them-to-yourself stories ...

Anyway, one night, when I was about seven, after a bedtime story, I said, 'Mom – where does my dad live?'

And Mom thought about it for a really long time and said: 'In the woods.'

So I went into school and told everyone my dad lived in the woods, which seemed legitimate because of all the *fairy tales*, and everyone laughed at me. I mean, it wasn't like I said my dad lived in a gingerbread house. But I think the problem was that I didn't mention ANY building ... because Mom didn't. So when I got home I was SO MAD at her and I said: 'You never SAID if it was a cabin, a house, a cottage or ANYTHING!' and that she HAD to tell me so I could tell everyone in school the next day.

And she said: 'You don't owe ANYONE an explanation.' And then I asked her if she was just lying about the in-the-woods thing. And she looked at me and said: 'I PROMISE you, I am not lying.' And I was going to ask her more about my dad, but I always felt like that just made her sad.

But when I was walking off I couldn't help it. 'Is it a TENT? Does he live in a tent?'

And Mom laughed out loud, and she looks at me. 'Do

you think maybe that's where your love of camping comes from?' Because even though I was only seven, we'd already had a camping situation where I was unhappy with the living conditions.

Mom reassured me that my dad did not live in a tent and that he never had. And that was a HUGE relief.

MY IDEAL DAD: kind, fun, happy, creative, gets me and Megsers and our weirdness, is chill, takes care of things, loves pancakes, cooks pancakes, isn't into rules but has some kind of boundaries so I don't go *TOO WILD* and end up on a reality show and losing Megser for ever.

Oh, and has a GREAT EXPLANATION for where he's been

FOR THE PAST FIFTEEN YEARS.

18 February (THURSDAY)

I use LOTS of Irish phrases and, in particular, Cork ones; not that I EXACTLY know which is which. Some could be CORK IN GENERAL or IRISH IN GENERAL or just BEARA. Lola gets so confused here. She has zero ability to work out what something means using the context of a sentence. But IN FAIRNESS they're not all obvious.

RANDOM LIST:

★ **GRAND OUT**: great

★ **FLYING**: great

★ **MOTORING**: great

★ **HAPPY OUT**: happy

★ **FINE OUT**: fine

★ **SAVAGE**: awesome

★ **DOTE**: anyone — male or female — who's really kind

★ **PASTED**: drunk (there are at least THIRTEEN ALTERNATIVES, which could be because of what Meg calls, in her discussions on books, a 'recurring theme')

Also:

★ **IN A HEAP** (rhymes with 'GRAPE' . . . I knowww): hungover

★ **HANGING**: hungover

★ **SHOOK**: hungover

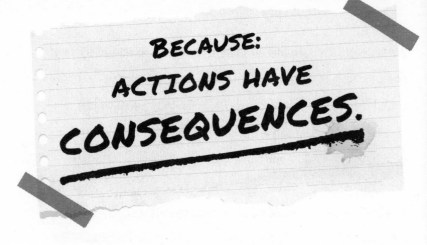

BECAUSE: ACTIONS HAVE CONSEQUENCES.

19 February (FRIDAY)

❀ • ❀ • ❀ • ❀ • ❀ •

Our school canteen is small and seats are at a premium. I always have one, because Meg is fast and loves soup. Today, though, she was stopped in her tracks by the girls' football coach to talk about her match on Sunday (Meg is the talkative Silent Johnny of the girls' football team), and I was left to fight my way to the front of the line, which for me means standing at the BACK OF THE LINE watching the soup run out. Next thing, I sense someone beside me and I do a quick glance and it's Oscar and I'm freaking out as if he DID send me the Valentine's card, which I KNOW he didn't. So I fling my head the other way and there's Silent Johnny and he looks down because he's, like, six feet two and gives me that upward nod of acknowledgement that the lads all

26

do. He's holding a folded up twenty-euro note in his big hand and scanning the counter.

'LITERALLY does any of the food here fill you up?' I say.

He gives me the same upward nod, so I think he's agreeing with me. His two friends are hovering by the wall watching his progress like he's buying lottery tickets in the last-minute window. He orders THREE ham and cheese rolls. And then he asks the lads what THEY want.

'I didn't think of the quantity option,' I say.

And he gives me a half-smile in fairness. But he's definitely feeling the pressure of talking. As far as I can tell, he only talks to the lads about sport or *Ear to the Ground* (a farming programme – highly respected).

'So, do you have a match tonight?' I say.

'No,' he says. And he walks off with ALL FIVE ROLLS in one hand.

I feel sorry for **beautiful** people sometimes. Because it can be all anyone sees. And maybe that makes beautiful people not bother developing any other skills, like . . . the ability to talk.

Megser and I went back to her house after school, which is what we do on Fridays. We allegedly babysit the Ferals, which involves letting them fight each other and destroy things while we roller-skate up and down the hall because they live in one of those really long Irish bungalows. Then when Susan comes home from work she makes us all dinner, and Megser and I go to her room to conduct our weekly sleep-deprivation experiment, which produces the same results every time: PEOPLE NEED SLEEP so they don't end up 'every Saturday like an antichrist' as Susan says to Megser.

20 February (SATURDAY)

'Here she is again,' says Susan this morning. 'Every Saturday like an antichrist.' And Megser goes: 'It's not like I'm a PRO-Christ any other day of the week.' Then the Elder Feral appears in the kitchen doorway doing this thing where he claps his hands, then rubs them together and lets us know how hungry he is by saying something like: 'I could eat the leg of the lamb of God.' I SWEAR he secretly hangs out with elderly farmers. Because there's also the sitting-down-expecting-his-meals-to-be-handed-up-to-him thing and the getting agitated when they're not. But in his defence, why wouldn't he expect something that happens ALL THE TIME?

Having your meals handed up to you by the woman of the house is the only element of outmoded oppression by the patriarchy that Megser goes silent on. Because: MEALS. And: NOT HAVING TO MAKE THEM YOURSELF.

After Megser's, I was meant to be doing something with Auntie Elaine but she had to work, so, instead, Susan took me, Meg and the Ferals to the cinema in Bantry (town: 58.7 km from here. I googled it). And SERIOUSLY it's the closest cinema. The Ferals slapped and elbowed each other through most of the movie. Megser and I moved seats. 'Not my circus, not my monkeys,' she says.

Susan followed not long after. 'MY circus, MY monkeys,' she says, sitting down beside me, 'but I HATE THE CIRCUS. And I definitely wouldn't be forking out FIFTY EUROS to watch—' And she glances at the Ferals.

And Megser goes: 'THOSE clowns?'

Then some random woman behind us leans in and says: 'You're just going to leave the lads there to cause a rack, are you?'

'Yes,' says Susan. 'Yes, I am. But that's the LAST time I'm taking THEM out to give the family a break. Their mother's in a psychiatric hospital.'

'Sure, is it any wonder?' the woman says, and she's patting Susan on the shoulder.

When I got home Auntie Elaine was asleep on the sofa. There was no sign of her laptop or any of her work stuff, and her eyes were all puffed up like she'd been punched. Punching without bruises. That's what I think grief is.

21 February (SUNDAY)

I don't usually see Meg on Sundays. They all go to her 'Nan' – Mrs Daly (first name unused). Mrs Daly is the **CRANKIEST WOMAN ALIVE.** If you can be a vicious mass-goer, that's what Mrs Daly is. And the weird thing is she *loves* me. She throws out these random compliments: 'There's a FIERCE SHINE off your hair, Ellery.' Then she uses her compliments to stealth-bomb Megser: 'You'd never see ELLERY going around with a FACE ON HER,' and: 'I'd say ELLERY always goes to bed at a reasonable hour.'

22 February (MONDAY)

My entire family is American. So I have an American accent. But I have an Irish accent mixed in. And, more specifically, a West Cork one. The Cork accent is so musical.

I LOVE, LOVE, LOVE it.

And it's contagious. There are people here from England, Holland, Germany, Poland, Lithuania, France, and they've got it too. You know the way there are mixers that go really well with lots of different drinks (I only know this from Lola)? Well, if accents were mixers, the Cork one is the best. It makes every other nationality sound friendly and on their way out for a drink.

The problem with my accent is, if you didn't know me, and you heard me for the first time, I represent what happens when you plonk your child in front of Nickelodeon and Disney. 'Plonk' means put something down like you don't care. I never heard that word in my life until I came to Ireland.

Obviously I don't know where the other side of my family comes from, which is **SO WEIRD.** I know I could ask Auntie Elaine about my dad, but I don't want her to think I'm looking for someone to replace Mom. As if anyone COULD.

But I'm FIFTY PER CENT someone else. That's a BIG MYSTERY per cent.

THINGS I WONDER ABOUT MY DAD:

- Does he know about me?
- Has he ever seen me?
- Do I look like him?
- Am I like him in any way?
- Would I like him?
- Would he like me?
- Where's he from?
- What would it be like meeting him?
- Do I actually want to meet him?
- Does he have other kids?
- What does he do?
- Is he famous?
- Is he responsible for these **AWESOME EYEBROWS?**

AND THE BAD ONES . . .

- Did he tell Mom to . . . Did he not want me?
- Does he have issues?
- Did he hate Mom?
- Did he and Mom break up because of me?

- Were they ever even together?
- Does he hate kids?

AND THE WORST ONES:

- What if it was . . . what if Mom just met him . . . like ONCE and doesn't really know who he is?

- ## IS THERE A **TERRIBLE** REASON WHY MOM NEVER TOLD ME WHO HE IS?

✳ 23 February (TUESDAY) ✳

RANDOM MUSINGS: Grandpa sees *beauty* in nature, in smiles, and in eyes. Lola sees beauty in bone structure, and bodies, in art, and in architecture, and in luxury items. I agree with both of them.

Mom saw beauty in words.

24 February (WEDNESDAY)

I do not get how people actively want to be mean. Like, HOW can it feel good?

SO, lunchtime, I'm coming out of the shop, and these two girls from second year are standing there, and I walk past them, and I hear one of them muttering something. So I go back and ask her to repeat it, and she's like, 'I just saaaid: Transformer.'

I'm like, 'Robots in disguise?'

And her friend laughs.

And the first girl goes, 'Nothing.'

And I'm like, 'What, though?'

And she says, 'You know . . . *Operation Transformation*.'

Operation Transformation is this TV show where people have to lose weight. What the actual?

'SERIOUSLY?' I say.

I realise then that Silent Johnny is hovering behind them, because we're blocking the footpath. He's heard it all. And I look at him, and say, '**WHAT IS WRONG WITH PEOPLE?**'

And he looks at the girls, and says, 'You'd want to grow up a small bit.'

He speaks. And his words are good. And it's Johnny.

And he's *HOT.* ⟵

So *DOUBLE-BURRRN.*

xox

26 February (FRIDAY)

'So,' says Meg,

'ARE YOU THE HERO IN YOUR STORY?'

I know where she's going, but I'm not sure I want to get on board.

'In your diary,' she says, 'are you writing only the things that make you look good? Like, is all the negative stuff "not in any mean way"?'

'I don't think so,' I say.

'You are God of all you write,' she says. 'And editor.' And this was her favourite realisation:

'YOU CAN BE FLAWLESS.'

And I'm like, 'I already am.' And she's saying, 'But you already are,' at the exact same time.

And we think we're **HILARIOUS.**

I a.m. update

THINGS I HAVE SAID TO MY MOTHER IN ANGER:

- Why are you always in my face?
- Why are you never around?
- I hate you.
- You hate me.
- No wonder you don't have a boyfriend.
- No wonder I don't have a boyfriend.
- All you care about is yourself.
- Why are you so obsessed with me?
- I am never talking to you again as long as I live.
- Get ... OUUUT.
- GO ... A ... WAY.
- LEAVE. ME. A. LONE.

Hmm ...

I think I prefer the hero thing.

2 March (TUESDAY)

Lola is arriving tomorrow. She and Auntie Elaine have taken to calling this The Changeover, like I'm the sheets in a B&B. They're meeting in Shannon Airport.

'I'll high-five her as I walk past,' says Auntie Elaine, and I'm not sure she's joking. Lola and Auntie Elaine have a fractious relationship. Grandpa and Lola have a fractious relationship. Lola and Mom had a fractious relationship. Common denom.: Lola.

You can trace Auntie Elaine's issues back to her christening. It was fine at the time but when Lois Elaine Brown started school and the other kids found out her full name they kept asking her where Superman was. Her second issue came later, and for YEARS all I knew was that she had arrived home from college one day and announced that 'Lois' was dead to her and she was ELAINE FROM NOW ON and that she would not stop correcting everyone until she **BROKE THEM.**

I finally found out why the name changed a few years ago in an accidental (I avoid drunk adults because you can end up knowing too much) eavesdropping situation feat. Mom and Auntie Elaine after nth glasses of something.

Mom goes: 'But I LIKE Lois, Elaine. I MISS Lois. You're a Lois, Elaine. You're a Lois.'

And Auntie Elaine was all 'STOP! Knives in my ears! STOP!' and 'You still don't get it, Laurie. You NEVER got it. I realised. You *know* this. We were ALL [like there are millions of them] given names beginning with L: Lois, Laurie . . . we are all just an EXTENSION of Lola: ONE LONG L. BROWN.'

AUNTIE ELAINE + ALCOHOL + LOLA = WORST COCKTAIL EVER

But the best bit was Mom GASPS and goes: 'Plot twist: LEX LUTHOR . . . our BROTHER? Could it BE?'

✳ 3 a.m. update ✳

Just: Auntie Elaine is leaving in the morning and I **HATE** goodbyes. Mom and I had way too many.

'Don't focus on the goodbyes,' Mom used to say. 'Focus only on the hellos.'

And I loved that. And it used to work. But now it's the middle of the night so all I'm thinking is GOODBYE, sleep. And HELLO to crying before school.

3 March (WEDNESDAY)

Auntie Elaine gives THE BEST HUGS.

'Stay strong, *beautiful* girl,' she says this morning. 'I love you to microparticles.'

'And *I love you* to nuclear matter,' I say. We've been saying this for years to each other and it automatically makes the goodbyes end in a smile, even though this time we're both taking these deep breaths and can't maintain eye contact.

But Auntie Elaine keeps it together and says: 'If you need me, you know where to find me.'

And I go, deadpan: 'JAIL.'

And she nods. 'And remember what I told you:

'I AM INNOCENT OF INSERT CRIME.'

And we laugh, and I wave and go off down the path then cry my eyes out as soon as I'm out of sight. THEN I had to go back to the house because I forgot my biology book but luckily Auntie

Elaine was in the shower so we didn't have to do that second goodbye weirdness. Then I realised the shower was on but Auntie Elaine was still messing with her phone in the bathroom trying to hook up the speaker. Next thing she just shouts at her phone: '&&&& YOU, BLUETOOTH!' and I can hear her sobbing. '&&&& you! Why do you ALWAYS get attached to the wrong thing?' And then she goes, 'WHY are you representative of my relationship with men?' because she was trying to make herself laugh, and that made me even sadder.

And then, in that pause before the speaker picks up, I hear her call out: 'Okaaay, Laurie – what's my SONNNG?'

What's My Sonnng? is this thing Mom came up with where, right before you turn on the radio, you say: 'What's my SONNNG?' and whatever song comes on next is your message. It can be so funny. And eerily relevant. But also: SO RISKY. And now I'm NERVOUS.

But there was no need to be.

Because this morning Auntie Elaine's message was:

♩ SHUT UP ♩ ♪ AND DANCE. ♫

2 a.m. update

Lola's flight was delayed, so I just hung around at Meg's after school, but then it was getting late and it was a school night so I was feeling awkward even though everyone was so nice. And NEXT THING Mrs Daly was in the living room. Seriously. That's how sudden it is. The front and back doors are always open in Megser's and Mrs Daly comes in unannounced like she's a health inspector. She could literally be sitting in a RANDOM ROOM in the DARK in her COAT for AGES before she'll let you know she's there. She just DOES THIS. It drives Susan insane but because she sometimes walks in to find Mrs Daly folding laundry or vacuuming, there's NOT A LOT SHE CAN DO ABOUT IT. The good thing about Mrs Daly's appearance tonight was that it meant Susan could drop me home – because she'd never leave just Megser in charge of the Ferals on a school night.

When we got to the house Susan came in for a little while, which was so sweet, but then I told her I was fine so she should go because it was late and I know how early she has to get up. She was insisting on staying so I just did all these fake yawns and told her I should probably go to bed, and that Lola would only be another two hours, and I could tell she didn't want to leave me on my own, but the yawns were getting embarrassing for both of us, so she did go but she made me PROMISE to call her if I needed ANYTHING.

And I was just nodding and trying not to cry.

Because the ONLY ANYTHING I need is Mom.

4 March (THURSDAY)

Oh my God — Lola has emptied the house of ALL FOOD that is not healthy. And what's worse is that Auntie Elaine had STOCKED the entire place before she left. And it is ALL GONE. There is no: pizza, ice cream, chocolate, biscuits, crisps, tortillas, sweets. Lots of: nuts, seeds, quinoa, powdered &&&&, buckwheat groats [no idea], lentils, psyllium husks [no idea], beans, wheatgrass (whyyy?), maca powder [no idea], vegan knock-offs. It literally feels like an army came in, overthrew the king and the kingdom is in ruins. And I'd save it, except I've no energy. Because there's **NO SUGAR.**

And I eat LOADS of healthy food, by the way. But I'm FIFTEEN. Junk food is my friend.

I am literally crying. And I know that's sad. Or a sugar withdrawal symptom. But still.

Then I go into the kitchen and do What's My SONNNG? It's 'A Church Is Burning'.

5 March (FRIDAY)

I told Lola at breakfast that I researched sugar withdrawal and it can cause depression. But Lola's a MARCHING ON person and a getting through the first days of things person. And it's feeling **HOPELESS** and I'm definitely LOOKING hopeless and she suggests THIS: 'Why don't you go for a walk?' And EVEN BETTER: 'Before school.'

And I'm just staring at her. SERIOUSLY: imagine traumatising someone with healthiness and then suggesting ANOTHER healthy thing to help the person get over it? That's like TOTALLY KICKING you when you're down. But kicking you into a YOGA POSITION.

Luckily, help is only hours away and comes in the form of the dedicated junk-food cabinet in Megser's kitchen, known as The Press (Irish for cabinet). We get access to The Press after dinner on Fridays when it is at maximum capacity because it's Susan's shopping day. So when you open the doors all these bags of tortilla chips or whatever THROW themselves into your arms in an act of desperation to escape their inhumane conditions and you feel SO GOOD because you're actually rescuing them.

6 *March* (SATURDAY)

Lola has this habit of fearing the worst. She keeps setting the alarm when she's leaving the house. And I told her the other day that Mom left the doors and windows open most of the time and I swear her eyes were saying, 'And look how that turned out.' Mom was NOT murdered by an intruder – it's just Lola is an expert in reacting to things facially in a way that creates intrigue for a soap-watching audience.

Today's drama that I discovered when I got back from Megser's was **A MAN IN THE BACK GARDEN.** Which – YES! – if it was *Legacy of Hate* starring Lola Del Monaco would be someone's evil twin bent on revenge. Not a neighbour dropping a package into the (unlocked!) shed because Lola hadn't heard the doorbell. She wanted me to print out a sign and put it in the front window saying **NO TRESPASSING.** I told her that would be the same as putting up a sign that said:

PARANOID NON-NATIONALS.

So I just explained to her that she is safe here. Men with chainsaws are from the council and they're trimming hedges. Flocks of sheep charging down the road in front of the house are not fleeing a natural disaster because they have a sixth sense.

'They're very free and easy, the Irish, aren't they?' said Lola. And that wasn't even about the 'trespassing' – it was later when she saw a woman at the shop with no make-up on.

After dinner this evening, Lola went to her room and came back with this big cloth tote from the bookstore in Rhinebeck. CONTEXT: when Lola comes over she usually brings me a big gift that she gives me at the start, but then she has all kinds of little gifts that she produces over the course of her stay and it is SO MUCH FUN. It could be anything – candy or a face mask or pyjamas or fluffy socks.

I just hope it's not ACTUALLY books.

You know that wallpaper that looks like bookshelves? Philistines' wallpaper, Meg calls it. Well, that's what our actual bookshelves look like to me. And they're in EVERY ROOM of the

45

house, apart from the bathrooms. Even the utility room has bookshelves.

'Before I give you the bag . . .' says Lola, and she hands me a page torn out of a magazine. 'Did you know Grandpa has a box of press clippings [no idea] of every single interview your mother gave over the years? Anyway, I found this before I left, and I thought it might make you smile.' And I'm thinking, ACTUALLY it's making me NERVOUS at the thought of what it might say.

And I'm like, CALM DOWN, ELLERY, and Lola lures me in with: 'She mentions *you* in it.' And I'm like, Whuttt? because Mom was super private in interviews, so she only ever talked about her writing or the world in general but never her personal life – even anything about her **AMAZING** daughter (!) other than to acknowledge that she had one. And I *LOVED* how she didn't talk about me in interviews. Because it made me A MYSTERY TO MANY.

'It's an interview about *Wildfire*,' says Lola.

Wildfire was the book that could have ended Mom's relationship with Lola because it was the one that turned Mom into the second American success story of the family. I found a congratulations card that Auntie Elaine sent to Mom when she made number one on the *NEW YORK TIMES* bestseller list and it started: 'Well . . . Lola's worst fear has come to pass . . .'

'Have you read *Wildfire* yet?' says Lola.

And I'm like: 'No, and Mom never had a problem with that. She knew it wasn't just her books I didn't read. It was ALL BOOKS.'

'Well, that's hardly a badge of honour,' says Lola.

And I HAVE A FACE ON ME then. Because you only have faces on you for your own family.

The headline of the article is **'THE REALITY OF LAURIE BROWN'** which I know right away will have nothing to do with Mom's ACTUAL reality because: SUPER PRIVATE IN INTERVIEWS.

Lola points to a paragraph. 'The interviewer asked her why she chose "tailor" as the profession for the hero,' says Lola.

And I read what Mom said:

Well, it might have something to do with my daughter – she was five years old when I was writing Wildfire *and we were chatting one evening and I said to her, 'What would you like to be when you grow up?' and she said:* **'A lover.'**

And I'm reading this like: Whutttt? And Lola's smiling and telling me to read on.

As you can imagine, I was quite shocked by this answer so I asked my daughter what she meant, and she said, 'I just want to love things.' She's always been very affectionate. And I asked her what she loved most in the world, and she flung her arms out and said – with enormous **passion** – 'Clothing.' Five years old. She didn't say, 'You, Mommy!', she didn't say 'dolls' or 'cookies' or even 'clothes': Clothing. So I asked her did she think that 'loving clothing' could be a job. And she said, 'You love books. But you write them too. Maybe I can be a clothing . . . maker.' So . . . maybe that was it – stitching things together: love and clothing . . . and loving clothing . . . and my little girl. Stitching things together made me a tailor.

FIRST THOUGHT: that explains me and the word CLOTHING. I thought that was Mom. Second thought: MOM MENTIONED ME IN AN INTERVIEW! And I didn't lose any MYSTERY! Even though I sounded creepy at the start.

But I did not dwell on that because Lola handed me the bag and I opened it to find – on the theme of clothing – a STACK of fashion magazines. *US Vogue, W* magazine, *WWD (Women's Wear Daily), Harper's Bazaar, Vogue Italia.* And yes it's old school but we've done this since I was small. And we love it. I spend the evening cutting out lots of pictures to put on my vision board on my bedroom wall that currently has as its main focus: Hunter Threat's face beside an Elie Saab gown that's not bridal AS SUCH.

7 March (SUNDAY)

I came into the living room today and Lola was perched on the edge of the sofa by the window with a little pile of books beside her.

'They really are **MAGNIFICENT,**' she says, pointing to the bookshelves. And they are. There are seven of them, and they're all slightly different, because they're hand-carved.

'What are they made from again?' I say.

'Reclaimed oak,' says Lola.

'Who claimed it first, though?' I say. 'And were they sorry to see it go, I wonder.'

And Lola's giving me Patient Face, and then she looks down at the next book on the pile, and goes: 'Hmm . . .' And she picks it up and reads the title out loud. **'ME, ME, ME & ME.'** And the bit underneath: **'GROWING UP WITH A NARCISSISTIC MOTHER.'** There were MILLIONS of Post-its sticking out of the pages and I could see Mom's handwriting all over them.

Lola looks up: 'Was your mother writing a book about a character with a narcissistic mother?'

AND EVERYTHING BECAME CLEAR. JUST NOT TO LOLA.

8 March (MONDAY)

• ★ • ★ • ★ • ★ • ★ • ★ •

Tonight Lola and I curled up on separate sofas to watch the Oscars and share our thoughts on the dresses. We're not always in the same location for this so this was **SPECIAL.** As was Lola's bottle of red wine. As were the MANY bags of food items I was surrounded by that Lola couldn't make eye contact with.

Anyway: THE DRESSES. You know when you see an evening gown at an awards ceremony or on the runway and you're like,

OHMYGOD. THAT IS THE MOST AMAZING DRESS I'VE EVER SEEN MY LIFE?

Every time that happens to me . . . it's Elie Saab. If you ever want an evening gown or a bridal gown – or a not a bridal gown as such – that looks like it was *made by angels*, then get an Elie Saab. But first: get an amazing job and have zero mortgage/rent/financial obligations of any kind. Speaking of jobs, Lola should TOTALLY be one of those red-carpet fashion commentators. Here were some of her comments:

'Was there an earthquake in LA this week that we missed?'

Pause. 'Because SOMETHING has to explain how so many of these women had no access to a mirror.'

'I'm the last person in the world to complain about skinny but –' and then SERIOUSLY she risks burning her retinas on my tortilla chips and says – 'maybe we could send her a care package of . . . those.'

Then: 'Do you remember making dresses and skirts for your Barbie doll out of strips of toilet paper and they never stayed on? You were ahead of your time.' Leading into THIS performance: *raises imaginary phone.* 'Hello – 911? I'd like to report a disappearance. The disappearance of MYSTERY.'

Then later, she points to one of the actresses accepting an award: 'I LOVE that woman! *LOVE* her! She has NO HOOTS to give! She is all out of hoots.'

And I'm cracking up because Lola does that: she randomly puts 'hoots' in a phrase that would normally have &&&&s in it.

When the actress finished her speech Lola is all wistful. 'You know your mother loved her too.' Pause. Then: 'And I think *she* would have . . . loved your mother.' Long pause, followed by tears, then: 'Maybe one day . . . they will meet in heaven.'

And THAT was the sound wine makes when it's gone from bottles.

9 March (TUESDAY)

There was no sign of Lola at breakfast this morning. But she was freshly showered when I got home from school and had made soup. Lola tries to look after me in a maternal/domesticated kind of way, but it doesn't come naturally to her. The thing is – Grandpa does **EVERYTHING** for her that their housekeeper doesn't. It's a *miracle* she is here without him. If he wasn't still recuperating from knee-replacement surgery and needing round-the-clock care, I'm sure he would be here.

But Lola does make juices that are DELICIOUS. And she's come all the way over here, and that's lovely because I know she wants to be there for me – it's just she doesn't really know HOW. When Lola asks you how you're feeling you can see in her eyes that there is a CORRECT answer and she's rooting for you to get it. It is any of the following: 'Fine!' 'Great!' 'Overjoyed!' 'Not Requiring Emotional Intervention!'

I mentioned this to Auntie Elaine before, and she nodded and said:

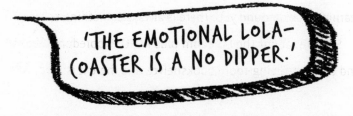

'THE EMOTIONAL LOLA-COASTER IS A NO DIPPER.'

9 p.m. update

MAJOR DIP

... that is costing Lola ZERO HOOTS.

The ***INTERNET HAS GONE DOWN.***

Meaning – MAINLY – NO NETFLIX.

And I'm just lying on my bed, staring at the ceiling, thinking about how much easier it is NOT to think about things when you can just WATCH things.

I'm about to mouth: I'm **SO BOOOORED.** And then I am horrified at how horrified Mom would be by that.

I said 'I'm bored' ONCE when I was small and Mom said: 'Only dullards get bored.' Obviously I had to ask her what a dullard was and Mom gave me some examples, which included Auntie Elaine's ex-boyfriend who played fantasy video games the way other thirty-something-year-olds drank wine. He also DRANK BEER the way other thirty-something-year-olds drank wine.

Then Mom said: 'I NEVER want to hear that sentence from you EVER again' and, 'If you are BORED, Ellery, it means you are not learning. Look around you. There is always something to learn.'

So: guilt about the boredom plus ACTUAL boredom means I end up at the living-room bookshelves and there it is: **ME, ME,**

I open it. Along with the Post-its, Mom had highlighted all these passages and answered all these questions in her JetPen (ink the colour of tropical island seas you don't believe are real until you're there, shouting at your mom: 'I'm SWIMMING IN YOUR FAVOURITE COLOUR!'). Mom always used this pen to write personal stuff – like greetings cards and letters and notes, and – it turns out – awful answers like THESE:

Q. Did you feel seen, heard, recognised, known by your mother?
'No!' Mom wrote.

Q. If you went to your mother with a problem, did she deny you had one?
'OMG THANK YOU YES!' Mom wrote.

Q. Did you eventually give up going to your mother with your problems?
'What problems?!!!' Mom wrote.

Q. Where did you go to feel loved?
'My dad' Mom wrote.

Q. If it was your father, did you sometimes find that he was unavailable to you, because your mother created a crisis to ensure that the attention was on her?
'SOMETIMES? LMFAO!' Mom wrote.

- **SADNESS:** there were tear stains in the ink.
- **NON-SADNESS:** I would have answered Yes! Never! No! Everywhere! And N/A: Not Applicable.
- **RETURN TO SADNESS:** one of the Post-its just had the words: 'Pouring love into a void.' And another one had: 'Who AM I? I am forty-two years old and I have no clue. I've been too busy making up who everyone else is.'

POOR MOM!

I need to be UNDEPRESSED, so I pull out the brightest book I can find: *THE HAPPINESS OF LESTER JOY BY LEON ADLER*. It's a yellow hardback with orange writing – and yellow and orange are two of my favourite colours. This is a Pulitzer-prize-winning novel. I turn it over, and it says on the back: 'There was no happiness in the life of Lester Joy.' What is wrong with people? Then a review at the top: 'A masterpiece where misery triumphs.' And another one: 'Lester Joy finds his home in sorrow; a discomfiting [no idea] tale for the suffocating positivity of our time.'

WHAT IS WRONG WITH WRITERS?

GOODNIGHT.

10 March (WEDNESDAY)

Megser came over after school today, and we're in the living room and Lola comes in and hands me an envelope – 'I meant to give you these' – and she disappears. And I'm deciding whether or not to open the envelope because I'm wondering what 'THESE' are because I'm getting nervous that Lola is going to keep surprising me with things about Mom that might make me sad.

But I open it obviously and it's got all these photos of me, at different ages, standing at the living-room bookshelves on my own like a loser. And I start dealing them to Megser like it's a poker game and I'm like, 'Is this normal?' And Megser goes: 'Yes, it's normal. The shelves are cool, your mom loves books, and you LOOK like you do.'

I'm thinking Mom set these all up to make me look more intelligent.

'She probably hid sweets behind the books to lure me in,' I say.

Meg rolls her eyes. 'What are you on about? You were **OBSESSED** with books when you were small. You're half the reason I got into reading in the first place. When you'd come over with Auntie Elaine in the summer, your mom used to have stacks of books waiting for you and I was always SO EXCITED calling in.'

THIS IS A **LOT OF EMOTION** FOR MEGSER

'About the BOOKS?' I say. And I'm HORRIFIED.

And Megser's shaking her head. 'And the caaandy. With the flavours we didn't get here.'

And then I remember: because I kind of went off reading when I was about nine, Megser ended up living the fairy years for both of us. Mom had got all these fairy books because she thought I'd love them, so I say to Megser: 'Do you realise I'm actually RESPONSIBLE—'

'Under no circumstances,' says Megser, 'are you EVER responsible—'

'For your love of *fairies?*' I keep going because I'm not letting her get away with it. Megser always goes a little quiet when the subject of fairies comes up and tries to LOOK! SQUIRREL! her way out of a conversation, even though I treat the whole thing respectfully. It's like she's bracing herself for the day where I'm finally going to laugh in her face about it.

So now she's just got her head down, looking at the photos. 'Awww. Look at you. Ellery's first visit to Ireland, 2007.' (Because that's what Mom had written on the back.) And the photo is ME and I'm two years old, in this adorable summer dress – pale yellow with a chicken on the front (a really cute one – not like a rotisserie chicken) and I'm just standing there and I'm looking up at all the books like I'm **ENTRANCED.**

Megser looks through the rest of the photos and there's another one of me in the pale yellow dress but on the back of this photo, it says:

The first place she went . . . like she was drawn to the missing part of her.

'My BRAIN!' I say and we're laughing but I'm like, SERIOUSLY . . . The missing part of me? And THEN: 'Hold ON. Does that mean . . . my DAD?'

And Megser is DELIBERATING.

And then it *HITS ME. OH. MY. GOD.* Because two-year-old me is looking at the bookshelves and I'm thinking about what Mom said about my dad living in the woods. And what's on the shelves? BOOKS! Made of PAPER! Which comes from TREES! Which grow IN THE WOODS!

And I'm FURRREAKING OUT. 'OHMYGOD, Megser!

I THINK MY DAD IS AN AUTHOR!
I AM – LITERALLY – A WORK OF FICTION!'

And Megser says, 'We are ALL works of fiction.'

And I'm like, 'I'm SERIOUS!'

Then Megser goes: 'OHMYGOD!' because she's holding up

another photo of me, this time holding on to one of the shelves, and Megser reads what Mom wrote on the back of that:

Her little hands so close to where his once were, as he signed his finest work.

And we're both like: OHMYGOD: Ellery is NOT insane. The RELIEF. And then I'm terrified because this falls under the category of Things I Can't Unknow. And that's a sub-category of Things I Might Furrreak Out About.

Megser's looking at me and says: 'So . . . what do you want to do with this information?'

'Unknow it?'

'The usual,' says Megser.

But we both know there is NOTHING usual about this. And Megser is looking like, I've encouraged Ellery's actings before but this one is a bit serious, so she makes her excuses and leaves. Her excuses were actually just ONE excuse:

'I can't be party to whatever is going on up there.' And she's pointing at my head.

And I'm like: 'The missing part of me?'

And she's laughing but she's also running out the door. And right before she slams it she shouts, 'GOOD LUCK!'

BUT _NOT_ IN A GOOD WAY

11 March (THURSDAY)

I got to work IMMEDIATELY. Megser was probably still on the property when I was upstairs at the printer scanning the photo of my first visit here and uploading the photo of the bookshelves I had just taken. Then I enlarged both of them and printed them out in sections because: A4. And because the spines needed to be big enough to read.

My plan was: find all those books and see which ones are signed. And then: know who my father is, find him, he's perfect, and we live HAPPILY EVER AFTER.

Kidding.

Because look at the MATHEMATICS that have just shown up:

SEVEN SHELVES with an average of FORTY-FOUR BOOKS PER SHELF = 308 BOOKS

To complicate matters: Mom used to randomly move books from the downstairs living room to the upstairs one or to her office or to the guest bedroom. PLUS . . . she always lent people books and donated them to the local hospital. So these books could be ANYWHERE. Mainly, though, what's on my mind is:

308 BOOKS

I gave Megser the printouts this morning.

'Did you not hear my "GOOD LUCK" last night?' she says.

But she's looking at the photos because she can't help herself. And then I tell her:

308 Books

Because to Megser, that's a positive.

And she goes: 'Well, obviously, we can narrow that down right away. First off, some of these authors are dead.'

And I'm like, 'YAAY!' (No offence to the authors' surviving loved ones. Especially because I AM an author's surviving loved one.)

'And easily half of them are women,' says Megser. 'And then there's ethnicity, which may not be a PRECISE tool. And then there are the openly gay authors – but we can't COMPLETELY rule them out ... just in case.'

'Mom TURNED them gay.'

And we're laughing. But then I feel guilty about laughing at something to do with Mom.

Meanwhile, Megser's eyes are moving across the photos

like advanced scanning technology and she has her pen in her hand and she is circling spines. Then she points out that some of the books are out of focus and we think we might be able to recognise them by their colours instead.

'It would make WAY more sense if we finished this in the living room,' I say. 'With the ACTUAL books so we can read the signed ones straight away.'

'Can I just ask here,' says Megser, 'what is the plan at the end of all this?'

'Define end,' I say, because I'm hoping she doesn't want me to go to the consequences part.

I Reject Consequences and All Their Works.

'I just mean after we check out the signed books,' says Megser.

And all I'm thinking is, SHE SAID WE! YAAAY!

But then she starts veering into consequences territory: 'You do KNOW,' she says, 'it's not like the book is going to be signed: "To Laurie, love from Ellery's secret father" and your mom just put it on a shelf where anyone could see it.'

'Terrrue,' I say. *But stiiill*, is what I'm thinking.

Then, like I'm someone's mom, I say: 'Why don't we cross that bridge when we come to it?'

'Only if you promise me we can BURN IT if things are not

looking good,' says Megser.

And I'm like, 'The bridge? Then we wouldn't be able to get back! We'd be stuck on the side that wasn't looking good!' And now I'm imagining this Island of Disappointing Fathers and me and Megser STRANDED there with the flames of a burning bridge at our back.

'What I'm saying,' says Megser, 'is if we arrive at the bridge and decide not to cross it, can we just **BURN IT** so that we don't have to KEEP coming back to it every time the mood hits you?'

But I don't want her to be attached to the outcome of that question – the answer NO. So I don't give her that.

After school, because it was a half day, Megser and I had four whole hours to destroy my living room before we had to be at Megser's for dinner. Thankfully, Lola was out. Megser finished her cross-referencing and I took notes as she called out the titles of all the books that were in both photos.

- **SADNESS:** there was a SECOND LAYER of BOOKS on some of those shelves.

- **FURTHER SADNESS/THRILL (DEPENDING ON WHETHER YOU'RE ME OR MEGSER):** this brought the NEW total of books up to:

421

Then we matched that list of books to the books that were on the shelves now, so we could see which ones were signed. And THEN I ran around to all the other bookshelves in the house to find any missing ones.

And THEN we looked at the blurry books from the photos and matched the colours to real-life books, and by the end we found all of them except three. Megser is staring at the photo because there's something vaguely familiar about the missing ones but – in a

SHOCKING TURN OF EVENTS –
I FIGURE OUT ONE OF THEM FIRST!

• **SADNESS:** it was *THE HAPPINESS OF LESTER JOY* by Leon Adler.

'OHMYGOD, LEON ADLER!' screams Megser. Then she goes COMPLETELY INSANE because – unlike me the other night – she actually OPENS the book and YES! It's SIGNED TO MY MOM!

8 October 2004

To my beloved Laurie,

True, I am broken. But even in the fall there were thrills like none I have ever known. And, oh, isn't every crash spectacular?

Always, L x

What's wrong with 'Hope you enjoy the book!'? But that

would involve JOY. And I'm going to guess that Leon Adler is JOY AVERSE.

Megser and I *LOVED* Mom's 'averse' thing. People could be 'shower averse' and 'manners averse' and 'tidying-your-bedroom averse'. The last two were me in case you were wondering. Because I love showers.

But Meg is all: 'ELLERY! Are you getting this? Your mom clearly had a thing with LEON ADLER! It looks like she DESTROYED him.'

'That's not exactly a positive.'

'Unless it led him to write his MASTERPIECE.' She checks the date. 'Nope. *Lester Joy* came BEFORE your mother CRUSHED LEON ADLER'S SOUL.' Then she's got **FLASHBACK EYES** followed by **SHAME EYES.** 'OHMYGOD . . . remember my third-year book review where I mortified myself going on about this book? I was OBSESSED. And everyone was just staring at me.'

'I DO remember that.'

And I'm like, 'That was THAT book? I blocked that out in your honour.'

'You said I was like a **TELEVANGELIST.** And then you had to explain what that was.'

'And that was probably the only time I ever had to explain something to you, which is probably the bigger mortification.'

And she's about to tell me to shut up, but I'm realising something about my potential new name: Ellery Adler sounds like diddly-eidly.

SERIOUSLY – try singing it on a loop to a jig or a hornpipe. And put in random *OHS!* and *AYS!* and **WHOOPS!** and some **CLAPS.**

And I start doing a hornpipe from my enforced childhood Irish dancing classes and we're singing, ELLERY ADLER ELLERY ADLER ELLERY ADLER ELLERY OH! ELLERY ADLER ELLERY ADLER ELLERY ADLER ELLERY AAAAAY, and we are crying laughing.

'As IF you'd be changing your name anyway,' Megser goes.

'Terrrue.' Even though I'm Ellery Threat on the inside.

And then Lola walks in, making no sound because she is so light on her feet, and I'm thinking she and Mrs Daly should do heists together. Lola's looking around the room, NOT HAPPY with the bookshelf situation. I tell her it was research. And she doesn't ask any more questions. Lola's not really an asking-more-questions person because she isn't interested in any great detail in the lives of other people.

And I know that Megser is trying not to laugh about the research thing because Mom used to say 'Everything is research!' Once, she had this massive deadline but it was a beautiful day, so she just abandoned everything, and took Megser and me to Kenmare (really cute town 48.1 km from here. I googled it), and we're at Sheen Falls Lodge (amazing hotel), and Mom goes: 'Everything is research.' And then she goes: 'And so help me God if I have to include a scene where an on-the-brink-of-collapse mother, her BRILLIANT daughter, and her BRILLIANT daughter's BRILLIANT best friend are having afternoon tea on the terrace of a luxury hotel, I'll do it.' And we all cracked up.

Next thing Megser's alarm goes off on her phone because there is a burrito situation about to kick off in her house and Lola has to drive us there. But just in case Lola gets curious later, I grab the dedicated-to-Mom pile of books and run to my room with them. Then I tell Lola not to worry about tidying up the other books – that I'll do it tomorrow.

I'm in Megser's then – in the kitchen helping Susan with the burritos and I'm thinking about what Mom wrote on that Post-it about being forty-two and not knowing who she was. And I ask Susan does SHE know who she is. And she looks at me and answers immediately with ONE HUNDRED PER CENT conviction.

'YES: A FOOL.'

And she points across the room with her spatula. 'For putting up with this lot.' And Megser and the Ferals are all sitting at the table holding their knives and forks up like it's a TV commercial, waiting to be handed their dinner.

'I studied law by night for FIVE years, you pups!' says Susan. 'I am a QUALIFIED SOLICITOR making burritos to order. And Ellery, ANOTHER FOOL, is grating your cheese.'

'She just wants to be beside the fridge,' says the Elder Feral.

'GRATE HIS FACE,' says Megs. 'DO IT.'

Susan just rolls her eyes.

'DO IT!' says the Younger Feral. 'Or give it to me.' And he starts to get up.

'I TOLD you the last day,' says Susan, 'that's a professional grater and it will CUT THE HANDS OFF YOU.' Then she says to me: 'Give it to him. See how he likes it.'

If this was America, every person in this kitchen would be under investigation by Child Protective Services.

The burritos were **AWESOME**. Which made it even worse for the Younger Feral when he dropped his on the floor resulting in a MASSIVE MELTDOWN which Megser reminded me was like the GREAT BIRTHDAY BURRITO MELTDOWN when I dropped one at my own party and 'ruined a GOOD HOUR of it, you SAP'.

After dinner Megser and I went to her room, and she revealed that when I ran upstairs earlier, just in case Lola was going to put the books back on the shelves, she photographed everything in the living room.

Next thing she jumps up and goes, 'I KNEW I KNEW IT!' And she dives for her bookshelf, pulls out a book, and holds it up triumphantly.

'*Kerosene* by Jay Evans! It's one of the blurry ones!'

And I'm reading the cover. 'The *New York Times* bestseller.' Like Mom! And underneath:

And my FAVOURITE thing to see on book covers:

NOW A MAJOR MOTION PICTURE

'So he's a crime writer?' I say.

'YES!' says Megser. 'But ... that's okay.' Megser does NOT read crime.

Then she opens the book, and COMPLETELY LOSES IT:

'OHMYGOD — Jay Evans could be your dad! Read this!'

She shows me the dedication he wrote to Mom and I'm like,

'OHMYGOD — JAY EVANS COULD BE MY DAD!'

January 2004

To Laurie,
And there we were, and it was perfect. You — starlight like peppered gunfire across me, the night sky.
    In your shining reflection, we are endless.
J x

And I go, 'Oh my God – ENDLESS! Because of a CHILD. They LIVE ON THROUGH ME.' Like I'm the saviour of humanity.

'Gunfire's pretty risky,' says Megser.

'Luckily Mom wasn't shot dead.'

'Or HIM – because she was the gunfire,' says Megser.

'Imagine Mom being gunfire,' I say. 'It would have to be one of those guns that fires out a flag that says **"END GUN VIOLENCE"**.'

'But seriously,' says Megser, 'Jay Evans is HUGE. He's written SIXTEEN books.' Then, to keep me interested, she adds: 'NINE of them have been made into movies!'

But I'm still wondering. 'How come you even have this here? It's CRIME. You HATE crime.'

'I wanted to TRY IT.' She says this like it was one of those fish that could poison you.

Then we look at his author photo.

'He is FIT,' says Meg. Then: 'Not that that's what people look for in a dad.'

'What I AM looking for is some sign of resemblance.'

And Megser is too. 'Your eyes have the same kind of shape?'

And I'm thinking there's not a huge range of shapes, but stiiill.

Then we look up all his author photos across the years. And Leon Adler's, while we're at it.

'It's hard to tell,' says Megser.

And I go: '"Never trust an author photo," Mom used to say. "My own included."'

Megser and I then agree that we need to write a list of things you get from your parents. 'And when we have that,' says Megser, 'we can do a compare and contrast.'

My second-to-least favourite exam question.

My LEAST FAVOURITE is:

Words to choose from:

CLOZE TESTS.

ELLERY'S PHYSICAL CHARACTERISTICS
by Ellery

- **SKIN** OLIVE TONES – TANS EASILY
- **EYES** GREEN – SEE EASILY
- **HAIR** CHESTNUT – CURLS EASILY
- **BODY TYPE** STRONG – OVERPOWERS EASILY
- **TEETH** STRAIGHT – WORE BRACES EASILY
- **IDENTIFYING MARKS** The 'M' FROWN. When I frown I have this kind of 'M' shape between my eyebrows. It's not angry/sinister-looking. It's a happy 'M'. It's like if you took the opening curly bracket that no one uses and rotated it left ninety degrees.

ELLERY'S SKILLS

by Ellery

(Megser's responses in brackets)

- **ROLLER-SKATING** (FLAT EYES)
- **MAKE-UP APPLICATION** (FLAT EYES)
- **NICE HANDWRITING** (That's your Rose of Tralee* party piece sorted.)
- **CAN SORT OF SING** (SORT OF? You're a SAVAGE singer.)
- **NOTE I:** Remember savage is a POSITIVE in Cork – it means AWESOME.
- **NOTE II:** Megser is TONE DEAF.

* Irish personality pageant but with an international element because Irish girls living abroad or girls of Irish extraction living here OR abroad can enter. If I entered, I could be the New York rose OR the Cork rose. Megser would be the CSI rose. Because: OVER HER DEAD BODY.

ELLERY'S PERSONALITY TRAITS
by MESSER

(Ellery's responses in brackets)

- **DISORGANISED** (Whuttt?!)
- **RECKLESS/FAILS TO SEE A PROBLEM** (Whuttt?!)
- **CONSEQUENCES AVERSE** (Terrrue.)
- **GETTING-TO-THE-POINT AVERSE** (STONY silence. Or PEBBLY maybe.)
- **A MORNING PERSON** (ELLERY A.M. would be my rap name.)
- **EASILY DISTRACTED** (Whuttt?! Followed by: OHMYGOD . . . check THIS out about insects and the jungle. I meant to send you this. DID I send you this?)
- **ANNOYING** (I'm not saying ANYTHING ANY MORE. Don't think I haven't noticed I'm giving you AMMO for your list . . .)
- **INSPIRATIONAL** (Stop! That's not FAIR! I went off and wrote my list and THEN presented my findings. You're live-writing yours and I'm live-responding really helpfully.)

But then she goes off and comes back with ALL THIS about me!

- **KIND**

- FUNNY
- LOYAL
- GENEROUS
- POSITIVE
- IMPATIENT
- ABNORMAL FEAR OF LAW ENFORCEMENT
- ABNORMAL LOVE OF LOVE
- GULLIBLE AND, NO, ELLERY – NOT ABOUT THE NICE STUFF ON THIS LIST

EVENTUALLY, because that was EXHAUSTING, we go to bed. And we're lying there, and Megser's in her weirdly small bed, and I'm on this weirdly small mattress on the floor. And I know she really needs to sleep because she has football training in the morning, and I know I'm really annoying, but I just ask her:

'Am I crazy trying to figure out who my dad is?'

And she leans up on her elbow and looks down at me. 'Why NOT? I'd want to know.'

'But do you think I'm ... betraying Mom?' I ask her.

'No WAY.'

'But ... Mom KNEW she was going to die and she STILL didn't tell me who my father is, so that must mean she REALLY, REALLY,

REALLY didn't want me to know. And I'm, like, going against her wishes.'

'She didn't make a wish that you weren't to look for him,' says Meg.

Which is an **EXCELLENT POINT**. And I flop back down, but then I'm lying there, and I just go: 'To the Universe! If I am to find my father, I want a sign! Not some feather or coin! A PROPER SIGN.'

'OHMYGOD,' says Meg. 'Not "the Universe" again.'

'And where do you think your TWENTY-SIX *fairies* live exactly?' I say.

And she looks at me. 'Behind my twenty-six fairy doors.' (She really does have twenty-six of them, and they're all up one of her bedroom walls like an apartment block. SERIOUSLY).

'You do know they fly off and that's the whole point,' I say. 'And that's what the keys are for. Where do you THINK they go?'

'Out into the normal world.'

'And what's so abnormal about the Universe?'

'You think the Universe is an entity that delivers things to you.'

'And what's wrong with that?'

And the two of us are just looking at each other. And I know we're both thinking that neither of us is going to be the other's

DREAMCRUSHER.

'I *LOVE* your fairy doors in FAIRYness,' I say.

'And I have no doubt that the Universe only wants good things for you.'

'SHHHH!' I say. 'Can you hear that? It's the *fairies!* They're on their way home!' And then I go: 'With their BAGS OF TEETH.' Because that FURRREEEAKS her out.

13 March (SATURDAY)

OHMYGOD . . . this morning! Megser and Susan! When I arrived down for breakfast it was ADORABLE . . . there was a special stack of pancakes there with a birthday candle stuck into the top because they won't see me tomorrow and tomorrow's my birthday and they sang 'Happy Birthday' right through to the Jolly Good Fellow awkwardness and even the Ferals joined in . . . with the Younger Feral – in bare chest and pyjama bottoms – standing with one foot up on a stool playing a guitar (made of air). And the Elder Feral on a kitchen chair playing the drums (made of Susan's head). And there were PRESENTS! Susan got me the most *beautiful* necklace with angel wings and it was so me and she gave me an extra-long hug and got a bit emotional. And Megser got me the matching bracelet and I said, **'YOU'RE ALL CRAZY!'** because I could tell they were really expensive and then I opened the Ferals' present and they looked as surprised as I was to see that they had got me a voucher for a manicure! And I'm THRILLED and I say thank you and they both kind of bounce off me in their version of a hug. Which was actually really sweet.

And then Susan dropped me home and I see – ANOTHER surprise! – because Auntie Elaine is back! And I'm, like, OHMYGOD! and ready to fling myself at her. Until I realise that she and Lola are standing there definitely amid tensions.

Then Auntie Elaine kind of jolts herself out of whatever and throws herself at me and gives me a huge hug and is all, 'Hey, gorgeous girl!'

And I'm like, 'Yaaay!' But then: 'Is everything okay?' because she looks TRAUMATISED. And so does Lola. At this stage I literally think they're about to sit me down and tell me who my father is, and that he's just been released from a **MAXIMUM-SECURITY PRISON.** And I now have a SECURITY DETAIL.

And Auntie Elaine says, 'I'm back because your mom wanted . . . I'm back for . . . tomorrow.'

Which is so adorable, and I'm thanking her and saying she

didn't have to because it's not like Sweet Sixteen is a thing over here and actually that makes it even cooler because then she can make a GIANT FUSS over me.

But there is now some extra-weird energy in the room and I catch Auntie Elaine and Lola exchanging these nervous glances. And then I discovered what was REALLY going on tomorrow and how come I had ZERO IDEA – because MEGSER had not allowed me to go into any shop all week. She literally kept producing drinks, and chocolates, and crisps from her locker whenever I said I wanted to go to the shop. She told me they were left over from the Younger Feral's birthday party. But it turns out that Megser had done some VERY DELIBERATE stockpiling of the Dietary Loves of Ellery . . . because if I HAD gone into a shop, I would have known EXACTLY what was happening tomorrow. The place would have been FESTOONED. And NOT because it was my birthday.

14 March (SUNDAY) MOTHER'S DAY

I can't even.

15 March (MONDAY)

I came down to breakfast this morning and it was just Lola.

'Where's Auntie Elaine?' I say.

'Gone for a run,' says Lola. 'She said she's sorry, but she has to fly to London earlier than planned, so she won't be here when you get back from school.'

JUST LIKE THAT. Auntie Elaine would have delivered news like that with some tonal anaesthetic (Mom's expression) that is not part of Lola's real-life range. And I'm so sad because I won't get to say goodbye and collect my hug and I tell myself THAT'S what the problem is.

Then Lola goes upstairs and I hear this **BANG** followed by one of her dramatic expressions of frustration and I know that she's just got involved with the door to the 'linen closet', which has driven her INSANE every time she's visited because you have to yank it open and shoulder-slam it closed. She also has an ongoing feud with a loose knob on one of my bedroom drawers. So when she comes back down she says: 'Do you know any carpenters?' Sometimes I think she alternates between thinking I'm nine and thinking I'm thirty-five. But I actually do know a carpenter. Silent Johnny works weekends for a guy called Dan and sometimes I see the two of them going by in the van, and Dan is always smiling, and chatting, and . . . pouring sentences into a void. Luckily, Dan used to live in America, so he'll be able to translate 'linen closet' for Johnny into his native Irish 'hot press'.

So I went up to Johnny in school today, and said, 'My grandmother – but don't call her that – needs some things done in the house – could I get Dan's number from you?'

Silent Johnny nods, takes out his phone, scrolls to the number, under Dan The Man (!), and holds the screen up to my face.

And that's that. Zero words.

THE END.

16 March (TUESDAY)

TIP: do NOT try to bond with an adult over any TV show you have not already watched FROM START TO FINISH. Tonight Lola and I curled up together on separate sofas to watch the new series *Daisy Season* on Netflix. Have you EVER heard a more grandma-friendly title in your LIFE? For a show whose pilot episode was probably informally referred to by the writers as The ALL THE AMPERSANDS episode.

Lola and I are SCARRED. Which is an extra level of scarring for me after the UNNECESSARILY ANATOMICALLY FAITHFUL ILLUSTRATION of what happens when two people love each other in the book Mom gave me when I was ten: *My Body is Amazing!* I'm like, BUT MY MIND! IS SCARRED! I have NEVER had such LITTLE FURTHER CURIOSITY about anything in my LIFE. To this DAY.

❀ *17 March* (WEDNESDAY) ❀

Today is: **ST PATRICK'S DAY.** Honouring the saint who drove snakes out of Ireland. And side-honouring Alcohol and All Its Works.

The Patrick's Day parade in town is AMAZING. It contains things like: tractors, transporters, Irish dancers and primary-school kids dressed as tiny disgraced politicians with signs hanging around their necks to explain their specific shame like those dogs on the internet who've chewed up sofas.

Lola is bewildered by everything.

And I'm RESTLESS. Because I had a float to commandeer.

Yes! That information was under embargo. As Creative Director I made all participants, including myself, sign non-disclosure agreements. Competition is FIERCE.

SO . . . our float was Netflix-themed. It was live action, played out on a flatbed truck typically reserved for live bands performing on the square at festivals, but secured for us by Silent Johnny (who approached Megser to volunteer his construction skills!) through his boss, Carpenter Dan, who was so sweet, because he also let Silent Johnny use his workshop to make the props. Plus he helped us carry the two sofas, and the bed, on to the truck. And he let us park it out the back of the workshop where we could keep it away from prying eyes (see above note re: COMPETITION, FIERCE). And he even watched a couple of the rehearsals, and at one point – when I **'LOST THE PLOT ALTOGETHER'** in the words of Megser – he even backed me up on a creative point.

But none of that matters now. Because:

WINNERS!
  OF.
    BEST.
      FLOAT.
        IN.
          TOWN.

So … **HIGH ON VICTORY** … Megser and I wander around town chatting to people and pulling the Ferals off lampposts and out of bars that are all PACKED.

Susan is having a blast day-drinking with her buddies and Meg loves it because unlike me she's always pumping drunk adults for information. She's convinced she'll discover some major family scandal, and she doesn't care if it could scar her for life. If she were me – not knowing who her dad was – she'd make it her business to go to a family gathering, wait until around 11 p.m. (because my family is American – probably 2 a.m. if we were Irish), then ask EVERY drunk adult, 'So, my dad . . . what do you think of THAT whole situation?'

I don't drink, and I have zero intention of ever drinking. Grandpa used to be an alcoholic. For the first ten years he and Lola were married he drank. A lot. I once heard Auntie Elaine say to Mom that Lola has made him pay for it ever since. Addiction is genetic, which FREAKS me out. Plus, when I was twelve, Mom read out this *New Scientist* article about alcohol causing damage to developing brains, and would I promise her that I'd wait until I was AT LEAST eighteen before I drank. Seriously – that was not hard. I don't want to ACTIVELY INVITE brain damage. I need my brain to make the wisest possible decisions on clothing, make-up and burrito fillings.

Meg doesn't drink because she's so sporty and looks after herself and thinks drunk people are idiots. Informative idots, but still. She has a theory: people who drink because they think they need to if they want to be ANY CRAIC are the people who are NEVER ANY CRAIC.

So today in honour of St Patrick's Day and The Irish, as Lola calls them, and CRAIC … and because you probably thought I left it out earlier …

CRAIC AND ALL ITS WORKS

CRAIC gets its own entry because it's the curling wand of Irish slang; hardly any non-Irish native knows how to use it but if a friend can help you, you won't get burned. Because Irish people get GREAT craic out of people who misuse CRAIC.

★ CRAIC = FUN

It's not ROCKET SCIENCE.

It is spelled: C-R-A-I-C. Yes, that's an Irish-language spelling because: IT'S AN IRISH-LANGUAGE WORD. You do NOT get to spell it: C-R-A-C-K.

'Have a bit of RESPECT,' as Mrs Daly would say.

★ CRAIC IN A SENTENCE

She's GREAT CRAIC. He's NO CRAIC. It was BRILLIANT CRAIC. We had GREAT CRAIC.

See how it replaces the word FUN so easily?

★ THEN THERE'S:

Any CRAIC? (Any news?)

We got GREAT CRAIC out of her (yes – we had fun with her but it was probably AT HER EXPENSE and she probably didn't realise it.)

★ NOW. PUT 'THE' IN FRONT OF 'CRAIC' AND THE WORLD GOES MAD.

★ NO SUCH THING AS:

It was THE CRAIC (it's not like The Bomb).

★ SUCH A THING AS:

What's/How's THE CRAIC? (How are you?)

THE CRAIC was mighty. (We had a great time.)

We had THE CRAIC. (This is a weird one because literally I think only non-Dublin people can say this the right way. It's about EMPHASIS.)

We just did it FOR THE CRAIC. (I think there is no MORAL CUT-OFF POINT for things you can do FOR THE CRAIC.) 'We had SOME CRAIC that night. WHAT? He DIED? J&&&&. We just CUT HIS BRAKE LINES FOR THE CRAIC.'

Then there's **THIS** CRAIC and **THAT** CRAIC (ANY form of bad behaviour/anything untoward).

EXAMPLE THROUGH CONVERSATION:

'If he thinks he's going to carry on with THAT CRAIC, we'll have SOME CRAIC cutting his brake lines.'

'What's THIS CRAIC? You're cutting brake lines?'

'What? You're NO CRAIC.'

Now I've read that back, I totally get the confusion. Plus, I've probably left out nine million other uses of craic.

❀ **BACK TO ST PATRICK'S DAY:** Megser and I are non-drinking our way around town, and doing some light stalking of Oscar, who is wearing some kind of sleeveless T-shirt thing and has muscles 'like frankfurters' says Meg. 'If it's about showing them off, he might want to wait a small bit. Like, if he's gone sleeveless because he's roasting, that's a different story. But he's definitely only about three weeks in on max 3 kg weights.'

Then we're distracted by the culinary highlight of the day because in a sea of green, white and gold Irish flags is: a green, white and RED one . . . with a COAT OF ARMS IN THE MIDDLE! YES! The Mexican flag. For the first time EVER there is a BURRITO VAN in town. St Patrick, the HERO: drives out snakes, drives in burritos. FAIR. TRADE.

Meanwhile, the whole town is continuing to get PASTED.

We meet Oscar while not actually stalking him (which proves that stalking is NOT always the answer) and he's with the lads, and they're all chatting to Megser. The lads *LOVE* Megser because she can talk about football and doesn't put up with their &&&&. Oh, and is **BEAUTIFUL WITHOUT EVEN TRYING,** and has ZERO INTEREST in any of them.

But Oscar . . . is talking to ME. And I'm being all cool until he looks at me for about two seconds extra, and I'm low-key FURRREAKING OUT. And then he tells me he was thinking about me earlier when he was on the pier because he saw a boat called New York Lady, which is literally the lamest name for a boat I've ever heard in my life, so there's this tiny PING in my brain that reminds me of Megser saying he's not very bright. But then it's overridden by the ping of the beautiful letter he sent me, and he's looking at me again with the extra seconds thing, and it's **IN-A-GOOD-WAY TERRIFYING.** I mean, it's BEARA HUNTER THREAT. And I'm suddenly thinking about kissing him. And that is definitely the biggest threat of all the threats. And because he's green through the lenses of my shamrock glasses, my stomach feels even worse. Then my St Patrick hat falls off, and we bang our heads together because we both bend down to pick it up at the same time. THEN I realise Oscar's breath smells of beer, which is GROSS, but it's OSCAR. And we're both just there, holding on to the St Patrick hat in between us, and he's just SMILING.

'Can I try on your glasses?' he says.

'Yes!' I say.

And he goes, 'Lads – shut UP! Take a picture!' and hands one of them his phone. Then he gets in between me and Megser, puts an arm around each of us, and gives peace signs. As soon as the photo's taken Megser RECOILS from him, and says: 'DEODORANT a small bit.' Then points. 'Spar's open.'

In fairness to Megser she rarely throws out a criticism without throwing in something helpful after it.

Next thing: Silent Johnny arrives and does the upward nod, and STARTS TALKING TO MEGSER! In bursts of three to four words. And with the volunteering and now this, I'm thinking he might LIKE-LIKE her. But he needs to do more than the upward nods to me. Because everyone knows that the way to a girl's heart is through her best friend's. But they do look AMAZING together. And this is the closest to high school it's ever been here. Captain of the boys' football team dates captain of the girls' football team. Except obviously in America, the girl would be captain of the cheerleaders, which is NOT a pyramid Megser would like to take a stand on ... despite her great admiration for cheerleaders' athletic and gymnastic ability.

'I'd DO it,' she says, 'if there was a PSYCH-OUT version, where you're not cheering your own team on, but you're trying to PSYCHOLOGICALLY ANNIHILATE the opposition. "FEARLEADERS". And you're doing all that "Give me an 'A!'" stuff but you're spelling out FAILURE and INJURY and HUMILIATION and DEFEAT.'

Megser would be an AWESOME FEARLEADING CAPTAIN.

Anyway, we go back to her place after, and she lets me talk about Oscar and things like HE HAD HIS ARM AROUND ME (I couldn't smell anything. I'm not sure he DID smell) and HIS HAIR WITH THE STICKY-OUT BITS, and his GLASSES. For FIVE MINUTES in total.

That night, Lola and I returned to our separate sofas and, because we are now **TERRIFIED OF NETFLIX**, this time we watched regular television. I had the remote control and I saw *Columbo* was on, and I went, 'Aw, *Columbo* always reminds me of Grandpa!'

And Lola, horrified, says, 'Grandpa? What about me?'

'But Grandpa introduced me to *Columbo*!' I said.

And Lola sat up very straight. 'Excuse me. I introduced you to *Columbo*, my dear. I remember distinctly. You were six years old. We were at the country club. You were in your pretty pink dress, your hair was in pigtails, you had your white sandals on. I was holding your hand, we were walking along the hallway towards the ladies' room, and there he was. And he said, "Lola, they haven't lifted that curse." Meaning how youthful I looked, bless his heart.'

'You mean the actor!' I said. 'Peter Falk!'

'Yes!' said Lola as if it was all interchangeable; every actor was himself and every role. 'I can't believe you don't remember!'

'I was six!' I said. 'Plus, I had never watched *Columbo* at that stage.'

'So you don't remember what Pete said to you?' said Lola. I swear Lola abbreviates or elongates every actor's name to flag their friendships. And if someone already has a shorter name for them, she'll go shorter again. 'Tony Hopkins? Oh, T and I have been friends for years.'

'No, I don't,' I said.

'Well, I could have killed you,' she said.

'Except my murder would have been solved ON THE SPOT!' I said.

Lola paused, and rolled her eyes a little. 'I coyly mentioned to Pete something about having a glass of champagne at lunch, and you looked up at me with those big green eyes, and said, "But Wo-Wa [I have never said it like that in my LIFE], your face only gets red when you have a BOTTLE." I had to explain to Pete that you didn't mean a *whole* bottle, but that maybe it was possible that I had consumed two or three glasses. And Pete crouched down in front of you, and looked you in the eye, and said: "Some day you're gonna make one helluva detective."'

I'D CALL THAT A SIGN.

In fact, I'd upgrade that sign to:

A BLESSING.
FROM GOD.

3 a.m. update

A good fictional detective works through the night, so that is exactly what I did. I went back to the shelves while Lola was sleeping and, using Megser's photos, finished what had to be done.

And just as I'm about to go to bed I find one last book in Mom's secret second layer: **HOW NOT TO SCREW UP YOUR CHILDREN**.

EERILY this one looks like it hasn't been read.

18 March (THURSDAY)

I tell Megser first thing about last night's sign from God. But I wait until after school for my next reveal. In my bag is a very special book – one of Megser's obsessions – the children's fantasy novel, *Overthrown*, the outstanding debut novel in the Overland trilogy. The first book was made into an award-winning TV series that Meg watched obsessively. Oscar was her Overland trilogy buddy when they were twelve, until the series ended and his purpose (discussing it with her in MIND-NUMBING detail) had been served.

Anyway, we're at Megser's, and I make her take a seat. 'Because,'

I announce, 'there is another author who you might be thrilled to discover has signed a book to my mom. In FACT, you might be OVERjoyed ... or maybe OVERexcited ... or possibly OVER—'

Megser goes SO INSANE that Susan came rushing into the room thinking that someone was KILLING HER (and with the Ferals, this is more likely than in most families). Then off she went, PROOF OF LIFE secured, to get a glass of red wine to bring her heart rate down.

'SO,' says Megser. 'We have our **FINAL CANDIDATES** and their dedications.'

And I'm like: *'YES. WE HAVE THREE POTENTIAL JOHN FOES: FATHERS OF ELLERY.'*

'Your mom was a PLAYAAH,' says Megser. Then: 'God rest her.'

POTENTIAL FOES:
THE THREE-AUTHOR SHORTLIST
FEAT. DEDICATIONS TO LAURIE BROWN
THAT HER DAUGHTER CAN'T UNKNOW

IN NO PARTICULAR ORDER:

- **AUTHOR:** LEON ADLER
- **GENRE:** LITERARY FICTION [Megser insisted on genre]

8 October 2004

To my beloved Laurie,
True, I am broken. But even in the fall there
were thrills like none I have ever known. And,
oh, isn't every crash spectacular?
Always, L x

- **AUTHOR:** JAY EVANS
- **GENRE:** CRIME/THRILLER

January 2004

To Laurie,

And there we were, and it was perfect. You — starlight like peppered gunfire across me, the night sky.

In your shining reflection, we are endless.

J x

- **AUTHOR:** QUENTIN SCHAEFFER
- **GENRE:** FANTASY

28 June 2004

To Laurie,

Born for oceans, but held in captivity, I watched you move through calm waters in a way that told me the waves were inside you. As they were in me. We were the cause; we were the effect.

Reckless, fearless and free.

Where did you go? I trawled the streets for you, stopping at seafood restaurants asking if they had seen my beautiful mermaid.

The only conclusion I could draw was that I conjured you.

But of course! The iridescent skin, the eyes dancing with the knowledge of what lay beneath the surface, the smile that caught me.

We told each other we were in love! The waterbabies we would have! And they would swim to shore each night. And write their stories in the sand.

'Wouldn't that be nice?' you said.

I THINK WRITERS ARE ALL INSANE.

19 March (FRIDAY)

There is something about being in pyjamas that lessens the seriousness of any conversation. Like, I'm in a pink pig-print onesie, trying to discuss my parentage. But then I realise Meg is in some dystopian-looking NIGHTMARE … which is about as serious as it gets.

'You know what we have to do?' says Megser. 'See if we can place any of these guys … at the scene of the crime.'

I knowww – EWWWWW. But obviously in order for me to exist … basically …

'You have to ACCEPT,' says Megser, picking up on this, 'that a MALE …'

And I'm like, 'Yes: had to have been in the SAME LOCATION AS MY MOM around June 2004.'

(Unless not finishing that *MY BODY IS AMAZING!* book has left me without CRUCIAL INFORMATION.)

Megser confirms I am **NOT WRONG.**

Online research shows that during that month Mom travelled to:

- **THE HAY LITERARY FESTIVAL** in Wales to speak on a panel
- **LISTOWEL WRITERS' WEEK** in Co. Kerry for a public interview
- **PARIS, FRANCE** for the launch of a French edition of one of her books
- **NICE, FRANCE** for a literary festival
- **DUBLIN, IRELAND** for a radio interview
- **NEW YORK, USA** for a reading

20 March (SATURDAY)

* ★ * ★ * ★ * ★ * ★ * ★ *

Megser holds up the Fathers of Ellery shortlist page and goes: 'It's time to give me your answer. What are you going to do with this information?'

'Go and MEET THEM,' I announce.

And I think Megser is waiting for me to laugh. And I'm DEFINITELY waiting for me to laugh. But it turns out . . . I'm SERIOUS.

And Megser's like, 'Whoa . . . ELLE . . . that's a bit . . . how are you even going to do that? ALL of them? And WHEN? And what are you even going to SAY?'

'I can get back to you on all those questions,' I go.

Then after the silence that Megser allows . . .

'Oh GOD,' she says. 'You're just going to GO. And expect SIGNS from the UNIVERSE. Just . . . NO. To all of it.'

And then I go: 'Imagine Quentin Schaeffer comes to Castletownbere! **HOW AMAZING WOULD THAT BE?'**

And she's got ALL KINDS OF EYES. But MAINLY: SPARKLY ONES.

99

21 March (SUNDAY)

CONTENT WARNING: CONTAINS SCENE OF A DISTURBING NATURE

CONTEXT: It is Sunday. So: NONE OF THIS SHOULD HAVE HAPPENED.

So, Susan drops me home this morning, I run upstairs to my bedroom, fling open the door and standing there . . . in the middle of my bedroom . . . is SILENT JOHNNY . . . holding the top drawer of my chest of drawers in THOSE ARMS.

I don't know how everyone else configures their drawers, but my top drawer is the underwear drawer. And it is NOW EMPTY. While my brain is also emptying, my eye is drawn to the bed, where the ERSTWHILE contents of my drawer are neatly laid out.

Both of us are ready to change our identities and leave the country. Separate hemispheres.

'Uh . . .' he says, 'your nan (!) said the loose knob had come off the drawer altogether, so Dan sent me up because he was doing the chair downstairs, and he's under a small bit of pressure, and—' He's got TRAPPED IN HELLHOLE EYES. Then he ALMOST glances at the underwear and says, 'I took no notice. I'm always in people's houses, in their drawers, and their bathrooms, and all kinds of things, and . . . sure, it might as well have been . . .'

There is like a **FIZZING** going on in my head. Partially because there are so many words coming out of, EFFECTIVELY, a mime, but mainly because DEFINITELY three of the most VISIBLE pairs of underwear are the giant flesh-coloured ones I wore under my dress for one of Lola's *glamorous* Christmas parties, the other giant flesh-coloured ones that I wore for one of Lola's summer parties, annnnd the MINIONS BOY SHORTS that are so faded I can't claim they were an unworn novelty gift. Flesh, flesh, Minions. Bullet, bullet, brain.

Oh, but it's not over yet. While he's saying all this, I slowly remember something else I keep in that drawer, and I look down, and there it is: YOU, Non-Judgemental Friend. Yes: YOU. You have BECOME the story.

'And I didn't read your diary,' he adds.

Then it is **STILL NOT OVER**, because I see the Tampax box, with two or three of them sticking out higher than the others. Like Minions.

'And I have sisters,' he adds.

'And a mam,' he adds after that. 'Obviously. I mean, EVERYONE has a—'

And he just STOPS. And his FACE. And now I am DYING FOR

HIM instead of myself, which really IS NOT BETTER.

So, we're both just standing there dying of independent but OVERLAPPING TRAUMAS, when Dan sticks his head in, notices the ROARING RED of our FACES and goes: 'J&&&&, lads. Have you the heating on?' and he grabs the ICE-COLD radiator, then goes, 'MAYBE NOT!'

And I just BURST OUT LAUGHING. And we all laugh. And then it was okay.

Until I went to bed, and lay awake for HOURS wondering what Silent Johnny was going to say to the lads. And then I turned to God.

'God, Mom and your NBF, Jesus, I pray to you and to all the angels and saints in heaven, and to St Joseph, King of All Carpenters. In fact, St Joseph, gather your carpenters and whisper in their ears as they sleep, a reminder of the oath – chipocratic? – they may not have sworn: To Uphold the Privacy of All Clients and To Never Speak of The Terrible Acts of Underwear they may have witnessed. I pray also that Saint Patrick might drive out the power of speech from any Silent People who suddenly developed it over the weekend, that they may be restored to their former WORDLESS glory.' Then I take it back because it's mean and pray for **WORLD PEACE.**

OHMYGOD. Minion &&&& (rhymes with 'farce') is going to be my nickname. Or Flesh-Coloured &&&&, which could be anyone's nickname. But they're going to go with Minion &&&&. It's not even a good nickname. But it's the lads.

22 March (MONDAY)

'Despicabutt,' says Meg. 'If they had a brain between them, that's what they'd go for.'

23 March (TUESDAY)

There was zero Minion talk in school today. My prayers were answered. **THANK YOU, THANK YOU, → THANK YOU,** St Joseph. I put €10 in the St Joseph box in the post office earlier. My fears, like Meg's make-up bag, were without foundation.

24 *March* (WEDNESDAY)

I bumped into Oscar after school, and we ended up going for a walk . . . and next thing I start telling him about Mother's Day. I thought – because of the letter – that he'd get it, but I think I just freaked him out because I got a bit upset, and it was **SO AWKWARD**. I mean, I haven't even told Megsers about Mother's Day. And I haven't even told you, Non-Judgemental Friend. But I think that's because I wanted to tell someone who could say something back. Like ALL THE RIGHT WORDS . . . like he did before. Just not today.

25 *March* (THURSDAY)

When I got home after school I walked into the hall and Lola and Carpenter Dan were standing in the living room. And Dan said a very cheery, 'How's it going, Ellery?' which I thought was nice because he remembered my name, but MAINLY because I figured he was making an effort to let there be no underwear-related embarrassment between us or – by association – Silent Johnny because I have to see him in school.

Anyway, I leave them to it but then I overhear the rest of the conversation from upstairs and Lola saying, 'Thank you SO MUCH again, Dan. You did a very professional job.' (Surprised tone.) Then she adds, 'I can see that you take GREAT PRIDE in your work.'

And Dan replies: 'Thanks very much.'

'My pleasure,' says Lola. And THEN: 'There is no reason, Dan, why you couldn't – some day – create something as MAGNIFICENT as these.'

AWKWARD SILENCE.

And Dan laughs, and goes: 'The shelves? I don't know about that. That's an awful lot of work: finding the right – WHAT wood is that?'

'Oak,' says Lola.

'Oak,' says Dan, 'and then there's all the cleaning, and sanding, and measuring, and cutting . . .'

'CRAFTSMANSHIP,' Lola explains. And I'm like, POOR DAN.

'Actually,' says Lola, 'do you know who built them?'

'Who?' says Dan.

And Lola goes, 'Oh! I was asking you, did YOU know?'

And Dan goes, 'I don't, no. But if I find out, I might ask him if he's looking for a forty-four-year-old apprentice.'

And Lola, I can tell, is not quite sure what she's supposed to say to that. So she goes with: 'You're never too old to learn!'

Dan will **NEVER FIX ANYTHING IN OUR HOUSE AGAIN**.

'I'm going to the playground,' I say to Lola afterwards.

'The playground,' she says.

'I like the playground,' I say.

'And what do you do there?' she says.

'Push little kids off the slide to make them cry.'

She looks at me.

'There's this giant round swing thing made of net,' I say, 'and I lie back and look up at the sky.'

'But would it hold your weight?' she says.

Seriously.

'No. I just break it every time, they fix it, I come back, break it, they fix it . . .'

SHE'S NUTS.

'But it's for children.'

'The stages of life are not that sharply defined any more,' Mom once explained to Lola when she saw me in a 'newborn's sleepsuit' (onesie) when I was twelve.

It's weird, though . . . I don't really FEEL sixteen. Or maybe I just don't WANT to be. But it's even weirder now. Because you know when you feel that way your mom can still give you hugs and tell you you'll always be her baby, and you're all, like, **GET OFF ME** but you don't mean it, and she knows you don't mean it. So it's fine.

But I think Lola doesn't get why I'm not renting my own apartment somewhere. I think she's only here because she has to be but she's thinking she wouldn't HAVE to be if Mom had been tougher on me.

Last summer when Mom and I were staying with her and Grandpa, I was flipping out because I had to take the train to Grand Central on my own – for the first time.

And Lola says: 'When I was your age, I had a one-way ticket to the Port Authority Bus Terminal, and a lipstick in my back pocket.'

'Didn't it melt?' I say. 'The lipstick.'

'Those were the days of real men and real lipsticks,' says Lola.

Mom is behind her, doing eye-rolls with Auntie Elaine.

'When I was your age,' says Auntie Elaine, 'I had a one-way ticket to Zero Authority, and a rock of crack in my back pocket.'

'Elaine!' says Lola. 'Don't LISTEN to her, Ellery.'

'When I was your age,' says Mom, 'I had terminal dyspraxia and a slapstick in my back pocket.'

Grandpa walks over, puts his arms around Mom and Auntie

Elaine, chuckles, gives their shoulders a squeeze, and says: 'That's my girls.' Then he looks at Lola, and adds: 'And that's my other girl.' And then he looks at me, and says, *'AND THERE SHE IS . . . MY BEST GIRL.'*

Anyway, the playground was cool. There was no one there, and I just sat on the giant swing thing and

watched the clouds.

26 March (FRIDAY)

When we get to Megser's she makes me wait in the living room for ages, then drags me down the hall to Susan's 'craft room', which is tiny, has one little window and smells of smoke. It used to be a walk-in wardrobe until Susan read a decluttering bible.

'Sit,' says Megser, pointing to the dressing table.

And she stands opposite me with a stick in her hand, pointing at a whiteboard with an A3 sheet of paper clipped to it. And written on it, in huge letters, is:

WTF?

Then she RIPS THAT SHEET OFF and there's ANOTHER SHEET underneath:

Who's The Father?
The Suspects

SUSPECT 1: JAY EVANS ★ ★ ★ ★ ☆
SUSPECT 2: LEON ADLER ★ ★ ★ ★ ☆
SUSPECT 3: QUENTIN SCHAEFFER ★ ★ ☆ ☆ ☆

Megser runs her stick under each name as she's calling them out.

'Why didn't you just write directly on the whiteboard?' I say.

'Because have you ever opened a whiteboard marker that wasn't dried out? And because we need a PERMANENT RECORD of all this.'

'What? For the celebrity stalker trial?' I say.

'I'm ignoring you.'

She tries to keep going, but I put up my hand. 'What are the stars all about?'

'Their average star rating on Amazon across all their books.'

'You actually worked that out,' I say.

'YES,' she says.

'But . . . why?'

'To get a SENSE of them. But the system's a mess – all it takes for you to lose stars is the book wasn't delivered in time for someone's birthday or because there was a dent in the corner of the box or – in the case of Quentin Schaeffer – you kill off the wrong dragon and you suffer the wrath.' And she picks up her notes: 'Literally: "I *LOVED* this book. But he KILLED MYANTHER!!!! WRONG, WRONG, WRONG". And gives him one star! And Myanther wasn't even killed off in that book: it was three books later.'

'WHAT IS WRONG WITH PEOPLE?'

Then she goes, 'If it helps, the suspects are all critically acclaimed. So really . . . they're all five stars.'

And DEFINITELY Megser cares more about that.

Because I'm like, 'We need DIFFERENT star ratings. We need to rate them on how likely they are to be my dad.'

And Megser, **WIDE-EYED,** says: 'That's not a bad idea.'

BEST COMPLIMENT that Megser could EVER give.

'Also,' I say, because I've been encouraged, 'we need a second star rating for how much I WANT them to be my dad.'

And **DEFINITELY** I care more about this one.'

But she lets me have it, and she's nodding, then: 'Based on what exact criteria?'

'The ZERO exact kind,' I say. Because: BORING. 'Carry on!'

'If you are serious about meeting your father(s) . . . the plan has to be FLAWLESS.' Then she looks at me. 'And FOOLPROOF,' she adds.

I notice then that there are MORE A3 pages hanging in the empty wardrobe on those trouser hangers with the clips. Megser takes the first one out and clips it on to the whiteboard. It has loads of colour-coded boxes and lines, and abbreviations, and dates, and arrows. I put my hand up and point to the red box in the top left-hand corner.

'What is M.O.C.?'

'Month of Conception,' she says.

'BEYOND creepy. Cross that out IMMEDIATELY. But you can leave the June 2004.'

Meg rolls her eyes, but starts scribbling.

'I can still see it.'

She scribbles again, until I give her the nod of approval.

'This,' says Megser, 'is the diagram that confirms that each suspect was in your mother's company during the—'

'APPROPRIATE TIME,' I go, because I can see her staring wistfully at where M.O.C. used to be.

Then she reaches into the wardrobe and pulls out Jay Evans' individual author page, which includes an author photo, a list of his books in order of publication, his movies in order of release dates, his upcoming speaking engagements, and a list of known associates.

She slams the stick against his face.

'Jay Evans may be your **BIGGEST** problem,' she says. 'He's the biggest star. He will have the most people around him . . .'

'Okay . . . it isn't an ASSASSINATION attempt,' I say.

'Let me have this,' she says.

'Carry on,' I say.

She points to a printout of our school calendar, with Xs marking the holidays, and a circle round any of the Xs that coincide with one of Jay Evans' public appearances.

There is ONE WEEKEND circled in the ENTIRE year.

'You have ONE SHOT,' says Megser. 'Jay Evans lives between New York, LA and Paris, but is guarded as to his whereabouts at any given time.'

This is because Jay Evans has millions of fans. They're called Jaystalkers. Megser has very thoughtfully included mugshots of the top-ten Jaystalkers just so I have a visual in case we converge, because we agree that I wouldn't stand a chance against these – mainly – women, such is the strength of their devotion and their belief in a long-term future with Jay Evans.

'Megser,' I say, 'promise me if I EVER start talking about Hunter Threat a little too much, you'll let me know.'

'I already have,' she says.

Terrrue.

'JAY EVANS!' she then shouts to focus my mind, 'comes to Europe once a year and this year it will be for: the Milan Festival of Literary Fiction, which is running the weekend of 24–27 August.'

I am BEYOND excited. 'You say Milan. I say: ONE OF THE FASHION CAPITALS OF THE WORLD.'

I am now sensing that Megser is waiting for something from me and I have ZERO idea what it is.

'ELLERY!' she says. 'You need to be on the ball. I SAID: the Milan Festival of LITERARY Fiction … **EMPHASIS ON LITERARY.**'

And I'm like, EMPHASIS ON FALL FASHION.

'THINK!' says Megser. 'WHY would a festival of literary fiction invite an author of COMMERCIAL CRIME FICTION?'

And I jump up. 'OH! I KNOW this! Because the festival organiser is a JAYSTALKER!'

'NO!' says Megser like I'm insane, even though I can SEE she's realising that it actually makes sense as a theory.

'It's because Jay Evans has gone ROGUE,' she says. 'He will be launching a book of ESSAYS at the festival. Essays on LOVE.'

I'm STILL waiting for her to explain the relevance.

'THIS IS GOOD NEWS!' she says, even more frustrated, because at this stage there needs to be an air traffic control tower for the stuff going over my head. 'FIRSTLY this means that Jay Evans *loves love* . . . Does that sound like anyone we know?'

'Terrrue.' Because Ellery says:

WHAT'S NOT TO LOVE ABOUT LOVE?

'And SECONDLY,' says Megser. 'Maybe he had . . . a MUSE.'

'I HATE that word.'

'No one cares.'

'Even when it's aMUSE-bouche, which I love.'

'OHMYGOD, I just don't know if you're ABLE,' says Megser.

'GIRLS! Are you fighting in there?' says Susan.

'No! We don't fight!' we both say. And she goes away.

And Megser gives it the full explanation: 'What I'm saying IS: this ENTIRE BOOK OF ESSAYS could be about your MOM. Or YOU!'

'Ohhhhhh!' I say. And then 'Eww.' Just in case: DETAILS.

'Over the course of the past week,' says Megser, 'I have SKINGED the works of Jay Evans – novels fifteen to twenty. I have also invented the word SKINGE, which is a combination of SKIM and BINGE. I have made notes that I will use to assign you a choice of relevant questions to ask him, leveraging details of the plots and characters of the aforementioned books to elicit personal information and/or views that might bring us closer to discovering whether or not he is your father.'

'Can you talk to me like this ALL THE TIME about EVERYTHING?' I ask.

'Under no circumstances.'

'So . . . me flying out of the country for an overnight stay under the radar of my family, your mom and everyone else will be handled . . . ?'

'Whatever way you come up with.'

'But . . . haven't you crafted my lies?'

'WHERE on this uniform (she's wearing a unicorn onesie) do you see the word LIAR?'

'UNICORNS ARE LIES,' I say. 'You're wearing a LIE-print uniform.'

'The lies are YOUR area,' says Megs. 'I'm Literary Enlightenment,

Transportation and Accommodation.'

I'm just looking at her.

'**OH MY GOD** — I skinged FIVE crime novels for you,' she says. 'Do you KNOW the kind of sacrifice that was for someone like me? They're like the McDonald's of the literary world.'

'Yeah, well, Literary Fiction is the PSYLLIUM HUSKS of the literary world.'

And Meg's like 'What? Psyllium husks are just FIBRE.'

And I'm thinking, *Whuttt?* (But it explains A LOT.) Then I'm like, **'HOLD ON A SECOND!** That could be MY DAD'S LIFE'S WORK you're talking about!'

'Jay Evans has SEVEN coastal homes across Asia, North America, South America and Europe,' says Meg, slapping the bottom of the whiteboard, then clipping on a new page. She points to the images of these magnificent homes, and their magnificent swimming pools, nods like some MAFIA guy and says: **'ALL IS FORGIVEN.'**

Then Susan knocks and just walks in. 'HEY! Is that my vision board?'

'Yes!' says Megs, who genuinely believes that everything Susan owns is also hers, but goes nuts if Susan even TOUCHES her stuff.

'What did you do with all my VISIONS?' says Susan. Then she leans into the seven coastal homes. 'But I like how you're thinking.'

4 a.m. update

Megser and I both wake up to Megser's phone beeping. And because I hate electronic sounds, I'm like: 'Whyyy wasn't it on silent?'

And Meg is like, 'It WAS!' but then she goes, 'Oh. It's a Google alert. I've never set them up before.'

'Alert about what?'

'Your potential fathers.'

And she's reading the alert, and she's checking other things on her phone, and then she takes this **BIG DEEP BREATH.**

'ELLERY!' she says. 'You no longer have just ONE shot at Jay Evans! He will be appearing at the Bridge Theatre in London . . . at 7 p.m., Wednesday, 31 March.' Then she pauses for effect. 'Four days . . .' Then she checks the time on her phone for effect. 'Fifteen hours from . . . NOW.'

'YES!' I say. **'I ACCEPT THIS CHALLENGE.** IS it a challenge? What's going on?'

'What is going ON,' says Megser, 'is you are going to FACE . . . YOUR –' then she says 'potential' like it's small print '– FATHER.'

'WE are, you mean!'

And she's shaking her head. 'I'm the stay-at-home savant, remember? I will be manning the Incident Room.'

'I think I'd feel more comfortable if we called it the Without Incident Room.'

'Comfort,' says Megser, 'has NO PLACE in this operation.'

27 March (SATURDAY)

After breakfast we devise our plan:

PART I

Compose FAKE letter from REAL orthodontist in Cork city with a date from three months ago.

'Hold on a second!' says Megsers. 'You're American. Your teeth are PERFECT. It needs to be something CONVINCING.'

We google alternative treatments that Lola believes in.

PART I (ROUND II)

Compose FAKE letter from REAL kinesiologist re: Ellery Brown's appointment on Wednesday, 31 March at 6 p.m. to coincide with time of the last bus back to Beara, thereby necessitating an overnight stay in 'Cork'.

PART II

Book Lola a day of pampering at the spa at Sheen Falls Lodge – to take place ALSO on Wednesday, 31 March.

We print out the letter and fold it in three, so it looks REAL and I'm about to stick it in my bag when I remember I told Silent Johnny I'd call to his house this morning to borrow his biology notes because they are *THE BEST*. Silent Johnny is the son of a sheep farmer (yes, he LITERALLY hauls sheep around) and I heard him tell the teacher that he would be busy with lambing over the holidays so that's when I saw my opportunity.

So, when I get back from Megser's, Lola and I get in the car, and I do *What's My SONNNG?* and the radio is on Lyric FM and 'Movies and Musicals' is on, and we LOVE that show. Then one of our all-time favourites (and Mom's too) comes on: Elaine Stritch singing 'I'm Still Here' and she was about eighty at the time and it's so brilliant and funny and I'm expecting to hear a **HILARIOUS** story about Elaine Stritch from Lola at the end but when I turn to her I can see that her lips are pressed together and she's kind of frowning. I know this face because it's when **EMOTIONS** are involved and I also know what she's thinking because it's the same thing I'm thinking: *We're still here. And Mom isn't.*

And then we arrive at Silent Johnny's so: DISTRACTION. And Lola asks me will she wait and I'm like, 'TOTALLY!' because, let's face it, Silent Johnny and I weren't going to get lost in conversation.

'Will you be okay here on your own?' I ask her because of the SADNESS.

And Lola looks at me like I'm nuts. Because WHAT SADNESS?

Then she points to the radio. 'I named your Auntie Elaine after her,' she says then. '"Lois" was after a kind old neighbour who used to take me in when I was a little girl and things were . . . tough . . . at home. And "Elaine" because . . . well, I had a feeling she'd be a **FIRECRACKER**. Even before she was born.'

And I'm like, why didn't she ever TELL Auntie Elaine all this?!!

'She used to kick SO HARD,' says Lola.

And I'm thinking, *She still does*. And then I realise Lola's thinking the same thing, so off I go up to Silent Johnny's door and his dad answers: 'He's inside in the shed.'

You're not just 'in' something down here, you're INSIDE in it. So I walk through the gate and across the yard and I stop dead in the doorway. 'Aw, maaan!' I say.

Silent Johnny looks up from where he's sitting against the wall with a NEWBORN LAMB tucked into ONE accidentally muscular arm, feeding it from the baby's bottle he is holding in the hand of the OTHER accidentally muscular arm.

'That's the cutest thing I've ever seen in my LIFE,' I say.

'Manly man caught in caring pastoral [no idea] nightmare,' Meg said later.

'Does he have a name?' I say, pointing to the lamb.

Johnny does a side-eye of **RELUCTANCE TO REVEAL PERSONAL INFORMATION** and says, 'S. Dodge.'

'He's a rapper.'

Even Silent Johnny's laugh is reluctant. 'He's a SHE.'

'Where did S. Dodge come from?'

'Slaughter Dodger.'

Okay – I did NOT think Johnny was funny. I thought if he had a lamb to name, he'd name it after a Cork county footballer.

'So she's not going to die?' I say.

'No. She's my pet now.'

'How did that happen?'

'Her mother rejected her.'

'OH, NOOOO,' I say.

This was the longest conversation I've EVER had with Johnny . . . if we completely block out the underwear one, which I have.

'Do you want to have a go?' he says.

'Sure,' I say, and we have this awkward exchange of lamb and bottle. And then I hold them both at EXACTLY the right angle, and he's just looking at me. Because he was DEFINITELY expecting: 'Ewww – animals! Hay! Smells! My nails!' But no. He got RANCH ELLERY. Food, water, shelter and warmth.

28 March (SUNDAY)

Megser came down with a fake flu this morning so she could skip the Weekly Daly Pilgrimage as Susan calls it.

So Megser and I are alone in the Without Incident Room and she solemnly hands me a brown folder marked with . . . NOTHING. Because that would have been a **ROOKIE ERROR.**

Inside it, though, the title page says:

SUSPECT 1
LONDON, ENGLAND

'Please tell me I get a briefcase of weapons,' I say.

'The only weapon you need is INTELLECT,' says Megser. 'MY intellect.'

I take this well.

The next page says: ITINERARY, and I IMMEDIATELY start PANIC-FLICKING through every page that follows.

'WHAT?' says Megser, and I stop. Then I panic-flick through everything again. In the BLUR I see CHOICE of flights and CHOICE of hotels.

'But I hate choices,' I remind her. 'Just tell me EXACTLY what flights I'm taking, and EXACTLY where I'll be staying. You SAID you were Accommodation/Transportation!'

'Yes!' she says. 'I deliver your choices! I don't know your BUDGET.'

'I don't really either, but . . .'

'I'm genuinely thinking this is a **DISASTER,**' says Megser. 'You hate books. You can barely focus on ANYTHING I'm saying, I'm making this BIG EFFORT, and what's the point?'

And then I go: 'Okay. I know you're making this big effort. And thank you. Seriously. But you have this like MAJOR capacity in your brain for information, and it kind of traumatises me.'

'YOU have a major capacity in your brain for information!'

'I knowww,' I say, 'but . . .' And I'm thinking her capacity is filled with WAY more boring stuff. Not in any mean way. She doesn't bore ME with it. It's just . . . give me bullet points. That's all.

'Okay – BULLET POINTS,' says Megser, because we totally read each other's minds. And she reveals a list of questions for Jay Evans. She also gives in on the flight situation and I go with whatever she tells me, then book it with Auntie Elaine's credit card (I KNOWWW) because Auntie Elaine doesn't really pay attention to things like statements.

Megser puts her foot down when it comes to hotels. 'Just PICK ONE. And BOOK IT.'

I go online, and I THINK I book one.

Then I have to leave and Megser is like, 'Whyyy?'

And I'm like, 'BECAUSE I HAVE TO DO BIOLOGY HOMEWORK and then meet Oscar.'

And she just looks at me and goes, 'ENJOY THAT!'

So I went for a walk down to the strand with Oscar and I did all the talking, which was **AWKWARD.** I did not get into anything about Mom, though. So it was cool.

Mother's Day: LET'S DO THIS

(PART 1)

So Mom wrote me a book. Like, just for me. And left it with Auntie Elaine. To give to me on Mother's Day. Poor Auntie Elaine. It's like . . . I mean, you could have a **LOT OF FUN** if you were dying, and you really wanted to get revenge on someone. Literally no one can refuse your DYING WISH. If I was dying, I'd grab someone's hand (only, like, one of those awful people who just show up to check you out with no hair) and I'd say, 'Please, please . . . for me . . . LIVE THIS.' And I'd hand them a bucket list that would literally be like handing them a bucket of

Anyway, Mom was NOT trying to be mean to Auntie Elaine – I know that. But the BOOK.

Oceans.

Oceans of tears.

And we had no boat. And no skipper.

● ONE MORE THING I SAID TO MY MOM IN ANGER

'Mother's Day is for the GOOD MOTHERS.'

29 March (MONDAY)

TWO DAYS TO OPERATION SUSPECT 1
IMPLEMENTATION OF PLAN: PARTS III TO V

PART III: Surprise Lola with luxury spa day. She is THRILLED and MOVED (yes . . . moved 93 km from Cork Airport and 945 km from London. I googled it). She will also be out of coverage, and disabled by aromatherapy oils (nature's chloroform).

PART IV: Rush downstairs two hours later brandishing 'newly discovered' letter from kinesiologist, and tell her she can't POSSIBLY miss her spa day to drive me to Cork – I'll get the early bus in the morning from right outside Megser's door. And I say that I can check with Susan (CRUCIAL ADULT PAWN) if I can stay with her sister in Cork on Wednesday night (EVEN MORE CRUCIAL **DISTANT** ADULT PAWN).

PART V: Tell the exact same story to Susan, whose sister OF COURSE agrees to host me for the night (despite doubts about kinesiology).

PLANNING OF PART VI OF PLAN (TO BE CARRIED OUT IN MY ABSENCE)

Megser to steal Susan's mobile and text her aunt to say that Ellery thanks her for her very kind offer of a room for the night, but she has decided to stay with a family friend who lives right beside the kinesiologist's office, and is going to drive Ellery back to Beara before school the next morning . . . unless SHE'D like to.

'That would push her over the edge,' said Megser. 'The thought of running into . . .' And she nods in the direction of the utility room where Mrs Daly appeared five minutes earlier, halfway through a pile of ironing.

And sure enough, Megser's aunt replied to the text INSTANTLY with a thumbs-up emoji and Megser INSTANTLY deleted the entire exchange.

31 March (WEDNESDAY)

OPERATION SUSPECT 1

Ireland is TINY. People don't believe you when you tell them this. And THAT is why I will be wearing a disguise. When I say disguise I mean my make-up will be **AWESOME** for a weekday, and my hair will ALSO BE AWESOME. And I will be wearing fake serial-killer glasses from H&M.

I get on the Harrington's bus to Cork city at 7.15 a.m. as Ellery – sixteen-year-old schoolgirl – and I get off the bus – still Ellery, sixteen-year-old schoolgirl. Then I go into the toilets in Brown Thomas, and emerge: Ellery, could-pass-for-eighteen-year-old flyer to London and literary enthusiast who can contour a face in a way that alters it beyond recognition.

'Hey, Ellery!' It's the bus driver. 'You're looking fierce dolled up. Was it not a doctor's appointment you were going to?'

'An *audition* to *play* a doctor,' I say. 'What seems to be the problem, sir?'

'How doctors are getting younger by the minute!' he says. 'Anyway – good luck! You look the part!' And I'm like, 'Thank you!' in the middle of this **INSTANT FAILURE.**

And then I hop into the first cab I see, and all I'm thinking about is what I'm going to say if someone catches me on a flight.

Cork Airport is one of my all-time-favourite airports because it is so small and everyone is friendly and you get through so quickly. I watch the boarding gate from the darkness of the café opposite to make sure there's no one I know on the same flight. (Seriously – you HAVE to believe people who tell you

Ireland is tiny. And Cork is even tinier while being MASSIVE. And Cork people travel A LOT.) Then I board and take my seat and it all happens Without Incident.

The flight attendants were SO lovely; they complimented my make-up and my serial-killer glasses, and then when I had this tiny meltdown because it was my first flight to London without Mom they brought me tea and Kit Kats, and the woman beside me tried to pay, but they wouldn't let her, and she gave me tissues, and told me I was doing great, and she made me laugh SO much. Then she talked to me about her amazing children's charity and I told her Mom was a writer and that SHE was amazing (but I didn't tell her Mom's name in case I would get arrested) and she was SO sweet and she took the Tube with me from Heathrow and walked me ALL THE WAY to my hotel because hers was on the next street (what are the CHANCES?!) and walked me right to the concierge desk and handed me over safely and told me how great I was. **PEOPLE ARE SO KIND.**

AND . . . MY HOTEL IS AMAAAZING!

BECAUSE I MESSED UP THE BOOKING! AND IT'S £700 PER NIGHT! NOT the room Megser INTENDED for me to book. But stiiill.

◊ *1 April* (THURSDAY) ◊

'I don't get it!' says Meg. 'You had ONE JOB.'

And I've got DOWNWARD-FACING EYES. And I'm like, 'I knowww, but I . . . fell asleep.'

And I look up at Megser, and she's looking at me, and the two of us are just standing there in the Without Incident Room and I'm only back in town ten minutes because I went straight there.

And Megser's like 'Is this April Fool's?' but she knows it's not.

'How could you fall asleep?' she's saying. 'James Bond doesn't FALL ASLEEP.'

'The bed! It was HUGE. And I had a bath and THAT was huge! And . . .'

Then I burst out crying. And Megser's freaking out, because I'm properly crying, and I haven't properly cried in front of her before, not like this, and **I HONESTLY CAN'T BELIEVE I HAVE ANY TEARS LEFT** after last night.

'Ellery, what HAPPENED?' she says, and she looks TERRIFIED. 'What happened? Did somebody do something—'

And I'm all no, no, because they didn't, and then I tell her.

Because . . . in really nice hotels if you stay there a lot, they have your file, and they know what you *love,* and they want

131

to cater to your every need, and when I paid for the room, the card was Ms L Brown's because some of Auntie Elaine's cards are still under her original first name and the hotel assumed it was Ms Laurie Brown because Mom has stayed there LOTS before, but I didn't know that, and . . . when I went into the room . . . it was just . . . FULL of everything Mom loves: Jelly Beans, and champagne, and salted-caramel chocolate, and roasted cashew nuts, and grapefruit shower gel, and lime bath oil, and lavender pillow spray, and a bergamot candle, and no television on, and it was this **beautiful, beautiful** room, with a view over the WHOLE of London, and just me, standing there in the **dark,** and it smelled like Mom. And it was gorgeous for this microsecond until I looked over at the bathroom door, and it was like this MASSIVE HORROR in my HEART because I knew she wasn't going to walk out and tell me something about the weird shower or how her make-up had been arranged neater than she had ever done it herself in her life or how she missed me for the entire half-hour she was taking a bath. And I couldn't BREATHE. And I literally was like, WHERE IS THE WOMAN FROM THE PLANE? And then I was like, **I AM NUTS**. And there were just **SO MANY TEARS** until I fell asleep. And then I woke up and it was one thirty.

2 April (FRIDAY)

LIES HAVE A WAY OF MULTIPLYING IN A WAY THAT THE TRUTH NEVER REALLY DOES.

Like there are all these offshoot lies. This afternoon Lola and I were walking down town, and next thing I hear this voice: 'Did you get the part?' and I know it's the bus driver and I'm like, OH GOD OH GOD OH GOD and, WHERE DOES HE KEEP COMING FROM?! and Lola is all confused and looking around and she can't see me shaking my head at him because I do it so quickly and then I say to her: 'I LOVE the Cork sense of humour.' And Lola's waiting for the RELEVANCE to kick in, so I go: 'He obviously heard you're an actress.'

Offshoot lies are like the instant coffee of lies – you know they'll satisfy something but you're ashamed to be serving them.

Anyway, now I'm just thinking about how much Mom hated lying, and how horrified she would be that I've turned into a PROFESSIONAL LIAR and what has become of me? And what WILL become of me?

'You are NOT going to end up a reality show contestant,' says

Megser when I arrive at her house.

'But this is not a good path I'm on.'

'It's only temporary lying with an end goal in sight.'

Hmm. 'Okay – that sounds **BRILLIANT** in fairness,' I say. 'You TOO could have a future as a disgraced politician.'

'Well, what are you going to do? TELL Lola?'

'Me? YOU'RE the mastermind in all this.'

And Meg's all no, no, no and Mam's a solicitor and she could jail me HERSELF, and I'm thinking if she hasn't jailed the Ferals yet . . . but I just say: 'NO ONE is going to jail.'

And Meg says: 'Which sounds EXACTLY like a line from a movie where everyone ENDS UP IN JAIL.'

✳ *3 April* (SATURDAY) ✳

Despite that concern, right before I'm leaving Megser's this morning, she grabs my arm and pulls me to one side. 'Okay – there's something I HAVE to tell you. Suspect Two – Leon Adler – is doing a reading on April 23rd . . . in Paris . . . in . . . Shakespeare & Co.'

And I'm like, **OHMYGOD!** It's a SIGN! SHAKESPEARE & CO.!

Where Megser says Mom is! Doing her AVENGER FAIRY GLINT!

And Megser is all, 'You don't have to do anything you don't want to do,' and, 'Do you WANT to go?' and, 'Do you want to have time to THINK about it?'

And I DO. Because my MAIN THINKING at this moment is: **?**

Who's the ~~Father~~ Failure? **?**

Ellery Brown **?**

❋ 4 April (EASTER SUNDAY) ❋

Lola and I went to the hotel for Sunday lunch, and I thought of the poor lambs who did NOT dodge the slaughter. It was pretty hard not to when one of them is dead in front of you. S/he was DELICIOUS. God rest him/her.

Lola handed me this ENORMOUS egg all wrapped up in thick gold paper and a beautiful red bow, and I was BEYOND excited until I realised the egg was plastic.

'Open the latch!' says Lola who has to be the only person in the world who could give someone an Easter egg WITH A LATCH.

'Be careful,' she says.

So I open it and **OHMYGOD**, IT IS THE BEST EASTER EGG IN THE HISTORY OF EASTER EGGS. I AM COMPLETELY HYPERVENTILATING. It is ENTIRELY FILLED with . . . MAKE-UP!

This is the flavour of crazy I love most about Lola. I jump up and give her a hug that almost BREAKS her, and she's the happiest I've seen her in ages, and so am I. But if I'm HONEST – for a change! – I did check everywhere for secret panels that might contain chocolate. **NEGATIVE.**

Grandpa FaceTimed us later, and his knee is doing great, and the horses are great, and he misses Lola, and he misses me. And it's all fine until he realises that something is on my mind, and he waits until Lola is out of the room to ask me.

'Come on,' he says. 'I know my girl's face . . . even underneath all that make-up.'

'I put it ALL on!' I say. 'And it's AMAZING. Thank you so much. *THANK YOU, THANK YOU, THANK YOU!'*

'Well, you don't need it,' says Grandpa. 'But we know you love it.' Then he says, 'Now . . . talk to me.'

I say: 'Is it okay to feel . . . a bit . . .'

'Sad?' he says.

And I just want to say, YES! That's what it is! Sad! Because sad is EASY. But I'm just shaking my head, and all these tears are happening, and then I just say, 'ANGRY'. And then I add in, 'at Mom'.

And Grandpa nods, and he's just SO adorable, and he says: 'Sweetheart, it's always okay to feel anything about anything. How about you tell me what it is you're feeling angry about?'

'I just . . . how could she . . . well, just . . . not in any mean way . . . but . . . how could she just LEAVE US ALL?'

His face. 'I know, sweetheart,' he says. 'I know. But it was not her decision to go.'

'But why would ANYONE make that decision? To take her away. Why? Because it's NOT FAIR. Because she LOVED US and WE LOVED HER and she NEVER HURT ANYONE. And terrible people get to live for ever. This guy was arrested in Texas last week for MURDER and he was SEVENTY-FOUR.'

'The same age as your grandmother.' And then he makes a face, and I don't even know what it is, except it's funny, and then we're laughing, and then I ruin EVERYTHING with this madness:

'And . . . HOW could Mom not TELL me who my DAD is?'

Poor Grandpa. I don't think he was expecting that. I mean, I wasn't even expecting it.

'Ellery, sweetheart, when you're sixteen years old I

can't imagine how you could wrap your brain around some of the decisions adults make. Hell, your *grandmother* still amazes me after all these years. But if Lola decides she's right about something, then that's that. No further discussion. Your mama didn't get it from nowhere.'

'But YOU'RE not like that,' I said. 'I don't know why she didn't even tell YOU who my dad was.'

'Well,' said Grandpa, 'if you can believe THIS – someone else came into this world who was a lot more important to your mama than anyone else in the entire **UNIVERSE** . . . including her old pa.'

'Nooo!' I say. 'That's not true.'

He smiled. 'Well, thank you for that.'

Then like a HORRIBLE human being I say: 'I don't BELIEVE you don't know who he is. You HAVE to know.'

And he doesn't even get mad at me for effectively calling him a liar.

He just says: 'I swear on the lives of all my darling girls that your mama never told any of us. What I do know is that she loved your father very much, and he loved her too – she told us that.'

And Grandpa KNOWS what I'm thinking and he's saying, 'I know things should be simple if two people *love each other,* but . . .' And then he looks sad. 'This was your mama's life, sweetheart, this was her baby's life – YOUR life. And, Lord knows, I lay awake enough nights, wracking my brains trying to figure out why she did what she did, but all we could do was respect her wishes.'

6 April (TUESDAY) HOLIDAYS

I call to Megser's and give her my formal permission to begin the research on Leon Adler. But it turns out that as soon as she mentioned the words SHAKESPEARE & CO. last week, my eyes were all the green light she needed.

I ask her has she been skingeing his books. And she goes: 'It would be a DISGRACE to skinge anything to do with Leon Adler ... but I DID read his novella, *Secret Daughter*—'

And I'm like, 'OHMYGOD!' And Meg is rolling her eyes.

'YOU'RE SO MEAN.'

'But what I DID do,' said Megser, 'was LOADS of things in great detail.'

(Happily for Megser that meant ordering the US edition of Leon Adler's latest book: *Elation*. SERIOUSLY.)

But reading *Elation* is the least of Megser's efforts. In terms of planning she is clearly taking ZERO risks ... because: MY TRACK RECORD. She has written CONTINGENCY plans. And EVACUATION plans. And EMERGENCY EVACUATION plans. And EMERGENCY EVACUATION CONTINGENCY plans.

I told her I was very disappointed with her anticipation of doom. And Mom would be too. Mom was Negative-Forecasting Averse.

We used to have this saying, Mom and I: 'Where's the neg?' She first said it when I was going to my friend MJ's birthday party/ sleepover in fifth grade (age ten). MJ lived in this MANSION, with a swimming pool, and her parents had cool jobs and knew all kinds of cool people and I was **FREAKING OUT** that morning because of pre-emptive party anxiety not helped by the privately held (MISGUIDED) belief that this party was happening on a boat. And Mom goes: 'Let me get this straight: you're going to one of your BEST FRIENDS' birthday parties, in a **MAGNIFICENT** house, you'll get to see a Disney movie that hasn't been released in theatres yet, there'll be a CELEBRITY DJ on the decks (this was why I thought it was happening on a boat), you'll be sleeping in custom pyjamas (SERIOUSLY), and a CHEF will prepare – and deliver to your room! – a **MIDNIGHT FEAST.**' I'm looking at Mom with the PROCESSING EYES. And she goes: 'Where's the neg?'

9 April (FRIDAY) HOLIDAYS

The GOOD NEWS is we located ALL THE NEGS!

IN LEON ADLER'S TWITTER ACCOUNT!

Recurring theme in Leon Adler's work: **MISERY**. Recurring theme in Leon Adler's Twitter feed: **ANXIETY**.

Meg and I are EXHAUSTED by it all. Here's ONE example:

@addledauthor you know you're anxious/depressed when you can't even eat your Death Row Meal #SteakBéarnaise [inc. photo of untouched Steak Béarnaise and his hand in the corner, thumb down]

And these replies:

My DRM is CHOCOLATE CAKE. For Brandy it's HUNGRY HOUND BEEF & SWEET POTATO STEW. But today . . . #NoAppetite #DownwardFacingDog

Wrap it up, hun, put it in the fridge. It will keep! Tomorrow is another day! Hugs! x

It's a SIGN. Get your cholesterol checked. Lots of butter in sauce. SORRY! Prob not what you want to hear! #hearthealth if its ur death row meal & u havnt eatn it yet . . . #hope

And THIS reply to the FIRST REPLY: give the dog the CHOCOLATE CAKE#OneBirdTwoStones

What is WRONG with people? In GENERAL. Because we KNOW what's wrong with Leon Adler.

Megser goes EERILY quiet and I find out why when she looks up from her laptop and announces: 'You're going to need a FAKE ID.'

And I'm like, Whutttt?! *BECAUSE THAT FEELS REALLY ILLEGAL.*

'Because it IS illegal,' says Meg when I bring that up. Then she goes: 'Where's the neg?'

'INCORRECT USAGE OF THE TERM,' I tell her. 'There are like a MILLION negs.'

'What are you on about?' says Megser. 'Loads of people have FAKE IDs.'

And I'm like, 'NO – loads of OTHER PEOPLE have them. I could be—'

'Don't tell me,' says Megser. **'ARRESTED.'**

And I'm like OBVIOUSLY because she KNOWS I am totally terrified of the law. Literally every time I hear a siren, I think the guards are coming for me – FINALLY! – to arrest me for [INSERT UNCOMMITTED CRIME].

'LOOK,' says Megser, 'you mightn't even have to use it. But what if . . . I don't know, you need to be an adult—'

'I don't want to need to be an adult even when I AM an adult.'

'What IF,' says Megser, 'you don't get to ask Leon Adler anything at the reading, and then he goes to some BAR afterwards, and you get stopped at the door?'

'OR,' I go, 'what if I need to rent a car? Like a GETAWAY VEHICLE?' And then I laugh to make her think I'm joking. But in my head I'm driving a Mini Cooper up the side of the Eiffel Tower.

'So . . . the ID,' she says.

'PLEASE tell me I don't have to do anything and you're just going to hand it to me in a brown envelope next week.'

And she's just giving me FLAT EYES.

'FINE!' I say. 'So what do I have to do?'

'This coming Wednesday, 14th April,' Megser announces, 'you will be paying ID Dean a visit.'

'Don't say "PAYING VISITS"! No one pays people visits unless it's SHADY.'

'It IS shady. OHMYGOD. Every bit of this is shady! Stop getting surprised by the shadiness.'

ID Dean operates out of the slot-machine corner of his

parents' bar in town. He looks like a Tim Burton-approved character sketch.

'WEDNESDAYS,' says Megser to focus my mind. 'ID Dean accepts clients between the hours of 3 p.m. and 5 p.m. No appointment necessary. Bring two passport photos and one hundred euros in UNMARKED BILLS.'

And we both know that neither of us knows what an unmarked bill is.

But we BOTH KNOW that we BOTH KNOW
→ it sounds AWESOME.

ALSO: Megser has started to read *Elation* by Leon Adler. Thoughts and prayers at this difficult time.

12 April (MONDAY)

So we're back at school and Oscar has new glasses. They're ADORABLE. He tells me they're Ernest Hemingway glasses, which I know because I'm EARNEST about accessories. I tell Megser about them later, and she goes, 'Safe enough living up to those.'

13 April (TUESDAY)

I literally spent TWO HOURS picking out an outfit to wear to meet ID Dean. I will be wearing black skinny jeans, black boots, a black long-sleeved T-shirt, and a green fashion combat jacket, so the military badges on it are all like: *Cutie!* and *Kiss! Kiss!* and **TRUE LOVE!** and *Be Love!* and I'm hoping tomorrow will be like a movie where you arrive and discover that the bad guy is SURPRISINGLY BLIND for contrast because he deals in IDs.

14 April (WEDNESDAY)

Because I don't have a lawyer (and Lola would have a coronary if I called her from jail), I tell Megser to stay by her phone because she will be my one phone call to which I am legally entitled. But Meg says it probably has to be an adult. And I'm like, well, come with me and get a fake ID, then. And she goes, SAFE ENOUGH. And I'm like, **I AM NOT SAFE AT ALL.** And she goes: YOU'VE TRAINED ALL WEEK FOR THIS. GO OUT THERE AND ... PUT THE BALL IN THE BACK OF THE NET.

So I step inside the bar. And the heads of all five drinkers at the bar JERK in my direction and they actually recoil! And I'm

FURRREAKED OUT — until I realise the problem was not me – it was the shaft of sunlight that accompanied me. So I quickly close the door behind me.

I carry on through the bar like a fugitive whose image has just been released to the media. Then I go around the corner (Meg drew me a floor plan) and ID Dean is slumped on this cracked black-fake-leather booth, with seventy-five per cent of his body under the table. He is unsurprisingly NOT BLIND, so I take off my jacket with the lame badges, and sit on the stool opposite him.

I then realise that ID Dean is wearing BLACK SKINNY JEANS, BLACK BOOTS and a BLACK LONG-SLEEVED T-SHIRT.

We literally look like the BEFORE SHOTS where the after shots are MUG SHOTS.

ID Dean drags himself up to a sitting position, lowers his forearms on to the table and presses his palms together. He leans in over his perfectly manicured hands (black nail polish). 'I've been expecting you.' And he sits back in triumph. And he smiles. And he actually has a really nice smile and white teeth.

'I knew you'd crack,' he adds.

And I'm like, *HOW DOES HE EVEN KNOW WHO I AM?!* And then I'm picturing his bedroom wall covered with grainy surveillance photos of all the kids in school, and Dean, smiling and drawing a red X on their faces as soon as they have their first taste of alcohol, but the photo of me is just me, no X, MOCKING him.

'I don't want it to buy ALCOHOL,' I say.

And he goes: 'I get it, I get it . . . some older guy. I can get you pepper spray too.'

OHMYGOD, EWWW. 'NOT an older guy.'

'A gun? That'll take a while. Japanese throwing stars? No problem: I know a guy in Bandon. Fireworks? Hotel room? Gambling? Driver's licence? Tattoo!' Then: 'Oooh! OOOH!' And he sits back. 'MARRIAGE LICENCE!'

I now think DEAN is short for deranged. So I do like in the movies, and slide this neatly folded square of money across the table as if THAT'S the only thing that's going to do the talking around here. And Dean nods with GREAT respect, sits up and holds out his hand for the passport photos and I give them to him, and he looks, and he nods again.

'Now, that's PROPER contouring,' he says.

And then I could hear something . . . which in hindsight was the sound of **IMPENDING DOOM** . . . and . . . SERIOUSLY . . . this happened:

The front AND back doors of the bar **EXPLODE** open, and in come . . .

THE GUARDS!

And I'm literally like: MEG HAS ORGANISED THE BEST, MOST **TERRIFYING PRANK** EVER AND I WILL KILL HER because that was WAY BETTER than focusing on the realisation that it REALLY WAS the guards. And I don't know how I did this, but I managed to grab my passport photos and the money and shove them into my jacket pocket. And I'm SERIOUSLY thinking about eating them. And the guards are all searching ID Dean's pockets and there is nothing in them. And I'm like, GREAAAT: I'M the one with the one hundred euro in cash and the passport photos.

And then Mom's words come to me: 'We can ALWAYS find evidence for what we WANT to believe.'

And the guards totally want to believe (the actual truth!) that ID Dean deals in ILLEGAL FAKE IDs and the evidence for MOST OF THAT is on my person but I'm thinking – thanks to Mom, which feels so wrong under the circumstances – what OTHER story can this evidence tell?

I AM A *WORK* OF FICTION!
AND IF I CAN'T DO IT, WHO CAN?

And then:

I. DO. IT.

Because I ALSO have something else in my bag . . . another

piece of 'EVIDENCE' (quotes by Ellery) that CHANGES EVERYTHING. It is an application form, not yet filled out, and it is the reason I had some passport photos to spare in the first place – and I pull it out of my bag, and I tell the guards THIS was why I was there: to sign Dean up for volunteering at the retirement home and that the hundred euros was for: associated supplies. And Dean is TOTALLY on board.

Lola came down to the station to pick me up and her face was like Fight Night. But . . . my story checked out because literally there was no way it couldn't have.

So ID Dean and I are saying our goodbyes – feat. HUGS! He is insane – and he's thanking me, and I'm thanking God and Mom in my head. And then he says: 'And good luck with the old guy. Sorry about the ID. But you don't need it. He'll totally believe you're over eighteen.'

EWWWWW!

And then he's walking off and goes, 'See you next week, so!' And he's RIGHT. Because that application-form lie has GUARANTEED that ID Dean and I will now be seen together EVERY WEEK and will become the kind of people you see together and go, **WHAT'S THE STORY THERE?**

Because, let's face it, there is ALWAYS a story.

15 April (THURSDAY)

Meg laughed SO HARD that I honestly think that what happened to me yesterday was the *best thing* that ever happened to her.

16 April (FRIDAY)

MOOD SHIFT: Meg was MISERABLE at lunch today.

'Are you still reading *Elation*?' I ask her.

She shakes her head. 'I finished it.'

'But . . . then you should be *ELATED.*'

She laughs. And still looks miserable.

'So what were your findings?' I ask her.

And she goes: 'I don't know what to say.' (Which always means she DOES know . . . but it will be AWFUL.) 'Just – I kind of hope he's not your dad.' Then she calls him Surprisingly Alive, which sounds like something I'd say. Then she expands on that: 'In that he hasn't dissolved into the "treacherous and endless darkness of the world".'

'He'll be no fun on our daddy-daughter dates,' I say.

And she laughs. Because we HATE 'daddy-daughter dates'.

Not just because we don't have dads or that we wouldn't DATE them if we did. Just because it's the CREEPIEST EXPRESSION KNOWN TO MAN. We also hate all the mum ones. Especially: MUMPRENEUR. Meg did a business presentation last year and called Richard Branson a DADPRENEUR for the whole thing.

'Do you still have it?' I say. '*Elation*?' But I can SEE the spine of it in her bag.

So I'm reaching out, expecting Megser to hand over the book. But she says: 'No.' Followed by eye dart to her bag. Rookie error. Rookie because Meg and I do NOT lie to each other.

'But is that not it?' I say, pointing right at it. 'In your bag?'

And I'm reaching down, but she YANKS the bag towards her!

'Oh no!' I say. **WHAT'S WRONNNG?** It's about Mom, isn't it?'

'No!' she says. 'No – it's NOT about your mom,' and she's looking RELIEVED.

'OH GOD,' I say. 'Does he say Mumpreneur? Or WORSE: daddy-daughter date?'

'It's set in 1898.'

'OH NOOOO! IT'S ABOUT HISTORY. WAY WORSE.'

And she laughs. And the bell starts to ring. And I THINK it's playing

'Let It go'.

17 April (SATURDAY)

Auntie Elaine – who was supposed to be here all this month but couldn't be because of work – called to tell me that she's booked flights for me to New York for the May bank holiday weekend. It's Grandpa and Lola's fiftieth wedding anniversary and the party is at their house on the Saturday.

I'm like (MUTED): 'Yaaay! Thank you!' And then there's this SILENCE.

And Auntie Elaine goes: 'I know. No one feels like throwing a party. But . . . the best thing is that all of us need to not feel like throwing a party TOGETHER.' And then she goes: 'And you and me SO need to be there to pin the medal of valour on Grandpa. Or if there's an endurance one. . .' And we laugh at that.

THEN I GET A BIT SAD when I think that there are only four of us left in our family. I mean: even five was small. The extended family, though, is big on both sides. But it's kind of like the extension on the dining-room table – in that it's an effort to pull out, and not everyone wants to get involved, but it has to be done every now and then, and then you're relieved when you get to push it back in again.

2 a.m. update

I woke with this thought. About my name. Because it's unusual and what if it has something to do with my dad?

And I realise I've never looked up what my name means, so I go to a baby names website.

And Ellery means JOYFUL! **HOW ADORABLE** of my mom!

And THEN . . . Oh GOD . . . now I realise: JOY!

THE HAPPINESS OF LESTER JOYYYYY!

19 April (MONDAY)

I am **NOT** proud of the plan Megser and I concocted to trick Lola so that I could go to Paris. PLUS, it involves ID Dean who reminded me – when I bumped into him slipping in through the fire door at school – he *'OWES ME'*.

So there's this personal development programme called Rollout, which basically involves doing good in the community and winning awards for it. Megser and I are Rollout Ambassadors which you would think would make us good people and upstanding citizens, which, in fairness, we used to be. But this

Thursday we will be rocking the rollout ethos to its CORE by using the innocent guise of a camping trip for ten-year-olds to our advantage. All because it is happening in woods located twenty convenient kilometres from Cork Airport.

22 April (THURSDAY)

So... NEW LOW. **I'VE WARNED YOU.**

First night at camp, I stage a fake meltdown over Mom. I knowww. I knowww. In fairness it DID spiral into a genuine meltdown once I got going. Megser – as Best Supporting Actress – is summoned by the scout leader to take care of me. She tells him that she has already put a call in to my 'Uncle Jeff' who flew in from New York this very morning as bird-nester of the coming week because Lola got a last-minute cancellation for a silent retreat in Dublin, something to do with GRIEF. I knowww. I knowww. **THE WHOLE THING IS DESPICABLE.**

'Uncle Jeff' is one of ID Dean's shady friends who does part-time extra work on movies and has a 'savage American accent'. In advance of this trip ID Dean sends me a photo of 'Uncle Jeff' for recognition purposes: big guy, broad-shouldered, grey hair, grey beard, gnarly face, friendly eyes, big strong arms that I will be running into to weep in the morning. Because – OH NO! – it seems 'Uncle Jeff' can't make it tonight (because then I'd have to pay for a hotel).

'He said he's SO sorry he can't be here any sooner,' says Megser.

'Oh, THAT'S okay, Megser,' I say, snivelling. 'I guess I can make it through the night. As long as I have you by my side.'

I make it through the night.

23 April (FRIDAY)

It's 7 a.m. and 'Uncle Jeff' arrives at camp looking approximately FIVE years older than me. ID Dean neglected to tell me the photo he sent me was from the set of the TV series, *Vikings*, where his hair is very convincingly coated in grey make-up. And then Jeff spoke. And YES! Yes, he DOES have a savage American accent ... clearly from repeat viewing of just one movie: *It's a Wonderful Life*. He sounds exactly like James Stewart. ('Golly, Ellery! You SURE are looking mighty lonesome!')

So, to sum it up: 'Uncle Jeff' looks like he's in his twenties, sounds like he's from the fifties, is wearing a tracksuit from the eighties and there are ninety-nine reasons why the scout leader should be saying: **'IS THIS SOME KIND OF JOKE?'**

But who wouldn't be charmed by JIMMY STEWART? And, in fairness, who wouldn't be charmed by Willy from Ballincollig – the man impersonating him. Because: **THE FRIENDLY EYES.**

We get away with it! And Willy from Ballincollig and I drive off into the sunrise and we get on like a tent on fire. He drops me off at the airport, but he comes in too so he 'can get changed for work in the jacks', and as I'm checking in I see him walking past – and I'd LOVE to do 'In Wild Guess Challenge: what work clothes DID Willy change into?' but I'm not sure even in your WILDEST OF WILD GUESSES you'd say: A GARDA uniform.

YES: Willy from Ballincollig is a part-time extra, full-time GUARD and full-time UNKNOWN ASSOCIATE of ID Dean.

And then he comes over to me, hands me an envelope, and I open it, and it has my fake ID in it!

I AM ELLERY BROWN AND I AM TWENTY!

And I'm like, 'But . . . howww?'

And Willy goes: 'Dean nicked the passport photos from your jacket pocket when he was hugging you goodbye at the station.'

24 April (SATURDAY)

PARIS: PART UN

I will be writing my account of the events that took place in Paris in parts. Or else my hand will fall off.

I blame LOLA (acting genes) for what happened. Lola, temporary insanity and . . . signs.

Merci-fully, there are zero *gendarmes* waiting for me in Charles de Gaulle. However, I do see several men in uniform: chauffeurs. And one of them is holding up a sign that says: M. LEON ADLER.

So I walk over to where he is and loiter with intent.

Beside the chauffeur is a tall, impeccably dressed man. He has to be the publicist with Leon Adler's publisher – written in small print on the sign – *MAISON D'ÉDITION DURAND DUVAL*. Though this man looks PERFECT on first glance, on second and third glances I can see that his eyes are a yellowy-red. And his hair is a little on end. And he is SQUIRMING. One word: **HANGOVER.** And two extra words: **FROM HELL.** He's chatting to the chauffeur, but his jaw is CLENCHED and his forehead is live-developing a sheen and his lips are now pursing, and I KNOW what's about to happen, then it HAPPENS. He SLAMS his hand against his mouth and RUNS.

Next thing: I find myself following through on my eerie compulsion to walk towards the chauffeur with great purpose.

'BONJOUR!' I say to him. 'I work with Monsieur Adler. There has been a SLIGHT change of plans. His publicist—'

And he goes: 'Jean-Luc?'

'Yes,' I say. 'Last name?'

'CatasTROFF' is how I hear his reply. And it takes me a moment to realise it's French, so it's CATASTROPHE (silent 'e').

'Unfortunately,' I say, 'Monsieur Adler is suffering from one of his well-documented [i.e. well gone on and on about on Twitter] anxiety attacks, and is unable to interact with ANYONE other than me ... for the time being. Is that his itinerary? Is it the same one I have here?' (A page from Silent Johnny's biology notes.)

And he hands me the itinerary, and I go: 'Let me check this against the PDF.' And I take it, faux scroll through the emails on my phone while taking a photo of it, then go:

'Yes. Perfect. I think what we'll do is let Monsieur Catastroph(e) enjoy his morning [*VOMIR* in peace!] and you and I will take Monsieur Adler to his hotel to get checked in. Then lunch: 1 p.m. to 2.30 p.m., after which we will depart for his first official engagement of the day at 3 p.m.'

And he's nodding. 'Oui, okay.'

And then I say: 'I would ask also for your discretion in this matter, and to extend the same request to Monsieur Catastroph(e). We would rather Monsieurs Durand *et* Duval not know about Monsier Adler's TEMPORARY anxiety issue in case they were to grow concerned about his ability to honour his future commitments.'

He nods. '*Bien sûr.*' Then: 'But – as you know – Monsieur Duval has been dead for ten years.'

'God rest him,' I say. Then: 'One more thing, IF I MAY. Because Mr Adler is currently in such a vulnerable state, if you wouldn't mind – could I ask that you kindly wait for us at the car?' And I get the details of where he's parked.

Right before he leaves, he pauses and says: 'Tell me, mademoiselle, how does a *JOYEUSE* young woman, such as you, work for a man such as Monsieur Adler? *C'est un MONSTRE.*'

WAIT. WHOA. WHUTTTT?

And in Too Late Now News – off I go to rendezvous with a *monstre.*

Mom once told me that sometimes the things she made up ended up happening in real life. This 'gift' is clearly genetic – because Leon Adler arrives into . . . Arrivals in PRECISELY the anxiety-ridden state I had just manufactured. His body is literally the shape of a question mark. And the questions it is asking are: WHY? Why ME? Why THIS? Why are we all really here?

I know why I am, so I'm holding my reclaimed M. LEON ADLER sign and calling out his name.

'Mr Adler,' I say, shaking his hand by actively reaching down, and pulling it up from his side. 'It is SO GOOD to meet you. I'm Victoria . . . THREAT. And here is your welcome pack . . .' Which contains a whole load of Leon Adler's favourite things. Then I look him in the eye and tell him: 'Don't worry. **EVERYTHING IS GOING TO BE OKAY.'**

(inspired by the 24 November 2018 tweet from **@addledauthor**:Sometimes all you need is for someone to look you in the eye and tell you EVERYTHING IS GOING TO BE OKAY.)

I can see SOME relief in his face. As we're walking to the car I tell him the **CATASTROPHE** about Jean-Luc and the PERSONAL MATTER he is attending to, and just as we're arriving at the car I add: 'I'm a little uncomfortable with the driver – it's PROBABLY JUST ME – so I've told him that you and I have worked together for MANY YEARS. So if you wouldn't mind NOT asking me anything PERSONAL while we're in the car . . . and then I mutter something about '**AS A YOUNG WOMAN**' and I trail off.

Leon Adler side-eyes me, and makes some remark about

me not looking like I was even BORN MANY YEARS AGO, but I choose to LOOK UNCOMFORTABLE so that he feels like it's an INAPPROPRIATE COMMENT to make to me...as a young woman.

Being a YOUNG WOMAN these days is like being a LANDMINE. So IN A WAY I am a walking BRIEFCASE OF WEAPONS.

Apart from the without-incident checking-in of Leon Adler to his hotel, the theme of the day remained: CATASTROPHE (NON-silent 'e'), beginning with Leon dismissing the driver, telling him he was going to his room to rest, and that they should reconvene in the foyer at 2.30 p.m.

These were the first of MANY of M. Adler's lies.

Okay...not LIES: **UNKEPT PROMISES.**

Okay...lies too.

Leon leaves his bag with the concierge, turns to me and says: 'Right, where shall we go?' And it's not said in the spirit of wild adventure, but more like, **PLEASE TAKE ME SOMEWHERE SO I DON'T HAVE TO BE ALONE IN MY ROOM.** And honestly I would have taken him to the moon if it would help BECAUSE: Ellery says NO TO SADNESS! And I'm thinking of Mom who would probably tell me to ALLOW SADNESS. But THE THING IS...if I SENSE SADNESS, I AM MENTALLY REACHING FOR A CLOWN NOSE. I am SADNESS AVERSE.

'Give me one moment,' I say, and I'm about to call Megser to ask her for a list of suggestions of Leon-Adler-friendly places in Paris when I realise that abducting an author is me going **ROGUE.** And you NEVER reveal to the head of the mission that you've gone rogue until the mission has been successfully completed and your roguery has proved instrumental.

'WHERE WOULD YOU LIKE TO GO?' I ask Leon.

And it turned out to be: EVERYWHERE. Leon and I literally did the most amazing sight-seeing tour of Paris and it was all so interesting, and he was so interested in everything. And he was in charge so what could I do exactly when – at 3 p.m. – he announces:

'Yeah . . . I'm NOT GOING back to the hotel.'

Hmmm.

We are standing on the street having just done a sidecar moped tour and Leon Adler is as happy as I've seen him all day and in any photo online. Then he looks around, and his eyes settle on a bar and he says he needs A DRINK.

Leon LIED. Because it turns out Leon needed MANY drinks. Leon talks about anxiety. I get anxious. Then distracted by a skate store across the street. Leon talks about anxiety. AGAIN. Leon talks about grief. Which reminds me:

I DON'T WANT TO TALK ABOUT ➡ **GRIEF.**

Which reminds me of Mom. Which reminds me of the

WHOLE POINT.

So I look across the street again – at the skate store, and go:
'I love roller-skating.'

And there's this PAUSE of **WHAT HAS THAT GOT TO DO WITH GRIEF?**

And I wait . . .

'I once loved a woman who roller-skated,' says Leon.

YESSS!

'Loved?' I say. Less casually than I'd intended.

'Loved,' he says.

'I'm so sorry,' I say.

And he's like, 'Why?'

GOOD POINT! I'm thinking. But also: HIS FACE. 'Because . . . you look sad about it.'

'Well, it's a sad story.' Pause. 'As most stories are.'

'Are they, though?' I say, because right now I'd rather save him from himself than do my actual job. 'My mom told me that sometimes people define themselves by their wounds.'

'Wounds' sounds like a big word. Wounds IS a big word.

'And she said that THEN what happens is – instead of someone bonding with the other person, it's actually their wounds that bond with each other.'

Leon is TAKEN ABACK. And now I'm thinking, Oh GOD: Mom said the exact same thing to him. And does he now feel like he's being haunted?

So I just keep talking. 'Like, everyone has "A STORY",' I'm saying. 'And they don't realise sometimes that they bring it out every time they meet someone new. And it's usually a SAD story. And the other person can't bring out a happy one then, can they? Like "Oh, no – you lost your whole family in a fire? WAIT until you hear about when I won the lottery!"

'SO THEY BOND OVER SAD STUFF.'

And he's really interested but it's also like he's figuring something out.

'I don't know,' I plough on, 'but I kind of like the idea of making friends with people over GOOD stuff.'

And he's looking at me, kind of amazed, and he says, 'That's really &&&&ing refreshing.' Then: 'THAT IS THE ENTHUSIASM OF YOUTH.'

And I'm thinking: more than you even KNOW. But I say: 'But I think you should never just go along with "You're whatever age therefore you have to be whatever". Like, responsible or mature.

Or serious. Like, just because you're a writer, you should . . . no longer be roller-skating . . . for example.'

And he is WIDE-EYED! 'That woman I loved? She was a writer!'

NO. WAY.

Then he looks bereft. 'She had the same attitude. She felt untroubled. And she made ME feel untroubled.'

'So . . . you didn't bond over your wounds,' I say.

'Actually we bonded over writing. The weirdness of it. The life. It's not weird for every writer. But it was weird for us. It was a compulsion. But the first thing I loved about her was that she could have looked at me a certain way, and she didn't.'

'What do you mean?'

'Well . . . my first book was an *ode to misery,*' he says. 'And she read it and she saw past it. She saw the pain behind it. And how misery was just the result. And she drew out . . . the pain. And everyone else just saw me as a dark, depressed, dejected wreck—'

'I'm sure they didn't!' I say.

He laughed. 'No – they did. And . . . I don't know . . . maybe I bled into my character somewhere along the way.'

I LITERALLY COULDN'T RESPOND TO THAT IT MADE ME SO SAD.

But then I remembered the two questions Megser had drafted

on hearing the connection between ELLERY and (*The Happiness of Lester*) JOY. So I ask them.

Q. Has JOY always held some significance for you?

A. In that it's the last name of the main character in my most successful novel. And, otherwise, something that's missing from my life.

Q. How did you arrive at the last name JOY for your character?

A. My editor arrived at it. **ZERO HELP.**

25 April (SUNDAY)

PARIS: PART DEUX

Here are the hours that passed us by: 4 p.m., 5 p.m., 6 p.m., 7 p.m.

And HERE is the number of promo engagements Leon Adler missed: FIVE.

His final scheduled event of the day – before the UNPLANNED ABDUCTION – is his reading at Shakespeare & Co. at 9 p.m.

It is now 7.30 p.m. and, at this stage, he can't even read the bar menu to find out which other red wine he can sample in full-glass format.

I go to the basement restroom and try to call Megser, but there is no coverage. I come back up and sneak out the back door to this laneway where the chefs are all smoking. Megser does not pick up so I leave her a voicemail: **'I HAVE GONE ROGUE. MORE TO FOLLOW.'**

I get back to the table and I sit down, and I just forget the whole mission thing, and I say to Leon because it ENTERS MY HEAD: 'It's really nice that we're just here, and you're an author, and you're just . . . RESPECTING what I have to say.'

And Leon just smiles, and says: 'Why wouldn't I?'

And I like that. 'Just . . . MALES (to use Meg's word) don't always do that.'

And he goes: 'We're led to believe that women are the weaker sex. MEN are weak. They live in this heightened state – this sense of . . . THREAT.' And he goes, 'Ha! THREAT.' And he points at me.

And I'm like, 'I'm NOT a threat.'

. . .

. . .

Until I remember it's meant to be MY NAME. And I laugh like a **CRAZY** person. And REALLY the only person I'm a threat to is MYSELF.

Leon is expanding on his point. 'That writer friend of mine?

Who roller-skated? She had a problem with males ...'

And now I'm like NOOOOOO! Because ONLY NOW do I realise PROPERLY that he's A DRUNK ADULT! And if Meg were here SHE could listen to the rest of that sentence, then deliver me the EDITED contents so I don't end up SCARRED.

But Leon is already telling me what this problem is:

'She said to me: "Leon, here's the thing: a lot of men like to think they support a woman like me. But they don't. Not really. They love my work ... until I put it BEFORE them."'

And I'm hoping I don't look too guilty about that.

Then he goes: 'ALL writers put their work before other people. Maybe not all the time. But they're lying if they tell you that they're not resistant to being pulled away from it, or interrupted, or that they're not getting plot inspiration while they're at their daughter's graduation, watching her and her boyfriend getting their photo taken.'

And now I'm all *HE ALREADY HAS A DAUGHTER!* And she's OLDER than me. And WHY WOULD HE WANT ANOTHER ONE? AND SHE'LL HATE ME! But he's still talking.

'It can make you feel like &&&&,' he says. 'Especially in that particular case ... because the plot inspiration I got there was about a girl who was graduating, and her father punches her boyfriend in the face because he's an arrogant 𝓫𝓫𝓫𝓫𝓫𝓫 [rhymes with "dosser"].'

And we laugh. And he has a great laugh. So it shouldn't be as RARE as it seems to be.

'Do you have a photo of your daughter?' I say.

So he gets out his phone, and I can see the TWENTY missed calls from PUBLICIST – PARIS and LOADS of missed calls from +33 NUMBERS but he's too drunk to notice, so it's perfect!

His daughter looks SO lovely. 'Her dress is beautiful!' I say. 'She looks SO like you.' Like literally she has almost entirely his face (without looking like a man), which makes me think he's one of those men who makes his mark on every child he has, and I don't look enough like him.

'But the boyfriend does look a bit SKETCHY,' I say.

And he laughs, and he's like, '**THANK YOU!**'

Then I go: 'I knew a writer, and she would drift off into her own world, and I didn't mind. Because I knew she was chasing magic. And at least she didn't just have her head in her phone randomly like some mothers, checking Facebook or Instagram or whatever.' I leave Twitter out on purpose.

And he nods. He's too drunk to notice my 'like some MOTHERS' giveaway stupidity.

169

'Do you like being a dad?' I ask him.

'I do,' he says. 'For something I'm really, really bad at, I love it.'

Then I ask him about Listowel Writers' Week in 2004 and who he was hanging out with and he definitely thought that was a really weird question and I threw Mom's name out there and he said, 'Ah, YES! Laurie Brown!' but then he looked really sad and asked me had I heard that she had passed away? And I got all these tears in my eyes, which was RIDICULOUS but understandable given the circumstances, so I had to pretend that I used to work with her too and then go to the bathroom to compose myself.

And then Megser calls, *THANK GOD!* And I go out the back again, and I fill her in on the madness, and she goes: '**I DO NOT CARE WHAT HAPPENED UP UNTIL THIS MOMENT.** But you MAKE SURE to GET THAT MAN TO HIS READING. I'm on Twitter, and people have been queuing outside Shakespeare & Co. since FOUR O'CLOCK and if he doesn't show, he is a DEAD MAN. It could really damage his career. PLUS, he is up for a HUGE French literary award at the end of the year. This could TOTALLY mess things up for him.'

'But he is SO drunk,' I say. 'That could mess things up WAY more.'

And Meg is like: 'You GO OUT THERE, and you POUR coffee

and water into him for the next two hours.'

And I'm like, 'OHMYGOD, this is TOO MUCH!'

And I realise that ONCE AGAIN she's giving me one of her ROUSING PRE-MATCH PEP TALKS. But I don't care where these words are from because they WORK! I stride into the bar and order coffee to arrive at our table every fifteen minutes. Then I order four litres of Evian. THEN I order Steak Béarnaise. Because if EVER there was a night Leon Adler should be eating his DEATH ROW MEAL, it's tonight.

Then I sit down next to him, lift his head off the table and deliver a recycled version of Megser's pre-match pep talk. And it kind of revives him!

Then I see this large white box on the table with a rainbow (*arc en ciel*!) on it. And he pats it and says: 'For you. To say thank you. Something has shifted in me today.'

And I'm thinking, *IT'S THE BARRELS OF WINE!*

But NO! He says: 'A CLOUD.' And then he looks at me: 'For a twenty-year-old you have many wise words.' And I'm thinking: THEY'RE ALL PLAGIARISED FROM THE WOMAN WHO BROKE YOU!

'So . . . I thought this might be fitting,' he says. And he gives the box a little push towards me. And OHMYGOD: he had gone across the street when I was on the phone to Megsers and bought me roller-skates. He probably wouldn't have done it if he was sober, but still. And it DID involve him coming CLOSE to violating the rule of NEVER looking in a woman's bag without permission by taking one of my ballet pumps out to get my shoe size. But I forgive him: a) Because, really, they were sticking out, but mainly b) HE GOT ME WHITE-LEATHER ROLLER-SKATES with RAINBOWS on the side and they are **SPECTACULAR.**

I feel a speech coming on. Instead I just go: 'WE are RAINBOWS, Mr Adler. So let's go out there and be ARCS DE TRIOMPHES.'

26 April (MONDAY)

PARIS: PART TROIS

Megser was NOT lying – Shakespeare & Co. is PACKED. And so is the street out front. Megser **LOVES** that in France writers are gods. Like, they're STARS.*

Leon meets the person in charge, and introduces me as his publicist, but she's SCEPTICAL. She brings us into the store, and there's a high stool set up, and that's where he'll be reading, and it's almost in the doorway so that the people standing outside can hear. And even though I really SHOULD leave, I kind of don't want to. And I kind of know Leon doesn't want me to either. So I stand there, just inside the door, knowing that as soon as everything is underway, escape will be effortless. But then I spot Leon HYPERVENTILATING behind a bookshelf as he's being introduced, and I'm way more focused on giving him the thumbs up. And he nods, and lets out this long breath and I give him a huge smile, and he gives me one back. And I'm REALLY proud like he definitely IS my dad. Leon Adler takes his seat and opens *The Happiness of Lester Joy* and slides out the VERY LONG bookmark (receipt from the bar). And what he reads is *SO beautiful.* And I look up as I'm listening . . . and then I see something in the corner. Like a GLINT. Like an advanced razor.

And OHMYGOD: my mom IS an avenger fairy.

AND MEGSER IS PSYCHIC.

And then everyone is clapping, and Leon is thanking them, and looking genuinely so thrilled.

And next thing – in the doorway, I see Jean-Luc Catastroph(e) and his face is *LES MISÉRABLES*. And then he spots me and his face is *PLUS MISÉRABLES*.

'And NOW,' says Leon, 'I will read from my novel, *Elation* . . .' And he looks up and catches my eye, and he gives me a small smile and it's SO kind. And I'm SO glad I have that smile still in my head, because then he reads THIS:

'When someone is lost to you, grief will find them, carrying them to you in a memory like a pearl from an ocean floor. You may not see this for the gift it is. But to honour grief, to honour love, is to take each memory in the shell of you, and let the beauty of then . . . shine through the tears . . . of now.'

And I have LOTS of the tears of now because: it is WORD FOR WORD the beautiful letter that Oscar sent me when Mom died.

I feel sick.

27 April (TUESDAY)

Megser and I are in the Without Incident Room.

'So you nearly ruin his career and he buys you roller-skates,' says Megser.

'No, no, no!' I say. 'Only HE was responsible for sabotaging his career. And I was – at first – **POWERLESS** to stop him. Until I was NOT. Thanks to YOU! And, in fairness to ME, wanting him NOT to ruin his career because he was SO nice.'

'Because he bought you roller-skates . . .'

'NO! Don't be so CYNICAL. And NO – he did not just buy me roller-skates.'

Because . . . um . . . there was MORE. Because . . . Jean-Luc Catastroph(e) didn't just stick his head in the door of Shakespeare & Co. He walked RIGHT in. And as I'm there silently crying he moves in beside me, and whispers: 'I saw you. At the airport. Who ARE you? I KNOW you don't work for Monsieur Adler.' Then he's like, **'AND WHY ARE YOU CRYING?** I should be the person who is CRYING.' Then he feels sorry for me and goes: 'Did that *MONSTRE* make you CRY?'

And I'm sobbing going, 'He's not a *monstre*. OSCAR is the *monstre*.'

And he's like, 'Who's Oscar?' and I'm like, 'It doesn't MATTER.'

And he's back to: 'Do you KNOW what you've done today? Monsieur Adler missed FIVE of his PROMOS! FIVE. My BOSS is *FURIEUX*.'

And I'm thinking that is SO close to the English word that it would have been so easy to learn it but I'm like: 'I'm sorry, okay?' And he goes: 'Well, my boss is on his way, and you can explain it to him yourself.' And I'm like: 'Okay, fine!' And THEN I see this man in a suit arrive at the door, and his face is like the Paris uprising of 1832 as depicted in *Les Misérables*, and he nods at Jean-Luc, and I know then that that's his boss, and I go in FRENCH: 'Excuse me for two minutes. I need to use the bathroom.'

And Leon Adler finishes his reading, and is getting a massive round of applause, so I squeeze through to the back of the store and get out through that door. And I check the time on my phone, and the time is PERFECT.

Because there's this THING in Paris . . . at 10 p.m. every Friday night. And if you needed another reason to love that city, FRIDAY-NIGHT FEVER is it.

It means that right about now, just across the street, thousands of roller-skaters and rollerbladers are about to roll right past. And to my left, I see Jean-Luc Catastroph(e) guide Leon Adler outside to where the boss is standing, and they're all **ANGRY BROWS**, and I saaaail by on my roller-skates de triomphe going:

'Thank you, Leoooon! They're AWESOMMMMME! Everything is going to be okay!'

And I look back over my shoulder and all I see is the HAPPINESS of Leon Adler and the RAGE of Jean-Luc Catastroph(e) and sooo . . .

Leon Adler did NOT just buy me roller-skates.

He bought me a GETAWAY VEHICLE.

Who's The Father?

SUSPECT 2: LEON ADLER

LIKELIHOOD ★ ★ ★ ☆ ☆

LIKEABILITY ★ ★ ★ ★ ☆

BASED ON THE FOLLOWING CRITERIA

(WHERE ◀ INDICATES A NEGATIVE):

PHYSICAL TRAITS ★ ★ ★ ☆ ☆

Hair colour ★ ★ ★ ☆ ☆

Eye colour ★ ★ ★ ★ ★

Height/Build ★ ★ ☆ ☆ ☆

Strength ★ ★ ☆ ☆ ☆

Awesome eyebrows ★ ★ ☆ ☆ ☆

PERSONALITY TRAITS ★ ★ ★ ☆ ☆

Consequences averse ★ ★ ★ ★ ★

Anxious ★ ☆ ☆ ☆ ☆

Spontaneous ★ ★ ★ ★ ★

Disorganised ★ ★ ★ ☆ ☆

Easily distracted ★ ★ ★ ★ ☆

SKILLS ☆ ☆ ☆ ☆ ☆
Writing literary fiction ☆ ☆ ☆ ☆ ☆
Wine drinking ☆ ☆ ☆ ☆ ☆

INTERESTS ★ ★ ★ ☆ ☆
Netflix ★ ★ ★ ☆ ☆
History ◄ ★ ★ ★ ★ ★
Wine drinking ☆ ☆ ☆ ☆ ☆

FOOD & DRINK ★ ☆ ☆ ☆ ☆
Steak Béarnaise ★ ★ ★ ☆ ☆
Green beans (hot AND cold) ★ ★ ★ ☆ ☆
Chocolate ★ ★ ☆ ☆ ☆
Dark chocolate ◄ ★ ★ ★ ★ ★
Broccoli averse ★ ★ ★ ★ ☆
Psyllium husks averse ★ ★ ★ ★ ★
Wine ☆ ☆ ☆ ☆ ☆

UNKNOWN UNKNOWNS ★ ★ ★ ★ ☆
Appreciation of roller-skating ★ ★ ★ ★ ★

Love of Paris ★ ★ ★ ★ ★

Belief in daughter's boyfriend's shadiness ★ ★ ★ ★ ★

Love of cloze tests ◀ ★ ★ ★ ★ ★

Love of Laurie Brown ★ ★ ★ ★ ★ ★ ★ ★ ★ ★

SUSPECT APPROVAL RATING ★ ★ ★ ★ ☆

Kind ★ ★ ★ ★ ☆

Fun ★ ★ ★ ☆ ☆

Happy ★ ★ ☆ ☆ ☆

Takes care of things ★ ★ ☆ ☆ ☆

Isn't into rules but has some kind of boundaries ★ ★ ☆ ☆ ☆

MISCELLANEOUS

Gift buyer: ★ ★ ★ ★ ★ ★ ★ ★ ★ ★ ★ ★ ★ ★ ★

NOTE:

I think Mom would have REALLY liked Leon Adler. She would have been fascinated by the mixture of **DARKNESS** and **SENSITIVITY**. Also . . . she was a broken-wing person. Buuut . . . she MAY have judged him to be WHOLLY unreliable and NOT parent material and Parent Most Likely to Leave Child Behind at an Airport.

Megser is frowning for pretty much the entire read. Then she looks up at me in **AMAZEMENT.**

And I'm thinking I KNOWWW: METHODICAL.

'OH,' I say, 'I forgot to mention one thing: I ROUNDED UP THE STARS so I didn't have to do those weird HALF STARS. And ALSO I ROUNDED SOME of them DOWN. Depending . . .'

'ON?' says Megser.

. . .

. . .

And Megser is just NODDING SAGELY through this silence.

Then she goes: 'So . . . which qualification do you think you benefitted from most when putting this together: a) Your Masters in Random Parameters [no idea] or b) your PhD in Statistical Analysis Through the Medium of Emotion?'

NICE TRY, Megser. 'Think AGAIN!' I say.

And she DOES. 'Oh. Okay. It HAS to be something to do with The Univ—'

And OBVIOUSLY – because CORRECT! – I cut in with: 'My ONGOING STUDIES at THE UNIVERSE-ITY.'

29 April (THURSDAY)

I KNOW I should not be thinking about Oscar.

Nevertheless I have **AN EPIPHANY** about him.

When Megser reviewed *THE HAPPINESS OF LESTER JOY* last year and was SO enthusiastic that it was MORTIFYING, Oscar was there. Which means he KNEW how much she *loved* it. So he must have got his hands on the US edition of *Elation* and used that bit in my letter. And he made me swear not to show it to Megser just in CASE. Basically, ALL he wanted was for me to tell Megser what a **BRILLIANT WRITER** he is. And **SENSITIVE GUY.** Like Megser would see that as a POSITIVE.

30 April (FRIDAY)

'Ewwwwwwwwwww!' but WAY longer says Megser when I tell her that CLEARLY Oscar is into HER.

And I'm like, 'Of course he is into you because you are **SUPER SMART**, and *beautiful* and **HILARIOUS** and **AMAZING.'**

'You're NOT WELL IN THE HEAD,' she says. 'YOU are SUPER SMART, and BEAUTIFUL, and AMAZING—'

'STOP PLAGIARISING ME!' I say.

And we're laughing and then I lay out all the evidence, and Megser just slumps down on the bed, and says, 'I am SO sorry.'

And I'm like, 'Whutttt? Why are YOU apologising?! It's not YOUR fault.'

'I feel like it is.'

'No it is NOT!' And I tell her this story about Auntie Elaine. So . . . years ago – Auntie Elaine was madly in love with this guy, and then she discovers that he's *madly in love* with one of her friends. And she's going NUTS about the BETRAYAL of it all. And Mom goes, really chill:

> ♥ ♡ **'LET PEOPLE LOVE** ♥ ♡
> ♡ **WHOM THEY LOVE.'** ♥

And Auntie Elaine went EVEN MORE NUTS. And Mom goes: 'You can't control the hearts of the world, Elaine. And who is ANY of us to ASSIGN love to ourselves? To EXPECT it? To hold it CAPTIVE. Or worse still to DENY it to the heart to which it has NATURALLY gone. . . as ALL love should?'

And then I kind of drift off thinking about all this, and Megser goes: 'And what did Auntie Elaine say?'

And I go: 'She looked at Mom and said, "OH, &&&& OFF,

LAURIE, with your *spiritual* BULL&&&&!'"

And Megsers is laughing now. 'That's why I asked, because I KNEW I'd have the EXACT same reaction.'

But there's more to it than that . . . Okay – you know I love Megser – but she is SO WEIRD about her mom meeting someone new. Susan has literally never had a boyfriend as long as I've known her. I asked Megser ONCE (and NEVER AGAIN), 'What would you do if your mom sat you down in the morning and said: "I've met someone"?'

And Megser looked at me in a way that was like she was trying to SET ME ON FIRE while CRYOGENICALLY FREEZING ME at the same time.

And she says: 'The same thing I'd do if she sat me down AT NIGHT and said it.'

And I'm like, 'Look at her the way you've just looked at me?'

'Until she dies. Yes.'

'My POINT,' I say to Megser, 'is it's ALSO not your fault that Oscar is a HORRIBLE human being and plagiarist.'

I mean, who thinks PLAGIARISM is the way to win the heart of a DEVOTED READER via her friend, the daughter of AN AUTHOR. **CONCLUSION:** As originally suspected Oscar is NOT bright.

2 May (SUNDAY)

Tonight I pulled out my box of **SENTIMENTAL THINGS.** It's full of cards and notes from Mom to me and I shouldn't have done it.

I love you, my precious girl! Xxxxx

Once Upon a Time: the MOST AMAZING DAUGHTER WAS BORN! And her mother REJOICED! Followed by THE WHOLE LAND ALSO REJOICING! The End.
Short Story by Mom xxxxx

I love you, my beautiful, smart, kind, warm, funny, perfect girl xxxxx

I must have SLAYED NINE MILLION DRAGONS, PUNCHED A BILLION AWFUL PRINCES WITH AMAZING HAIR BUT NO PERSONALITIES IN THE FACE TO FREE THE FIVE POWERFUL PRINCESSES THEY KNEW COULD OVERTHROW THEM, CURED A MILLION PLAGUES, TIDIED UP AFTER THIRTY MILLION VERY MESSY CHILDREN, READ THAT AWFUL BEDTIME STORY ABOUT THE CREEPY BAT A HUNDRED THOUSAND TIMES, THEN SAVED MULTIPLE CIVILISATIONS FROM EXTINCTION TO BE GRANTED THE GIFT OF YOU AS MY DAUGHTER.

XXXXX

Do you know what it's like, Ms Ellery Brown, when you tell me that you love me from the bottom, the top AND the sides of your heart? Well, because I know the GINORMITY of that heart I have NO DOUBT – in the bottom, the top AND the sides of my brain – that I am the LUCKIEST MOM who EVER STRODE THE EARTH LOOKING FOR HER CAR KEYS because she was SURE SHE LEFT THEM SOMEWHERE. XXXXX

I'm sorry for making you cry today, Ellery Bellery. So now . . . it's my JOB to make you LAUGH. Because that is my FAVOURITE JOB (WAAAAAY more than writing). So . . . I found this in one of my old notebooks. When you were small I used to write down the things you came out with that cracked me up:

8 July 2007

I made Ellery cry today (told her she couldn't wear the dress with the ENTIRE BOWL OF SPAGHETTI stuck to it from the night before). And she's sobbing. And she says: 'You're a JERK!' And I, of course, was HORRIFIED. And she says it AGAIN! 'You're a JERK!' And she's pointing at her face. And I say: 'ELLERY! That's not a very nice thing to say.' And she says: 'Well, it's NOT VERY NICE to be a TEARJERKER!'

So, I'm sorry, Ellery. I will do MY VERY BEST to aim for LAUGHJERKER AT ALL TIMES. I LOVE YOUR LAUGH. Mom xxxxx

And this randomness but I LOVED it. And it WORKED . . .!

Ellery!!!! HOW did you not HEAR that TORNADO?!!! Have you SEEN what it's done to your BEDROOM? YIIIIKES. I'd get in there and STRAIGHTEN IT OUT if I were you! Because I heard ANOTHER TORNADO is on its way. And it's the MOTHERTORNADO. And THAT one LEAVES NOTHING IN ITS WAKE.

Do you KNOW what I love most about you, Ellery? Your LIGHT. And it is EVERYWHERE. In your eyes, and in your heart, and in how you see people, and in how you see the world. And I thank my LUCKY STARS every day that I get to be in that world with you. xxxxx

And now she's not. And where did the lucky stars go? And WHY did they go?

And now I won't ever get any more cards from her. EVER AGAIN. She won't EVER WRITE DOWN ANY MORE WORDS FOR ME. I can't. I just . . . can't.

And I hate these kind of thoughts. I HATE THEM. I HATE THEM. I HATE THEM.

I can't BREATHE.

3 May (MONDAY)

OHMYGOD: Oscar. He KEEPS texting me. What a **WEIRDO.** I didn't go there with him about the whole plagiarism thing because what would be the point? And I made Megser swear not to say anything to him either. So if you can violently ignore someone, that's what Megan has decided to do to Oscar. And now it seems he is even MORE *in love* with her, which is making him even more desperate to get in touch with ME! What is WRONG with people? **WHY WOULD YOU WANT TO BE WITH THE PERSON WHO TREATS YOU THE WORST?**

4 May (TUESDAY)

OHMYGOD I have NEVER been so embarrassed in my entire life.

END OF ENTRY.

Okay . . . I'm back. Because I have to tell SOMEONE.

A PACKAGE arrived in the post today. From:

LEON ADLER!

I METAPHORICALLY DIED. I thought it was going to be

a LAWSUIT about IMPERSONATING a PUBLICIST. It was SQUISHY like all it had inside was documents and it was REGISTERED and I was looking at the envelope in slow motion because I could see his name and address on the sticker in the corner. And OBVIOUSLY the envelope was addressed to ELLERY BROWN – NOT Victoria Threat! And HOW did he have ANY of this information? And my hands were shaking and it was all TERRIFYING.

BUT . . . BASICALLY . . . LEON ADLER FIGURED OUT WHO I AM.

And he got in contact with Mom's agent and got my address and it was actually the sweetest letter ever because he figured out with my weird question about Listowel and my roller-skating and the fact that I was dumb enough to imply I was working around the time of Listowel even though I clearly would have been a child at the time. And he was NOT – as originally thought – too drunk to notice my 'like some mothers' comment. And not only did he figure out who I was, he also figured out WHY I had tracked him down. And even though he didn't spell that out EXACTLY, he let me know that he hadn't met my mother at Listowel because they were appearing on different days. And that he hadn't met her at all over that **ENTIRE YEAR.** Then he said: 'The thing was – there was something so familiar about you, and I realised afterwards what it was: you have your mother's **beautiful** smile.'

And there I was focusing the WHOLE time on what I inherited from my DAD that I hadn't even THOUGHT of all the things I inherited from my MOM.

Who's The Father?
Elimination Round I

SUSPECT 1: JAY EVANS

~~**SUSPECT 2:** LEON ADLER~~

Because he told me and I want to DIE of embarrassment as a direct result.

SUSPECT 3: QUENTIN SCHAEFFER

SADNESS: I have lost a potential father.

NON-SADNESS: I am one step closer to having an answer.

FURTHER SADNESS: I'm not even sure that's the case. Because: statistics.

5 May (WEDNESDAY)

Tonight I was packing because I leave for New York in the morning for Grandpa and Lola's anniversary. And it's so weird when you are a Lover of Clothing and you're picking out something to wear to a *party*, but you don't really want to go to the party in the first place but you HAVE to and it's in New York and you're flying first class and SERIOUSLY ... has anyone ever sounded so spoiled in the history of mankind? You don't need to answer that. But I'll be adding 'being ungrateful' to the list of things that are making me feel so bad right now.

The second thing on the list is that Megser is now SERIOUSLY questioning my abilities as a spy. Even though I reminded her that a NORMAL spy would never be assigned a case in which they have an **EMOTIONAL INVESTMENT.** And she's like, 'Your emotions better be invested in a time lock vault by the time you face Suspects 1 and 3.'

And I don't know if that's going to be the case.

Because the one OTHER item on the list of things that are making me feel so bad right now is:

My mom died and I loved her and I miss her so much.

7 May (FRIDAY)

WELCOME TO RHINEBECK, NEW YORK, NON-JUDGEMENTAL FRIEND!

Thank you SO MUCH for coming! **I LOVE RHINEBECK** (countryside – 103.7 miles outside New York City. I googled it. And switched to miles because: AMERICA)! My bedroom, as you can see, is EXACTLY how you would picture a bedroom at an American ranch: oversized Princess and the Pea bed, patchwork quilts, nine million pillows, weird American glass lampshades that I love, preserved childhood adorableness in the form of photos stuck into the sides of mirrors featuring teens with braces on their teeth.

The last time I was here was at Christmas. But the last time I was here in this kind of weather (I don't know why that matters) was last summer with Mom. When i *truly believed* she was going to get better. And I have NO idea if it's better to think that or to be told that someone you love won't EVER get better. Because if you know someone won't ever get better, then the time you have left with them might be all **FEAR** and **PANIC** and **TEARS.**

BUT . . . if you truly believe that someone is going to get better . . .

BETTER

BETTER

BETTER

BETTER

BETTER

BETTER

BETTER

WHY DO I KEEP WRITING THAT?! IT IS **NOT** A MAGIC SPELL.

Just . . . if you have all this amazing time together and you actually manage to love them even more than you ever thought possible, then it might be even more unbearable to lose them. Like, it could be THE MOST HORRIFYING SHOCK IN THE WORLD and your HEART could be: LEVERS DOWN ON DEMOLITION SITES.

8 May (SATURDAY)

It's the morning of the party. And even though event planners with headsets are spreading out over the property like they're searching for a missing child (adding tasteful touches to the search area as they go), Lola is having these random moments of hysteria like she's **OUT OF HER MIND** with worry about the missing child.

Grandpa and I are curled up on the sofa watching faded television shows. And we hear Lola from the kitchen: 'Maaax! MAAAAAAX! I NEED YOU IN HERE! RIGHT NOW!' And I'm thinking, *The child has been found dead.*

And Grandpa goes to me: 'Men were sold a lie. I always thought the damsel's distress was supposed to end when you rescued her.'

6 p.m. update

It is what Lola would call a balmy evening. The house looks BEAUTIFUL. The garden looks *beautiful.* The flowers growing there are BEAUTIFUL. There are MORE beautiful flowers in vases all over the house. The doors are open on to the terrace and everywhere is strung with beautiful *fairy* lights.

And I'm sitting here at the mirror in my bedroom trying to make myself BEAUTIFUL. And I *love* beautiful. And Mom loved beautiful too. And Mom is NOT here.

AND I DON'T WANT TO GO.

1 a.m. update

Lola gave the most SURPRISINGLY non-emotionless speech about Grandpa, and I'm thinking how exhausted she must be going around hiding all those feelings the whole time. And Grandpa was so kind and soooo funny about Lola in his speech and he said that thing about the damsels in distress and everyone laughed for SO long. And they both thanked each other for the gift of their **wonderful** girls. And they also mentioned ME.

And then Auntie Elaine is giving a speech and I'm not listening because I'm thinking, *There are only four of us left!* And suddenly I'm like: *What if they all died? What if Auntie Elaine's plane goes down next time she's flying somewhere? What if Grandpa and Lola are in a car wreck?* And then I'm like, *What if ALL THREE OF THEM are in the car? And where are all these thoughts coming from? And why won't they leave me alone? I'm at a PARTY.*

Then the speeches are over and people are moving around again and I'm on my own but I'm also surrounded and I can feel this meltdown about to happen and then someone comes up beside me and he's this lawyer second-cousin person, and I manage to smile and say hi and he is DEEPLY uncomfortable at having to talk to a female, and PARTICULARLY a teen girl because we're so poorly portrayed in fiction. But we're chatting, and then he goes: 'So . . . what are your career goals?' SERIOUSLY.

And I say: 'Not to be obsessed with my career, number one.' But I was being light about it.

And he looks at me with PITY EYES and says, 'Is that because of your mom?'

And I say, 'You mean . . . because I lost my mom?' I'm thinking he means that now I know life's too short, why spend it working the whole time?

But NO!

'Actually,' he says – WAIT FOR IT – 'I meant: because your mom was so focused on her career, that maybe you felt that you lost out on time with her . . . because of her . . . priorities . . . and now . . .' And he SHRUGS! Instead of using his words to finish his hideous sentence, as if the action of SHRUGGING is in some thesaurus as an alternative to 'she's dead' or 'she's gone' or 'she's with the angels' or 'she's in the library in the sky'. And I could feel these tears coming like BAM! But I would literally rather dive into the rosebush in front of me than let him see that. Then I'm GENUINELY thinking about kicking him down the terrace steps.

Instead I say: 'Do you have kids?'

'I've three boys.' And he points over all PROUD to these MASSIVE preppy idiots.

And I go: 'And how do you think THEY feel about you PRIORITISING being a _____?' (Rhymes with whatever YOUR favourite term of insult is because I want to involve YOU in this moment, Non-Judgemental Friend.)

And then Auntie Elaine comes up as he's staggering back over to his FINE SONS, who I will one day hear have been kicked out of Yale or Harvard because of some hazing incident that their father failed to buy their way out of.

Me and Auntie Elaine sit down on the steps and we're watching the crowd, and she turns to me, holding her nth glass of wine, and her eyes are swimming and she says, 'I know, right? You're having a WONDERFUL time too.' And across from us, a group of people burst out laughing. And then one of them starts singing a few lines from a show tune and they all laugh again and then we realise that Lola is in the middle of them and Auntie Elaine says: 'A "MUTED" celebration, says Lola. The only thing muted about Lola is her lipstick.'

I want to say that actually ALL Lola's make-up is muted. And that even though she LOOKS happy, when all eyes are off her hers are SO sad. But maybe you can't really see anyone else's eyes when your own are swimming. And now that the volume of the group is rising – Auntie Elaine's eyes are now swimming in Lola's direction like *Jaws*. But I pretend I can't see the fin in the water.

'Lola's speech!' I say. 'She adores Grandpa. It's so weird how—'

'She treats him so badly?' says Auntie Elaine, and she empties her glass.

And I'm like, UH-OH. Auntie Elaine is OUT OF WINE. And HOOTS.

'For YEARS,' says Auntie Elaine, 'I thought that was how you were supposed to treat guys. You can see how THAT worked out for me. NO ONE'S going to marry me.' And she's shaking her head. 'We didn't stand a CHANCE, me and your mom, did we? What did WE know about love?'

And I'm like: ***THIS IS WHY THE DRUNK ADULT THING!!!***

And I'm like, 'Mom knew LOADS about love!'

'Oh, **sweetheart** – ROMANTIC love!' says Auntie Elaine. 'Not you! She ADORED you. You know that.'

And I'm like, 'OBVIOUSLY. But . . .' And I'm like, DON'T DO IT DON'T DO IT but I DO DO IT: 'Did she love my dad, though?'

And Auntie Elaine gets a FRIGHT, I think. 'WHAT? YES!' she says. 'Of COURSE! YES! WHAT?' But she wants to keep going with what she wants to say, so I just LISTEN.

'We were scuppered on TWO fronts, your mom and me,' says Auntie Elaine. 'We have this amazing adoring father that – let's face it – no man can live up to and then our "wife role model" is Lola.'

And I go: 'But that's PERFECT. Because if no one will ever marry you, then you won't BE a wife so it doesn't matter who your role model is.'

Luckily she laughs.

Then I say: 'It must be strange to hear Lola being so open about her feelings.'

Auntie Elaine, **EYEBROWS RAISED,** turns to me and goes: 'Last WEEK? I tried on the dress I bought for tonight and she told me it was "hitting me in all the wrong places".'

And I'm like, Whuttt? 'No, it's not,' I say. 'It's STUNNING.'

'Because I bought a new one,' says Auntie Elaine. 'And some Spanx.'

And I'm like, 'I'M wearing Spanx!' And then I tell her that I read a very interesting study that said if you gathered up all the Spanx at any formal occasion, you could catapult every living woman into space and they would circle the globe at LEAST fifteen times.

And Auntie Elaine laughs out loud. And Lola is safe from the FIN.

But then Auntie Elaine goes all serious. 'Ellery, you're not thinking about your dad, are you?'

And obviously the CORRECT ANSWER is 'No'. So that's the one I give.

Because tonight everyone's riding the big dipper.

9 May (SUNDAY)
· · · · · · · · · ·

I am SO TIRED after last night. I don't come down until after lunch, and the place has been all tidied up. And I don't know where Grandpa and Lola have gone, and I'm guessing Auntie Elaine is in bed, and will be for days. So I'm just wandering around the house. And I end up in Grandpa's study. And I go to the box of press clippings that Lola told me about and I open it. And YES . . . it really does seem that Grandpa saved every one of Mom's interviews.

I pick out one magazine interview, and it has this cool photo of Mom when her hair was long.

I ask Brown if any of her characters are based on real people.

'Of course not,' says Brown with great solemnity. For a moment I believe her. And then she laughs. 'I don't think any writer has written a book that hasn't been "inspired" by people they know or events that have occurred in their own lives. It's real life, and that's what we write about or, at least, want to reflect. But it's not like I'll put an entire person in there – it might just be one stand-out trait. If, perhaps, I wanted to "use" – which sounds terrible – more of a person than just one trait, then I might add five or ten years to them, change their physicality, use opposites – in gender, description, clothing, ethnicity. But it has to be realistic. I couldn't have, for example, a narcissist in the role of tender, loving mother.'

(I LITERALLY glance towards the door when I read this bit.)

'Does that mean,' I ask Brown, 'there's a real man out there who inspired one of our most beloved romantic heroes?'

Brown laughs and says, 'I love how you said "our".'

'But that is the magic of Wildfire, the magic of the man,' I tell her. 'I do believe your readers feel like they, we, own Joshua Land now.'

Again Brown laughs. 'What is it about him, do you think?'

'Perhaps we are all starved of the kind of man who lets a woman breathe,' I say, 'who sees love as a strength, not a capitulation [no idea]. But enough about my dating hell.'

Laurie Brown gives a warm, throaty laugh, and it's infectious.

'Maybe it's not that we think Joshua Land is ours,' I suggest. 'Maybe we just wish he was.'

And Brown, looking wistful, says, 'Maybe . . . he's my wish too.'

'So . . . are you saying you wrote your ideal man into existence? Are we all holding out hope for a man who exists only "on paper" – to quote the book?'

Brown smiles, and it's like an end point.

But I ask, 'Have you anyone special in your life right now?'

'Everyone in my life is special,' she says. 'That's why they're in it.'

'BAM! Shut downnnn!' I say.

And then I read this other piece, which is just on its own – one of those long columns.

Seriously. Read THIS:

What I decide will happen, happens. At a time and place of my choosing. I raise the arm of the winner, and laugh at the loser at my feet. Then I hold out my hand, and pull him up to his standing. Until once again, I send him down. And if I hold out my hand again, it will be for someone new. Bright and shiny. I create people. I make people, I break people.

I abandon them. I forget them. I love them. I hurt them. And I dig my fingers into their wounds. I shine lights where they are unwelcome. I conjure monsters and I introduce them to my friends. I sit back and watch spectacular collisions, and my eyes are bright.

The words of a psychopath? NOPE. The words of my MOM! About being a writer! And she didn't even write crime! I'm just picturing her roller-skating around the kitchen with me and we're singing 'Blank Space' while this madness is going on in her head.

My point IS: maybe I'm a test-tube baby. Maybe NO man was involved in my conception. Seriously. Would YOU date her?

HOW am I SO NORMAL?

3 a.m. update

I'm here – CRYING. I'm CRYING at all the: 'I love you, my precious girl!', 'I love you, my beautiful, smart, kind, warm, funny, perfect girl' cards and about being 'the most amazing daughter' and . . .

I CAN'T STOP CRYING.

Because . . . ←

What if she created me too? What if I'm none of those things?

11 May (TUESDAY) 🌟

Auntie Elaine and I arrived home tonight – she's here until the end of term. We got to the house right when the sun was going down. Beara sunsets are the most **beautiful sunsets** in the world. I still remember the first time I really noticed one. It was the beginning of July and I was nine years old. Mom and I were sitting on the sofa in the living room, and the light changed, and she jumped up, and reached out her hand. 'Come with me,' she said, 'for tonight's performance.' I literally thought we were going to the cinema. We went as far as the wall at the front of the house. She sat me up on it, and stood behind me, and wrapped her arms around me, and kissed my head. **And we watched the sky**. It was PINK! And there was ONE star in the middle . . . and now I'm crying.

14 May (FRIDAY)

Megser is **OVERJOYED!** Susan finally got planning permission for the extension she wants to build on to the house.

When Megser explains the plans to me I'm thinking Susan

is LITERALLY building a FERAL SANCTUARY. The extension will contain: the Ferals. They will have a bedroom each and will be separated by a Jack and Jill bathroom (those shared ones with two access doors). The Ferals are the LAST people in the WORLD who should share ANYTHING that involves PLUMBING, MULTIPLE ACCESS POINTS and LOCKS.

Megser is **SO HAPPY** about the extension, probably secretly because of the sanctuary element, but OUT LOUD it's because she's getting the Ferals' old room, which is massive and has the best view in the house. She's also getting a double bed, a proper desk ... and a single bed for visitors i.e. ME.

'Look, though,' says Megser, and she's showing me the plans. And I'm like, I have NOT developed the part of the brain that deals with floor plans. Or having an interest in them. Until I see she's pointing to a little box.

SADNESS: there is a question mark over the Without Incident Room. LITERALLY.

26 May (WEDNESDAY)

— MOM'S BIRTHDAY —

OHMYGOD . . . ID DEAN.

So remember when we were part of a Garda sting operation? Remember the form I had in my bag about the retirement home volunteering? Well – it was specifically about doing makeovers on the elderly ladies to cheer them up. I do make-up. Dean does nails. We go in every Wednesday after school, and Dean always brings homemade scones because he says the scones in the home could be put to better use smashing windows.

Dean is **SO MUCH FUN**. He is a brilliant singer and dancer, and all the old ladies LOVE him. On his third week on the 'job', he came up with this routine because the ladies' nails were smudging almost immediately and they had to keep coming back to get them re-done. So now every time he finishes a manicure, he stands up, and gets the 'client' to stand up too, and he says: 'Put your hands where I can see them.' And then he pretends he has a megaphone. 'It would be a CRIME, Eileen [or whoever], if those pretty nails got all smudged now, wouldn't it?' And then he puts Sinatra or Tony Bennett on, and he walks up to the lady, all smooth, and holds his palms up against hers, and they DANCE! And while they're dancing he shouts things at them like he's pretending he thinks they're deaf: 'HOW ARE YOUR ADULT CHILDREN TREATING YOU? DO I NEED TO HAVE A WORD WITH ANYONE?' Then at the end of the dance he examines their nails and tells them: 'DRY AS A SCONE!' And off they go, DELIGHTED.

And he told me he'll never stop doing it, even though he switched to gel top coat ages ago, so their nails are now SCONE-DRY INSTANTLY.

Anyway, I told him last week that I wasn't going to come today because it was Mom's birthday. And he said, 'No problem – you do what you need to do.' Then he called me this morning and said he was SO sorry but he had to cancel, and please could I fill in, because it was an EMERGENCY: Eileen had some visitors coming tonight, and she wanted to look her best. But when I got there, Eileen was waiting for me in the hall, and she was definitely already done up, and then she brought me into the day room, and ALL our 'clients' are in there . . . and they're ALSO done up. And there's a VERY *fancy* afternoon tea set up, and ID Dean is bowing me towards a seat because apparently I'm also having afternoon tea because – NO JOKE – ID Dean had gone to Kenmare, had a word with someone in Sheen Falls Lodge because he knew I used to go there with Mom, even though I literally have **ZERO** memory of ever telling him that, but WHO CARES? Because ID Dean managed to answer the question that EVERYONE had been asking me: how did I want to spend Mom's birthday? CRYING ALL DAY was all I could think of, but it turned out that crying for SOME OF the day in the company of kind old people and a kind criminal was EXACTLY how I wanted to spend Mom's birthday.

28 May (FRIDAY)

BANK HOLIDAY WEEKEND!

But also: LAST WEEKEND BEFORE EXAMS. But also: TRANSITION YEAR so no one really cares. Except OBVIOUSLY adults.

29 May (SATURDAY)

STUDY.

30 May (SUNDAY)

STUDY.

31 May (MONDAY) BANK HOLIDAY

STUDY.

1 June (TUESDAY)

EXAMS. What's not to love? **ANSWER: EXAMS.**
   COMPARE AND CONTRAST: Exams and No Exams.
   ANSWER: One is GARBAGE. It's the FIRST ONE.

2 June (WEDNESDAY)

Exams.

3 June (THURSDAY)

Exams.

4 June (FRIDAY)

FINE . . . it was only three days of exams. But stiiill.

And NOW: **SUMMER! HOLIDAYS!**

I'M GOING TO MISS MEGSER SO MUCH.

5 June (SATURDAY)

It's my last day with Megser and I'm packing for New York, and there are clothes all over my room, and my suitcase is like the world's BIGGEST suitcase and, next thing, Megser is inside it and I'm like, 'You are SO flexible.' And she's like, 'An elephant would fit inside of this.'

And then her phone beeps and she looks at it, and goes: 'Where is Albany, New York?'

And I'm wondering about the **INTENSITY** of this question.

'Like – is it NEAR you?' she says.

And I'm like, 'About an hour away. Why?'

And she goes, 'JUST . . . my . . . cousin lives there.' Then: 'Like . . . moved there . . . recently.'

And I'm thinking this cousin sounds like s/he could be related to 'Uncle Jeff', but Megser is keeping up the weirdness. 'JUST,' she says, 'I was going to get you to take some stuff over. But . . . it doesn't matter. You won't have room.'

I'm like, give me the stuff. But she's acting all 'I don't want to put you to any trouble' like she's someone's mom. And I CAN'T do that Irish thing where you have to ALLOW REFUSAL a million times before the person accepts whatever it is you're offering them.

So I just zip Megser into the suitcase, and she lets me, and I call Auntie Elaine in. 'I think I have ALL I NEED in this suitcase.' And I OPEN IT, and Megser just smiles up at her because she's too cool to say 'BOOO!' and Auntie Elaine is laughing, and next thing Susan is in the doorway, which is WEIRD, because she's that person who parks outside and leaves the engine running . . .

EVEN WHEN THE FERALS ARE IN THE CAR!

Then Auntie Elaine goes to Megser: 'LUCKILY you won't have to curl up that small when you DO go to New York.' And she pulls out A PLANE TICKET from her back pocket.

And Megser and I are like 'Whuttt?'

And Susan is BEAMING from the doorway.

And Megser is STUCK INSIDE THE SUITCASE.

And I pull her out, and we're just standing there going,
'WHAT IS HAPPENING?'

And Auntie Elaine goes: 'Megser O'Sullivan! On 1st August
you. are. going. On your first. ever. plane. ride to NEW YORK
CITY where you will be met by me and Ellery Brown and driven
to Rhinebeck, New York – where you will spend a WHOLE TWO
WEEKS at The Brown Family Ranch.'

And she throws her arms up in the air, and I'm SCREAMING
because: NO ONE TOLD ME ANYTHING. And Megser is also
screaming probably because: STAY-AT-HOME SAVANT. And Auntie
Elaine JOINS IN the screaming.

Susan joins in the celebration in her own way (MUTED) and
then she goes to Megser: 'You'll miss Regatta though.' Regatta is
the highlight of the social calendar in Beara, and it's in the first
week of August, and everyone does activities like wife-carrying
competitions and a car treasure hunt, and net making.

And Megser just looks at Susan and goes: 'SAFE ENOUGH.'

And Susan is thinking, *Ellery has destroyed our family tradition.*

And then she goes: **'I'LL MISS YOU TERRIBLE.'**

And this – I KNOW – is what Irish Mammies specialise in: GUILT.

And Megser goes: 'You'll miss having a BABYSITTER so you can go out and get PASTED.'

And that is what Megser specialises in: **BRUTAL TRUTHS.**

4 August (WEDNESDAY)

Welcome back to Rhinebeck, Non-Judgemental Friend. I am so sorry I left you behind.

I missed you. I've had some terrible nights without you. And some even worse days. And there was a whole 'therapist' situation.

Please don't be mad at me. I really need you to remain your wonderful non-judgemental self. It's what makes you so *special*. I await your reply . . .

Oh, thank God, you got back to me so soon. And with no hard feelings! **YOU'RE AMAZING.** Thank you, NJF,

thank you.

5 August (THURSDAY)

I have never seen Megser so just . . . **AMAZED BY NEW THINGS.** She told Grandpa that being here was like being on the set of loads of movies. And he said to her: 'Megser! [I LOVE THAT HE CALLS HER MEGSER!] When you were little and you were watching American movies what all captured your imagination?' And she STRAIGHT AWAY goes: 'S'mores.' And then she goes: 'Sleeping by a campfire but close to a house and nowhere near bears.' Then: 'Cooking beans over a campfire.' Then: 'Singing around a campfire.' Then: 'Someone playing a banjo around a campfire.' Then: 'People telling ghost stories around a campfire.'

And Grandpa promised Megser he would make ALL those dreams come true. And then he probably went around the house when we had gone to bed and hid all the lighters.

6 August (FRIDAY)

Megser is jet-lagged. I'm letting her sleep so she won't be an antichrist. Even though she hides it SO well (eats breakfast with her head bowed).

So, it's just YOU and ME, NJF.

⟹ DRAMAS of the SUMMER

DRAMA 1: THE ATTEMPTED NEW NJF SITUATION!

Lola knew that I left you behind, and that I was upset because I missed you. So we were in this amazing stationery store and Lola saw . . . a 'replacement' you. **AS IF THAT WAS POSSIBLE.** I had only been here FIVE days. It literally was like being handed a new puppy after my FIRST AND ONLY OTHER BELOVED PUPPY was run over by a truck. Or left behind at home by horrific accident.

I surprised myself – and the entire store – with the intensity of my rejection.

But that did NOT deter Lola. Because a few weeks later she 'liaised' with the therapist who clearly told her I was the Rhinebeck Silent Johnny, and that maybe there was another way for me to 'process'. The other way – in Lola's mind – was to continue what she had tried to start that ended SO badly and just go ahead and BUY ME that 'replacement' you! I had a HEAVILY SIGNPOSTED bad reaction to that and there were SCENES and Lola was all, **IT'S SUMMER AND YOU CAN'T JUST SIT IN YOUR ROOM CRYING FOR DAYS ON END** and, **THE SUN IS SHINING** and,

I'M NOT SURE BLACK IS REALLY YOUR COLOUR, SWEETHEART.

Grandpa was staying out of it. Just providing hugs without saying a word. And we watched faded television shows. And he didn't ask me ONCE how I was FEELING. And I *loved* him EVEN MORE for that.

DRAMA 2: THE DAWN OF THE RUNAWAY HORSE

A little while after this, Grandpa came in one morning at DAWN. He's in his overalls and his plaid shirt, and he shakes me awake, and he's like: 'ELLERY! ELLERY!' And I have no idea what's going on, but then I think something's wrong with Lola and he's like: 'No, no, she's in the thick of her beauty sleep. I'm afraid it's Twister. I've just been down to the barn. And I don't know WHAT happened, but he must have broken free, and we're going to need ALL HANDS ON DECK.'

My HEART was: WARRIORS CHARGING.

Mom got Twister when I was about six years old ('my brave boy' Mom called him) and *I LOVE HIM SO MUCH.* And so did Mom.

216

But now I'm like, 'GRANDPA! You're not going to ride, though, are you?' Because he hasn't been able to since his new knee. But he looks me in the eye and goes: 'You BET I am.'

So I jump up and I get dressed and RUN. And ALL the ranch hands are out, and they've woken up their kids, and people are going out searching on horseback. And Grandpa saddles up Lumbo for me. And I was, like, hugging him, going in his ear: 'Lumbo! Twister has been by your side ever since you arrived (my ninth birthday!), so I don't care what it takes – we are going to go out there and bring Twister home, alive and well (and possibly surprised by all the attention).'

And Grandpa rode ahead on his huge black stallion, Teddykisssparklepony (the result of asking a five-year-old girl to name your horse), and I followed, and I was SO worried about Twister, but I was also just . . . breathing, and the air was warm, and the sun was rising, and I was thinking about how beautiful it is here. And I only realised that night that the one thing I didn't remember that **WHOLE DAY** was the one thing I remembered EVERY OTHER DAY since I got there: that Mom and me, and Twister, and Lumbo would never, ever ride together again. Because when I found Twister, I really DID feel that Mom was right there with us.

7 August (SATURDAY)

DRAMA 3

As suspected, Megser does NOT have a cousin in Albany, New York. While I was packing, she received a Google Alert announcing that Suspect 3: fantasy writer Quentin Schaeffer would be making a special guest appearance at a convention called OVERCON, taking place in? YES: Albany, New York on Friday, 13th August: **SIX DAYS FROM NOW**.

'I wasn't sure if you'd be ABLE,' she explains.

'And why do you think I am NOW?' I shouldn't have said.

'Oh, GOD,' she says. Because she KNOWS it's In Too Late Now News.

8 August (SUNDAY)

Megser and I were having breakfast on the terrace this morning and Grandpa appears and goes, 'What are you two out here scheming about?' And Megser and I did that jump of guilt because that's EXACTLY what we were doing: SCHEMING. About the upcoming appearance of Quentin Schaeffer.

We are able to legitimately go . . . because when we explained to Grandpa and Lola it's a cosplay convention, and we would be dressing up as dragons, and talking about books, plus meeting an esteemed author to get a book signed, we had their **FULL APPROVAL**. Because: BOOKS. Grandpa is going to drive us there. And the only effort we have to make is getting the bus home.

13 August (FRIDAY)

QUENTIN SCHAEFFER: ADVENTURES IN OVERCON: PART I

OH god . . . this MAN.

Twenty minutes in, and I ALREADY have Ellery's Approval Rating for Quentin Schaeffer: ☆ ☆ ☆ ☆ ☆

Megser and I are observing the suspect in letterbox format through the clear plastic face panels of our costumes, as we hide behind one of those divider things you see in convention centres.

Quentin Schaeffer is a small, round, furry BALL OF RAGE. With a bald head. And **AWESOME** eyebrows! He keeps returning things that he's being handed: coffee, water, food, opportunities to be nice. People are then coming back (or sending minions back) with new versions of whatever he rejected first time around. And I'm now thinking REJECTION is his thing, which makes me feel a little better because that means he did not single me out for rejection – after meeting me as a child and not liking what he saw, for example.

So . . . our COSTUMES. Do you ever get DRAGONS and DINOSAURS mixed up? Probably not. But I have some kind of mental block about them. And I was tired. Soooo . . . when I ordered two dragon costumes online, what I ACTUALLY ordered was DINOSAUR costumes. Plus, also by accident, they are inflatable. Basically Megser and I look like giant pool toys from a celebrity five-year-old's birthday party . . . pool toys he refuses to play with because they are lame. He doesn't even want them in the background of any of the photos. PLUS, MY dinosaur has REALLY DOPEY EYES, and Megser's has **BEWILDERED EYES.**

'Girlfriend INCOMING,' says Megser. 'Valentina from Venezuela: thirty-two years old.'

'THIRTY-TWO? She looks ten years younger,' I say.

'No rumours of plastic surgery,' says Meg.

And I'm thinking Megser has to be THE most OVER-RESEARCHING person in humanity because HOW is the level of plasticity of Valentina from Venezuela relevant to whether

Quentin Schaeffer could be my dad?

'Which COULD mean,' Megser is explaining because we read each other's minds, 'that if Quentin Schaeffer were to favour "girlfriends" of a "particular body shape" that included "any or all of the various types of enhancements available on the market" then your "late mother" would "not have been his type".'

Then she goes – as if she has an earpiece to a **STANDBY SWAT TEAM**: 'Subjects on the move.'

14 August (SATURDAY)
* ★ * ★ * ★ * ★ * ★ * ★ *

OVERCON: PART II: LINES OF ENQUIRY

Megser and I have been standing in line SO long that I can feel our summer, youth and beauty slipping away. But now we're finally within close observation distance.

Description of Quentin Schaeffer: sweaty brow; despair in the eye at non-diminishing line of fans.

Description of Valentina: stunning and blank in the eye; smile like red elastic band that is too short to reach (feline) eyes. Said eyes showing instead feline mistrust of all fans, plus NERD OVERWHELM. Dressed like sexy pirate but it's not a costume.

Also wearing jewellery like she has **EMPTIED ENTIRE TREASURE CHEST** from pirate ship over her person.

'Imagine her at mass in Castletown,' says Megser.

And the queue is moving, and we're shuffling/bobbing forward.

'And she probably would go to mass,' says Megser. 'Venezuela is seventy-one per cent Catholic, which is only SEVEN PER CENT less than IRELAND. And some of those necklaces she's wearing are crucifixes.'

'To ward off superfans,' I say.

We finally get to the top of the line and that's when I see the SIGN:

AUTOGRAPHS: $50!

QUENTIN SCHAEFFER IS A **MULTI-MILLIONAIRE.** YET ... – I REPEAT –

AUTOGRAPHS: $50!

Megser and I have EXACTLY $50 to get the bus home.

But in Wild Guess Challenge ... is it TOO LATE TO BACK OUT NOW?

Quentin Schaeffer glances up at us. 'Hey, drag—' he says, then he looks properly. 'Hey, DINOSAURS...' he says and his face is like:

YOU HAVE DANCED A JIG ON A DRAGON'S GRAVE.

And Valentina laughs and says: 'Isn't it the Barney convention you're looking for?'

And Meg goes: 'Barney's PURPLE.' Then: 'Unless he's green in Venezuela.'

And Valentina is like: 'WOW! How did you guess I'm from Venezuela?'

I step in: 'I love your work,' I say. Then: 'Sorry, Mr Schaeffer. But I'm here as a fan of Valentina's fantasy art. But my friend, MEGAN, loves your books.'

So Megser and I swap places, which takes AAAGES because: we are GIANT, INFLATABLE and are BOUNCING OFF EACH OTHER. And have TAILS. The positive is that even though I can't see Megser's face, I know that her current status is **AMAZED** that I read the research on Quentin Schaeffer all the way down to the bottom, where Valentina lay. PLUS – independently of Megser – I went online and WILLED myself through the gallery of Valentina's fantasy art. ☆ ☆ ☆ ☆ ☆

I feel SO mean writing that because Valentina's eyes are now NO LONGER BLANK – they are shining with validation. But I can see that Quentin Schaeffer is not liking this MISAPPROPRIATION

OF ATTENTION. His hand is in mid-air, waiting for the book to be handed to him. So Megser hands it to him. And he opens it. And we hear the sound of pages coming unstuck, and possibly ripping, and he goes:

'THIS IS ALREADY SIGNED.'

And Megser and I try to look at each other but it's too hard.

And he's frowning. 'WHERE DID YOU GET THIS?'

And I have to go: 'A charity shop.'

And he goes: 'WHERE?'

And I am PANICKING because I have ZERO idea what the problem is or who exactly is in trouble: me/the charity shop/the person who GAVE it to the charity shop.

And I channel my Inner Disgraced Politcian and go: 'I can't remember.'

And Quentin Schaeffer goes: 'Can I keep this? I'll swap you for a brand-new one.'

And Meg goes: 'NO.' (Her theory shared later was that it's worth **MILLIONS OF DOLLARS.)**

And he just shrugs and says: 'Well, I can't exactly sign an already signed book, can I?'

And I literally don't know if he can. Then – to mine and Megser's GREAT SURPRISE – I go: 'You knew my mom.'

'Who's your mom?' says Quentin. And Valentina looks pre-jealous in the eye.

'Laurie Brown. She was a writer too—'

'You don't need to explain to ME who Laurie Brown is,' he says, and he sits back. 'I didn't know Laurie had a daughter. So how old are you back there, Mr Dinosaur?'

'Sixteen,' I say. And I'm all **NERVOUS.** 'I think you and my mom were on a panel in Nice together years ago when her fantasy novel came out.'

'Ah, YES,' he says. And he turns to Valentina, and goes: 'Her mom wrote a fantasy novel and it was –' PAUSE – 'gooood,' and he nods. 'Actually, I think our panel at that convention was about whether female authors can write fantasy. Or SHOULD. I can't remember which. But she . . . held her own.'

I'm imagining Megser's costume filling up with steam that turns into sweat that rises up to chin level so she has to stab her own head or she'll DROWN.

Quentin is nodding in a reminiscing kind of way. 'That was a very *special* time.'

'What do you mean "SPECIAL"?' says Meg. And it's like this HISS of WILD ACCUSATION.

But Quentin Schaeffer just shrugs. 'We were young writers

starting out: hopeful and unburdened. We had four days in Nice, drinking champagne, partying, being treated like rock stars. We hadn't a care in the world.' Pause. 'No kids.'

And Megser who likes to **MOVE THINGS ALONG** just goes: 'The dedication you wrote to Ellery's mom . . . we don't have that book with us . . . SAYS . . .' And then pauses long enough for Quentin to realise Valentina might need to go pick him up lunch. In reluctant obedience, as Mom used to say about my room-tidying, she leaves. Then Megser RECITES an extract from the dedication: *We told each other we're in love! The waterbabies we would have! And they would swim to shore each night. And write their stories in the sand!*

And even I'M thinking she's a **WEIRDO** for knowing it off by heart. 'What did you MEAN by that?' she says to Quentin Schaeffer.

But he's just *LAUGHING*

and *LAUGHING*

 and *LAUGHING.*

And then Valentina, having delegated the lunch job to a minion, comes back, probably thinking, WHO IS THIS LAUGHING GUY? and he's explaining to us: 'They were the lyrics to a VERY, VERY, VERY BAD – as I'm sure you can tell – French song. And

SERIOUSLY if THAT was the way I went about seduc—' And then he STOPS HIMSELF, thank God, and says, 'It was from an album that was playing through the speakers when we got back to the hotel at the end of our night together in Nice.' PAUSE. 'The soundtrack to our skinny-dipping.'

Responses to this Last Statement:

Me: What a weird title for an album.

Valentina: Pre-jealousy of the eye now BACKDATED JEALOUSY. Feline eyes now **LASER EYES.**

ME, AGAIN: Heart bound for centre of earth due to sudden placement of Quentin Schaeffer at SCENE OF CRIME. WHILE NAKED.

Megser, I discover later, has not got past 'whether female authors can write fantasy. Or SHOULD'.

'I probably shouldn't have mentioned skinny-dipping,' says Quentin.

'No one,' says Valentina, looking up from her phone, 'wants an image of their mother skinny-dipping.'

'My mother is in pretty good shape,' says Quentin.

Then Valentina turns the phone around to me and says, 'Is THIS your mother?'

And I'm like, she will MURDER that man in his bed in a jealous rage some day.

'Yes,' I say.

'She has a *beautiful* smile,' says Valentina. Then, SHOCKED (with possibly a TOUCH of relief), 'Oh, noooo. Your mother has passed away.'

And I'm like, YES – YOU HAVE BEEN JEALOUS OF A DEAD PERSON.

Instead I try to nod. It is TRICKY to nod in a dinosaur costume without looking like Barney.

And Quentin Schaeffer goes: 'Yeah . . . I felt bad. Your mom and I hadn't been in touch for such a long time. She left a TON of messages with my agent after Nice, but I was busy. I was writing. And then I had that whole issue with the . . .'

And Valentina is giving him **STOP-SIGN EYES.**

'ASSAULT,' Meg announces.

And I'm like, Whuuuttt? Because this was UNDER NO CIRCUMSTANCES in the research she provided me.

AND MY HEART IS: machine at the country club that rapid-fires tennis balls but has malfunctioned so they can't get out.

'YES,' says Meg, because she is now in NEGATIVE HOOTS. 'In 2005 Quentin Schaeffer assaulted a guy in a bar. It went to court, but he avoided prosecution.'

And Quentin is nodding. 'True story. It's available for all to read on the internet. I have to own it. But I paid my dues. I went to anger management. I stopped drinking . . . publicly. I can talk about it now because I was a DIFFERENT GUY back then. I was arrogant. I was angry. I thought THE WORLD OWED ME A LIVING.'

'NOW,' says Megser, 'the world only owes you fifty dollars PER AUTOGRAPH.'

'*You poor girl,*' says Valentina to me, still scrolling through photos of Mom to reassure herself. She looks up, then: 'It is very hard for a young woman to lose her mother. A girl NEEDS her mother. Even more at that age. I am deeply sorry for your loss. And if I have your permission, I would like to light a candle for your mother, and include you both in my prayers.'

And she really is SO SINCERE and SO COMPASSIONATE.

Then this random nerd lurches into her personal space for a selfie and she turns around, grabs him by the neck of his costume (genial peasant) and goes: '*GET YOUR &&&&ING HANDS OFF ME, YOU TRAGEDY.*'

So, NO to VALENTINA as a STEPMOM. But YES to calling people TRAGEDIES.

We still go ahead and get an autograph, but just on a piece of paper.

And we're about to leave, but then the minion arrives with

Quentin Schaeffer's lunch: a buckwheat groats salad, a smoothie that the minion spoons maca powder and psyllium husks into. And there's a separate WHEATGRASS shot.

There's this awkward pause because of the **HORROR** of the lunch. And then Valentina raises her head from where it had been bent over the table, and she hands me a cartoon she's just drawn of two dinosaurs.

'THANK YOU!' both dinosaurs say.

'It's AMAZING!' I say. And it IS.

And then I can't help myself. 'You are SO LUCKY,' I say to Valentina, 'that you are with a man, who DESPITE HIS MASSIVE SUCCESS, has not forgotten that HE TOO started a creative career from NOTHING, as EVERY CREATIVE PERSON does, not really knowing if they're any good until someone TELLS THEM that they are. You are LUCKY because Mr Schaeffer KNOWS the bravery it takes for you to put your creations out there. Whether you're an AUTHOR, an UNSURE FANTASY ARTIST or a GIFTED CARTOONIST, it's all the same. Mr Schaeffer has CLEARLY remained HUMBLE, and will NO DOUBT be a huge support to you and take GREAT PRIDE in your achievements.'

'And feel UNTHREATENED as a MALE,' adds Megser. 'And not feel that he can only hang on to a woman as *beautiful* as

YOU if you are LESS successful than him, and/or DEPENDENT ON HIM FINANCIALLY.'

* And just to remind you: all of this is coming out of the mouths of inflatable dinosaurs *

So I'm not sure how powerful the message was . . . until I see TEARS in Valentina's eyes. And she squeezes Quentin's (RIGID) arm. And says thank you . . . TO HIM!

And then I hand over the $50.

And in Wild Guess Challenge: did he take it?

15 August (SUNDAY)

OVERCON: PART III

So Megser and I stagger out of the convention centre into the blazing sunlight and deflate our costumes, and we're both bright red, with hair like linguine with that ink from seafood in it.

And I am **TRAUMATISED.**

! 'OHMYGOD, MEGSER. ! ! QUENTIN SCHAEFFER IS MY DAD.'

'You're going STRAIGHT TO "DAD",' says Megser.

'YES!' I say. 'That HAS to be why Mom was trying to get hold of him after Nice! To tell him! But he ignored her calls. And THEN she found out he had assaulted someone, and she was like NO WAY IS MY DAUGHTER HAVING THAT GUY AS A FATHER.'

'I'd say she was thinking that before the assault too,' says Megser.

'I KNOW,' I say. 'But STILL . . . I don't know WHAT TO THINK. Do people go skinny-dipping PLATONICALLY?'

'How would I know?' says Megser.

'I'm HOPING,' I say, 'that Valentina's prayer for Mom will be a retroactive "STAY AWAY FROM MY MAN" and because time is irrelevant in the spiritual world the skinny-dipping will never take place.'

'Then you WOULDN'T BE ALIVE,' says Meg.

'OHMYGOD — YOU think he's my dad TOO!' And I'm panicking because I want Meg not to dismiss my concerns, but I also want her to NOT VALIDATE them.

Next thing I hear: 'Ellery?'

I turn around, and there's this guy standing there, and I KNOW I KNOW HIM. But it's from years ago . . . like when I was eight or nine. And he's in a proper non-inflatable dragon costume with the head under his arm, and also with the sweaty hair.

And then I GET IT:

IT'S AUNTIE ELAINE'S FANTASY-VIDEO-GAME-PLAYING-BEER-LOVING EX-BOYFRIEND.

And I'm like, HEY! Because he was a GREAT GUY. And he was FUN. And THREW ME AROUND THE SOFA and didn't treat me LIKE A GIRL. Then I add: 'GABE!' when I remember his name.

'YES!' says Gabe with this big smile. 'I recognised you from your Auntie Elaine's Facebook page.' And he looks at me and Megser. 'Are you two ladies okay? You look a little stressed.'

So we tell him about Quentin Schaeffer BLEEDING HIS FANS DRY one $50 bill at a time.

And Gabe says: 'I will NEVER forgive him for killing Myanther. I even wrote this review on Amazon and gave him one star . . . if that makes you guys feel any better.'

And it makes us laugh our heads off and we're looking at each other like WHAT ARE THE CHANCES of meeting the guy who wrote the review AND of actually having a connection to him?

And then I look at Gabe's costume PROPERLY. And I see that he is a dragon covered in wounds with swords sticking out of them, and I realise: GAMEBOY WENT TO OVERCON DRESSED AS A SPOILER!

233

'That is SO COOL!' I say. And then I register that I remembered Mom's nickname for him without even thinking.

And Gabe is laughing too, and he goes: 'Damn RIGHT I'm dressed as the slain – THREE BOOKS INTO THE SERIES – Myanther! SUCK IT, SCHAEFFER!'

And YES, this guy is late thirties, but anyone who goes to a convention dressed as a spoiler is a LEGEND. And anyone who drives us home safely to Rhinebeck when he hears we have no busfare is **ALSO A LEGEND.**

So we're getting out of the car and Gabe calls out the window: 'Tell your Auntie Elaine that Gabe says "Hi!". She is a great person.'

DRIVEN OUT OF YOUR LIFE BY LOLA, I'm guessing.

Then he shouts, 'Say Gabriel actually! GABRIEL says "Hi!"'

'Don't,' says Megser when he's gone.

'But maybe NOW,' I say, 'he and Auntie Elaine could have a second chance!'

'I just meant no to GABRIEL,' says Megser. 'The name – not the person.'

'And I mean NO to SCHAEFFER, the name AND the PERSON.'

Oh, and the book that was already signed? We looked at it later and it was signed to Quentin Schaeffer's favourite creative writing professor at NYU, thanking him for inspiring him and being the reason he wrote this book. But AT THE BACK – what Quentin Schaeffer DID NOT see – was a handwritten note FROM the professor . . . who had clearly sent the book to one of his friends: 'If I am any way responsible for this overwritten mess of a crowd-pleaser, shoot me now and strip me of my tenure.'

Who's The Father?

SUSPECT 3: QUENTIN SCHAEFFER

LIKELIHOOD ★ ★ ★ ★ ☆
LIKEABILITY ★ ★ ☆ ☆ ☆

BASED ON THE FOLLOWING CRITERIA:
PHYSICAL TRAITS ★ ★ ★ ★ ☆
Hair colour ★ ★ ★ ★ ☆
Eye colour ★ ★ ★ ★ ★
Height/Build ★ ★ ★ ☆ ☆
Strength ★ ★ ★ ★ ☆
Awesome eyebrows ★ ★ ★ ★ ☆

PERSONALITY TRAITS ☆ ☆ ☆ ☆ ☆

Rude ☆ ☆ ☆ ☆ ☆

Angry ☆ ☆ ☆ ☆ ☆

Arrogant ☆ ☆ ☆ ☆ ☆

Aggressive ☆ ☆ ☆ ☆ ☆

Dismissive ☆ ☆ ☆ ☆ ☆

SKILLS ☆ ☆ ☆ ☆ ☆

Dismissing things ☆ ☆ ☆ ☆ ☆

Dismissing people ☆ ☆ ☆ ☆ ☆

Overpricing autographs ☆ ☆ ☆ ☆ ☆

FOOD & DRINK ☆ ☆ ☆ ☆ ☆

Buckwheat groats ☆ ☆ ☆ ☆ ☆

Psyllium husks ☆ ☆ ☆ ☆ ☆

Maca powder ☆ ☆ ☆ ☆ ☆

Wheatgrass ☆ ☆ ☆ ☆ ☆

UNKNOWN UNKNOWNS ★ ★ ★ ★ ★

Inappropriately naked at appropriate time ★ ★ ★ ★ ★

'Companion' similarly attired ★ ★ ★ ★ ★

'Companion's' efforts to make contact after the fact ★ ★ ★ ★ ★

SUSPECT APPROVAL RATING ☆ ☆ ☆ ☆ ☆

Kind ☆ ☆ ☆ ☆ ☆

Fun ☆ ☆ ☆ ☆ ☆

Happy ☆ ☆ ☆ ☆ ☆

Takes care of things ☆ ☆ ☆ ☆ ☆

Isn't into rules but has some kind of boundaries ☆ ☆ ☆ ☆ ☆

MISCELLANEOUS ◀ ★ ★ ★ ★ ★ ★ ★ ★ ★ ★ ★ ★ ★

'Whether female authors can write fantasy. Or SHOULD.'

[The REASON that – DESPITE ALL THE ZEROS and NEGATIVES – Quentin Schaeffer gets a two-star likeability rating was because Megser made me give one star for the **MILLIONS OF DOLLARS** element. And one star for IF HE DOES END UP BEING MY DAD, THEN DIES and I AM A NAMED BENEFACTOR IN HIS WILL.]

16 August (MONDAY)

In Informed Guess Challenge: CLOZE TEST edition:

After meeting Quentin Schaeffer, Megser and Ellery woke up in a state of ABSOLUTE _____ and, as a result, made a **ONE HUNDRED PER CENT COMMITMENT** to the planning stage of Ellery's trip to the Milan Festival of Literary Fiction on 27th–30th August in order to _____

Suspect 1: Jay Evans and _____ him into the role of FATHER of ELLERY even if there turns out to be _____ evidence.

WORDS TO CHOOSE FROM:

PLEASE DO NOT QUENTIN LET SCHAEFFER BE MY DAD

SO . . . this plan is the first that will be carried out through the medium of EMAIL. It is also the first one I don't feel guilty about. Which is making me worried that we have become SEASONED LIARS and GUILT IS DEAD TO US.

So . . . here's what we did. We set up a fake email account for Susan.

SusanOSullivanSolicitor@gmail.com

Then we composed a) OURSELVES and b) an EMAIL:

Dear Lola and Max,

I trust you are both well and enjoying your summer. Thank you so much for looking after Megan so well during her two weeks with you. She had the most wonderful time in Rhinebeck, and your generosity meant so much to both of us.

I'm emailing to ask a special favour of you, regarding the girls. As you know, Ellery and Megan are dear friends, and Megan misses her very much during her absences. In fact, this summer, I would go as far as to say Megan turned inward. It was clear to me that she was becoming increasingly anxious about going into the fifth year, something perhaps that may not have happened were Ellery to have been by her side. Now that Megan is soon to return – after her amazing American adventure! – I'm concerned that, without Ellery, she may revert to her prior anxious state. I know that having Ellery back will make a huge difference to her, and with that in mind I was wondering if you would allow Ellery to return a week earlier than scheduled, and stay with us for the final week of the holidays. I'm aware that someone will be due to fly back with her, but, if your flights have yet to be booked or are flexible, I have taken that week off work to be there for Megan, and I would be more than happy to do the same for Ellery – to pick her up at Shannon Airport, and perhaps to take the girls on a short break in the area, maybe a trip to Bunratty Castle to keep their spirits up, and get them ready for the new school year. I would be more than happy to help Ellery with all her school preparations for the following week: books and uniforms; all the trips back and forth to Cork that will necessitate. Having done this many times for Megan, it's a familiar process that, were you not to know your way around, could end up being an ABSOLUTE NIGHTMARE!

If, however, you'd prefer to stick to your existing plans, please let me know, so that I can reserve tickets for the Parents/Guardians V Teachers KARAOKE CHALLENGE on Friday, 3 September at 6 p.m.

Also – with the rising popularity of NETFLIX among students – there is a scheduled talk by a psychologist that will take place on Saturday, 4 September that all parents/guardians are expected to attend: ISSUES RAISED IN THIS EPISODE: BROACHING SENSITIVE TOPICS WITH YOUR TEEN. Tea and sandwiches in the sports hall after!

If you need to contact me, email is the best option. But you can also reach me on my new mobile number: +353 55 5273840 – though the service has been unreliable due to works being carried out in the area.

Kindest regards,

Susan O'Sullivan

SOLICITOR

BREAKDOWN OF INSPIRED WORD CHOICES:

- 'I trust ...'

  I love Susan but she doesn't trust ANYONE or ANYTHING. This was to implant the general concept of trust.

- 'ask a special favour of you'

  Lola *loves* when 'SPECIAL' is connected to her in any way. And Grandpa can never say no to a favour request.

- 'turned inward'

  As if Susan would EVER use this expression. But Lola will RELATE because EVERY SINGLE SCRIPT EVER WRITTEN features someone TURNING INWARD.

- 'anxious x 2'

  Anxious: the Get Out of Jail Card that never expires.

- 'more than happy x 2'

  I love Susan but I've never seen her 'more than happy'. But Lola LOVES, LOVES, LOVES ENTHUSIASM.

- 'Bunratty Castle'

  This will evoke FOND MEMORIES for Lola and MAXIMISE the STARK CONTRAST of:

- 'all her school preparations'

  Invocation of Lola's PERSONAL HELL: First Circle

- 'all the trips'

  Invocation of Lola's PERSONAL HELL: Second Circle

- 'back and forth'

  Invocation of Lola's **PERSONAL HELL**: Third Circle

- THE ENTIRE SECOND-LAST PARAGRAPH

  Invocation of Lola's PERSONAL HELL: Circles Four to Nine SUPER-

SIZED by trigger words: KARAOKE, CHALLENGE, 6 p.m., NETFLIX, EXPECTED, ISSUES, TEENS, SANDWICHES, and SPORTS HALL [x 2].

NOTE I: there are ZERO EVENTS taking place before we go back to school. LITERALLY ZERO PARENTS, TEACHERS or STUDENTS want to LAY EYES ON EACH OTHER until the BITTER START.

NOTE II: the mobile phone was acquired through ID Dean. We recorded Susan's existing voicemail message on to it. This phone is DIVERTED AT ALL TIMES. If Lola DOES leave a voicemail, we plan to reply BY EMAIL ONLY.

Then COMPLETELY PANIC if that doesn't work.

17 August (TUESDAY)

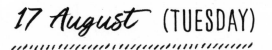

I came down this morning and Grandpa is watching this show from the seventies called **THE SIX MILLION DOLLAR MAN.** He cost that much money because he's filled with advanced technology after some accident. I mainly love him because he can run faster than anyone on the planet but when they were making the show his running was shot in slow motion because it looked too weird and jerky when it was sped up.

Anyway, Grandpa and I were watching it and Megser walks in and goes: 'Ha! Look! It's Dan!' (Carpenter Dan!) and I knewww he looked familiar. And even LOLA can see the resemblance but unfortunately has no real-life story about Lee Majors (the actor who played the Six Million Dollar Man). But I'm getting the impression she WISHES she had.

Megser and I are now LOVING going around running at high speed in slow motion, and Grandpa cracks up every time he walks in on us doing it and he goes: 'Twelve million dollars just HANGING AROUND MY KITCHEN.'

Then Lola walks in and takes Megser and me by 'TOTAL SURPRISE' (quotes by Ellery) with an email she just got from Susan and how would I feel about travelling back early alone? Would I be okay?

And I just go:

'DON'T WORRY ABOUT ME, LOLA!

I'm going to WALK OUT OF HERE with a **ONE-WAY TICKET** to SHANNON AIRPORT and a LIPSTICK in my BACK POCKET!'

18 August (WEDNESDAY)

SADNESS: Megser went home today.

NON-SADNESS: I'll be seeing her in five days' time. Then living with her for a week.

REALISATION I: I have just become the liar that FALLS FOR THEIR OWN LIES.

BECAUSE: REALISATION II: I'm OBVIOUSLY ACTUALLY going to be LIVING ALONE for that entire week. For the first time ever. And why did it even need to be a week?

21 August (SATURDAY)

Lola announces she will ALSO be travelling to the airport tomorrow, because she's flying to LA – one of her friends broke her arm and Lola would like to be there for her.

'She's a regular Florence Nightingale,' says Grandpa and he gives me this WINK.

22 August (SUNDAY)

Grandpa's driving me and Lola to the airport and I'm in the back of the car looking at him in the rear-view mirror, thinking,

FOCUS ON THE HELLOS.

NOT THE GOODBYES.

THEN: ⟶

FOCUS ON THE TRUTHS.

NOT ON THE LIES.

And the truth is that Lola is definitely looking way happier than she should for someone about to administer to a broken-armed friend. And I'm thinking there's NO broken-armed friend and, in FACT, Lola's happiness is the result of me CLEARING HER SCHEDULE to make way for a **VACATION**.

Which makes me able now to FOCUS ON THE LIES and feel

WAY BETTER ABOUT THEM.

23 August (MONDAY)

I slept almost all the way home but I was still spaced out enough to think Susan and Megser were actually going to be there at the airport to pick me up. And I'm feeling sorry for myself, thinking I wish I was arriving to a familiar face . . . and **BE CAREFUL WHAT YOU WISH FOR** is my advice. Because STANDING THERE in ARRIVALS is the VERY familiar face of:

OSCAR.
SERIOUSLY.

With his ENTIRE FAMILY. I hate to say bad things about people because that's not how Mom brought me up and I NEED TO SAY THAT because I ALSO NEED TO SAY: Oscar's Mommmm! Is SO FAKE!

'ELLERY!' she says. 'Are you ON YOUR OWN?'

Simple question, you would think. But this is Nuala. So I need to know EXACTLY how my lies might be distributed across the peninsula so that I do not FALL AT THE FIRST HURDLE.

My mind is like the whiteboard in the Without Incident Room, and a photo of NUALA'S FACE is now on it, with all these RED STRINGS coming out of it and I'm trying to see if she can be linked in any way to SUSAN or AUNTIE ELAINE or LOLA whose photos are ALSO now on the whiteboard.

OHMYGOD, IS NUALA STILL HERE? YES! OF COURSE SHE IS! RIGHT IN FRONT OF ME! With the face with the WORRY all over it! Which is a **DISASTER** because it tells me I AM SO CLOSE to being A DISCUSSED CHILD . . . I have to END this NOW.

<u>CONTENT WARNING:</u> this is BAD.

I drift back into reality. And I say: 'OHMYGOD, Nuala – I am SO sorry. I . . . it's . . . just . . . when you asked me that . . . you sounded . . . JUST LIKE MY MOM.'

I knowwww. I KNOWWW.

- **NON-SADNESS:** I got a lift back to Beara.
- **SADNESS:** Oscar was in the car too.
- **FURTHER NON-SADNESS:** I got the front seat.
- **ULTIMATE NON-SADNESS:** I got to tell Nuala an AWFUL STORY I heard about a boy who plagiarised the letter he sent to this GRIEVING GIRL I knew. But how, when this girl found out, she VERY QUICKLY got over it, because she knew that was more about HIM than it was about her. In FACT, I add, it was the girl's **beautiful,** BRIGHT, SPORTS-STAR BEST FRIEND who was the MOST DISGUSTED, and how SHE WAS THE ONE BENT ON

REVENGE.

'Well, we know where Oscar gets his brains from,' says Megser when I get back. 'Nuala sounds no more like your mom than the man in the moon.'

And we're laughing, but I'm also starting to freak out because we're in my house and I know Megser will have to go home soon but ALSO because WHAT IF NUALA TELLS SUSAN I'm back? But Megser says she won't because Susan thinks Nuala's a WEAPON, so they don't talk to each other. Then I realise ANYONE could notice I'm home – it's a tiny village where people go for WALKS [no idea] right by my front door. And I'm not planning on sitting in darkness for the week. THEN I realise I can just tell people that Auntie Elaine is here because it's not like they're going to come into the house and carry out a SEARCH.

There are SO MANY CONSEQUENCES to lying that I can see why Mom was so obsessed with the truth. Plus, you get a better night's sleep if you have no lies going on.

ANYWAY, when Megser is leaving, I'm MENTALLY CLINGING TO HER ANKLES AND BEING DRAGGED DOWN THE PATH.

BECAUSE: HOME ALONE.

2 a.m. update

I'm terrified.

3 a.m. update

IT IS SO QUIET.

It always is.

But stiiill.

z z z z z

4 a.m. update

Okay ... QUIET apart from the **WEIRD MOVEMENT** of TIMBER.
Timber SOUNDS LIKE INTRUDERS.

24 August (TUESDAY)

It is so strange to be able to do whatever you want. Tonight that involved watching nine million episodes of randomness on Netflix. And eating most of the week's supply of junk food. And I loved EVERY MINUTE.

Apart from the minutes that contained the thoughts: INTRUDERS.

That was MOST OF THE MINUTES.

25 August (WEDNESDAY)

Today, while trying to relax in the home I am not currently supposed to be living in, Grandpa FaceTimes me. And I PICK UP! And he is UNSURPRISINGLY SURPRISED I'M HOME. I am AN IDIOT! But BECAUSE I'm an idiot I have a track record of forgetting things, so, stopping by to pick something up is a believable excuse for why I'm not at Megser's.

Grandpa's telling me he's watching a Western about a sheriff in some two-bit town and we're laughing because when I was small and he explained what two-bit meant, I kept using it to describe ANYTHING that didn't impress me, and he's telling me he wishes I was with him because the outlaw is about to come into town, and I'm thinking I'M AN OUTLAW IN TOWN TOO and then I'm telling him HOW MUCH I miss him because I DO SO MUCH ALREADY and I'm looking at his **SMILEY EYES** with ALL THE LOVE in them and thinking, I'M LYING TO YOU ALL THE TIME AND NEXT WEEK I'M FLYING TO MILAN AND YOU HAVE NO IDEA AND I HATE LYING TO THIS MAN WITH HIS *gorgeous* SOUL WHOM I *adore,* AND THEN . . .

THIS comes out.

Of NOWHERE.

LIKE ₴UNFIRE ACRO₴₴ THE PERFECTLY LOVELY LOVE.

'Grandpa? Can I ask you something? Was Mom ever going to give me up for adoption? Did you and Lola MAKE HER keep me? Did she NOT WANT ME really?'

And Grandpa actually gives me this BIG HUGE SMILE. 'Now,' he says. 'Imagine your picture on a poster –' and he draws this frame around the screen with his big finger – 'and, right above your picture, a big old WANTED! sign. And right under your chin: REWARD!'

I'm probably looking at him like, Whuttt?

'Ms Ellery Brown,' he says, 'you'd have caused a HELLUVA lot of confusion in the Wild West because you were WANTED – one hundred per cent. And you were the reward. The BEST reward any of us could have EVER DREAMED OF.'

Grandpa is the **BEST MAN I KNOW.**

26 August (THURSDAY)

'What do you mean you've CALLED OFF THE SEARCH?' says Meg.

And I'm like: 'I JUST HAVE.'

Who's The Father?
Who Cares Edition

SUSPECT 1: JAY EVANS

SUSPECT 2: LEON ADLER

SUSPECT 3: QUENTIN SCHAEFFER

Because who needs a TWO-BIT FATHER when they have a **SIX-MILLION-DOLLAR GRANDPA?**

6 September (MONDAY)

Well, HELLO, SCHOOL! And HELLO,

glorious sunshine!

Why do you guys ALWAYS get together the same week?

❀ 8 September (WEDNESDAY) ❀

Silent Johnny only arrived back to school today. He has a tan. And he has clearly been carrying a lot of boxes and sheep. PLUS, the first-year girls have now **LAID EYES ON HIM.** And seriously Silent Johnny does not even notice. Even though it's literally like AND EVERYWHERE THAT JOHNNY WENT THE LAMBS WERE SURE TO GO. Which reminded me when I bumped into him to ask him how S. Dodge was. And his face LIT UP!

S. Dodge has his heart, First Years.

Which I FEAR will put her ONCE AGAIN at RISK of **SLAUGHTER.**

9 September (THURSDAY)

Oh my GOD! So ... that day at Overcon when we met Gabe? Well, he was SO FURIOUS that Quentin Schaeffer took $50 from two young women, thereby leaving them without bus fare home, which could have put them in ***EXTREME DANGER*** that he went back to the convention centre and CONFRONTED HIM about it! WHILE DRESSED IN HIS SPOILER COSTUME! And BASICALLY ... Quentin Schaeffer ASSAULTED HIM! SERIOUSLY! And there's talk of a LAWSUIT. **HOW HILARIOUS** is THAT (as long as no one was injured)?

AND ALSO HOW **BEYOND AWFUL** IF **QUENTIN SCHAEFFER** TURNS OUT TO BE **MY DAD?**

17 September (FRIDAY)

Oh GODDD. Megser is DEVASTATED. Because the overlooked part of the whole renovation/extension situation is the fact that ALL HER *fairy* DOORS WILL HAVE TO COME OFF THE WALL.

And Megser is all: 'I don't want a new room now! Let's just FORGET THE WHOLE THING.'

And Susan is all: SPACE! DOUBLE BED!

And Megser is all, 'I don't NEED a double bed!'

And Susan is all, 'You'll be doing your EXAMS in two years' time and you'll need PROPER SLEEP and a PROPER DESK and then you'll be GOING TO COLLEGE' and that was like PUNCHING MEGSER IN THE FACE because that was about a GROWN-UP FUTURE and no longer being a stay-at-home savant when she's already in the middle of an eviction nightmare with the *fairies*. And Susan is being **so lovely** about it, even though you know she's thinking, THIS IS ALL COMING FROM A SOON-TO-BE-SIXTEEN-YEAR-OLD FOOTBALL CAPTAIN who calls men MALES. And then Susan tells Megser that the best she can do is have a word with Carpenter Dan about the fairy doors, but Megser is like, 'I KNOW there'll be no way of taking them off without them all falling apart because they've been there SO

LONG' and now **SHE'S FALLING APART.**

And then the Ferals arrive into her bedroom swinging hammers and singing 'Wrecking Ball'. So Susan WRESTLES THEM OUT and sends them to bed, and then comes back to us with the glass of wine she wasn't intending to drink. And she looks REALLY SAD that Megser is so sad when this was supposed to be SUCH A *special* THING but Megser is just NOT THE BEST at ACKNOWLEDGING that Susan has emotions. Probably because Susan POWER-WALKS through her own emotions and throws food at everyone else's. Which is probably because Mrs Daly treats emotions like WHAC-A-MOLE.

❀ *29 September* (WEDNESDAY) ❀

I wake up with *divine* INSPIRATION for Megser's birthday present. It is **AWESOME.** And unsurprisingly involves COVERT OPERATIONS.

*Because that's who
I am now.*

257

1 October (FRIDAY)

OH. MY GOD. YOU WON'T BELIEVE THIS! QUENTIN SCHAEFFER IS DEFINITELY ⟹ NOT MY DAD.

After the whole GAMEBOY ASSAULT SITUATION at Overcon, Quentin Schaeffer has clearly gone on a PR rehabilitation mission. Megser and I just watched this video of him online and he's with Valentina from Venezuela on a visit to Africa where they have SURROUNDED THEMSELVES with children and then it cuts to them being interviewed in this JUNGLE SITUATION, which is probably the pool area of the five-star hotel they're staying in that was paid for by AUTOGRAPHS. They are engaged now, and talking about ADOPTING because . . . WAIT FOR IT . . . it turns out that, due to a CHILDHOOD INCIDENT, Quentin Schaeffer is unable to have children. And I'm thinking A GAME OF DODGEBALL but that's where that train of thought ended.

Because the only thing that matters is **QUENTIN SCHAEFFER CANNOT POSSIBLY BE MY FATHER!**

I have LOST a FATHER. And GAINED a RELIEF.

And Megser and I **SCREAM SO LOUD** at this positive development that Susan comes rushing in. And then she stops dead and goes: 'Ah, for God's SAKE! There's NOTHING WRONG WITH YOU.'

Who's The Father?

Elimination Round II

● ~~SUSPECT 2: LEON ADLER~~

Because he told me he wasn't.

● ~~SUSPECT 3: QUENTIN SCHAEFFER~~

Because he can't have kids.

● ~~SUSPECT 1: JAY EVANS~~

By order of Ellery. Because: GRANDPA .

2 a.m. update

THANK GOD Quentin Schaeffer is not my dad . . .

So there are NO BUTS. Except it's just . . . the idea of DADS DISAPPEARING – even one from the Island of Disappointing Fathers – is making me . . . I don't knowww. Because I'm looking at JAY EVANS being crossed off the list BY ORDER OF ME, so maybe ALSO BY ORDER OF ME, he could be REINSTATED just so he can be **OFFICIALLY INVESTIGATED** so he can be OFFICIALLY crossed off because of PROOF.

2 October (SATURDAY)

Megser and I go down for breakfast this morning and realise that Carpenter Dan and Silent Johnny are putting down floors in the Feral sanctuary. Luckily – because I'm in a koala onesie and Megser is in her **DYSTOPIAN NIGHTMARE** – the kitchen is at the other end of the house, so the chances of running into them are slim.

But Susan has different plans. She's standing there with this massive bowl of pancake mix and sends the Younger Feral down to them to see if they'd like pancakes, that she's made plenty of batter. When he comes back he says they're FINE OUT, i.e. they don't want any. And Susan is like, 'Did you tell them there's plenty of batter?' And he says, 'I DID! And I even said my brother was gone on a playdate, so there was even more on the go.' And BASICALLY . . . he is SO lying about **EVERYTHING** to do with the pancakes. All of it is LIES. And then it's like this wildlife documentary where Susan **LOCKS EYES** with him and she's seeing the lies and he knows it . . . and he SPRINGS UP and BOLTS, and Susan flings down the spatula and charges after him, shouting, 'You PUP, you!' And next thing there's some kind of crash in the hallway and the Younger Feral is shouting, 'My head! My HEAD!' And we rush out and he's lying on the floor and Susan's standing over him roaring, 'My GOOD VASE! J&&&& C&&&&& ALMIGHTY, are you a **SAVAGE ALTOGETHER?**'

Then we all realise Dan has arrived on the scene. And now Susan is crouching down to the Younger Feral, all soothing and – 'Sure, it's only a vase, and as long as YOU'RE okay' and Dan is reassuring her that he saw EVERYTHING and that the Younger Feral definitely did not hit his head. And the Younger Feral has BETRAYAL EYES and CHECKING-FOR-AN-EXIT-ROUTE EYES until

Dan says to Susan: 'You know yourself how you take a fall and in the shock of it you don't know WHAT'S going on, or what hit where or IF YOU'VE BEEN HIT AT ALL...'

And Megser is looking *SO WORRIED.* Because: HURRY UP WITH THE PANCAKES.

Then Susan roars: 'The PAN! The GAS!' just as the smoke alarm goes off. And Dan gives the CALMING HANDS to everyone and strides off to the kitchen and we go in after him and SERIOUSLY he does ALL THIS: turns off the gas, gets rid of the smoke so the alarm stops, washes and dries the frying pan, puts it back on the gas, puts some butter in it, makes a cup of sweet tea for Susan while the butter is melting, gets a bag of peas for the Younger Feral's FAKE HEAD INJURY and then starts making the pancakes!

Until Susan says: 'DO YOU THINK I'M PAYING YOU TO STAND AROUND FOR THE DAY MAKING PANCAKES?'

I'm SO HOPING that she's joking, even though there was zero evidence of that. And Dan is looking **MORTIFIED.** And SERIOUSLY it feels like about three weeks before Susan lets out a laugh. And the RELIEF on Dan's face.

And then I have this **TERRIFYING REALISATION.** Was that SUSAN... FLIRTING?

4 October (MONDAY)

OH.MY.GOD: MOMMM!

Auntie Elaine got a call from the Irish Book Awards people and they are honouring Mom with a Lifetime Achievement Award in November! And Auntie Elaine is going to collect it on her behalf! And I'm going to be her DATE!

But we are SWORN TO SECRECY.

5 October (TUESDAY)

WHAT AM I GOING TO WEAR TO THE IRISH BOOK AWARDS? has been a RECURRING THEME for the past twenty-four hours.

6 October (WEDNESDAY)

OHMYGOD: the Younger Feral. AGAIN. I was at Megser's this evening and he **THROWS THIS CURVEBALL** into the renovation situation. So . . . Susan promised them all that they could design their rooms any way they wanted and she gave them furniture catalogues and colour charts and it was a NORMAL-BUDGET-type situation.

But the Younger Feral (reminder: he is NINE) appears after dinner with his choice of furniture and paint. From totally different catalogues from the ones Susan had given him. And the paint is FARROW & BALL. I don't know ANYTHING about paint because: SIXTEEN YEARS OLD. But I have since learned that Farrow & Ball is basically the CHANEL of PAINT. So imagine the Younger Feral in black polyester football shorts, no top, long fingernails, holding a banned energy drink and standing in a country home in front of portraits of his ancestors against a MUTED BACKGROUND of 'WEVET WHITE' walls with 'RECTORY RED' accents.

SERIOUSLY.

AND THE FURNITURE HE WANTS:

- MAHOGANY BED with MATCHING NIGHTSTANDS
- MAHOGANY and GREEN-LEATHER-TOPPED WRITING BUREAU
  (and I'm thinking TO SCRATCH HIS NAME and 'UP, TOWN!' into)
- MAHOGANY and GREEN-LEATHER WINGBACK CHAIR

When questioned by Susan he points out that she didn't SAY there was a budget. And she didn't SAY they had to pick ONLY from the furniture brochures she gave them.

So . . . now Susan is a bit stuck because Megser and the Elder Feral are getting what THEY wanted and the Younger Feral is now talking about NOT BEING LOVED AS MUCH AS HER 'OTHER CHILDREN' as he has started to call them.

The SUM TOTAL of the Younger Feral's RENOVATION VISION is €6,500.

Susan hands him back the list, shaking her head, and goes: 'Look at that! Look at it PROPERLY. What have you not taken into consideration?'

And he looks all solemn and goes: 'Money?'

And Susan goes: 'NO! The LINE OF LITTLE BELLS across the wall to SUMMON THE HELP.' And points to herself.

Then Megser leans over to him, pats his head and goes: 'YEAH, Downton SHABBY.'

And he JUMPS UP from the table and so does Megser because he's gone Maximum Feral. She RUNS and he BOLTS after her and tries to kick her in the shins, but Megser stops and holds the top of his head and keeps him at arm's length and he's SNARLING at her and trying to SCRATCH her and it's like watching those LIONS at the ZOO who have reached **BREAKING POINT**.

And Megser goes to him. 'What's wrong with you? Do you need HELP? Ding! Ding!'

And Susan comes out and says, 'Ah, don't be PROVOKING him at this hour of the evening.'

But SERIOUSLY he's actually CRYING everyone realises. And it doesn't seem like rage, which is USUALLY why.

And Susan's face gets all relaxed and she says, 'Ah, he's worn out, the poor pet. I think bed for you.'

And that's like someone throwing a lollipop into the LION ENCLOSURE.

'I AM NOT GOING TO BEDDDDDD!' he screams.

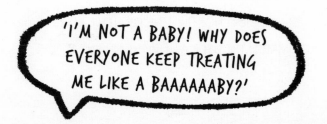
'I'M NOT A BABY! WHY DOES EVERYONE KEEP TREATING ME LIKE A BAAAAAABY?'

'Is that why you want all that granny furniture?' says Megser. 'To make you seem OLDER?'

And he goes BALLISTIC again. But Susan separates him and Megser and half carries him down the hallway to his bedroom and I bet she's considering some kind of ELECTRIFIED DOOR SYSTEM for the Feral Sanctuary.

Twenty minutes later, Susan reappears, screwing the cap back on a bottle of cough syrup. 'WHAT was that about?' she says. 'Does he not feel *loved* or WHAT'S going on?'

Then she looks at Megser. 'What's he watching?'

And I go: '*GRAND DESIGNS*?'

And we're laughing.

'Maybe he's gay,' says Megser.

And Susan is horrified. 'I did NOT raise a child to buy into stereotypes. He likes INTERIOR DESIGN equals he's GAY?'

'THE GAYS ARE A NICER CLASS OF PERSON,' says Mrs Daly. **'GENTLER SOULS,'** and we all turn around and she's just SITTING THERE IN THE DARK IN HER COAT.

7 October (THURSDAY)

I came home from school today and Lola's FACE. And she says, 'Sit down, but everything's FINE now, so there's NOTHING to worry about. But, Saturday night, Grandpa had to go to the hospital—'

My HEAD IS **STARTING TO FIZZ** and the SHEETS of TEARS have been PUT OUT ON MY FACE and POOR LOLA is all STEADYING MY ARMS: 'Nooo! Ellery, no! He's FINE!' And 'Look at me! Listen to me!' and 'KEPT HIM IN FOR OBSERVATION' and 'ALL-CLEAR—'

'From WHAT?' I'm saying.

'He had CHEST PAINS, but—'

And I'm thinking NOOO! Because: HIS HEART!

And Lola's panic-talking over me. 'But it WASN'T HIS HEART! ELLERY! He's as HEALTHY AS EVER! It was probably just STRESS.'

'GRANDPA DOESN'T STRESS! GRANDPA NEVER STRESSES!' And I'm thinking if GRANDPA is stressing then NO ONE IS SAFE.

AND MY HEART IS:

ALL THE DIPS.

3 a.m. update

I'm wide awake for HOURS, thinking about NOTHING EVER HAPPENING TO GRANDPA EVER again. And I actually go down and wake Lola up, which I've never done in my life because: *beauty sleep*. And I BEG HER to let me FaceTime Grandpa on her phone because he hasn't been picking up my calls and I secretly don't believe that he's okay, but I don't say that out loud. And Lola says YES to FaceTime, so we do and he looks a little pale but as handsome as ever, and he's DEFINITELY at the ranch and it's not a FAKE BACKDROP because I make him push against it to prove there's not a whole CRITICAL-CARE UNIT behind him.

And then I go back to bed and I CRY about him BEING PALE. And then I tell myself EVERYONE AROUND HERE IS PALE and THEY'RE ALL ALIVE. And NOBODY DIED from BEING PALE.

And THANK YOU,
PEOPLE OF IRELAND,
for helping me go back to sleep.

8 October (FRIDAY)

Megser and I win Puffiest Eyes in Class Today. She was ALSO awake half the night . . . because Carpenter Dan was back yesterday and took her aside to gently break it to her that TODAY is THE DAY he'll have to remove the fairy doors from her wall. And how gorgeous is this: he PROMISED her he would be as careful as possible and that he would put them safely in a box for her.

And POOR MEGSER thanked him a million times before telling him in the nicest way possible that she never wanted to LAY EYES on that box so to please give it to her mam to put in with the LADS' BIRTH CERTIFICATES in **MEGAN'S BOX OF CHILDHOOD TRAUMAS.**

ANYWAY, because we are BOTH like antichrists we go to bed a little earlier than normal, and we STILL can't sleep, and I end up telling her about Grandpa which I didn't want to bother her with earlier on account of the fairies, and I'm trying to be all cool, but I'm not, and I go: 'But what if Grandpa—'

And she WON'T LET ME FINISH the sentence! And she tells me he's STRONG AS AN OX and LOOK AT HIM and IT'S GRANDPA and he's a COWBOY and she's right and I feel better.

SADNESS: later I hear this sob in the dark and then this LITTLE VOICE and Megser's telling me that her dad bought her her first *fairy* door.

9 October (SATURDAY)

Susan went to Cork this morning to buy house stuff, so it was just me and Megser and the Ferals. And Dan and Silent Johnny who were 'hanging doors'. The Ferals were going BALLISTIC all morning and you can totally tell that Dan's thinking HOWWW is this BEHAVIOUR ALLOWED TO GO DOWN? And next thing I hear him come out into the hall: *'LADS, LADS, LADS!'*

I stick my head out the bedroom door, and he's crouched down between the two of them with a hand on each of their arms and they flash a glance at each other, and go:

'DANNN, THE MANNN!' like they're in some TRIANGLE OF ADMIRATION when actually all Dan wants is a ZERO FATALITY work place.

'Will ye tell me what's going on altogether?' he says to them.

And Megser walks by with a bowl of Cornflakes and goes, 'DAILY LIFE,' and keeps walking.

And Dan is looking at the Ferals. 'Surely, you're not carrying on like this the whole time.' And they're looking at each other like, 'Well . . .'

'Ah, now – that's not on,' says Dan. 'We need to have a chat here about all this.' And the Ferals don't know WHERE to look. But he's **DEFINITELY** got their attention, so he lets go of them, and points at the Younger Feral. 'You first. What's going on?'

'I'm FIGHTING HIM,' he says, like duh.

'You're angry with him,' says Dan.

'Yes!' says the Younger Feral, delighted Dan's GETTING IT.

'And why's that?' says Dan.

'Because I HATE HIM.'

'Right,' says Dan, taking this very seriously. And he turns to the Elder Feral and says: 'You next.'

And the Elder Feral says: 'Same as.'

'And do ye enjoy fighting?' says Dan.

And they're both nodding, and Dan is nodding away with them. And he goes, 'What's your favourite part? The punches, the kicks, the roars out of you –' and then he PAUSES – 'or is it upsetting your mother who got me in here now and made me promise to give the pair of you THE BEST BEDROOMS in the WORLD?'

OHMYGOD . . . HE IS A LEGEND. Plus, he doesn't even wait for them to answer, because – LET'S FACE IT – they'd probably say: 'The PUNCHES!' And instead he goes: 'The reason I'm asking is that I'm two men down at the moment. And I'm going to need a team here to help me on this. And if the pair of ye can't get on . . .' And he shrugs.

And the Ferals are **FLIPPING OUT** at the thought of missing out on playing with POWER TOOLS, which is where BOTH their heads DEFINITELY went, so they go EERILY STILL, like soldiers prepared to take orders.

'Right,' said Dan. 'Can ye shake hands on that, so, lads?'

And the Ferals shake hands. Because: POWER TOOLS.

And Dan stands up and pats them on the head.

'You're fine strong lads,' he says, 'and you've a lot of energy, and the best thing ye can do with all that is work hard. FORGET ABOUT ALL THAT OTHER NONSENSE.' And then he's walking away, but shouting back at them, 'I HAD TO FIRE THREE SEVEN-YEAR-OLDS ON A JOB LAST WEEK, SO DON'T THINK I WON'T DO IT IF I HAVE TO.'

13 October (WEDNESDAY)

❋ • ❋ • ❋ • ❋ • ❋ •

Today is the Irish Book Awards shortlist announcement day. And there's a reception in Dublin, but we don't have to be there, but me and Lola watch it on THE NEWS [no idea].

AND NEXT THING: in the middle of all these Irish authors being interviewed . . . is one of the nominees in the Radio One Listener's Choice category:

SUSPECT NUMBER 1: JAY EVANS!

And he's saying he WILL BE THERE ON AWARDS NIGHT! IN DUBLIN!

IN IRELAND!

~~ONE-SHOT, TWO-SHOT~~, THREE-SHOT JAY EVANS!

And I BOLT for my bedroom because I'm thinking, OHMYGOD. JAY EVANS IS BACK IN THE RUNNING – and YES I called off the search but maybe what I was ACTUALLY calling off was GOING on the search. Now that the search has COME TO ME – well . . .

So I call Megser because I want to find out how I should feel about this and I tell her that ONE-SHOT JAY EVANS will be in the SAME COUNTRY as ME in the SAME ROOM in ONE MONTH'S TIME and that this makes him THIRD-TIME-LUCKY JAY EVANS! And IS THAT—

But Megser is already saying:

'It's A SIIIIIIGN!'

15 October (FRIDAY)

We decide that for the purposes of approaching Jay Evans at the Irish Book Awards I have to know just enough about him to be a convincing fan but **NOT ENOUGH** to raise JAYSTALKER flags.

So my suggestion is that we read *Kerosene* by Jay Evans in VISUAL FORMAT.

You know the way you hear the word LIKEABLE and how important it is for a BOOK or NOW A MAJOR MOTION PICTURE to have a LIKEABLE character? And how you don't usually hear the word HATEABLE? Well, watch *Kerosene* . . . and meet THE MOST HATEABLE CHARACTER you have EVER come across in YOUR ENTIRE LIFE. And? She's a TEENAGE GIRL . . . who ends up being set on fire . . . BURNED ALIVE . . . effectively to get her out of the hair of the narrator *WHO YOU TOTALLY SYMPATHISE WITH!* Like you ACTIVELY WANT her to be set on fire.

And in **FURTHER WORRYING NEWS**, the narrator bears an eerie resemblance to Jay Evans. Which did NOT help when we hear this PSYCHOTIC WHISPERED VOICEOVER right at the start:

'There is a lightness to teenage girls, an easy laughter, a playfulness.' This was all going so well. Until: 'But it's not for you. Because even if they do turn their gaze outwards, its purpose is only . . . to BURN.'

'J&&&&,' says Meg. 'Does he know that, mainly, we're just sitting around talking about burritos?'

'This is NOT GOOD,' I say. But I have my first question: 'What did a teenage girl EVER DO TO YOU?'

'We need to remember,' says Meg, 'it's FICTION. And he wrote it EIGHTEEN YEARS AGO. He could *love* teenage girls now.'

Then we both look at each other.

'Not great either,' we agree.

16 – 17 October (ENTIRE WEEKEND)

ONLINE DRESS SHOPPING.

18 October (MONDAY)
★ ★ ★ ★ ★ ★ ★ ★ ★ ★ ★ ★ ★

EPIC PHONE CALL FROM GRANDPA!

'Ellery, sweetheart,' says Grandpa. 'I've said the following three words only a handful of times in the course of my life. And it'll be the first time ever I have said them to you.'

'Well, I know for a fact it's not "I love you".'

'No,' he says. 'It's WAY MORE FUN than that.'

And then he says:

And I'm like, 'On WHAT?'

And he says, 'Your GOWN, Ellery! For the awards!'

I **SERIOUSLY** don't think Grandpa knows how much dresses cost.

19 October (TUESDAY)

I FIND A DRESS! On an American website. And I decide to blow $200 on it. Grandpa is just TOO KIND. PLUS you don't need to WEAR Elie Saab to wear the EXPRESSION of SOMEONE WEARING Elie Saab.

22 October (FRIDAY)

MEGSER'S BIRTHDAY!

THIS was THE BEST NIGHT.

Not JUST because it was Megser's birthday, but also because: HER FACE when she opened her present. The present that involved COVERT OPERATIONS and ADULT COLLUSION in the form of Susan and Dan.

Susan retrieved the box of Meg's prised-off *fairy* doors,

delivered them to me, who delivered them to Dan, who made sense of my crude drawing.

So ... TONIGHT I got to watch Megser unwrap 'Fairy Towers': a luxury nine-storey apartment block with twenty-seven fairy doors mounted on the front in three columns of nine (twenty-six PRE-ADORED and one NEW birthday addition). On top of this freestanding building is a light-up sign that reads FAIRY TOWERS.

Then I gave her the TOUR while reading from the TINY BROCHURE I wrote:

Welcome to fairy towers, an exceptional new living experience — a place where fairies can retreat to at the end of a long night, hang up their bags of teeth, and lay their heads on pillows that no one has to root around under.

What makes Fairy Towers particularly special is that — weighing in at a mere 12 LBS — it is one of the lightest designs in portable fairy living. Meaning it can accompany its owner, MEGSER O'SULLIVAN, wherever life may take her.

HER FACE! And the sweetest thing – Susan made Dan stay for the big reveal, and when Megser opened it he said that, if she wanted, he could put hooks on the side to hang her football boots on. And Megser said, 'NO!' Then: 'Thank you. Because . . . just . . . **IT'S PERFECT.**'

I have NEVER heard Megser say ANYTHING was perfect before IN MY LIFE. And clearly Susan hasn't either and she's *FULL OF JOY.*

Next thing we all stop breathing because the Younger Feral who had SEPARATED HIMSELF from the group is now standing with his head bowed and his arms wrapped around Fairy Towers . . . which is UPSIDE DOWN.

And after what feels like ten years he looks up at Dan and says, 'What's this CRACK?' which was even more terrifying because the Ferals are WIRED to EXPLOIT WEAK POINTS and I'm imagining him just smashing his chin off it to see if it will shatter and we ALL KNOW that things shattering is the soundtrack to the Ferals' LIVES and at this stage WE ARE ALL FROZEN.

Except Dan, who – NOT A BOTHER – holds eye contact with him and starts walking towards him like a bomb-disposal expert, then – BAM! – does this sudden CROUCH in front of him and slides his big hands under Fairy Towers. Now that it's secured,

Megser LEAPS FROM THE CHAIR to grab the Younger Feral by the hair but he springs back and lets Fairy Towers go and poor DAN ends up DROPPING and ROLLING with his arms in the air holding Fairy Towers up like a SACRIFICE to the gods or ST JOSEPH PATRON SAINT OF CARPENTERS and we are all frozen AGAIN – until we see Dan safely lower Fairy Towers to his chest.

'OHMYGODOHMYGODOHMYGOD,'

says Megser. 'You &&&&ing LEDGE [short for LEGEND]!'

'MEGAN! LANGUAGE!' says Susan. 'Sorry, Dan.'

And Megser is standing over him, tilting her head, staring at the bottom of Fairy Towers while it's on view.

'Would you HELP THE MAN UP?' says Susan.

But Megser is frowning and pointing at the bottom of *Fairy* Towers: 'There's NO CRACK. What's he ON ABOUT?'

And Susan is looking around. 'Am I the ONLY sane one in the place?'

And Megser goes:

'UNDER LITERALLY
➡️ **ZERO** CIRCUMSTANCES.'

And she's so serious that Dan starts to laugh, and Susan tries to but instead she looks at him and goes: 'I'M NOT PAYING YOU TO ROLL AROUND MY FLOOR FOR THE NIGHT PLAYING WITH DOLL'S HOUSES.'

OHMYGODDD.

And Dan climbs to his feet and goes: 'Sure, you're not paying me AT ALL. I was just dropping in the—'

'Thing he spent AGES making, Mam,' says Megser. 'Would you COP ON TO YOURSELF?'

And Susan is *REALLY STRUGGLING.*

'And,' says Megser, 'you TOLD him, "Stay for a glass of Prosecco and a slice of cake".'

And we all know that Dan has been standing around empty-handed since he arrived and Susan's there with her ALMOST EMPTY glass of red wine. But she's got that DEFIANT look in her eye (that MEGSER gets too) and she's lining something up and here it is:

'I'm docking you the cake and Prosecco for the crack in *Fairy* Towers – in the BASE of all places – that even a child of nine, whose eyes can hardly settle on a thing for more than two seconds, managed to spot.'

And Megser is shouting: 'There is NO CRACK. I TOLD YOU.'

But Susan was half smiling as she was saying all this and she's cutting the cake and she's popping the cork on the Prosecco and Dan is DEFINITELY going to bring some kind of gauge thing with him the next time because the **ONLY EXPLANATION** for the MADNESS in this house is a carbon monoxide leak.

31 October (SUNDAY)

HALLOWEEN

MOM AND I WERE OBSESSED WITH HALLOWEEN.

Everyone loved calling to our house. It was like a movie set. The garden had gravestones and mummies, and a creepy fog machine, and these cackling witches with red-laser eyes. INSIDE, EVERY YEAR, we would scare ourselves OVER AND OVER with motion-sensor lights that played *THE EXORCIST* theme tune

when you walked past – EVEN THOUGH they were always in the same place. We also had bloody handprints and footprints all over the walls and floors, and we hung skeletons from the stairs and **YOU GET THE PICTURE.**

Tonight I made Lola turn out all the lights and sit in the dark and wait until all the trick or treating was over and all the kids had gone home.

Because **NO ONE TELLS YOU** about WHEN CALENDARS ATTACK. Because if you lose someone you love, your calendar will attack you every month. The first Christmas without Mom. The first New Year's Eve without Mom. The first Mother's Day without Mom. My first birthday without Mom. Mom's first birthday without herself. And if you actually thought about it, you would have a COMPLETE MELTDOWN. I'm SIXTEEN – I could have a SIXTIETH Mother's Day without Mom and even the thought of that makes this

OFFICIALLY THE SCARIEST HALLOWEEN I'VE EVER KNOWN.

1 November (MONDAY)

NOOOOOOOO! Auntie Elaine called to say that she won't be able to make it home for the book awards because of WORK! And I was like, 'Whutttt? That's INSANE!' I can't BELIEVE they wouldn't give her time off for this. But Auntie Elaine is already saying, 'I know that sucks when I'm letting you down, but . . . LEAVE IT WITH ME,' and she says she'll talk to Mom's publisher and the book awards people and come up with a **PLAN.**

2 November (TUESDAY)

OH.MY.GOD. THE PLAN!

So I got down on one knee today, and I took Meg's hand.

'May I, Ellery Possibly Evans, take THEE, Megser Hundred Per Cent O'Sullivan –' and then I pick up this After Eights box from the floor beside me, slide it open to reveal the ticket – 'to the –' pause for effect – 'IRISH . . . BOOK AWARDS?'

'Oh. Sweet. J&&&&. YES! YES! YES!' Megser is saying and there's this WILD mix of PANIC and THRILL and DOOM on her face and she's grabbing my arms and pulling me back up to my feet.

And I'm like, **'BUT YOU'RE HORRIFIED!'**

'Oh, I AM,' says Megser. 'I AM. It's like getting WILLY WONKA'S GOLDEN TICKET and you're chill, but you know in your soul that when he throws open the gates, you're going to fling yourself inside and LICK ALL THE CHOCOLATE and you're VIOLET BEAUREGARDE 2.0 – Violet NO REGARD. For her OWN DIGNITY.'

'But you'll have LICKED THE CHOCOLATE,' I say.

'I don't want to LICK the chocolate,' says Megser.

'I WANT TO BE THE CHOCOLATE.'

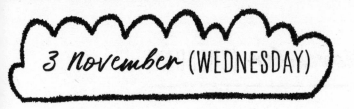

3 November (WEDNESDAY)

Where's MY DRESS?

4 November (THURSDAY)

Not obsessed with DRESS . . . but NO SIGN OF DRESS. And where's MY DRESS?

5 November (FRIDAY)

Is it better to write **NOTHING** than say the same thing OVER and OVER? **LIKE:**

? ?

Where's MY DRESS?

?

6 November (SATURDAY)

My DRESS has been **DETAINED IN CUSTOMS!** Grandpa calls to tell me this because I asked him if he wouldn't mind getting on the case. And APPARENTLY the problem is: something, something TAXES something DUTIES something, something INVOICE something, something PAYMENT.

8 November (MONDAY)

Dress **STILL IN CUSTOMS.** Someone HAS to be wearing it at this stage.

9 p.m. update

Grandpa called re: dress. Something, something PROBABLY NOT UNTIL WEDNESDAY. I'm like, Whutttt? THE MORNING OF THE AWARDS. SERIOUSLY. The dress will be going directly to the hotel.

That is HIGHLY UNLIKELY to GO WELL.

9 November (TUESDAY)

'ENJOY THE AWARDS!'

We're getting all day in school because EVERYONE knows we're going. And I'm like, 'I'll be the naked one!'

10 November (WEDNESDAY)

I bid farewell to Lola this morning because she's flying home tomorrow, leaving Auntie Elaine next in line for the throne. But it's not TOO sad because we'll all be in Rhinebeck for Christmas, which is not TOO far away.

Susan drives me and Megser to the train in Cork, and WHO CARES until: Megser and I arrive at the Shelbourne Hotel in Dublin, which I LOVE because it's old school and charming and there to meet us is the Irish team from Mom's publisher – Winborne. They are ALSO CHARMING. They help check us in, and Megser and I go to our room and get changed, then we all get a cab to this UNBELIEVABLY COOL RESTAURANT ON THE TOP FLOOR OF THIS UNBELIEVABLY COOL HOTEL.

Some of the London team are already at a table in the bar, waiting for us to join them, and there's this GAZELLE-LIKE CREATURE in a slip dress at the end of the table who gives us this BIG WAVE and SMILE, and then raises her glass and makes a little **SAD FACE** (which I think was in honour of Mom), and knocks back the last of her drink. Then she gets up because she realises she's supposed to (based on orders from the eyebrows of the older woman opposite who has to be her boss) and she comes up to us. And Chloe, the Irish publicist, goes to me and Megser: 'This is Will. Short for Willow. She's—'

And Will goes: 'THE NEPOTERN.'

And all the Irish team laugh but her boss is now behind her and her face is **STONE MOUNTAIN.**

Then Will goes to us, SUPER POSH: 'Yes. My mum is head of . . . something incredibly dull in Winborne, plus Dad IS the actual Winborne, so I'm now suddenly "EMPLOYED" (quotes by Will).' Then she pauses and says: 'YES: Willow Winborne. Seriously. That's what they called me. And they're supposed to be into words. Anyway, SPRINTING TO THE POINT, I will be looking after you LOVELY LADIES for the next X NUMBER OF HOURS.' Then she turns around to her boss and goes, 'Mummy, you're going to HAVE to explain to me again what it is you do. It's getting AWKWARD.'

I INSTANTLY LOVE WILL.

Megser is . . . not so sure. But for context: Megser is upset that the Union Jack emoji is higher up than the Irish flag one on her phone.

Anyway, dinner was **AMAZING.**

AND THEN . . . Megser and I get back to the hotel. Annnd . . .

OHMYGOD.

OHMYGOD.

OHMYGOD.

(SKIP THIS SECTION IF YOU HAVE NO SOUL)

We get to our room, and on my bed is this giant grey box with a charcoal-grey silk bow. And beside THAT box is a black bag with a red ribbon . . . and I know straight away what's inside, **WHICH IS WHY I SCREAM.** Then I untie the ribbon, pull out the brown box inside it, fling off the lid, and the first thing I see are the RED SOLES.

And, oh my GOD, they are **THE MOST MAGNIFICENT LOUBOUTINS** I have ever seen. They are the colour of WISPY GREY WINTER CLOUDS that some heavenly angel has lightly strewn with *magical snowflakes* that have crystallised overnight. Even Megser is looking moved.

And now we move on to the BIG BOX and I CAN'T EVEN. Because as soon as I open it and RESPECTFULLY, DESPITE MYSELF, smooth back the PALE BLUE ENTIRE PACKET (DEFINITELY) of TISSUE PAPER, I behold this *celestial* FABRIC that I have ONLY EVER SEEN ONCE BEFORE IN MY ENTIRE LIFE. Which is why I scream for easily four minutes.

IT IS AN ELIE SAAB.

LET'S TAKE A MOMENT.

BUT NOT JUST *AN* ELIE SAAB. IT IS *THE* ELIE SAAB. VISION-BOARD ELIE SAAB!

AND, NOW, HERE IT IS . . . IN A BOX . . . ON MY HOTEL BED.

WHICH MAKES IT: **MY** ELIE SAAB.

I HAVE AN ELIE SAAB NOW.

AND I CAN'T. I JUST CAN'T.

AND I DIDN'T EVEN HAVE TO GET A JOB!

So . . . here's exactly what this dress is: it is *every beautiful winter sky* you looked at when you were a child, EVERY SNOWY WOODLAND you walked through and sensed the magic in, EVERY ICY PANE OF GLASS you rushed to at the faintest sound of sleigh bells and THE REFLECTED SPARKLE IN YOUR EYE from your hope that – this time! – you would see FATHER CHRISTMAS.

Or 'the grey dress', as Megser calls it.

Then I FIND THE NOTE IN THE BOX! And it's GRANDPA'S HANDWRITING!

Ellery, darling,

Someone had to blow the budget. But I'm not going to lie to you: me and your grandmother [it's allowed not to be LOLA when it's written down] are still trying to figure out your punishment for disobeying a direct order. Personally I think wearing heels that high for a whole night is enough. Your Auntie Elaine is telling me to say 'Sorry not sorry' for revealing the details of your vision board. My best girl, have a magical night. You go up there, be yourself, speak from that big heart and that big brain, and know that your mama is with you. We all are.

We love you so much.

Grandpa and Grandma

All the Xs and Os

And I'm CRYING at this stage. OBVIOUSLY.

And THEN: a card from AUNTIE ELAINE:

I am SO sorry I can't be there with you to celebrate, Ellery Belle. And please know: you are ALLOWED TO CELEBRATE. Your mom is a WINNER! You can be as HAPPY and PROUD as she would be. Tears of joy ONLY. I will be thinking of you the whole time, and sending you lots and lots of love. And a little . . . GLAMOUR. Or maybe: A LOT. Because: ELLERY! And LAURIE! My GIRRRRLS! And MEGSER – my Irish girl!'

Auntie Elaine xx

It turns out that Auntie Elaine has booked the BEST hair stylist and the BEST make-up artist in the ENTIRE COUNTRY to come to our hotel room tomorrow to turn me into my best self and to turn Megser into . . . a SELL-OUT.

So I call Grandpa, and I'm crying my eyes out **IN A *GOOD* WAY,** and I thank him a million times.

Then I try to call Auntie Elaine, but she doesn't pick up, so I just leave her this INSANE voicemail.

And then SECURITY KNOCKS ON THE DOOR because of 'REPORTS OF SCREAMS.' And he adds: 'HIGH-PITCHED.'

11 November (THURSDAY)
• ★ • ★ • ★ • ★ • ★ • ★ • ★ •

IRISH BOOK AWARDS

Where do I START?

THE HEROES: NEPOTERN WILL

THE VILLAINS: ME and MEGSERS. I'm not joking.

THE PLOT TWISTS: Like I'm going to put them AT THE START.

THE TEARS: ME and MEGSERS. I'm not joking.

THE LAUGHTER: Not me. Not Megser.

THE TRIUMPH: MOM!

6 p.m. update

Meg LITERALLY looks like a SUPERMODEL. We are in the lobby and everyone is staring at her. And, in fairness, everyone *loves* my dress. And then, obviously, I have to show them my shoes, and everyone loves my shoes.

NINETY MILLION of Meg's favourite authors are swarming around the place, so she disappears for AGES and when she comes back she is HYPER. 'It's like the OSCARS!'

And I'm like, 'They're just PEOPLE. Who MAKE STUFF UP.'

Megser then REACHES OUT and stops this tiny elegant woman in her sixties who's walking by.

'Excuse me!' says Megser. 'I just wanted to say: **CONGRATULATIONS ON YOUR NOMINATION.**'

And the author is taken aback. 'Thank you!' she says.

And Megser goes: 'This is JEANETTE LITHGOW. Jeanette, this is my BEST FRIEND, Ellery Brown.' Then she turns to me: 'Jeanette is up for an award in the Non-Fiction Category for her AMAZING Non-Fiction Book: ***NOTHING MEANS WAR: DIPLOMACY IN***

THE AGE OF AGGRESSION. It's about her career in CONFLICT RESOLUTION and INTERNATIONAL PEACEKEEPING. And it's beautifully written and honest and inspiring, and I hope you win, Jeanette.'

And Jeanette is VERY surprised and I'm guessing it's because Megser looks a LOT younger than the rest of her readers, but at the same time she can't look TOO surprised because Megser is a YOUNG WOMAN and, for young women, offence is like the chocolate bars right by the till – VERY EASY TO TAKE. And MESSY in the wrong hands.

So I sweep in with: 'Your DRESS, Jeanette, is STUNNING.' Because it is. 'Lanvin's tailoring is the best known to man,' I add. 'Woman,' I also add.

'Well,' says Jeanette. 'You've made my night. Compliments on my brain AND my gown. And from two such *beautiful* and BRIGHT . . . YOUNG LADIES.'

Then she politely excuses herself. And, in hindsight, it was probably because she spotted the early signs of a conflict that she was under no contractual obligation to resolve.

And when she's gone I turn to Megser and go: 'I was just trying to make a JOKE. It's not like I don't respect what my OWN MOTHER did or don't know there are people who write NON-fiction. Mom used to joke about making things up too. And you KNOW that. **WHY ARE YOU BEING SO SERIOUS?'**

And Meg's all WHAT IS WRONG WITH YOU and I'm like, NOTHING WE JUST NEED TO BE FOCUSED because THIRD-TIME LUCKY has gone right out of my head at this stage because ALL I'm thinking is: **LAST CHANCE. THIS IS YOUR LAST CHANCE. AND I HATE LAST CHANCES.**

7 p.m. update

Nepotern Will has been drinking champagne for an hour, I'm guessing, at HIGH SPEED. The foyer is filling up, and the red-carpet interviews are kicking off.

And I'm scanning the place, and then I realise: WILL! And go: 'Will! Do you know the author JAY EVANS?'

And she says, 'YES! But not personally. Are you fans?'

'Meg is,' I say. 'She loves him as much as she loves McDonald's.'

And Megser is giving me **FLAT EYES.**

And Will is looking at her like, 'There is NO WAY you eat

McDonald's. And if you DO, I HATE YOU.'

And Meg goes, 'I do in my &&&&e [rhymes with "kite"].'

And Will laughs. **'I LOVE THE IRISH.'**

'So,' says Will, 'in the course of the two weeks of my working life, I've learned that **SUPER-FAMOUS AUTHORS** arrive late and leave early, so there's THAT. But . . .' And she checks her schedule, which was a SURPRISE ACTION. 'Okay . . . Jay Evans' category is up after the interval, which could be tricky, because he might not appear until the end of the interval. But . . . shall I see if I can locate him?'

'Shall away!' says Meg. Probably because she wants to be free to STALK AUTHORS.

Meanwhile, I'm internally freaking out at the prospect of meeting Jay Evans, so I go: 'I need to use the bathroom. I'll be right back.'

So . . . I'm in the bathroom, BREATHING, and thinking HOW am I going to get to **TALK TO HIM?** And then I'm like, I'll have to take him aside first. But 'Excuse me, Mr Evans, can I have a word with you IN PRIVATE?' sounds TOTALLY creepy. Or do I go, 'I'm LAURIE BROWN'S DAUGHTER SLASH POSSIBLY ALSO YOURS and . . .'

Then I'm like: **WHAT IS WRONG WITH ME?** Because I

REALISE I'm acting like he's definitely my DAD! Like, I'm skipping the ENTIRE PART where I have a **NORMAL** under false pretences CONVERSATION with him in order to find ANY evidence that might REMOTELY back this up.

And then I say to myself: 'YOU SHOULD NOT BE ON YOUR OWN RIGHT NOW. GET OUT THERE.'

But when I DO go out Will sweeps past: 'Sorry! AUTHOR CARE! Won't be long! Megser's gone THATAWAY!' And I EVENTUALLY find Megser standing in front of Derek Landy like Mrs Daly in front of a STATUE OF OUR LORD. And I'm like, WHY ISN'T SHE SCANNING THE ROOM FOR JAY EVANS? And I get right up in her peripheral vision, and I'm making gestures and I KNOW she can see me, but she's actively ignoring me, so I just go up and say, 'Excuse me but I need to borrow my best friend,' and Megser is introducing us and can barely remember my NAME and Derek Landy is being so nice even as I'm physically dragging Megser away, and we go out of the side door and I'm like, **'WHAT ARE YOU DOING?'**

And she goes, 'Just MEETING MY HERO.'

'But ... what about MY DAD?' And she's got this look on her face and I know she's thinking **I SHOULDN'T BE CALLING HIM THAT YET.**

'You really need to CALM DOWN,' says Meg and she's

genuinely looking at me in a CONCERNED WAY. And then she goes: 'Maybe this isn't a good idea.'

'Whutttt?'

AND NEXT THING: Will sweeps past AGAIN with this fly-by news: 'Jay Evans is IN THE BUILDING! Don't worry – I'm ON THE CASE!'

And I'm just STARING AFTER HER.

AND MY HEART IS:

GUNFIRE UNDER A GREY DRESS.

Then Megser grabs my arm. 'This is a BIG NIGHT. Don't forget you have to present an award later. In front of **MILLIONS OF PEOPLE.'**

'I'll BE FINE!' I say.

'You don't know that.' And she's glancing over to where Will disappeared, and I'm like: 'NO! DON'T YOU DARE!'

'I'm NOT,' says Meg. 'I just ... maybe we need AN ADULT here.'

And I'm like, 'Whuttt? No we DON'T!'

'I think we do. I'm just AFRAID—'

'OHMYGOD – YOU'RE afraid? You! Who's **NEVER AFRAID OF ANYTHING?'**

'I'm NOT AFRAID. I ... I keep thinking about ... about what if something ... goes wrong.'

'But YOU'RE the one who was ENCOURAGING ME to do this! You said it was A SIGN!'

'YOU'RE the one who made me BELIEVE IN SIGNS!'

I could have thought this was **so *lovely*.** I could have said: 'Oh, MEGSER!' and we could have HUGGED and MADE UP because WE REALISE WE ARE BEST FRIENDS. AND WE GET EACH OTHER. AND WHY ARE WE FIGHTING?

But no! I CHOOSE FIGHTING!

'OHMYGOD!' I say. 'Now it's MY FAULT!'

'NO!' says Megser. **'*NOTHING IS ANYONE'S FAULT!*'**

'Well, that MAKES NO SENSE.'

'Stop,' says Megser. 'PLEASE stop.'

'But you're SUPPOSED TO BE HELPING ME,' I say.

'I WAS HELPING YOU.'

'No, you WEREN'T.'

'I WAS, but—'

'You were SO BUSY just going around doing what YOU wanted to do.'

'Yeah, well, you were treating me like your ASSISTANT!'

'OHMYGOD – NO I WASN'T.'

'It's just … this is all a bit REAL.'

'YES – MY REAL LIFE!'

'It's just all a bit INTENSE,' she says.

'LIKE: IT'S TOO MUCH.'

And then a bell rings. And we have to go into the ballroom for the main event and sit side by side while television cameras are all around us. And I will be Lola-channelling for the entire thing. And Megser doesn't have it in her to put on a show. Which is one of the reasons I love her. But stiiill.

• 8 p.m. update •

We're at the Winborne table and I'm sitting beside Nepotern Will on one side and Megser on the other. And beside Megser is an Irish Debut Literary Fiction author called Daimhin Mac an Airchinnigh so I know the whole **PSEUDONYM** conversation didn't go in Winborne's favour. Daimhin (DAW-VEEN) is twenty-six years old and has just signed a massive book deal and I hear Will lowering the literary tone by asking her about guys.

This is what Daimhin replies: 'Dating creates a CHEAP THEATRE out of the search for **REAL INTIMACY.'** Will's nodding but her eyes are like TRAPPED IN HELL. 'And when I say THEATRE,' says Daimhin, 'it's Punch and Judy: just this exchange of blows, really. Collapsible bodies on a collapsible stage that's just going to move on to the next town, the next night.' And Will is giving **RELATING EYEBROWS,** and I have NO IDEA where she managed to pull them out of. And Daimhin THEN goes: 'All that these Punches and Judys are doing is jolting their jaded hopes to life once more with the PADDLES of PUTRID SHOTS from a WEARY HOTEL BARMAN.' And Will literally looks like she's just knocked back a putrid shot and wants to keep knocking them back until she dies. Then she goes: 'Well, PUTRID SHOTS ON YOU, tonight! But seriously . . . **CONGRATULATIONS** on the book deal, you lucky duck!'

'Luck has nothing to do with it,' says Daimhin. 'TALENT, INSTINCT and HARD WORK. When I wasn't getting my fingers stuck down the back of the sofa looking for coins so I could buy tins of beans, all I was doing was WRITING.'

'Good for you!' says Will.

'But it was never simply WRITING,' says Daimhin. 'Anyone can WRITE. We've all BEEN TO SCHOOL.'

'Not if I could help it!' says Will to me and Megser.

'I WAS TERRIBLE.'

But Daimhin is in the zone: 'I am my characters' CONFESSOR. They want me to HEAR them: REALLY HEAR THEM. And what they have to say is IMPORTANT.'

'Tell me about your CONFIDENCE,' says Megser. 'Did you have that BEFORE your massive book deal or AFTER? Like, can you be THAT CONFIDENT before a monetary value is placed on your work?'

'YES!' says Daimhin's agent. 'Oh YES!' Then she turns to Daimhin with the FEAR EYES. 'I'm not talking about YOU, obviously.' And her face is THE HEATING SYSTEM OF THE ENTIRE HOTEL. And then she turns the **FEAR AND RESCUE EYES** on us and says, 'I'm just saying in GENERAL. You'd be AMAZED at how cocky young writers can be.'

'Not after TONIGHT,' says Megser.

And Will goes: 'I HATE COINS. I just THROW THEM OUT.'

And then the meal arrives, and we eat, and it's delicious, and half of the awards are given out and **ZERO EYE CONTACT** is made between me and Megser.

❀ 9.30 p.m. update ❀

At the interval there is this **MASS EXODUS** from the ballroom into the bar like it's Macy's on Black Friday.

I turn to Megser and say: 'We shouldn't be fighting. Let's just—'

And then Will comes up with **BIG EYES,** striding ahead of Daimhin. 'Well, she was a BARREL OF INTENSITY.'

And we laugh and Will goes: 'I'm looking at her like you're minted, critically acclaimed, loads of publishers bid on your book . . .'

And I go: *'WHERE'S THE NEG?'*

And Will is like 'Where's the neg? I LOVE that. Sigh. I wish I was creative.'

And I'm like 'Whuttt? EVERYONE IS CREATIVE. Mom used to always say that. It's just that not everyone is in a WELCOMING ENOUGH ENVIRONMENT to release it.'

Mom said people should look back at what they loved to do when they were small – when they were FREE and FEARLESS and had yet to discover the JUDGEMENT and OPINIONS of OTHERS.

'WILL!' I say. 'When you were SMALL . . . what did you LOVE?'

And Will goes: 'How small?' And that's such a BRILLIANT thing to ask: 'HOW small?'

'SEVEN?' I say.

'Gosh. Seven . . . GOBLINS definitely.'

I LOVE WILL.

And she says: 'I used to make little trousers and tunics for them out of felt. But what I loved most was getting these massive sheets of cardboard and painting these BACKDROPS in RIDICULOUS detail: forests and bridges, and underwater things for the seagoblins or haunted houses on stilts. And there were LADYGOBLINS with TRIPLE-BARREL SURNAMES like Flissy Barrington Bilgley Bluebottom.'

'Did you like READING?' says Megser.

'Well,' says Will, and she kind of twists her mouth to one side. 'Let's just say BOOKS . . . were THE ENEMY.'

And Meg is like 'Whuttt?!'

But Will and I have **LOCKED EYES.**

'I was only small,' says Will. 'So this was my CHILD'S-EYE VIEW OF THE WORLD. Mummy won't be home tonight because: BOOKS. Daddy is running late because: BOOKS. Mummy and Daddy SO WISHED they could have been at your INSERT CHILDHOOD MILESTONE but: BOOKS.'

When Megser and I are on our own we ONCE AGAIN reject

the opportunity to make up. And the moment everything TOOK A TURN FOR THE WORSE was when she said I'd got OBSESSED about my dad.

And I go: 'In a movie if someone "stops at nothing" to find someone—'

'We are NOT IN A MOVIE,' says Megser. 'We are IN REAL LIFE.'

'OHMYGOD that was MY WHOLE POINT EARLIER!' I say.

And Will comes up and goes: **'GIRLS, GIRLS, COME WITH ME!'** And she takes us by the hands and we start walking, and there we are, suddenly entering the smaller bar, and coming up to a dark corner where two people are sitting.

'I FOUND HIM!' says Will.

And she gestures towards the man facing us: JAY EVANS. FINAL POTENTIAL FATHER.

And I am NOT JOKING: that was NOT THE BIGGEST SURPRISE. NO!

Because . . . SERIOUSLY. In Things You Actually Couldn't Make Up:

The person with his back to us turns around. And as I see him I turn to Will and quietly go: 'That will be all, thank you, Will.'

SERIOUSLY. I SAID THAT TO HER!

And she thinks this is **HILARIOUS** and *adorable* and

she BOWS and LEAVES.

And Megser is looking at me like Elie Saab has changed you, but I'm giving her MORE-TO-THE-STORY-FILL-YOU-IN-LATER-BACK-ME-UP-IN-THE-MEANTIME EYES.

Because THERE – ironically looking at ME over HIS shoulder when the last time I was looking at HIM was over MY shoulder as I roller-skated to freedom – was: JEAN-LUC CATASTROPH(E).

All the way from PARIS, FRANCE.

AND MY HEART IS:

EXPLODING PIÑATA FILLED WITH SHOCKED EMOJI FACES.

And he says: 'Ah, USURPER.'

HOW COOL IS THAT, IN HINDSIGHT? But at the ACTUAL TIME TERRIFYING.

'*Elle est BELLE!*' he says to Jay, and gives three relaxed-casual claps like bad guys do in movies.

'*Merci!*' I say.

And I can hear him explaining to Jay Evans in French that THIS is the **CRAZY PERSON** (*MALADE MENTAL*) who FLED (*qui S'EST*

ENFUI) on ROLLER-SKATES (*sur DES PATINS À ROULETTES*), as I'M explaining to MEG who HE is. But now he's getting up REALLY SLOWLY and looking around REALLY SLOWLY in a way that makes me think he's going to fling a protective arm across Jay Evans' chest and shout, '*SÉCURITÉ! SÉCURITÉ!*'

And Meg HALF RAISES HER HANDS and goes – IN REALLY SLOW ENGLISH – 'She. Has. NO. ROLLER-SKATES' like it's French for 'She is unarmed'.

NEXT THING: Will's mom picks the BEST TIME EVER to come over and wish me luck with my speech! And Jay and Jean-Luc are looking at her and each other like: WHO IS THIS GIRL? And why is EVERYONE in publishing being duped by her? And WHO the *L'ENFER* has she tricked into allowing her to give a speech? And WHY?

But their MAIN concern is clearly DISTANCING THEMSELVES FROM THIS TEEN FREAK because as Will's mom and I are talking, they take the chance to DISAPPEAR.

Then it's Megser and me alone again, and we go back into the main bar and even the craziness of what just happened doesn't automatically unite us. But I'm afraid to say ANYTHING at this stage and, in fairness, this time, Megser gives it a go.

'What I was TRYING TO SAY EARLIER about your DAD was

just . . . there's FANTASY and REALITY—'

And that word — *fantasy* — sets my EYEBALLS ON FIRE.

And Meg knows it. And she's like, 'Nooo!' And: 'What I'm saying is you don't KNOW—'

'WHO MY FATHER IS!' And my voice is this PSYCHO HISS. 'WHY CAN'T YOU GET THAT?'

And I'm thinking, if she actually knew all the awful stuff that goes through my mind . . . like what if my dad already met me when I was too young to remember . . . and he didn't like me or maybe he saw a photo of me and I was this massive let-down and at least tonight I look the best I could ever look so maybe that might make a difference, but all I kept saying to her was I HAVE ZERO PARENTS. I HAVE ZERO PARENTS.

And Meg's crying. And I'm crying.

AND MY HEART IS:

ROPES UNRAVELLING ON A PIER and the ship is sailing away.

And I storm off in the only direction I can: down the slope into the underground car park and everyone who has ever worn heels KNOWS you can't storm anywhere on an incline. So what I actually did was place one foot in front of the other like a SHOW PONY, and I'm holding up the skirt of my dress and hoping I don't trip and LUCKILY, I make it down to the bottom without incident which – paradoxically – marked the start of the **INCIDENTS.**

Because as I'm walking across the car park, I see, sitting on the hood of a car, the elegant form of JEAN-LUC CATASTROPH(E), which FURRREAKS me out. But not as much as the shock of the – SLOW MOTION! – identification of the person who is stepping back from KISSING HIM.

'YOU ARE GAY,' I announce. To JAY EVANS. My ERSTWHILE FATHER. Who obviously is already aware of his gayness.

And Jay Evans says PRECISELY NOTHING. And stands MOTIONLESS.

But there is now a WALKING CATASTROPHE/(E) coming my way, forcing me to QUICKLY curve a question around him to Jay Evans: 'Were you always gay?'

And I literally feel like I'm confirming his **WORST FEARS** about teenage girls as featured in *Kerosene* and that I really SHOULD be set on fire and STILL I'M TALKING!

OVER Jean-Luc saying, with an accompanying clap on each word: 'Never. Been. With. A. Woman.'

'But why aren't you OUT?' I'm asking Jay Evans. 'I don't get it. You're a WRITER. No one CARES.' Then I turn to Jean-Luc. 'Why can't he be OUT?'

And Jean-Luc looks at me: 'Because of YOU, chérie. Because of all the girls, all the women, all the FANS, all over the world.'

'Well, that's AWFUL,' I say, 'but I'm NOT A FAN.'

I SHOULD NOT BE SPEAKING.

'But, *ma pauvre*,' says Jean-Luc. 'How is it that you look so ARSE-BROKEN?'

AND MY HEAD STARTS TO FIZZ.

'How many TIIIIMES?' says Jay Evans, exploding to life and striding over to Jean-Luc: 'No one's ARSE IS BROKEN!'

And I'm like, WHAT IS HAPPENING HERE?

And Jay Evans is going: 'It's HEART. ENDING IN T. HEART . . . BROKEN!'

And I'm like **OHMYGOD. THANK GOD. THE CONFUSION IS OVER.**

'So, ANYWAY,' I say, starting to walk away from them backwards, 'I am so sorry to have disturbed you both.' And then I look at Jay Evans and I'm like, 'I'm not crying about YOU . . . I mean, I DID enjoy *Kerosene* . . . the MOVIE . . . and obviously I'm sure the book was way better.'

And then I look at Jean-Luc and go: 'Sorry again about . . .' And in this Nepotern Will kind of CHEERY delivery: 'ALL THAT STUFF IN PARIS!'

Then I'm back to Jay Evans saying, 'And I don't FANCY you. I swear. It's just . . . you were friends with my mom.'

Jean-Luc is now giving me the SERIOUSLY?-YOU'RE-GOING-TO-GO-WITH-THAT-NOW? EYES.

But Jay Evans asks me: 'Who's your mom?'

'Laurie Brown,' I say. **TRIUMPHANT.** But waiting to be asked for DNA-level proof from Jean-Luc.

'How did I not SEE IT?' says Jay. 'You have her beautiful smile.'

Then I keep going because I have his attention, 'Your dedication to my mom – you gave her *Kerosene*. It said something about a night sky and peppered gunfire . . .'

And Jay Evans smiles. 'Yes! I was in such a **dark place** when I met your mom. And after our event that night I was planning on going back to my room to feel sorry for myself, but your mom INSISTED I came out with her. And it was honestly one of the BEST nights of my life. We stayed up until dawn wandering around Paris, stopping in different bars – don't drink, it's bad for you –

and I told her all about Jean-Luc and me. She was just SO light about everything and apologising for her enforced positivity and I said it was like being SHOT BY AN AUTOMATIC RIFLE LOADED WITH STARS.'

'OHMYGOD – I LOVE THAT!' I say.

And even hearing about Mom made me feel better. Then APROPOS of EVERYTHING, I announce: 'I've got to go!' Because I need time to BREATHE and CRY and FIX MY MAKE-UP before I stand up and give a speech. Jay and Jean-Luc want to accompany me back up, but I politely decline and off I go towards the slope with my head down because I'm trying to manage a whole heel and hem FIGHT NIGHT SITUATION and I've got a story going on in my head about that and I'm thinking this is what going insane with grief is. And now . . . tears are trying to come out again and my whole body feels slowed down and it's like my brain is filled with this weird gel that nothing can really move through but there's this one thought trapped there and the gel is clear so I KNOW what the thought is and it's:

! I JUST LOST THE LAST FATHER I NEVER HAD. !

And when you put it like that – which I DID – you really couldn't be anything other than . . .

ARSE-BROKEN.

★ *10 p.m. update* ★

I fix my make-up in the bathroom and when I come out the bell is ringing to make sure everyone goes back into the ballroom for the second half. As I'm walking through the bar I cross paths with JAY EVANS and JEAN-LUC, walking along with a foot between them. Not an ACTUAL FOOT. A GAP that was one-foot wide. And we exchange glances. Because we all know that thing that everyone knows:

THE SHOW MUST GO ON.

And it DID. And JAY EVANS did HIS THING. And I DID MINE.

12 p.m. update

You know when you have a fight with someone . . . and you try to make up? But then THAT conversation turns into a fight? They are THE WORST FIGHTS EVER. They are worse than the original fight.

Well, this was Megser and me at the end of the night: Round Three of trying to make up. I couldn't bring myself to tell her about Jay Evans because I didn't want her to feel sorry for me and it was SO cringe. Plus, why talk about Jay Evans when I could go RANDOM?

'And I know you KNEW,' I say, 'that Oscar liked YOU! Before I EVER said it to you.'

And Megser's giving me **PANIC EYES.** 'Let people love whom they love!' she says. 'And I DID try to tell you in LOTS of ways that I wasn't sure about him.'

'What about the TRUTH WAY? Or what about telling me what you WERE sure about? That he liked you!'

'HOW could I have told you that?' said Megser.

'WITH YOUR WORDS!'

'But . . . you were in bits about your mom! And . . . I don't KNOW but it was like he was giving you something to LOOK FORWARD TO.'

'But you knew that what I was ACTUALLY going to be looking forward to was: NOTHING. Or REJECTION.'

'No, I did NOT!' says Meg. 'I honestly thought he would fall in love with you.'

And that was the **sweetest** thing EVER and I could tell she really meant it.

'And then it would have been fine!' she says. 'And he'd have forgotten all about me.'

And you'd think that NOW would be a good time to make up, but no!

'You're just saying that to make yourself feel better!' I say.

And Meg's face is VOTED-OFF-REALITY-SHOW-FAVOURITE.

'I'm not!' she says. 'I SWEAR TO GOD that's what I thought.'

'You don't even BELIEVE in God!' I say. Which was SUCH a ridiculous thing to say. And for a moment I'm thinking she's going to swear to *fairies*, which would be BEYOND awful, so I quickly go: 'HOW could you have thought that?'

And Meg goes, 'Why WOULDN'T I?'

And I'm like, 'Because . . .'

And she goes: 'WHERE has your SELF-ESTEEM GONE?'

And now there's another bell ringing. And it's seriously like some boxing match at this stage. Except . . . no one is going to be raising ANYONE'S arm at the end.

ELLERY'S WORDS OF WISDOM:

SOMETIMES YOU HAVE YOUR BIGGEST LOWS IN YOUR FANCIEST CLOTHES.

12 November (FRIDAY)

I wake up effectively an ORPHAN. I have no Mom and I have RUN OUT OF DADS. And my best friend Megser is GONE. There's a note in my shoe – an INSIGHTFUL or POINTED location – telling me that she was getting the early train, and Susan was picking her up in Cork, so I didn't have to worry about sharing a tiny bus home with her.

And I'm just packing and crying, and the last thing I put in my bag is the WHOLE POINT: Mom's beautiful award picked up by **ELLERY MEANING JOY**.

So it all should have been?

JOYFUL.

Instead, it's me and Megser and a burning bridge.

THE ISLAND OF DISAPPEARING FATHERS

Population: 3

- **SUSPECT 1:** ~~JAY EVANS~~

  Because Never. Been. With. A. Woman.

  [And one person's Catastroph(e) is another person's catastrophe.]

- **SUSPECT 2:** ~~LEON ADLER~~

  Because he told me.

- **SUSPECT 3:** ~~QUENTIN SCHAEFFER~~

  Because thank you, the Universe.

13 November (SATURDAY)

I arrived home last night to no Auntie Elaine! And in her place: Lola!

And I immediately went PLANE CRASH in my head. And I'm all **WHAT HAPPENED TO AUNTIE ELAINE? IS EVERYTHING OKAY?** And lots more questions until I come to a normal one: 'When IS she coming?'

And Lola says, 'She's not, sweetheart. I'm sorry.'

And I'm like, Whuttt? And Lola says, 'She's still very busy in work and we tried to figure it out but we can't seem to do that, so you're stuck with me!'

'Until WHEN?'

'Well . . . until Christmas,' says Lola.

'Christmas! But what about Grandpa?' I say. 'He was expecting you back! Won't he MISS YOU? Won't you miss HIM?'

'Oh, I think it's a huge relief for him,' she says. 'Another month to himself.' And she laughs, even though she looks **SAD** and **TIRED** and then she makes me sit down and tell her everything about the awards but we both know Lola never wants to know everything about anything, so I give her the highlights and that's all the everything that either of us needs.

Then Lola takes Mom's award and goes: 'Okay, Ellery Belle – let's make space for THIS.' And that's what we do – and it looks **PERFECT.**

14 November (SUNDAY)

★ ★ ★ ★ ★ ★ ★ ★ ★ ★ ★ ★ ★ ★

I miss Megser SO MUCH.

OHMYGOD – is this what it feels like to break up with someone? Because that plus Oscar plus anatomical drawings means I now have three reasons NEVER to have a boyfriend. And the ONLY reason I have to have one is: HUNTER THREAT.

But that might not be until next year.

The WORST part though, is: Mom looking down on all this. Plus, she knows I can't unknow her wise words: 'If you have a fight with someone, the first person you look at is YOURSELF.'

Myself is LITERALLY the last person I want to look at . . . I'd rather look at Oscar.

Plus, Mom knows I can't unknow her strict guidelines on

apologising and even the THOUGHT of having to LOOK MEGSER IN THE EYE and take *FULL RESPONSIBILITY* for my WORDS and ACTIONS is HORRIFYING.

Why couldn't Mom have been a HORRIBLE PERSON who didn't make it into heaven? Then I wouldn't be in this position.

KIDDING, Mom! That was one of my jokes to defuse the situation: the ones that drove you *CRAZY* when I tried to use them to avoid apologising.

OHMYGOD, I'm SO SORRY, Mom. And I'm just crying now because I can't look you in the eye to apologise for letting you down at the book awards in so many ways. And literally everyone's honouring you EXCEPT ME. And I know you always said that nothing could ever make you love me any less. But . . . I think you were too nice to even IMAGINE I could treat someone so badly. Because I know better. Because of you.

xoxoxoxoxox

15 November (MONDAY)

I have **TOO MANY EMOTIONS.** And no one to talk to them about. With whom to talk to them . . . about. Emotions about which to whom no one can talk.

That's it.

I AM SILENT ELLERY.

The Statistics of My Life: Moms: 0. Dads: 0. Best Friends: 0. Number of Black Mascaras in My Make-up Bag: 7?!

16 November (TUESDAY)

OHMYGOD. What is Silent Johnny doing calling to my house? I know he is because I am live-diarying from my bedroom window while watching him having some kind of conversation with himself. He's taking a few steps, then stopping, blinking, going again. 'Right!' I can lip-read him saying to himself, and he walks on, and I dart across the hall into my mom's bedroom to creepily watch him from that window as he struggles with the front gate, pauses, gets distracted testing the hinges, and then keeps going up the path. And I can see that he has an A4 padded envelope in his hand. The doorbell rings, and I'm now creepily standing in the upstairs hallway. (I'm no longer live-diarying because everything's happening too fast, but I'm sticking with the present tense for effect.) I hear the opening of the front door.

'Johnny,' says Lola.

'Is Ellery . . . uh . . .' he says.

'Is that a gift?' says Lola in a way that shows she is unable to pick up the cues of **GIANT TEEN AWKWARDNESS** that I can sense even from here. Like I could break out in a sweat from the hot fear that's radiating up the stairs from Johnny.

I think what is actually happening is Silent Johnny is returning my *To Kill a Mockingbird*.

'Uh,' says Johnny again. 'Could you give this to . . . uh . . . Ellery?'

'Uh – yes, I can,' says Lola, because she can't help herself. 'But she's here. Why don't you give it to her yourself?'

BECAUSE HE WOULD RATHER EAT HIS PET LAMB.

'Thanks very much!' says Johnny cheerily, but it's a distant sound mixed with the sound of the gate opening and closing.

'Eller-EEEE . . .' calls Lola in a thrilled way. 'Someone has delivered a gift for you.'

I'm already halfway down the stairs. 'Oh my God, Lola! It's my

English book! You totally embarrassed him!He's really shy, and—'

Lola **TRIUMPHANTLY** raises the envelope that's not, I now realise, an envelope. Nor is the shape inside that of a paperback novel.

She ALSO raises one of her amazing eyebrows. 'I think this falls under the category of GIFT . . . don't you?'

And I'm like, 'Whuttt? No! Why would Johnny . . .'

And I take the package from Lola, run upstairs, then sit on my bed, just looking at it like I'm an army bomb-disposal expert who failed basic training, but is now in too deep.

I open it. Oh God.

IT IS SO NOT AT ALL WHAT I EXPECTED.

I EXPECTED NOTHING. But stiiiill. I'm in SHOCK.

It's a framed photo of me and Mom. From when I was nine. We're on the pier, it's Regatta week, and I'm in her arms, and we're looking at each other, and we're laughing so hard, and it's the evening, and the sky is PINK and there's a STAR in it. A tiny one. Right between our heads.

And I run down to show Lola. And we're just standing there, tears in our eyes. And she's just pointing at this *one star.*

And it's *magical*. And if you don't believe in things like that, then you should. Because I think that when you do,

✦ MAGIC WILL ALWAYS FIND YOU.

'Remind me where this young man lives.'

'Kilmacowen,' I say. 'Why?'

'Get in the car,' she says, like we're going to rob a bank. Then she looks at me. 'Brush your hair.'

Fine, then. I do.

'This was an incredibly thoughtful thing to do,' she says. 'We must thank him IMMEDIATELY.'

So we get to Johnny's, ring the doorbell, and we're standing there like weirdos. And his dad answers.

'Hello, Mr . . .' said Lola. Then she looks at me. I'm completely blank because Johnny's two names, to me, are Silent and Johnny, so it kind of feels complete without the surname.

'Johnny's father?' says Lola.

'Yes – Jimmy,' says his dad.

'I'm Ellery's . . . Lola,' says Lola. 'It's a pleasure to meet you. Is Johnny here?'

'He's inside in the shed.'

I look down at Lola's nude ballet pumps. Lola looks down at the welly collection by the door. 'Do you mind?' she says.

'Not at all – fire away!' says Jimmy.

I'm proud of Lola being so chill. She lets herself down a small bit by handing Johnny's dad the ballet pumps without even making eye contact, but he takes it well.

'You have a wonderful son,' says Lola, pulling on the boots.

'Yerra, he'll do,' says Jimmy.

'He gave Ellery the most ***beautiful*** gift,' said Lola. 'And we wanted to thank him.'

Jimmy clearly has no clue.

'It was a photo of me and my mom at Regatta,' I say.

'Ah, go 'way,' says Jimmy. He looks at me. 'When you called THE LAST DAY (at Easter!) I said to Johnny after: "Is that that American girl with the mother the writer?" And Johnny said yes. And I said to myself, I'm sure I have a photo of the two of them from Regatta long 'go – I used to take the photos – and, sure enough . . . I only wish it was in better shape. Johnny gave you that, did he? I suppose however faded it is, whatever cracks or creases are in it, 'tis a great memory all the same.' He looked at us both. 'I'm very sorry for your loss. She was a *lovely* lady.'

But Lola and I were just looking at each other. Because the photo in the frame was pristine.

1 a.m. update

I just cannot stop thinking about it. Silent Johnny, without a word to anyone – that part shouldn't be a surprise, let's face it – went to the trouble of getting a photo of ME and MY MOM retouched. And not only that, he had fled the shed before we got there, in case he'd have to hear:

THANK YOU.

Actions: 1. **Words:** 0.

17 November (WEDNESDAY)

MOM'S ANNIVERSARY

CONTEXT.

20 November (SATURDAY)

There was mass for Mom in the village church tonight. And it was
SO WEIRD because Megser was there and so was Susan and
Mrs Daly and even the Ferals, and, STILL, Megser and I weren't
talking, even though she did give me a kind look at one point.
Which was gorgeous and AWFUL. But what was so beautiful was
that the church was packed and there were loads of people from
school, and the principal, and the teachers, and Silent Johnny
and his family, and Dan, and people from the coffee shops and
the restaurants. Lola was so touched. She invited everyone to
Causkey's – the pub across the street – afterwards and I went
over for a little while, and I got to thank Silent Johnny properly for
the photo and it was SO awkward but that was fine because all I
cared about was him knowing what a lovely thing that was to do.

And then I just wanted to go for a walk down to the pier. It
was OUR WALK – me and Mom. Especially when I was younger,
and it was summer, and it was just the two of us, and we'd
go after dinner every evening. It's down this winding country
lane – those ones with the strip of grass down the middle and
foxgloves growing in the ditch, and I used to pluck off the tops
and put them on my fingers. There's also a river with a bench

you can sit on, but we always just kept walking until we came to the sea. If you didn't know the pier, you'd be happy to just sit on the wall, but if you have inside information you'd climb over the fence, and walk up over this little hill, and there's this spot and it's just . . . perfect.

Tonight it's FREEZING, but when Jay who owns the pub heard I was going to the pier she gave me a flask of tea, and half a packet of chocolate biscuits and I thought that was the **sweetest thing ever.** People are SO KIND.

Anyway, I'm walking down the lane, using the torch on my phone, and when I get to the pier Carpenter Dan is walking up and I'm like Mrs Daly: 'You're SO GOOD for coming to mass' and, 'Did you get a drink in Causkey's?' And, 'Go, get a drink in Causkey's!' And then, 'It's ON LOLA!', so then maybe he will because it's the least she could do after her accidental insults on his work.

And he goes: 'Thanks, but I'm fine out,' and, 'No bother' about the mass. 'Sure, of course,' he says. And I realise how lovely it is that it's 'of course' as if 'why WOULDN'T you do something kind?' like that's the default setting.

'Are you all right down here by yourself?' he says, looking around. 'In the dark?'

'I am, thank you,' I say.

Anyway, it's SO awkward, because all I actually wanted to do was to go and sit on the rock and drink my tea and think about Mom. But I'm guessing Dan thinks I should have company on the walk back up, but then he's probably thinking OLDER MAN WITH TEEN GIRL IN DARK COUNTRY LANE. And I feel really sorry for good men who have to feel afraid because of what bad men do. It only has to LOOK bad for people to BELIEVE bad. Then he notices the flask, so he knows I have some kind of plan. And then it's even MORE AWKWARD because he doesn't know WHAT to do.

Next thing: he is DELIGHTED, because he has found this flat torch thing in his wallet, and he tries it and it works. 'Take that. I have my phone. You should probably have a hi-vis on you, though.'

'Like yours?' I say, because he's not wearing one.

And he laughs and says, 'Will you be all right now with that?'

Then he's all MAN ABANDONS TEEN GIRL IN DARK COUNTRY LANE ONLY TO DISCOVER LATER THAT SHE WAS MURDERED. 'Or do you want me to wait and walk you back up? Like, I could just sit over there.'

And I'm like, 'No, but thank you. I'll be fine. The light is perfect.'

And then we both looked at the moon, and there was that ONE STAR in the sky again, and the light really was perfect.

21 November (SUNDAY)

Breakfast with Lola was SO WEIRD, and I was wondering what was going on because Lola was trying to be nice but there was something underneath it all that she was struggling to suppress, and it turns out it was a WHOLE RANGE OF EMOTIONS.

Breakfast ended with four of the WORST WORDS IN A ROW that when you hear them on a television show always spell disaster for the person on the receiving end: 'WE NEED TO TALK'.

And she makes me go into the living room and sit down with her. ON THE SAME SOFA.

'I spoke with Susan last night,' she says. 'And she thanked me for the lovely gifts.'

And I'm thinking what lovely gifts? But also: that's very nice of Susan. And also: what has it got to do with me?

'And I told her she was welcome,' says Lola, 'but it soon became clear that Susan thought the gifts were a GENERAL thank you. For how good she is to you in GENERAL . . . and not

SPECIFICALLY because you stayed with her for an entire week at the end of the summer.'

And my **STOMACH IS:** TRIPLE BACKFLIP with a BAD LANDING.

So Lola knows about the following: the fake emails, the home-alone incident, and the DANGER I put myself in. And she tries to tell me that she, and Grandpa, and Auntie Elaine are DISAPPOINTED in me for ALL THE LIES but the irony is that THAT'S a total lie, because there is ZERO disappointment in Lola's eyes: Lola's eyes are **STEEL FURY**.

And I can feel my face on FIRE and I don't know how to react apart from run away and **START A NEW LIFE SOMEWHERE** but I do manage – because it's fresh in my mind – to LOOK HER IN THE EYE and SAY SORRY. And the worst part about THAT is I can now see the HURT in her eyes which is like an **ECLIPSE:** NOT SOMETHING YOU SHOULD LOOK AT DIRECTLY.

'What were you doing here ON YOUR OWN?' says Lola. 'Why did you WANT to be here on your own?'

And I'm thinking it's clear she has no idea about the dad situation, which is the only relief in all this and then it gets just a **WHOLE NEW LEVEL OF TERRIBLE** because she says: 'I know I'm not very easy to live with, Ellery, but I'm doing the best I can.'

The thing about CONSEQUENCES is: some of them can be SURPRISES. And the thing about SURPRISES is they can have their OWN set of CONSEQUENCES.

'I read that book,' says Lola. 'The *Me, Me, Me & Me* book. And I know that it wasn't for research. I know your mother wasn't reading that for a CHARACTER.'

I FEEL SICK.

'So I want to apologise, Ellery, if, while I've been here, I've been focused on myself and not on you.'

I WANT TO DIE.

And I just ROAR at her: 'YOU HAVEN'T! YOU HAVE TOTALLY FOCUSED ON ME! SO THANK YOU! I APPRECIATE IT!'

And she HAS. And you know she has too, NJF. And I'm CRYING and **HATING MYSELF** and **EVERY SINGLE THING I'VE DONE** just so I could TRAVEL AROUND THE WORLD to find out that actually NO ONE IS MY DAD. And then I'm like: Why would anyone want to even BE MY DAD when LOOK AT HOW I TREAT THE PEOPLE WHO LOVE ME? THE PEOPLE I LOVE RIGHT BACK.

AND MY HEART IS:

AIRCRAFT HANGAR. AND ALL THE FLIGHTS HAVE TAKEN OFF.

22 November (MONDAY)

I wanted to go up to Megser in school today because I know she had to have got in serious trouble with Susan. Plus, I have no idea how she explained any of it or if she ended up confessing to Susan about the whole dad thing but made her swear not to tell Lola, which doesn't mean Susan is NEVER going to tell Lola, which is making me TERRIFIED AT THE THOUGHT, which is making me feel SO SELFISH. And Megser won't even look at me and she's right because ALL of this is my fault.

And how can I possibly figure ANYTHING out when the FIGURING-OUT PART OF ME is MEGSER?

24 November (WEDNESDAY)

I Reject Tense Silences and All Their Works. But they are stretching between Lola and me like a CATAPULT made of SPANX.

25 November (THURSDAY)

THE NIGHT THE CATAPULT SNAPPED

I hate Lola. I hate her. I HATE HER. I hate her. I hate her. I hate her. HATE HER. HATE. HATE. HATEY. HATEY. HATE. EY. HATE. Multiplied by a ZILLION.

SERIOUSLY: THIS IS LOLA'S SOLUTION TO THE PROBLEM OF NO LONGER BEING ABLE TO TRUST ME: 'We've decided to put the house up for rent, and—'

WHUTTTTTT? 'You've WHAT?' I said. And I'm looking around. 'Is this real life? Are we . . . is this . . . are we . . . in an episode of *Legacy of Hate*? Or are you just ON YOUR OWN IN ONE?'

And Lola goes, 'ELLERY!'

'But – why would you DO that? Put the house up for RENT?'

'You know exactly why!' said Lola.

'Because you CANNOT HELP YOURSELF AND YOUR ENTIRE LIFE HAS TO BE A SOAP OPERA?!'

And she SCOOTS on by that and says the second set of FOUR WORDS IN A ROW that, when you hear them on a television show, always spell disaster for the person on the receiving end.

'EVERYTHING HAS BEEN ARRANGED.' Followed by a sort of

rapid-fire: 'You'll be moving in with a family in town.'

Whutttt? 'A FAMILY? In TOWN?' I say. 'What is THAT supposed to mean?'

'You will CHRISTMAS IN RHINEBECK—'

'Nooooooo,' I say. 'NOOOOO to Christmas being a verb.'

'Now you sound like your MOTHER,' says Lola.

'THANK YOU!' I roar. 'THANK YOU!'

'You'll return to Ireland in the New Year,' says Lola, 'and stay with this family until summer, when you will return to Rhinebeck—'

'Who is this RANDOM FAMILY you're talking about?' I say.

'They're not a random family for goodness' sake – don't be so dramatic!' says Lola.

LOLA!

'Who is this SPECIFIC FAMILY?' I say.

'The O'Sullivans,' says Lola.

'OHMYGOD, NARROW IT DOWN!'

She's looking at me like I'm crazy.

'There are NINE MILLION O'SULLIVANS in Beara,' I say. 'And you would have SAID if it was Megser. So I need a NICKNAME, a TOWNLAND or a MEDICAL CONDITION.'

'The mother's name is Nuala,' says Lola, 'and she has a lovely son about your age—'

THE FIZZING IN MY HEAD IS NOW IN MY EARS. Lola HAS narrowed it down. Into a very fine point that I want to use to STAB MYSELF IN THE NECK, so I can BLEED TO DEATH at the prospect of sitting in my pyjamas at breakfast looking across the table at OSCAR O'SULLIVAN.

1 a.m. update

I WANT MY MOM.

Mother's Day: LET'S DO THIS

~~~~~~~~~~~~~~~~~~~~~~~~~~~~~~~~

(PART II) ◄ • • • • • • •

So the book Mom wrote for me was . . . a PICTURE BOOK. And it's illustrated by my FAVOURITE ILLUSTRATOR in the whole world, who was one of Mom's best friends and he never said a WORD and there's only one copy of it in existence and it's *beautiful* and *magical* and . . . it's called **WHO I AM**. And . . . I can't.

26 November (FRIDAY)

I stayed home from school today. I am 'sick' (quotes by Ellery). Lola 'believes me' (quotes also by Ellery). Lola has, nevertheless, been leaving clear liquids and dry toast at my shut bedroom door. Like I'm in a women's prison. Which I feel like I am. Even if it is OF MY OWN MAKING. And I'm curled in a ball crying. And it is EXHAUSTING. Then Auntie Elaine calls and I DON'T WANT TO ANSWER, but I DO, and she starts with: 'Ellery, I love you so much.'

NOOOOO! Because that's TOO MUCH with all the GUILT going on.

'Please try to understand what's going on here,' she says. 'Your mom was PRECIOUS to me. She was my BIG SISTER. We made each other's lives hell over the years, we really did, but I loved her so much there are days now where . . .' And she takes this BIG DEEP BREATH and says, 'You know those days.' And she goes: 'But you are JUST as precious to me, Ellery. More. And you make my life WAY LESS HELL.' Then she goes: 'My big sister entrusted you to us – me, and Grandpa, and Lola. And we failed her. And we failed you too.' And then she goes all quiet, and says: 'God, you are too young to have to deal with any of this. And I'm so sorry. None of this should have happened.'

And she's SO UPSET.

But it wasn't her FAULT and I tell her that and I say sorry for everything because I AM. I'm still not telling her about the dad investigation, though, because that would be a whole other bunch of lies, and it's over now anyway. And then she says: 'I know you are heartbroken, Ellery. We all are.

But we have to keep the pieces of all our hearts together.

We HAVE to.' And she sounds so exhausted and so sad and I want to let her go but ALSO I want to beg her not to make me move in with the O'Sullivans, so I DO.

And Auntie Elaine is like, *WHUTTTTTT?*

And I tell her about Oscar, and it's NEWS TO HER, and then I hear this SOUND that's like a growl and a scream mixed together. And she HANGS UP!

Then I hear Lola downstairs. On the phone. And I can't make out what she's saying, but I think it's Auntie Elaine she's saying it to. And then the call is ABRUPTLY OVER and I hear the front door open and SLAM. And I'm thinking DOORS ARE THE

INNOCENT VICTIMS IN ALL THIS. Which reminds me of the BACK door. Which is unattended so I RUN FOR IT.

I arrive at Megser's, even though I know she's out or maybe BECAUSE I know she's out. And definitely because I know the Ferals are out: having their once-a-month 'treat' of dinner at a restaurant with Mrs Daly.

Susan opens the door and she's got a glass of red wine in her hand, and I'm thinking, **LEAVE HER ALONE, IT'S FRIDAY NIGHT** and she has TWO HOURS' PEACE ahead of her. But it's too late. I'm all, 'Susan, please, please, please, please, please. Please HELP. I CAN'T. I JUST CAN'T. I'm going to BE DEPORTED.'

'What?' she says. 'But aren't you an Irish citizen?'

'No idea,' I say. 'But, I mean, by Lola.'

'What?' says Susan. 'Come in, come in.'

And then I add: 'And I'm SO SORRY about the lies. And involving you in them. I'm so embarrassed. And Megser was just going along with it because I was SAD.'

And Susan's like, 'What's going on, pet?'

We go into the living room and she sits beside me on the sofa and takes my hands, and I look at her, and then I hang my head in shame. And next thing I'm just ... **THE EMBARRASSMENT** and ...

SERIOUSLY why am I writing any of this down? Feelings are bad enough at the time.

Anyway, I tell Susan about Lola's plans. And I can tell she's horrified, but totally trying to hide it. And she's apologising for thanking Lola for the gifts and pressurising Megser into confessing about the emails! And I'm like, 'You're SO not to blame for anything ever.' (Except for the Ferals, I do not say.)

And Susan's like, 'Thank you,' but I'm just looking at her and she's being so kind, even though I lied to her and said terrible things to her daughter, and I'm thinking Susan HATES me now. And she's my SECOND-BEST MOM. And I've already lost **THE BEST MOM IN THE WORLD.** And WHO LOSES TWO MOMS? When they have **ZERO FATHERS** as backup?

I HAVE A COMPLETE MELTDOWN AT THIS STAGE.

27 *November* (SATURDAY)

I wake up and I'm in Susan's bed and the duvet is tucked all around me, and she's standing there holding out her hand to me. 'Come on,' she says. 'There's a pancake downstairs with your name on it.'

And I held her hand all the way down to the kitchen. And the pancake LITERALLY DID have my name on it. And Megser did it, and she's done another one that's got a NO-ENTRY SIGN meaning NOT with a '1st' after it, indicating it is NOT THE FIRST PANCAKE. And I take the bottle of chocolate sauce and one of the pancakes off the Elder Feral's plate because he hasn't shown up yet, and I write SOZ on that because it's a smaller pancake. Then he walks in and goes ballistic at me. And Susan TURNS ON HIM: 'How DARE you behave like that to a VISITOR?'

And he looks at me and goes, 'She's NOT A VISITOR. She's part of the—'

And I'm like, aw, he's going to say FAMILY and I will be so moved that I'll start calling him by his proper name [no idea] from now on. But NO! He says, 'She's part of the FURNITURE. The furniture you're SICK LOOKING AT at this stage.'

And then I'm like, I got 'AT THIS STAGE' from a FERAL?

Anyway, after breakfast, Megser and I go to her room and I follow Mom's horrific apology guidelines, which is so hard when the other person is following the Daly Family apology guidelines: eye contact with the floor, followed by – if relevant – 'Lookit. Same as', followed by: 'Have you eaten? Do you want something from the press?'

Then Susan sticks her head in and sees Megser tolerating a hug from me and says, 'Thank God – she's been an absolute NIGHTMARE. If I hear ONE MORE of those songs . . . every time I went past the door. Was it just the ONE song or was I imagining it? I was afraid to ask. I'd get the head eaten off me.'

And Megser is all, 'GET OUT, MAM – you just missed Ellery yourself!'

And Susan is like, 'Sure, of COURSE I did! I've NO PROBLEM admitting that.'

But the two of them are **MORTIFIED.** And Susan just goes, 'Right, girls – I'm taking the lads to the cinema.'

Then when they're gone, we're roller-skating up and down the hall, and then we go in to watch television and Megser goes into Planner where all the recorded stuff is, and we both see it: **IRISH BOOK AWARDS**.

And we look at each other.

'Did you watch it?' I say.

And Megser goes, 'No!' Then, 'Did YOU?'

And I'm like, 'No! Obviously!'

Then her thumb is hovering over PLAY, and I just PUSH IT DOWN, and this was what it was like to watch:

There you are! There's me! Pause! Pause! There's Derek Landy! You look AMAZING! My ELBOW! IS that my elbow? It IS! *OHGODOHGODOHGOD!*

And then Mom's bit is about to happen. And the presenter comes out and Megser and I are all: 'I LOVE herrr!' and 'Her DRESS!' And she gives the most gorgeous introduction about books being so much more than books, and authors being so much more than authors – that they're capturers of hearts and holders of hands and how they bring order to disordered thoughts and how they walk the path first to make the way safe and she's saying how Mom epitomised all this in her writing.

And I glance at Megser and she's all, 'Shut UP! I hate people looking at you when you're . . .' And she can't even SAY the word crying, but I can't even DO the crying, so then we're both Shut up! Shut UP! because the presenter is talking about how in the same week that the Irish Book Awards is honouring Mom, one of her characters is ALSO being honoured: JOSHUA

LAND, hero of her bestselling novel, *Wildfire*, was voted in an **INTERNATIONAL READER'S POLL:** The Most *Romantic* Fictional Hero of All Time!

Then they put in these video bits that they didn't show on the night of the awards.

And this stunning blonde author appears on screen with the book open on her lap. And she smiles and says, 'I LOVE this book. This extract, about Amandine, I loved – not just because of what it says, but also because of how I imagined Laurie Brown – as an author – writing it with a wry smile: "To Amandine, there was a sense of ending in being 'on paper'. It was where people could be born and die, yet live for ever, yet extend no further. She knew of one woman who had written a list of the qualities she hoped to find in a man, as though to commit him to paper were to commit him to real life, and then, of course, to commit him to her. 'May he be rich', 'may he be generous', 'may he be handsome'. Amandine had never considered what she hoped to find in her future love. Until she met Joshua Land and, without inventory, thought, 'May he be you'."'

'Wow!' says Megser.

And I'm like, **'I KNOWWWWWW!'**

And we're both like **WE SHOULD ACTUALLY READ HER BOOKS.** And I think Megser is surprised at what popular fiction actually IS.

Then the next author comes up, and it's Daimhin Mac Can't Remember! And she looks really awkward and I'm like, OHMYGOD, she has been made to do this for publicity purposes, and popular fiction has to be her idea of hell. There's this big pause and she says, 'This is not going to be easy,' and her voice cracks. And she holds up this battered copy of Mom's book and says: 'I first read *Wildfire* when I was fifteen years old. The following year, I was lucky enough to meet Laurie Brown, and to have her sign this beloved book of mine . . . well, of hers. But . . . I'm not going to read an extract. I'm going to read what she wrote to the desperately shy sixteen-year-old girl, standing in front of her in her school uniform, spelling out her strange Irish name.

'"Dear Daimhin, there is magic out there and it is our task, as writers, to capture it. Know too that the best magic is within. Never give it away. But always . . . share it. Love, Laurie". And a kiss. And underneath, she drew this little asterisk and wrote, "Next time we meet I'll be the one standing in line."' And she looks up and she's got all these **TEARS IN HER EYES.** 'That moment never did happen,' she says, 'but in a way it feels like it did . . . because any time I was struggling with this "task" that at times seemed insurmountable, I pictured a future moment where I was signing my book for Laurie Brown. And, every time, that's what got me through.'

And then she pointed up . . . like TO HEAVEN . . . and said, 'So, thank you, Laurie Brown.'

And Megser and I HATE OURSELVES. And Megser hits PAUSE and she's like: 'Why didn't she SAY anything on the night?' We decide it's because she was anxious and then we think about setting her up with Leon Adler but we agree that would be some sort of COMBUSTION situation where the end result is the two of them in some sort of **DYSTOPIAN COLLAPSE.**

And we go back to watching and the next author comes up, and Megser is overjoyed. 'A MALE! Who is not afraid to say he has read a *love story* . . . written by A WOMAN.'

'*Wildfire*,' he says, 'is a book that brings hope to readers searching for love, and a soft landing for those who are reeling from its loss. What I love most is its essence of fairy tale, and how it is rooted in the simplicity of a bucolic [no idea] village, a woman, a tailor, a gown, and from that . . . a beautiful and timeless love story. This is about Joshua Land and how he never feared "the fire of Amandine".'

And he starts to read: "'In Amandine was a fire by whose hearth a man could sit, day and night, to guard, and to stoke. But only the vain would offer a hearth to a wildfire and call it a gift. And only a fool would expect Amandine to take it. Joshua was neither. His gift to her, made under the light of many moons, was a gown of inky black so that all the world could better see her flames.'"

Then it's back to the presenter and she's saying all the sad stuff about Mom before I come out and the backdrop on the stage, which I couldn't see on the night, obviously, is this massive photo of Mom and in it, she's sitting down, but one knee is up, and her hands are kind of wrapped around it. But her FACE. It's so beautiful. She's really laughing, and her eyes are so green with the gorgeous laughter lines, and her skin is GLOWY, and her lashes are PERFECT, and her hair is all *bouncy and shiny*, and she's wearing this beautiful pink silk top that kind of drapes at the neck. And the ring on her finger is a STAR: platinum with a beautiful diamond at the centre. And I'm walking out on the stage in front of her . . . RIGHT UNDER THE STAR! And the audience is giving Mom a STANDING OVATION, which I obviously saw on the night and I'm looking out on it all with this massive smile.

BUT MY HEART WAS: RACEHORSES.

And then I just GAVE MY SPEECH. This was it:

'Mom would have laughed. She would have said: "This should be called the Deathtime Achievement Award" as she is receiving this during a time in which she is dead.'

Then I gave this big smile so everyone knew it was okay to laugh. Luckily, they did, because then I could keep going with this:

'If I learned one thing from my mom, it was how important it is to LAUGH. And if I learned *TWO THINGS* it was

how important it is to LAUGH
and how important it is to LOVE.

'But the thing is: I learned **MILLIONS OF THINGS** from my mom.

'To accept this award on her behalf is a HUGE honour. And for anyone out there who knew my mom, THAT was a huge honour too. And for anyone out there who read her books, that was a huge honour for Mom and for all our family.

'Mom didn't want to die. I miss her every day. And so do

Grandpa and Lola, and Auntie Elaine. We are all so proud of her. But we always have been.

'I know that when people win an award they love saying that they put it in their bathroom, or in storage, or they can't remember WHERE they put it, but NO WAY. I'm going to go home, and make a space RIGHT IN THE MIDDLE of Mom's bookshelves, and I'm going to put this there to honour her, and to honour all the words of all the authors she loved, and all the words of all the authors she had yet to love.

'Mom died too soon. But all good mothers die too soon. So this is for all the moms and the lifetimes they devote to their children. THAT'S some achievement.

THANK YOU,

THANK YOU,

➡ THANK YOU.'

And Megser rewinds and pauses at the part when I arrive on stage.

'LOOK!' she says. 'LOOK!' And then she scrambles over to the television and she's pointing at it and her other hand is over her mouth, and there are tears pouring down her face and she **DOESN'T CARE.**

And there it IS! And I never told ANYONE about it because it was right after I thought I was losing my mind with grief, but when I came out on stage I could see – out of the corner of my eye – the AVENGER *fairy* GLINT. But even though I thought I imagined it, I knew I didn't.

BECAUSE MY HEART WAS:

magical . . .

comfort.

After all that, Susan and the Ferals arrived back from the cinema and all I could think was I DON'T WANT TO GO HOME. And it turns out I actually said that out loud. And Susan called Lola for me again because she had to call her Friday night too, in case Lola reported me missing, and I became even MORE known to the gardaí.

So Susan asked Lola if I could stay over in a way that made it sound like Lola would be doing SUSAN a favour. And I could hear Lola giving a VERY ENTHUSIASTIC 'OF COURSE!'

I found out why the next day.

I KNEW something was wrong as soon as I walked in. The house felt DIFFERENT. Then I started wandering around downstairs. And things were MISSING.

'Where is . . . EVERYTHING?' I say.

'I need to prepare the house for renting,' says Lola. 'So I put away some of the BREAKABLES.'

'WELL,' I roar.

'HOW COME I STILL HAVE MY HEART?'

2 a.m. update

NO MOM.

NO DAD.

NO HOME.

NO WORDS.

28 November (SUNDAY)

████ ████ ████ ████ ████ ████

I come out of the shop this morning holding a LARGE BOX of **EMOTIONAL SUPPRESSANTS** in salt and sugar flavours and I hear: 'Ellery!' And it's Silent Johnny, and I keep walking and he knows why.

'Ellery!' he says. 'Are you okay?' And he's darted around and he's standing in front of me.

'Did you help Lola to pack up my house yeterday?' I say.

And he gives this nervous shrug and says, 'Yes, BUT NOT ON PURPOSE. I swear to GOD. All she said to Dan was she needed some boxes moved. We didn't know what she was up to. It was only when me and Dan were nearly finished that she told us. And, to be honest, we both thought she was . . .' And he shrugs. But I know he means NUTS and he's too nice to say it.

And he looks **SO SINCERE** and **SAD** on my behalf. And I feel TERRIBLE.

'Thanks,' I said. 'Sorry for being so . . .'

And he says, 'No bother.' Then: 'I . . . uh . . . have something for you, though. I . . . took something.'

And I'm like, Whuttt?

'From your house,' says Johnny. 'It's a box. I think it's your mam's. I kind of found it by accident.'

'Where?' I said.

'In this sort of secret compartment.'

And I'm like, 'SECRET COMPARTMENT? Where?'

'Just . . . it's under . . . where the hoover is.'

'Well, that explains that.'

And he smiles. 'Do you want it? The box?'

And I'm like, 'YES. But . . . why did you take it?'

'No – it wasn't like that. Like, how it sounds. I don't know . . . well, I do. Because I opened it, and it had cards and stuff in it. And I didn't read them, but a few of them on the top were . . . like cards . . . "to my daughter" . . . and all that.'

OHMYGOD, he is so kind.

And then he goes: 'Your nan was just sending everything up to the attic and she wasn't being very SENTIMENTAL, I thought . . .'

Seriously – he said that. And then: 'There were some notebooks too. One had "Random Musings" written on it.'

And he's shrugging like he knows that might be something I'd be into, which it totally is. Then he goes: 'Sure, maybe you'll just throw the box up into the attic too,' because he can see that I've got the **NERVOUS EYES.**

'NO! I won't,' I say. 'Not yet! I'd love to see it. Where is it?'

'Inside in the shed.'

29 November (MONDAY)

'Oh my GOD!' says Megser. 'Is it going to be CLEAR whether these are your mom's random musings or her CHARACTERS'?'

'What difference does it make?' I say.

'Are you SERIOUSLY ASKING ME THAT?' says Megser. 'Let me break it down. Random musing: "I want to strangle my daughter for not knowing what an ampersand is."' Then she looks up at me. 'Would you think that was about you?'

'Well, it obviously WOULD be about me.'

And Megser's just shaking her head. 'Okay ... forget that. Just – if you read something and you think it might be about you and it's NOT GOOD, you'll have no way of knowing for SURE. And you will be **TORTURED FOR LIFE.**' And then she adds, 'And I'll have to listen to you.'

And I'm like, 'You're going to be WITH ME FOR LIFE!' Because that was the main message I got.

And Megser's like, 'I'M SERIOUS. Like, what is it you think you're going to find in there? What do you WANT to find? Because you might be disappointed. Or WAY WORSE.'

And I'm like, 'Well, what do YOU think I'm going to find in there?'

But I can see the **MEGSER-WORRIED-I'M-NOT-ACCEPTING-HAVING-NO-FATHER EYES.**

And obviously she's right. But ALSO there's no way I can stop myself because I can't UNKNOW THAT THESE NOTEBOOKS EXIST.

1 a.m. update

OK: something **WEIRD** is going on. I just tried Auntie Elaine's phone for the nth time this week, and STILL it went to voicemail, so I emailed her on her work email . . . and I got an out-of-office reply that says she's on ANNUAL LEAVE until JANUARY! And it's dated the week of the Book Awards – which she was too busy to go to because of WORK! And I'm like, Whuttt? Has Auntie Elaine been going around LYING TO EVERYONE, flying off WHEREVER, without letting ANYONE know where she really is, and . . .

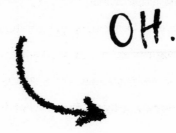

OH.

3 a.m. update

I think I'm just this **MASSIVE BURDEN** that everyone's lives have to revolve around now. And that was bad enough as it was, but then they find out I'm a LYING UNGRATEFUL BURDEN too. And I'm like, have they all just been sitting around and I'm like this PASS THE PARCEL that no one wants to end up holding when the music stops?

And that's pretty much the **WORST THOUGHT EVER,** so I do what Mom used to tell me to do with my imagination: make beautiful pictures.

So I LITERALLY think about the *beautiful* picture of me and Mom on the pier that Silent Johnny gave me. And I think of him putting the box of Mom's stuff aside for me. And how BEYOND THOUGHTFUL that was. But now I'm feeling terrible for calling him Silent Johnny. Even though it wasn't in any mean way. But it's still a name I have for him that that he doesn't know I have . . . and it's not exactly positive.

Because I remember the wise words of Mom: 'You don't always know what lies behind someone's silence.' And I remember her raising her finger and saying, 'AND you don't always know what lies behind someone's words.'

Oh, Mom. Have I learned ANYTHING?

Oh, but I HAVE!

Because then I remember the wise words of MYSELF: 'The way to a girl's heart is THROUGH HER BEST FRIEND'S.'

Oh, Silent Johnny: you have WON! You have won me over and in so doing, you have **won the heart** of my BEST FRIEND, Megser, but it's a **CAGED HEART SO THERE'S SOME WORK TO BE DONE, BUT STILL.**

Oh, do I now want to start every sentence with OH?

Oh, Megser. Silent Johnny WILL be yours even though you show zero signs of wanting that. But:

Oh, how that could all be *about to change.*

30 November (TUESDAY)

'Are you WELL IN THE HEAD?' says Meg. 'Silent Johnny: NO.'

'What do you mean "No"?'

'Johnny and I are FRIENDS,' says Meg. 'End OF.'

'But ... but ...'

'Whyyyy,' she says, 'are you so resistant to Silent Johnny being just a friend? He is YOUR FRIEND too. He gave you that lovely photo because he's a NICE LAD. And his mam's a counsellor. So . . . he's fairly copped on.'

'Oh NO,' I say.

'What's wrong with you NOW?'

'It's . . . CULTURAL CONDITIONING,' I say. 'American High School Hell. Where the girl is only complete when she has been CHOSEN by the guy. Even a guy she has ZERO INTEREST in.'

And Meg is nodding.

'I should be – and AM – **ASHAMED** of myself,' I say. 'I am an American idiot.'

'Thank you!' says Meg. '**THANK YOU.**' Then: 'You're TOTALLY Irish by the way.'

And I say NOTHING, even though I am DYING TO KNOW why I'm totally Irish. But I take a leaf out of Silent Johnny's book. And Mom's Allow Silence book. Because I don't want to hear that it's because I've lost the ability to pronounce my THs.

1 December (WEDNESDAY)
❀ • ❀ • ❀ • ❀ • ❀ •

OHMYGOD . . . this AFTERNOON. Lola wasn't home when I got back from school. And there was no note, which she would always leave if she wasn't going to be there when I got home.

And then the doorbell rings.

And when I open the door, standing there are Carpenter Dan and Lola **WITH THEIR ARMS AROUND EACH OTHER.**

And my head is about to start FIZZING until I realise Lola is actually SLUMPED against him, and her left leg is bent, and she's holding her foot off the ground. It turns out that Lola went out for a walk, dived – I'm going to guess unnecessarily – into a ditch because of an oncoming vehicle, and twisted her ankle. Dan was driving by in the van a little while later and spotted her, and came to her rescue. She was **MORTIFIED. BECAUSE:** DO NOT SHOW ANY SIGN OF WEAKNESS. Anyway, Dan brought her in, set her up on the sofa, then insisted on making tea and couldn't believe there was no sugar in the place, and none of us knew if coconut sugar has the same impact on a shocked body as white sugar. So Dan goes out to the shop, buys sugar, comes back, makes tea, organises a cushion and finds one of those creepy flesh-coloured bandages to strap up Lola's ankle because he won't HEAR OF HER going to the hospital because that's a TOTAL WASTE of money, and they 'WON'T DO NO DIFFERENT'. He then POISONS Lola with the sweet tea but she's an amazing actress so it's literally like she's shooting a commercial promoting the sugar industry. Then, as Dan is about to leave, Lola tries to pay him 'for his time'. And he just laughs and says, 'Sure, how can you pay a man for the TIME OF HIS LIFE?'

And I'm laughing and Lola is confused and off he goes and I run out after him. 'Nice try, mister!' I say. 'Nice distraction game.' And that makes him stop.

He laughs. 'Sure, I was hardly going to take money from the woman. And I wasn't going to stand around arguing with her about it.'

'I knowww,' I say, 'but she's thinking that was two hours out of your working day, and she hates being an inconvenience . . . to ANYONE other than Grandpa . . . and all other family members.'

He laughs at this. 'I wouldn't dream of taking money. Sure, she'd do the same herself if it was me lying in the ditch.' And I'm so close to laughing in his face. I'm picturing Lola seeing him in the ditch, driving on by, arriving home and saying: THERE IS AN ADDICTION CRISIS IN THIS COUNTRY THAT NO ONE IS TALKING ABOUT. IF A TALENTED CRAFTSMAN CAN'T GET THROUGH THE DAY WITHOUT FALLING DOWN DRUNK IN A DITCH . . .

Dan asks me what's so funny. And I go: 'Lola.'

He laughs. 'She's SOME WOMAN.'

'SOME WOMAN' can LITERALLY MEAN ANYTHING – Dan could

love Lola like a mother or he could ACTIVELY want to FINISH THE JOB OFF next time he sees her in a ditch. We may never know.

BUT HE DID ADD THIS: 'It must be fierce hard on her at the moment. With the anniversary.'

Mother's Day: LET'S DO THIS

(PART IIII)

Lola wasn't at breakfast on Mother's Day morning. And she didn't come back for dinner. Or even after that. I didn't see her before bedtime. But then . . . I went to bed early with my new book.

I woke up, though, at 11 p.m. And 1 a.m. And 3.30 a.m. Then I just went downstairs. The living room door was open a crack, and I walked in. Lola looked up at me, and she had no make-up on, and she looked old, and her eyes were red, and the **SADDEST EYES I'VE EVER SEEN.** And she looked so disappointed that I had seen her. And the moonlight was on her face, and she was beautiful, and she was in her nightgown, and she just looked so skinny. And her hands were gripping a photo frame on her lap.

I looked down at it. It was Lola and Grandpa and Mom when she was about five. Grandpa was holding Mom in his arms, but Mom was kind of in the middle of them with her arm wrapped around Lola's neck, and she was smiling. And they all looked SO HAPPY. I'd never seen the photo before. There was bubble wrap on the sofa. Lola had bubble-wrapped this photo and packed it in her suitcase. And I sat down beside her, and I realised: **IT'S MOTHER'S DAY.** Lola's a mother too.

2 December (THURSDAY)

Lola and I made up.

3 December (FRIDAY)

Tonight was the OFFICIAL UNVEILING of THE FERAL SANCTUARY. And MEGSER'S NEW BEDROOM.

IT IS ALL  AWESOME.

SADNESS: the Without Incident Room has been returned to its original status of Walk-In Wardrobe.

'What's THIS,' says Mrs Daly, stepping out of it, and closing the door behind her, 'about LOLO packing you off to those AWFUL O'SULLIVANS?'

(We have ALL agreed never to correct Mrs Daly about the Lolo thing.)

'Has she LOST THE PLOT ALTOGETHER?' says Mrs Daly. And she looks at Susan. 'You know that's all about the pay cheque with that one,' and she's doing the fanning-out-cash thing with her fingers like she's in a rap video. And Susan is giving her **WARNING EYES.**

'Watch now,' says Mrs Daly, 'Nuala'll be billing Lolo for gourmet THIS, THAT and the OTHER and it'll be CAT FOOD and HORSE MEAT on the dinner table.'

And Megser is 'NAN!'

And Susan is 'MAM!'

And I'm 'MIAOW!' Then: 'NEIGH!' Because the whole thing is **SO CRAZY.**

And then Mrs Daly is looking at me and it's so kind, and she says: 'Do you want me to have a word with Lolo?'

And I'm like Whutttt? But also: YES.

She is then talking about people and GRIEF and being in NO FIT STATE to make decisions. 'NO BIG DECISIONS for the first year at LEAST,' she says. 'Because it won't be the right one. And you won't be making it for the right reason.' And then she SIDE-EYES Susan. 'But you WON'T HEAR A WORD AGAINST IT. You'd get the HEAD EATEN OFF YOU. Even if you only want what's BEST for them.'

Then she and Susan LOCK EYES. And there's this MOMENT.

And Mrs Daly goes, 'The wallpaper in the en suite is ROTTEN.'

And Susan goes, 'DO NOT GO NEAR ANY OF ELLERY'S FAMILY.'

'FINE, SO!' says Mrs Daly. Then she looks at me: 'That goes for you too: NO BIG DECISIONS THE FIRST YEAR. Do you hear me?'

And I'm thinking: BIG DECISIONS LIKE TRYING TO FIND YOUR FATHER? And I can feel Megser's eyes on me, probably because she's thinking the same thing.

'And the WORST PART ABOUT IT,' says Mrs Daly, 'is whoever it is you've lost won't be there to help you pick up the pieces at the end of it all.'

AND MY HEART IS:

THE GRAND CANYON.

3 a.m. update

I FaceTime Grandpa. Finally. And I look him in the eye and I tell him I'm sorry about all the lying, and he is the most serious he's EVER been with me, which was REALLY OFFPUTTING in the sense of putting me off lying for LIFE, but I'm definitely still okay with lying by omission, so I don't mention ANYTHING about the reason for all the lying.

Then I tell him about Auntie Elaine, because I need to know if she hates me now, and has to make up excuses not to come to Ireland, while going on vacation to HAWAII for MONTHS, just to get away from me.

And this is so sad I don't even want to write it.

Because Auntie Elaine is NOT ON VACATION – she was just having such a hard time after Mom died that she had to get some proper help and check in somewhere.

And my HEART is: dominoes.

And the next one to fall is going to TIP ME ON TO A CHAIR AT OSCAR O'SULLIVAN'S KITCHEN TABLE FOR BREAKFAST for the next two years. Because even though I don't want to make anything worse because everyone has all these things going on, I just have to check if Grandpa definitely knows about Lola's Oscar decision because I can't IMAGINE Grandpa thinking that makes sense, and if Lola DID say it to him, DEFINITELY he would have tried to TALK HER OUT OF IT.

But then he says THIS: 'And I'm SO SORRY, *sweetheart*, about the house, and the move.'

BECAUSE: LOLA NOT HEARING A WORD AGAINST IT.

And he's saying: 'You know HOW MUCH we love you, but there are OTHER FACTORS at play in the coming year. And your grandmother and I felt this was better than the alternative: having you move here to Rhinebeck and go to high school here.'

And he is RIGHT. But I'm crying, and making him promise me that the other factors were NOBODY IS DYING and he one hundred per cent did, so I could SLEEP TONIGHT, NO MORE WORRYING, which I obviously couldn't.

BECAUSE: Auntie Elaine.

4 December (SATURDAY)

OHMYGOD . . . POOR SUSAN. Night One in the Feral Sanctuary and the Younger Feral has already vandalised it with some wood-burning tool he took from Dan when he was helping him pack up his stuff! Apparently, he FIRED IT UP last night and burned some 'IMAGES' into his new furniture. Seriously. Everyone is calling them 'IMAGES' and no one is saying what they actually are. Megser thinks he's going to be a SERIAL KILLER. Susan is **TRAUMATISED.** And Megser BEGS ME to come over, so I do.

When I get there Dan and Silent Johnny are in the hall, apologising to Susan and Susan's apologising to them. And Megser goes: 'I don't know why you're all apologising. There's only one person responsible: THIS FREAK.' And she points to the Younger Feral. 'REMEMBER THIS MOMENT,' she says to the rest of us. 'For the CRIME DOCUMENTARY. Because we're ALL going to be interviewed. Because even though everyone suspected for years, this is the first TRADITIONAL SIGN that he's going to end up—'

And Susan **BURSTS INTO TEARS!** And goes to her room! And Megser follows her RELUCTANTLY.

So it's me, Silent Johnny, Dan and the Younger Feral, and I go, 'RIGHT! Would anyone like tea?' like I'm IRISH.

And Silent Johnny goes, 'Yes, please!' even though I know he doesn't mean it, so we head for the kitchen. Dan says he wants a word with the Younger Feral and he'll follow us in. And I'm like, to Silent Johnny, 'Is Dan going to kill him?' And he goes, 'Not a HOPE.' And he didn't mean it to be funny but it was and we're trying not to laugh while the rest of the household is **FALLING APART**.

And then we can hear Dan outside talking really low to the Younger Feral, so we sneak over to the door to listen. And we stick our heads out, and the poor Younger Feral is just staring at the ground and nodding and shame-faced and silently crying, and Dan is crouched down in front of him and looking at him with SUCH KINDNESS it's RIDICULOUS and the Younger Feral is just **WIDE-EYED** at whatever Dan's just said to him and he's nodding FURIOUSLY now, and muttering, so we can't HEAR, which is frustrating. Then Dan stands up and says: 'Do you feel better now you've got all that out?' And the Younger Feral is nodding again and he looks up at Dan and gives him a little smile and then he's wiping his eyes, and Dan goes: 'Right, so. Will we go and tell Mammy the whole story? And maybe you could give her a big hug and say sorry. What do you think?'

And OFF THEY GO in the direction of Susan. And Dan pats the

Younger Feral's head, and says, 'GOOD MAN.'

Later, Megser was like: 'And you DEFINITELY saw him showing emotion to Dan? Because THESE PEOPLE can be VERY MANIPULATIVE.'

And I'm like, 'I diiid!'

And I'm dying to see the 'IMAGES', but I don't want to ask. But as soon as Susan is gone Megser goes, 'WAIT till you see what he did.' And she sneaks me down to the room and opens the door and at the end of his bed, all across the entire wood panel, he had drawn – with the wood-burning pen – all these FLAMES. And I'm seriously reconsidering whether or not I DID see him show emotion.

2 a.m. update

POSSIBLY because of the power of suggestion, I started reading *Wildfire* tonight.

And I read this, which I loved. It's a fairy tale that Amandine's mother used to read to her when she was small and she would put her name in it as the *princess*.

And it's so *sweet*. And so Mom.

'We must choose carefully,' said the queen, 'whether our mind's eye is to be our friend or enemy in life. Because, whichsoever you choose, its power is great. Do you understand?'

And the young princess nodded, and the queen smiled.

'Make beautiful pictures, my darling Amandine,' she said. 'Let your imagination carry you, always, into the light. For my part I will imagine the inside of your mind as gleaming with all the colours of the rainbow and radiant with hope. The world around you will change, but come with me.' And she took Amandine's hand, and led her to the window. The night was wild and the sea raged. A beam of light swept across mother and daughter as they stood in the darkness.

'Look over there,' said the queen, pointing to its source, and they watched as the waves crashed against the rocks beneath. 'Be the lighthouse, my darling Amandine. Be the lighthouse.'

5 December (SUNDAY)

I told Megser I was going over to Silent Johnny's to check out Mom's notebooks, and she's trying to put me off again. NOW she's warning me about 'PRIVATE THINGS' I could discover. And I'm like, 'AS IF I'm going to READ ANYTHING LIKE THAT!'

And Meg's like, 'Yeah! As if your mom WROTE IN DETAIL about ALL THESE GUYS she—' But I'm not laughing any more so she doesn't finish that sentence. Instead she says, 'You're ON YOUR OWN, girl.'

So I call over to Silent Johnny's this evening, and he gets a torch and we go out to the shed and he unwraps the plastic and pulls out this beautiful pale blue cardboard box that I've never seen before – the size of a file box but much prettier, and he asks if I want to take it home.

'Noooo,' I say. 'I don't want Lola to see it.'

'Okay, so,' he says.

And I'm like, what am I supposed to do now? Does he think I'm going to sit inside in the shed for the night?

'Right!' he says, looking around. 'I'll bring in the heater. And the big light.'

INSIDE IN THE SHED IT IS!

Then he heads off and comes back with the heater. But also:

a ham sandwich and a Fruit 'n' Nut.

HOW ADORABLE IS THAT?

'Stay as long as you like,' he says. 'S. Dodge will keep an eye on you.'

And S. Dodge bleats, and we're like, SHE IS HUMAN.

And off Silent Johnny goes.

I can't call spending time inside in a shed underrated because I'm guessing no one has rated it in the first place. But if I were to be the first person to rate it, I'd give it a ten for novelty value. And a ten for the **SPEED AT WHICH THE NOVELTY WEARS OFF.**

So . . . 'as long as I liked' turned out to be FIVE MINUTES (the length of time it took to eat the sandwich and chocolate). But I waited FORTY minutes before I knocked on Silent Johnny's door to let him know I was done (the length of time I decided could justify NEEDING to eat the sandwich and chocolate).

I took three of Mom's notebooks home with me, and started with Random Musings. Obviously, I had no idea what to expect when I started reading. But it was DEFINITELY not this, the answer to a question I've been asking **ALL MY LIFE:**

What's not to love about LOVE?

IT TURNS OUT: MILLIONS OF THINGS.

&&&& [rhymes with 'book' if you're Irish] this &&&&!!!! [rhymes with 'bit'] [Though Mom WROTE IT so I don't know why I'M being so faithful to the non-swearing.] I'm sitting at this &&&&king desk and I don't have the &&&&king WORDS for this. I'm a &&&&king writer! No wonder I never read love stories. I knew the &&&&king endings. I wanted to have some &&&&king HOPE.

AND:

My HEART is like a &&&&king rock. I can't remember what it used to feel like. And all the words for this horror feel out of reach . . . like there's a cliff up ahead and they're beyond it. They've gone over the edge down into this little black seam that sucks the &&&&king joy out of the world, and the sun from the &&&&king sky. And it's dark and it's miserable. And I can't BREATHE. And I want to go back to the library to those shelves I ignored and find out how? How, romance authors, do you do it? How do you find the &&&&ING words?

AND:

How can a **heart** be so light when you carry someone in it, and so heavy when they're gone?

And I'm thinking I KNOW THE FEELING.

✳ 6 December (MONDAY) ✳

Megser is in charge of what I am insisting on calling Secret Santa, because Kris Kringle sounds like some guy in a red sweater who shows up at your house for Christmas drinks and no one knows who he is. Anyway: I got Silent Johnny!

After school, we go back to Megser's and there, on her brand-new nightstand, is *Wildfire*! And I'm like, 'No waaay!'

And Megser goes: 'Yes way – just because I've never read popular fiction before that doesn't mean—'

And I'm like, 'No – I meant no way because I'm reading it too!' And Megser's got the **NERVOUS EYES** and then – because I can see that her bookmark is further into the book than mine – I'm wondering if it's because she knows something I don't.

1 a.m. update

I may now know the thing that Megser knows … that I no longer don't.

Which is that *Wildfire* by Laurie Brown might be more **'INSPIRED BY REAL EVENTS'** than the author may have led me or any of us to believe.

So SERIOUSLY . . . I'm going to do a COMPARE and CONTRAST.

COMPARE and **CONTRAST** the below passage, from *Wildfire* by Laurie Brown, with the recently quoted passages from the notebook Random Musings by the same author, as violated by the author's daughter.

Amandine sat in the candlelight, her heart like a fist she was afraid to open. She reached for her diary and her pen and began to write.

I know now that the love I had only read about exists. And so too does heartbreak. But those were the books whose spines I would run my fingertips along in the hush of the library without stopping. I wonder if some part of me knew that one day I would live it, and I could find my own words. Let her believe just in love for now. Or, at least, try. Because she will be quicker to believe stories of heartbreak. And they will shatter her; her heart is too fragile, her imagination too great.

Amandine wanted to go back now and find those books, and see how others had captured what felt to her was something beyond the horizon, nestled deep in a black seam. And she imagined that same black seam was what sucked the sun from the sky, and that was how night fell.

AND:

> How can a heart be so light when you carry someone in it, and so heavy when they're gone?

Because sometimes you can get it right first time.

7 December (TUESDAY)

Okay . . . I'm reading more of *Wildfire* . . . and even though I know that authors make things up completely, it's pretty clear that Amandine was COMPLETELY MADE UP by COMPLETELY BORROWING HEAVILY from Mom's real life. The point IS: does that MEAN Joshua Land is based on MY DAD? Obviously, I want to just skip the whole way through *Wildfire* to find out if they had an **AMAZING DAUGHTER** with **AWESOME EYEBROWS** or maybe a son with really thin ones if Mom was trying to DISGUISE me but I'm hoping the answer will come, as it often does, from: MEGSER.

8 December (WEDNESDAY)

OHMYGOD, the Younger Feral. Because that was the first mystery that was solved today. You won't believe what the whole story was about the IMAGES. It turns out that because the Elder Feral was spending more time on 'PLAY DATES' with his own friends over the summer, the Younger Feral felt rejected, and when he got upset about this, the Elder Feral told him he was a BABY, and no WONDER he didn't want to hang out with him. And now that they wouldn't be sharing a room any more, the Younger Feral was terrified he would never see his big brother again. And that was what all the expensive furniture was about – he thought Susan would CALL THE WHOLE RENOVATION THING OFF! And when it looked like it was all going ahead, mahogany or no mahogany, his last ditch effort was to **DESTROY** the place after the fact, so he'd have to be moved into the Elder Feral's room. The POOR GUY.

Hearing ALL THIS was the distraction that meant Megser didn't notice what I had noticed: poking out from under her bed, her copy of *Wildfire*, which, since we last spoke about it, had LOTS more Post-its in it.

So as Susan is leaving, I VERY CASUALLY reach down, pick it up, and, when she's gone, go: 'Soooo . . . the Post-its?'

And Megser DIVES for the book while also trying to tell me that she's just 'marked passages I particularly love'.

And because **OBVIOUSLY SHE'S TOTALLY LYING,** I start to open it, and Megser goes, 'Noooo!' but I'm holding it up high and trying to read ANYTHING WRITTEN ANYWHERE, but luckily all I need is to flip to the page where the most DRAMATIC Post-it is: the one with three GIANT RED EXCLAMATION POINTS on it.

AND: *OH*. *MY*. *GOD*.

Remember that bit the male author read out in the Book Awards video about Joshua Land not fearing the fire of Amandine? Well, HERE is the sentence BEFORE it. ALSO about Joshua Land:

He lived in the woods and in the woods he breathed.

HE. LIVED. IN. THE. WOODS. (see entry Feb. 16: 2 a.m. update)

And I look at Megser. And she looks at me. And now we KNOW.

Who's The Father?

Joshua Land

★ ★ ★ ★ ★

NOW, ALL WE HAVE TO DO IS

FIGURE OUT WHO JOSHUA LAND IS.

9 December (THURSDAY)

There's this song called 'Last Night a DJ Saved My Life'. And it's AWESOME. Mom got it once when we played What's My SONNNG? and the message we took from it was just: DANCE.

I have my own version of that song now:

'LAST NIGHT A FERAL SAVED MY LIFE!'

Actually BOTH Ferals did. Actually the ENTIRE O'SULLIVAN FAMILY saved my life. It turns out that, following the Younger Feral's post-vandalisation admission, the Elder Feral made an admission of his own: he was ALSO sad about being split up from his archenemy. But he was too cool to admit it. So Susan – having laid out strict guidelines that will be completely ignored – has allowed them to be reunited. BUT . . . they don't want to be in the Feral Sanctuary because they feel TOO FAR AWAY FROM THEIR MAM! Which is HILARIOUS. So they're getting their old room back . . . and Megser is being moved to THE FERAL SANCTUARY! And the only reason she agreed to this is because the person at the other side of that dangerously designed Jack and Jill bathroom is?

ME!

And the **sweetest** thing is THIS: Susan said that as soon

as the boys said they wanted to be back in their old room . . . her first thought was ME MOVING IN. And Megser said she just came out with it on the spot but then she tried to TAKE IT BACK in case Lola said no!

But Megser told Susan there's no WAY Lola would say no . . . and not just because she casually mentioned to Lola last week that Oscar made her **UNCOMFORTABLE AS A YOUNG WOMAN** but because Lola KNOWS that Megser's house already feels like home to me. PLUS, she knows that Susan has already busted us for bad behaviour, which gives us no option but to resort to our BEST BEHAVIOUR.

So Lola said YES! And Grandpa said YES! And now they can be reunited! And Auntie Elaine can get better! And SERIOUSLY – WHO GETS TO LIVE WITH THEIR BEST FRIEND? This is *THE BEST NEWS EVER!*

And when I get home, I FLING myself at Lola and she's apologising for her WRONG O'SULLIVANS idea, and I'm thanking her for the RIGHT O'SULLIVANS idea, and then she's telling me she had another idea too, but that it's one I'll definitely like, which is that instead of going to Rhineback, the entire BROWN FAMILY – me and Lola, and Grandpa and Auntie Elaine – will 'Christmas in Ireland' and I TOTALLY FORGIVE HER THE USE OF A NOUN AS A VERB.

10 December (FRIDAY)

I have a LEAD. From Mom's notebooks. And they are the initials:
TM.

SKINGE these if you like running your fingertips over romance spines without stopping.

> TM
> There are people who have lost loved ones, people grieving for the dead. We are alive. We have chosen grief. You are gone; I am gone. But we didn't have to be.
> Laurie xxxxx

> TM
> I must accept that you are gone. But today is not the day. Today I would like to breathe. Today I am postponing grief.
> Laurie xxxxx

> TM
> Who am I to watch your brave heart carry you to my door, then send it away broken? Back down the only straight path that had ever separated us.

And she couldn't even SIGN that one!

And Megser starts to put her hands over her face as I'm reading them out, and I'm like, is any of this familiar? Does any of this sound like *Wildfire*?? And she just nods, and she's like, Yes! All of it! And she's like, do you want to know?

And I DON'T KNOW is the answer. But I'm saying, 'YES!'

And Megser says: 'So after they break up the FINAL TIME . . . Amandine is back in France in her parents' house in the countryside on some massive estate. But Joshua follows her over and she can see him walk up the drive. And she tells her mother to send him away. Because she can't let Joshua see her, because . . . **SHE'S SIX MONTHS PREGNANT.'**

And I'm like, 'Why? Why didn't she want him to KNOW?'

'If it's like the book,' says Megser, 'because it MIGHT NOT BE ALL LIKE THE BOOK, Amandine doesn't want him to feel trapped or her to feel trapped.' Then she goes, 'but you get the sense there might be another reason too.'

'And what does Joshua DO?' I want to know.

'He just . . . LEAVES. Because he believes she doesn't want to see him ever again.'

And I'm like, 'OHMYGOD – that is SO SAD.'

And Megser looks terrified. **BECAUSE:** *emotions*.

So she goes STRAIGHT to researching authors whose initials are TM and there are none who were alive at the 'relevant time', and I tell her I've already looked up all Mom's contacts for a TM because they were on an old phone she gave me, and there were NONE so then I'm like: 'What if TM stands for something . . . like The Mystery . . . that I'll NEVER SOLVE . . .' And then it's hard to breathe. So I just LAUGH because I can't SPEAK at the HORROR of THAT thought, but also because it would DEFINITELY prove that making big decisions **REALLY WAS A DISASTER**, which would make Mrs Daly RIGHT, which is something I don't think Megser could ever really come back from.

❄ *11 December* (SATURDAY) ❄

MRS DALY BEING RIGHT has stayed with me. And made me realise that she's a source I cannot BELIEVE I overlooked. Mrs Daly: HISTORIAN OF LOCAL SCANDAL where LOCAL includes INTERNATIONAL WATERS. And LANDMASSES. And basically, if you've EVER lived on the Beara Peninsula, you become like a PIN on a whiteboard in MRS DALY'S MIND, and she'll be pulling red string from you and attaching it to other strings

FOR THE REST OF YOUR LIFE.

MY POINT IS: she could EASILY KNOW STUFF about Mom.

And my ADVANTAGE is: she's down a bingo buddy (no – that's not a thing) because the Younger Feral is currently grounded.

Do not let ANYONE tell you that bingo is just for old ladies. It is for old ladies AND their YOUNG CHAPERONES . . . who love it way more than they will publicly admit. Because bingo is **AWESOME.** And involves TEA and CAKE.

The first three numbers out of the drum are: 13, 16 and 17. In BINGO LINGO (yes – that's a thing) 13, 16 and 17 are: UNLUCKY FOR SOME, SWEET SIXTEEN AND NEVER BEEN KISSED, and DANCING QUEEN. I'm like, 'ELLERY BROWN: An Autobiography in Bingo Lingo.'

But ENOUGH ABOUT ME. Because the bonus outcome of this bingo trip was that Mrs Daly won €400, which put her in TOP FORM. And **CHATTIER THAN USUAL.**

I start the drive home by telling her I'm suffering from travel sickness so she will slow down, which will a) buy me time and b) possibly save my life.

If I've learned ONE thing from my time spent in Mrs Daly's company over the years it's her ability to retain vast amounts of gossip. And her willingness to share it. It's a form of PRIDE.

The result is that no question is too CREEPY or INAPPROPRIATE for Mrs Daly.

She DID NOT BAT AN EYELID at this:

'Beara is **so beautiful,**' I say. 'I'm sure Mom had LOTS of visitors. Who probably had to stay OVERNIGHT as it's so far away from everywhere.'

'Sure, of COURSE,' said Mrs Daly.

'She had a lot of GUY FRIENDS, Mom.'

'You could LOSE TRACK of THEM,' she replies.

SERIOUSLY.

Then I go, 'Did you ever hear of Mom having a friend called TOM or TIM or TONY or THEODORE . . . MARSHALL or MATHERS or . . .?'

'No,' she says, and looks at me like, NEXT QUESTION.

'Do you know ANY MAN with the initials TM?' Because: GETTING TO THE POINT.

And she goes: 'Tobey Maguire.' SERIOUSLY.

And I'm like, 'A REAL PERSON.' Even though I KNOW he's real but at the SAME TIME I'm picturing WEB-SLINGING through town.

'No,' says Mrs Daly. NEXT QUESTION!

'Do you remember much about my mom . . . in the early days?'

And Mrs Daly gives me this GLANCE.

And I'm like, **WHERE IS THIS GOING?**

'I MIGHT AS WELL TELL YOU,' she says, 'that myself and your mother didn't get off to the best start. God rest her.'

And I'm like Whutttt? 'I NEVER noticed anything.'

'No, no, no – we were PAST ALL THAT by the time yourself and MAGSO (!) got together,' she says. 'It was YEARS back – when your mother bought the house. I was getting a bit of work done on my own place and it was Dan doing it and I was under FIERCE pressure and there was no sign of him one of the days after me TELLING HIM I had visitors coming, and how was he to know otherwise? ANYWAY, there were floors to be put down, and there's **NO SIGN OF HIM,** and next thing I hear he's out in Eyeries working on your mother's place! So I hopped in the car, out to Eyeries, and landed on your mother's doorstep, and, sure enough, there's Dan, working away, happy out, and me with my CONCRETE FLOORS.'

SERIOUSLY, you'd think she was having a FLASHBACK to VIETNAM.

'BOOKSHELVES she was getting!' says Mrs Daly. 'As if SITTING AROUND READING A BOOK was more important than having a FLOOR UNDER YOUR FEET.'

And I'm like, 'NO – the ones in the living room? Dan didn't make those. I heard him telling Lola.'

'He DID OF COURSE make them,' says Mrs Daly. 'Didn't I see him MYSELF!'

And I'm thinking she was **BLIND WITH RAGE** so I'm NOT CONVINCED.

'And I remember at the time,' she says, 'it was off with that AWFUL "B" (short for B&&&&, rhymes with rich) and they'd been GOING OUT YEARS, so I was giving Dan a bit of leeway, thinking no matter what anyone ELSE thought of the woman, the man could have been in bits, and I didn't want to be putting him under any pressure. But anyway, there he was NOT A BOTHER ON HIM – in YOUR FRONT ROOM!'

But I'm still at 'AWFUL "B"', so I go, 'Who was the "AWFUL 'B'"?'

And she goes, 'THAT AWFUL NUALA ONE!'

And I'm like, 'NUALA O'SULLIVAN? But Dan's SO NICE. HOW was he going out with HER?'

'Because I TOLD YOU she knows how to say WHATEVER IT IS A PERSON WANTS TO HEAR to get WHATEVER IT IS SHE WANTS TO GET, which in YOUR CASE, was HER HANDS ON LOLO and MAX'S MONEY, and in DAN'S CASE, on a NICE PLOT OF LAND up by the school, with her view out over the harbour's mouth.'

And I'm like, 'HARBOUR'S MOUTH? You mean . . . looking across at the LIGHTHOUSE?'

And she's like, 'YES! And I know I was annoyed with him that day, but you couldn't meet a nicer fella than Dan the Man and—'

The more she's saying, the more I'm thinking, WHAT THE ACTUAL, and BE THE LIGHTHOUSE, and by the time I get back to Megser's I'm running in the door and Susan thinks I'm NUTS and I RUN TO MEGSER'S ROOM and BURST IN and I can barely breathe and she's like, 'WHAT?' Then she's sitting up. 'WHAT?'

'IS LIGHTHOUSE A RECURRING THEME IN *WILDFIRE* BY LAURIE BROWN?' I go.

And she's like, 'YES! WHY? WHAT ABOUT IT?'

And I'm like, 'Did Joshua live near one, and he knew Amandine loved them? And is there some "B" who wants to get her hands on it?'

'LITERALLY her name begins with "B",' says Megser, 'BEATRICE – Joshua Land's ex! But they broke up, and he fell in love with Amandine, and promised her that he would build her the most beautiful home, and together they would look out on a lighthouse for the rest of their lives. But Béatrice was INCANDESCENT WITH RAGE.'

And I'm like, 'IS FIRE A RECURRING THEME IN *WILDFIRE* BY LAURIE BROWN,' even though it's PRETTY OBVIOUS because: TITLE OF THE BOOK. But at THIS STAGE, I'm ALREADY walking over to *Fairy* Towers and Megser's following me and we TURN IT UPSIDE DOWN to look at where the Younger Feral did when he was asking, 'What's THIS CRACK?', which I now know was actually 'What's THIS CRAIC?' because, seared into the base, with the wood-burning pen, there were THREE LITTLE FLAMES.

And Megser GASPS: 'THAT'S WHAT JOSHUA LAND STITCHED INTO THE HEM OF THE INKY BLACK GOWN OF HIS BELOVED AMANDINE!'

And you KNOW what happened next, NJF, don't you? You know that Megser and I went straight over to my house. And ran to the bookshelves in the living room. And lay down right where my little two-year-old hand went the first time I walked in the door. And saw where someone once took a wood-burning tool and SIGNED HIS FINEST WORK.

Who's The Father?

UNSUSPECTED SUSPECT 1:

DAN O'SHEA

★ ★ ★ ★ ★

SERIOUSLY.

THE FIVE STARS . . .

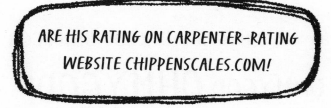

ARE HIS RATING ON CARPENTER-RATING
WEBSITE CHIPPENSCALES.COM!

MY DAD IS CARPENTER DAN!

★ SMILEY-EYED DAN!

★ CREATIVE DAN!

★ LOLA-RESCUING DAN!

★ PANCAKE-MAKING DAN!

★ FAIRY-TOWER-BUILDING DAN!

★ FERAL-PSYCHOLOGIST DAN!

★ SIX-MILLION-DOLLAR DAN!

**YOU LITERALLY COULD NOT MAKE HIM UP!
BECAUSE YOU WOULDN'T NEED TO!**

OHMYGOD OHMYGOD OHMYGOD OHMYGOD

OHMYGOD **OHMYGOD!**

I KNOW WHO MY DAD IS!

I HAVE A DAD! A REAL DAD!

AND HE'S ALIVE! AND WE *love* HIM! AND HE DOESN'T LIVE IN A TENT! OR ON THE ISLAND OF DISAPPOINTING FATHERS! UNLESS HE REJECTS ME AND ALL MY WORKS. BUT STIIILL.

And BECAUSE COLUMBO NEVER LEAVES YOU IN ANY DOUBT HERE'S ALL THE EVIDENCE some of which I missed:

TM stands for THE MAN! DAN THE MAN!

The FROWN! (My FROWN that's shaped like an M – IT'S FROM DAN! It's just you HARDLY EVER SEE IT! Dan also SAYS NO TO SADNESS!)

That night after Mom's mass when I met Dan on the pier, it wasn't the COLD that was making his eyes water – it was the ANNIVERSARY SADNESS.

And that SAME NIGHT ON THE PIER he said he'd wait for me 'OVER THERE', which means he KNEW where I was going even though I HADN'T SAID . . . because THAT'S WHERE HE USED TO GO WITH MOM and THAT'S HOW she had the INSIDE INFORMATION.

That day he took over making the pancakes, he told the Younger Feral he was giving him the FIRST ONE because he hurt his head. But being given the FIRST PANCAKE was his PUNISHMENT for LYING about HITTING HIS HEAD!

When Lola FELL and Dan brought her home and he was getting bandages and looking for sugar and making tea – I didn't realise at the time – he KNEW HIS WAY AROUND ALL THE KITCHEN CABINETS!

He's where I get my BROAD SHOULDERS FROM . . . and my FIERCE PHYSICAL STRENGTH.

12 December (SUNDAY)

SO . . . I INVITE Megser to JOIN ME when I tell Dan THE NEWS and she WRITES her response and hands it to me while giving me SAFE ENOUGH and **GOOD LUCK EYES.**

Dear Ellery, I'm sorry I am unable to attend your Pop-Up Birth Announcement, but I will CRY LIKE A BABY AND DAN in your honour. REGARDS, Megan O'Sullivan.

2 a.m. update

The books *How to Tell Someone They Are Your Father* and *How to Tell Someone You Are Their Daughter* were written by the well-known duo: NO ONE & NO ONE.

So it's up to me.

I have ONE LINE (UNUSABLE): 'Hey, Dan: Jesus' father was ALSO a surprised carpenter.'

13 December (MONDAY)

I decide to TEXT Dan. I do this before school so Megser can't talk me out of it. It takes me half an hour to come up with THIS:

Hi Dan! It's Ellery. I was wondering if I could call to your workshop tomorrow after school? I want to organise a surprise for Lola. **TOP SECRET!**

And I hit SEND. And now I'm TERRIFIED. And it takes him a whole hour to reply, and I've been thinking the whole time that he's there thinking, WHAT is this girl's OBSESSION with SURPRISE WOOD-BASED gifts?

FINALLY HE REPLIES: Not a bother. Wld 4.30 suit?

AND I REPLY: Not a bother.

Because it's not a bother. ***IT'S A TRAUMA.***

When I get to school, there are signs of another trauma . . . on Megser's FACE.

It turns out that she finished *Wildfire* this morning. WHO READS BOOKS IN THE MORNING? And she can barely speak. 'The END, Ellery. The END. You won't be ABLE.'

CHALLENGE ACCEPTED. So I immediately excuse myself to go to the 'bathroom' (quotes by Ellery) and instead go STRAIGHT to the library and to the multiple copies of *Wildfire*. And grab one. And . . .

OH. GODDD.

The END, NJF. The END. You won't be ABLE.

But stiiiill.

It's SIX YEARS after Amandine and Joshua break up.

Amandine stood on the beach at the end of the flagstone path, watching as Elodie danced in the sand towards the waves. Joshua stood in the doorway behind them, looking out at his first love, and his second. How bare his view would have been without them, how empty his house and heart. To think they might only have been echoes there, still, could steal the breath from him. He left the house and, barefoot, made his way silently towards Amandine who would always sense his approach, as he did hers, who would feel, as he did, the comfort in it. He came up behind her and wrapped his arms around her, pulling her close, kissing her head.

Amandine bent to plant kisses in the crook of his elbow, and he drew her closer still.

Across the water the tall white lighthouse gleamed in the sunlight.

'Do you remember promising me that lighthouse?' said Amandine. 'And then you were gone.'

'Let's not talk of our darkest time,' said Joshua. 'The nightfall that stole the light, and held it for six long months.'

Amandine shook her head. 'No,' she said. 'I know now.' She looked to where Elodie was running up the beach towards them. 'I held it,' said Amandine. 'I held the light inside me all that time.'

And I'm like, OHMYGOD . . . MOM . . . she WROTE HER HAPPY ENDING because she DIDN'T GET IT IN REAL LIFE.

Have you ever read anything SO SAD?

1 a.m. update

WORST-UPDATE-EVER ALERT

Oh, GODDD. Megser was RIGHT. I should never have gone NEAR Mom's notebooks.

Because it turns OUT I CAN'T TELL DAN. It turns out that Dan is **NEVER SUPPOSED TO KNOW ABOUT ME.**

READ THIS:

TM

She is your beautiful girl, and she is a joy. She has your frown and its similar rarity. I have taught her things I learned from you. We are a little island, me and Ellery B., on which I fly your flag. That's the best I can do.

I'm sorry for keeping her from you. You are the book with too many endings that I never would have written, that I never would have read. You feel so distant now, faded in ways I could never have imagined. Then in runs our little twist, and her light brightens me, and the picture I hold of you in my mind.

She asked me today where you live.

'In the woods,' I say. 'And in my heart,' I don't.

I know now that we were never fighting each other. We were fighting to the surface through waves that were drowning us . . . only to stand barefoot and bleeding on the rocks. You were afraid of love, and so was I. You couldn't trust love, and nor could I. But this little girl does. With all her heart. If you knew her like I know her, you would feel a love so powerful you might run from her, further than you did from me. And I know how fiercely she loves for one so small. And I could never let her know the pain of losing you. Or the hope of finding you again.

I have imagined too much of who we could be, and I have imagined too well.

This is my last letter.

Laurie xxxxx

OHMYGOD. What is WRONG with people? NO OFFENCE, Mom and Dad, **BUT YOU ARE WEIRDOS.** I am actually the WORK OF WEIRDOS.

What were you SO AFRAID OF?

And THIS from the woman who told ME NEVER TO MAKE A DECISION BASED ON FEAR?

Oh.

14 December (TUESDAY)

This is WORSE than not knowing who my dad is. This is KNOWING WHO HE IS, and SEEING HIM ON THE STREET or DRIVING BY or FIXING THINGS SOMEWHERE but NOT EVER BEING ABLE TO SAY ANYTHING!

I went for a walk. THAT'S how bad things were.

And I just kept walking, and I was crying, and I went down to the strand but there are two ways and I took the one I don't normally take, and I was walking by some of the houses, and I saw DAN'S VAN. And then I realised THAT'S where he lives unless he's still working at 9 p.m. . . . which he COULD be considering he works the morning after *ST PATRICK'S DAY*.

And it's the *cutest* HOUSE.

And THE DOORBELL HAS A LOVELY RING.

YES.

And I'm SO sorry, Mom. But you once told me: 'Moms don't ALWAYS get it right.'

SO MY IDEAL DAD:

★ *KIND*

★ *FUN*

★ *HAPPY*

★ *CREATIVE*

★ *GETS ME AND MEGSERS AND OUR WEIRDNESS*

★ *IS CHILL*

★ *TAKES CARE OF THINGS*

★ *LOVES PANCAKES*

★ *COOKS PANCAKES*

★ *ISN'T INTO RULES but has SOME KIND OF BOUNDARIES*

And when you look at it that way – a RECORD-BREAKING TEN-STAR WAY – I'm sorry, Mom, to throw THIS PARTICULAR ONE back in your face, but: WHERE'S THE NEG?

So I'm in Dan's kitchen, and I start by apologising for

not showing up at the workshop and then we talk about the Younger Feral and his PYROMANIA and Dan is so kind about him while also being funny and then I get sliiightly closer to the point with: 'You made the bookshelves in our living room, didn't you?'

And Dan has **WHERE'S-THIS-GOING EYES.**

So I say: 'Everyone calls them MAGNIFICENT,' because who WOULDN'T want to lay claim to magnificence?

'I did make them,' he says.

And the funny thing is I know that's not even why he actually admits it. He just admits it because it's the truth.

And I go: 'You were just teasing Lola that time – when she said some day you'd be good enough to make something like them and you asked her what wood they were made from!'

'Yes.' And the sheepish face.

And I'm like, 'I could HEAR what she was saying to you. And I was, like, **AAAAGH.**'

Dan just laughs and says, 'Yerra, she meant well.'

And I'm like, 'I know. We give her a hard time.'

And then we FALL INTO SILENCE. And obviously he's waiting for an explanation as to why I'm actually there. And I can't get JESUS and SURPRISED CARPENTERS out of my head.

And then OUT COMES THIS: 'Did you and my mom ever—' And I'm like, BACKTRACK, BACKTRACK, and then I'm like, FORWARD TRACK, FORWARD TRACK, because that was a weird question to leave hanging. 'Did you and my mom ever DATE?' I manage.

And Dan's looking at me and he's weighing it up and REALLY Dan knows that I KNOW the answer to that already or WHY WOULD I RANDOMLY BE ASKING ABOUT IT NOW?

'We did,' he says.

'And that was . . . 2004?' I ask him.

And he nods and says: 'It would have been, yes.'

And then there's this PAUSE and I shoot out this SINGLE LAUGH because he sounded like he was answering in a court of law and it was SO embarrassing because I'm too nervous to NOT LAUGH and then Dan JOINS IN because he's TOO NERVOUS PROBABLY ABOUT HAVING A YOUNG WOMAN IN HIS KITCHEN.

'And . . . what happened with you and Mom?' I say, like I'm just curious and not how I suddenly feel, which is PANIC-DESPERATE.

And Dan is **DEFINITELY UNCOMFORTABLE** but I'm not really knowing where I'm going at this stage, so I'm hoping he'll just answer the question.

But he has **BREACH-OF-PRIVACY EYES** and it's awful because I know the normal part of me would never put someone in this position but the ORPHAN PART OF ME is crying somewhere in the distance.

And Dan is now Silent Dan.

And the clock is SO LOUD.

And Dan is still not speaking.

And I'm like THIS CONVERSATION COULD END WITH NO RESOLUTION and the orphan baby is SOBBING and GRIPPING THE BARS OF HER CRIB and AFRAID that no one is going to come. No one is going to pick her up. And WHERE HAS THIS ORPHAN BABY COME FROM? Because she was quiet before. She was SLEEPING. But NOW . . . she's AWAKE. Because SOMEONE'S HERE NOW. SOMEONE COULD PICK HER UP.

And I'm ON MY FEET KNOCKING THE CHAIR OVER and the ORPHAN BABY is CRYING but it DOESN'T SOUND DISTANT ANY MORE and that's because *I'M* CRYING and Dan RUSHES OVER TO ME and I DON'T KNOW WHERE TO LOOK but he's concerned so he's FROWNING and I'm now getting MESMERISED by the M between his eyebrows, which I know from THE MIRROR.

'What is it?' says Dan. With so much kindness that if everyone spoke that way, it would **END WAR.**

And I'm SHAKING MY HEAD and doing that thing where you press your lips together to seal your mouth shut in case anything escapes. **LIKE:** SOBS, WORDS, BREATHS. Except you have to let breaths out, so I DO and these SOBS HITCH A RIDE! And SERIOUSLY, POOR DAN.

But he manages to sit me back down and for a moment I think I'll be able to control myself.

Until he delivers SOME MORE human-race-rescuing kindness: 'Do you want me to call someone? Do you want someone to . . . PICK YOU UP?'

SERIOUSLY. He said: PICK YOU UP.

And THAT was THE GENTLE PUSH THAT SENT ME AND THE ORPHAN BABY OVER THE EDGE.

And I'm like, 'No (SOB) . . . it's . . . (SOB) . . . (SOB) Okaaaaaaaaaaaaaaay (SOB).' SERIOUSLY.

And Dan goes, 'You can stay here a while, there's no rush or I can take you home myself, drive you back, or if you want to walk, I'll walk up with you.'

And now he's handing me this pristine old-fashioned handkerchief JUST LIKE GRANDPA. And STILL GIVING ME OPTIONS: 'Or will I get Megser for you? Would that be the best thing?'

And he looks a bit surprised that THAT'S the option I have the extreme negative reaction to (because of GOING ROGUE again) so he logically concludes that Megser and I have fallen out, but

I'm shaking my head and Dan goes off to find tissues. Instead finds ENTIRE TOILET ROLL. But stiiill. And there's NO SIGN of my tears stopping and then, because Dan has to be THE NICEST MAN IN THE WORLD APART FROM GRANDPA, he puts the kettle on and I'm thinking any other man would be running out the door shouting into the dark for female assistance or looking for ANY WAY to PASS THIS NIGHTMARE ALONG, but Dan is actively doing something that will make me his problem for EVEN LONGER.

But at least – because I'm distracted by TEA-MAKING – I've stopped crying. And I can't hear the orphan baby. And Dan comes over with two mugs of tea and a plate of biscuits.

And I manage to drink some tea and then I let out this MASSIVE BREATH and then I have this **REALISATION: 'I'M SUCH A WEIRDO.'**

And Dan laughs and says: 'You're your mother's daughter.'

And I'm thinking HE THOUGHT MY MOTHER WAS A WEIRDO!

Dan notices my face and goes: 'No – she used to say that too. "I'm SUCH A WEIRDO".'

'But I really AM one,' I say. 'I just show up at your house like I'm some DOOR-TO-DOOR MELTDOWN DELIVERY SERVICE and you're like YOU'VE GOT THE WRONG HOUSE. I HAVEN'T EVEN ORDERED ONE.'

'Not tonight,' says Dan. 'But I had three over the weekend.'

And I LAUGH OUT LOUD and he's DELIGHTED.

'I'm so sorry,' I say.

'Don't worry about it,' says Dan. 'You're better off. When I was growing up feelings were OUTLAWED in Ireland.'

And I laugh, and he goes: 'Have you seen *The Exorcist*? They'd bring THAT guy in.'

And I'm laughing and I go: 'That movie FURRREAKS ME OUT.'

'Try LIVING it.'

And I'm laughing so hard now and then I'm like: 'You DID order the **MIXED MELTDOWN SPECIAL** tonight, right?'

And Dan shakes his head: 'I thought it was the DON'T-KNOW-WHETHER-TO-LAUGH-OR-CRY SPECIAL.'

And this is what I said: 'ACTUALLY, if that IS what you ORDERED . . .'

And Dan's looking at me like, Whutttt? And the ORPHAN BABY'S just SITTING IN THE CRIB with her HANDS OVER HER FACE.

And I go: 'Well . . . it's just there is SOMETHING. I just. . . I have something to TELL YOU. And I don't know whether it'll make you LAUGH or CRY.'

And Dan goes: 'Okay . . .' But he's got the FEAR EYES. But I've got the **WAY MORE FEAR EYES,** so then he adds, 'Well, whatever it is, it won't be the end of the world.'

And I'm thinking DEFINE THE WORLD while FOREVER ALTERING HIS by announcing:

'I'm your daughter.'

Then in case that wasn't clear enough:

'You're my father.'

SERIOUSLY. THAT'S WHAT I SAID.

And I have **NEVER BEEN SO TERRIFIED IN MY ENTIRE LIFE.**

I'm just looking at Dan and he's looking at me, but at my FACE like he's trying to FIND HIMSELF IN IT. And it's all happening in ABSOLUTE SILENCE. And I'm thinking of Mom telling me: 'We don't always know the reason behind someone's silence.' BUT I DEFINITELY KNOW THE REASON BEHIND DAN'S SILENCE: HORROR. And that just SPIRALS into imagining me telling this story to people in nightclubs at 5 a.m. for the **REST OF MY LIFE.**

But NO! Because SOMETHING ELSE is UNFOLDING before me. There's this FLICKER OF SOMETHING and then the PROCESSING EYES and now I'm thinking that somewhere inside him maybe he had a FEELING. Because even though he didn't KNOW I was his daughter until I TOLD him, I wouldn't have called him a SURPRISED CARPENTER.

Now he's just looking at my face like he's EXPECTING to find himself in it. And during the NINETY LIFETIMES this was going on, I had all these QUESTIONS GATHERING like racehorses at gates but I can't OPEN the gates because WHO ASKED FOR THIS RACE?! And it's a CONFUSING analogy so here are the questions:

What would you have done if Mom had told you at the time?

Are you happy I'm your daughter?

Do you wish you'd never met my mom?

Do you wish you'd never met me?

And then I CRACK TOTALLY, and ask him ONE.

'Are you happy I'm your daughter?'

And I'm TOO ATTACHED TO THE OUTCOME.

And Dan looks at me like I've lost my mind. And says THIS: 'Who WOULDN'T BE HAPPY to have you as a daughter? Sure, look at you! I'm DELIGHTED. I'm . . . I'm . . . *FIERCE PROUD.*'

SERIOUSLY. He said all that.

He SMILES.

And my HEART is:
SKY LANTERNS.

15 December (WEDNESDAY)

Grandpa and Auntie Elaine arrived today! And Auntie Elaine does not look as bad as I was TERRIFIED she was going to. She's a little pale and a little skinny and a little sad. But she looked really happy to see US. EVEN to see Lola who gave her a HUGE HUG that lasted way longer than expected.

And I decided that NOW EVERYONE WAS HERE . . .

'Grandpa,' I say, 'have you got a strong heart?'

'I'd have to,' he said. 'How else could it hold all this *love* for my BEST GIRL?'

'And how about you, Lola?' I say.

'I've just had my annual physical exam, so yes,' says Lola without even looking up from the newspaper.

Then she pauses and looks up. 'Hold on – why are you asking us about our hearts?'

And I'm smiling, *BECAUSE I HAVE BIG NEWS*.

And Lola puts the newspaper down and looks like she's going to slide onto the floor. 'No more!' she says. 'No more! I'm DONE with news. Bring back the OLD.'

And I'm like, 'Well, this is SIXTEEN YEARS OLD . . . news. I have *FOUND OUT WHO MY FATHER IS.*'

Then I break it to them, and ALL THE REASONS WHY.

And Grandpa and Lola are STILL looking at me like, Whutttt?

And Auntie Elaine lowers her head and starts BANGING IT OFF THE TABLE!

And we're all like, Whuttttt?!

'Oh, thank GOD,' she says. '*THANK GOD, THANK GOD, THANK GOD, THANK GOD, THANK GOD.*' And she looks up and says, 'Your mom gave me this LETTER before she died and told me to give it to you when you turned eighteen. And she gave ME a letter too. But I COULDN'T DEAL so I just put them both in a drawer. Then I plucked up the courage to read MY letter one night . . .'

And I DEFINITELY KNOW that involved NTH GLASSES OF WINE.

'And,' says Auntie Elaine, 'because I didn't have my glasses on . . . I opened YOURS. And it was already in my hand and it was just . . . it took me a LONG TIME to realise it was yours and . . . you're RIGHT. Dan IS your father.'

And I'm like, 'Wait. Mom *WANTED ME TO KNOW?*'

'When you turned eighteen, yes,' says Auntie Elaine. 'And when I opened MY letter, there was one in there for Dan too.'

'And she wanted DAN to know?' I say. 'BUT . . . she wrote down that she DIDN'T!'

'Maybe at one point she didn't,' said Auntie Elaine. 'I don't know. But things change. Hearts change. And I'm so glad you are SO HAPPY, Ellery Bellery. I am so, so glad. I had all this information and I was TRAUMATISED because I knew Dan was living nearby again, which your mom didn't know at the time. And I knew he was working here and in Megan's, so you were around him. And I thought, "What if he goes away again? What if he's gone by the time Ellery is eighteen?" And I was like, I HAVE NO LAURIE TO RUN THIS BY.'

AND I REALISE: Mom was Auntie Elaine's Megser.

And Lola goes to Grandpa, 'Dan is the knight in shining armour I told you about – when I sprained my ankle.'

And Grandpa looks at me: 'Lola's Damsel in Distress game is FIERCE.'

I LOVE GRANDPA!

And he squeezes my hand and says. 'I heard ALL ABOUT Dan. And I have to say I was very impressed. He sounds like a VERY NICE MAN.'

'He is,' says Lola. 'He is.' And she's wiping away tears.

16 December (THURSDAY)

I woke up with this FRIGHT that Dan was just being polite because how ELSE is any decent human being going to reply to the question: 'Are you happy I'm your daughter?'

'"Not so much" is what Lola would say if I asked her,' said Auntie Elaine over breakfast. 'But of COURSE Dan is happy about you.' And I'm nodding, but when she's not there to monitor my musings, I'm like, OH GOD, DAN HATES MOM for keeping something like this from him. **BECAUSE:** HEARTBREAK. And HURT. And REOPENING WOUNDS. And then I'm like, **OHMYGOD:** LIVING REMINDER OF WOUNDS. That's ME.

And, SERIOUSLY, I arrive on Dan's doorstep AGAIN like I'm Mrs Daly. And I'm pretending I'm just calling to give him an UPDATE. Which I do – about me telling Grandpa, and Lola and Auntie Elaine, and how they're all looking forward to meeting him, but obviously Lola's already met him, and I tell him the Knight In Shining Armour thing, and then I ask him if he's going to tell his family, and when, and has he any last-minute Christmas shopping to do, and is the overnight bag by the door because he's leaving the country, and what's the smell in the oven, and all these RANDOM QUESTIONS that I'm not even giving him time to ANSWER because NONE of them is the REAL QUESTION I want to ask. But he KNOWS there's something and he ALLOWS SILENCE and I say: 'OK, I know you said you were happy that I'm your daughter . . .' and Dan goes: 'DELIGHTED. I said "delighted".'

And I'm smiling and saying thank you because that's so lovely, but then I add the next bit: 'Even though you *DON'T REALLY KNOW ME?'*

And he looks at me AGAIN like I've lost my mind and says: 'Your best friend is Megser, your favourite colours are orange, yellow, green and blue in that order, your favourite chocolate is Fruit 'N' Nut, your favourite food is burritos, your favourite TV show is *Terrors*, you're in *love* with some actor called Hunter Danger—'

'THREAT!' I say, as if that's the point.

'Threat! That's it,' he says. 'You hate mean people, you volunteer at the retirement home giving old people makeovers, you hate sport of all kinds, but you don't count horse riding, Lola drives you nuts, your Grandpa Max is your hero.'

I LITERALLY CANNOT SPEAK.

'But . . . ?' I say EVENTUALLY. 'Howwww . . . ?'

And he shrugged in a way that was asking me to THINK HOW.

'Are you like SHERLOCK HOLMES when you go into people's

417

houses?' I say. 'Like you see: stuck linen-closet door and you KNOW: THIS PERSON EATS BURRITOS.'

And he's LAUGHING.

'Don't make the same mistake your mom and I made, maybe,' he says.

STILL NO IDEA.

'JOHNNY,' he says. 'He never stops talking about you.'

11 p.m. update

SILENT JOHNNY NEVER STOPS TALKING ABOUT ME.

12 p.m. update

SILENT JOHNNY **NEVER STOPS** TALKING ABOUT ME.

1 a.m. update

SILENT!

2 a.m. update

TALKING!

3.30 a.m. update

NEVER STOPS!

17 December (FRIDAY)

Megser puts ZERO time limit on how long I get to talk about Silent Johnny. And I'm like, THANK YOU. And she goes: 'MERRY CHRISTMAS. That was your present.' Then, 'It's a ONE-OFF.'

Then, 'Did you think you got him in KRIS KRINGLE by ACCIDENT?'

And I'm just BLANK. **THEN:** 'SECRET SANTA.'

And Megser's rolling her eyes. 'I KNEW,' she said, 'you'd get him something CLASS and THEN the two of you might cop on. You always give **AMAZING** presents or you make something cool, and it's really PERSONAL and you make this HUGE EFFORT.' Pause. 'What DID you get him? Have you wrapped it?'

AND ALL I'M THINKING IS:

UH. OH.

18 December (SATURDAY)

Megser and I skipped over the SECRET SANTA FIASCO that followed and went straight to her bedroom to get ready for the Rollout Ambassador 'social event' that's on in the sports hall tonight that Megser and I – because we have **ZERO SHAME** — are attending.

We're in Megser's bedroom in the Feral Sanctuary and we're both vying for the full-length mirror. Me, because: LASHES and Megser because: PREPARING THE SURFACE FOR A NEW FOOTBALL STICKER.

And I'm looking at her with her window-cleaner spray and her cloth and her intense focus and disinterest in my lashes . . . and Megser is five feet nine, and a sports-star athletic size eight. And she's in her JEANS and JERSEY and NO MAKE-UP on her STUNNING FACE, and her TOTALLY NON-FASHION PONYTAIL and her GLASSES. And I'm five feet six and a half with my

AWESOME SHINY HAIR, and my **AWESOME EYEBROWS** and my AWESOME MAKE-UP, and my GLOWY SKIN somewhere underneath it, and my KILLER DRESS and HEELS, and—

'Stop looking at us!' says Megser. 'WHAT?'

And I'm like, 'NOTHING!'

And she goes: 'SAY WHATEVER IT IS!'

'I just had a realisation,' I say. 'So . . . you're a size eight. And I'm a size sixteen . . . so that's twice your size.'

Meg rolls her eyes. 'Yeah: NOT HOW IT WORKS.'

'I knowwww,' I say, 'but this is GOOD. I'm thinking I might be twice your size, buuuut your BRAIN is TWICE THE SIZE OF MINE. So we kind of cancel each other out.'

And Megser's nodding. 'And how does that fit in with you being ten times more TAPPED?'

'I don't know,' I say, 'but I HAVE just remembered Silent . . . I mean . . . just . . . Johnny—'

'Oh no,' says Megser. 'Are we calling him Johnny now? Or is it "Just Johnny"?'

'Yes! Johnny!' I say. 'And do you know what's WORSE? He came to my rescue that day when those second-years were calling me Transformer.'

'You never need to be rescued,' says Megser.

421

'Terrrue,' I say.

Then Megser shakes her head. 'Still, though . . . I'll miss the SILENT.'

'FINE then!' I say. 'Keep it. Make it a silent SILENT.'

And she applies her new sticker to the mirror, and she's side-eyeing my face.

'You weren't being mean about him, calling him Silent Johnny – just so you know,' she says. 'You were just being . . . descriptive.'

The Rollout 'social event' started with a trip down memory lane – the kind of memory lane that has been blocked off with crime-scene tape. 'How is your UNCLE JEFF?' Megser and I hear as we walk right into the Scout Leader. 'Myself and the wife were watching some auld episode of something – *VIKINGS* maybe – the other night, and there was a fella on it THE IMAGE OF HIM,' he says.

And Megser goes, 'Your wife's NAME or at least "MY WIFE" – not "THE".' And we're gone by the time he processes that.

- **NON-SADNESS:** Johnny was there.
- **SADNESS:** he looked SO BEYOND HURT AND EMBARRASSED when he saw me that I had to look away.
- **EPIC SADNESS:** what if he never forgives me?

19 December (SUNDAY)

Why does wrapping paper always run out when you have ONE PRESENT left to wrap? And it's for DAN. It's not like a BEST DAD IN THE WORLD mug or anything CREEPY. But I wanted to give him SOMETHING. And then I remember I kept the tissue paper that came with my Elie Saab (OHMYGOD! I HAVE AN ELIE SAAB!) and because there was ZILLIONS of it, I can use some of that. So I go to my DRAWER OF JOY, which is also obviously home of the photo of me and Mom that Johnny got me, and OBVIOUSLY I take it out when I see it, because I'm thinking maybe THIS TIME I won't be afraid to actually display it in my room. I love it SO MUCH. And next thing I see this piece of paper stuck to the end of it, and it looks like those really thin handwritten receipts, but there's too much writing on it and I pull it out and it's a NOTE. From JOHNNY. HOW did I not SEE THIS BEFORE? But then there was a bit of glue on the top of it that must have stuck it to the inside of the envelope.

And I would GLUE THIS ENTIRE NOTE INTO HERE IF I COULD, but I WON'T. Because I want to PRESERVE IT EXACTLY AS IT IS. Because **I THINK I MIGHT WANT TO LOOK AT IT FOR EVER.**

Here's what I remember about your mam: it was in the summer I was seven in the shop trying to get a Twister out of the freezer but I couldn't open it because there was a pile of Sunday papers on top and the place was packed because it was right after mass and the lady behind the counter was asking me what it was I wanted and everyone was looking at me and because of the stammer (I used have a stammer) I said 'T-T-T . . .' for so long my legs started shaking like mad and there were lads laughing and I was looking around, panicking, and I'll never forget how this lovely American lady took this giant stack of papers off the freezer out of the way and then crouched down in front of me with the nicest smile and the kindest eyes, and she must have checked the whole fridge in two seconds because she knew the ice pop I wanted beginning with T and she wouldn't let me drop eye contact with her because she knew I was so terrified, and she says out loud, 'Little man, you and me have impeccable taste in ice pops but I'm going to need those muscles of yours to get this freezer open,' and I slid back the lid but probably she was the one doing it, then she took four Twisters out, I think just in case I might have wanted more than one and she didn't want to have to make me say anything the state I was in, and then she took my hand and she went up and paid and then she took me out to my dad outside and he was feeling awful because he'd seen the whole thing and he was the one sent me in on my own on purpose to be brave and she said to me, 'So what's your name, little man?' and I said Johnny not a bother and she said I've got *a little girl about your age and she's back home in New York and we're missing each other very much and I'm going to tell her tonight about the big strong boy I met today and how we should try our best to be brave just like him.*

Anyway I thought that was class.

PS *Dad said that for ages I thought if I couldn't reach an ice pop in the freezer it was because it was INPICKIBLE!*

I'm IN BITS at this stage and SERIOUSLY how are there any more tears left in my body?

I'm just so proud of my mom and I'm so proud of Johnny and how he was EXACTLY AS BRAVE as his dad hoped he would be and how Mom saw it when he was seven years old because he stayed in the store and he didn't run away and I know that look Mom had when her eyes were on yours and she was willing you, willing you, willing you on and you couldn't tear yourself away and you wouldn't want to anyway because it was like this **SUPERHERO THING** where Mom's eyes were the source of all your strength and there's something about knowing Silent

Johnny got to feel it too that's just making me . . . I don't even KNOW what this is about but seriously I'm like: is there some guy up there in a control room who's in charge of people's emotions and he's in jeans and a T-shirt and he's got this mixing desk like in a recording studio and he's just RANDOMLY sliding the dials up and down and sometimes he's lying back in his chair with his eyes closed and he's got his BARE FEET on the dials and he's using his TOES to just WHATEVER and right now, he's slid the COMFORT one, the JOY one, the LOVE one, the HOPE one, and the SADNESS one ALL UP TO THE MAXIMUM.

And I just need him to drag the SADNESS one down, even a little bit. Even with his little toe. Because I know it won't go down the whole way. And now I'm thinking it will NEVER go down the whole way again so instead I think about Johnny and how he goes and fixes a photo and picks out a frame, and sits down and hand writes a non-plagiarised letter (that was really one big long lovely sentence) for ME . . . the girl who called him Silent Johnny behind his back. Not in a mean way, but still.

He was Johnny because he was too afraid to speak. Because speaking hurt him when he was small.

And then I'm like, **DEFINITELY** the guy in the control room's boss has just walked in and given him a fright and his foot has spasmed and he's kicked the BUTTON of HEARTBREAKING REALISATION. **AND IT FIRES OFF THIS:** TWISTER. Mom's HORSE. Mom's BRAVE BOY. That's where she got his name. Oh, GODDDDDDD.

24 December (FRIDAY)

✳ CHRISTMAS EVE ✳

We are ALL in Megser's for Christmas Eve dinner – me and Lola and Grandpa and Auntie Elaine, and Susan and Megsers and the Ferals and Mrs Daly. No one outside the family is allowed to know the news about Dan until he tells his own family and probably really because Lola wants to have some kind of certificate from a lab before GOING PUBLIC as she keeps calling it.

So it was understandably awkward on multiple levels for many people when Dan and Johnny showed up, filling the entire doorframe that they installed themselves.

And I'm thinking, why didn't Susan tell anyone they were coming until I see Auntie Elaine mouth 'Thank you' to Dan. So SHE knew. And then she squeezes Susan's arm and mouths

'Thank you' to her. And Auntie Elaine needs to try mumbling her mouthing if she wants no one to understand what's going on.

And I could see Lola whispering to Grandpa, and Grandpa rising from his seat and Dan's got his arm out to shake Grandpa's hand.

AND MY HEART IS:

AS FEATURED ON MONITOR IN TV HOSPITAL DRAMA EMERGENCY SCENE.

Until they SHAKE HANDS but ALSO Grandpa pulls Dan in and gives him that slap on the back that he does for awesome people.

AND MY HEART IS: CHARGED BY PADDLES.

Until it's FLATLINING when Johnny and I look at each other.

And then I have to go to the bathroom, and Megser has to follow me, and she goes: 'WHAT is going ON with you?'

And I'm like, 'NOTHING!'

And she goes, 'Okay . . . you're going to have to tell me. WHAT was the story with Kris Kringle ?'

And I'm like, 'OHMYGOD SECRET SANTA! What is WRONG with you?'

'But . . . his FACE,' Megser is saying.

And I'm all, 'SHUT UP! SHUT UP! CRINGE!'

But she WON'T LET IT GO. 'I know you don't want to talk about it. But . . . you have to tell me. How could you just FORGET?'

And I want to CRY because I did NOT forget. It was the TOTAL opposite. I thought about it SO much I think it fried my brain. And Megser is STILL LOOKING AT ME (OBVIOUSLY). And she goes: 'I mean, he was the ONLY person in the class with NO PRESENT.'

And one of the lads slagged him and everyone started LAUGHING which is a memory I DO NOT want.

And now I'm imagining him AGED SEVEN IN THE SHOP WITH HIS INPICKIBLE BRAVERY while lads are laughing at him. And his INPICKIBLE BRAVERY when he was talking to himself outside my house, MAKING himself walk up my path to give me the most THOUGHTFUL GIFT EVER. Which included the most BEAUTIFUL NOTE EVER (that I have not even THANKED HIM FOR!)

And me with **ZERO BRAVERY** — not giving him his ACTUAL present. JUST IN CASE the whole class might know how much EFFORT went into it. Or EXACTLY HOW NUTS I am. But stiiill.

And Megser's like, 'Just give it to him tonight! What's the big deal? Where is it? Someone will drop you out for it.'

And I'm like, 'No.' And, 'I can't.' And, 'IT'S NOT AS SIMPLE AS THAT.'

And Megser looks at her watch and goes: 'SORRY. I'm giving you TWO HOURS to make the NICE LIST.'

☆ 8 p.m. update ☆

Megser took on the role of filler of awkward silences over dinner. Some fillings were more random than others. This one was while she was piling Brussel sprouts onto her plate: 'You are SO LUCKY, Mam. Having a teenager who actively seeks vegetables.' And Susan laughs out loud and goes: 'Yeah . . . because her mother snuck them into her food for her ENTIRE CHILDHOOD.' And Megser is like, Whutttt?!! And Susan tells us all about liquidising vegetables at night and slipping them into pretty much everything Megser and the Ferals ate. And Megser is horrified by the **BETRAYAL OF IT ALL.**

And I'm laughing at Susan's air of triumph and Megser turns to ME and says: 'I don't know what YOU'RE laughing at.' And I'm like, Whutttt? And she DOES AN IMPRESSION OF ME! 'Oh, I'm Ellery, and I have no interest in reading or writing.' Then she says: 'And have you had any trouble writing in that diary?'

And I'm like: 'No . . . what's that got to do with anything?'

And she goes: 'Yeah . . . because YOUR mother snuck words

into your vocabulary for your ENTIRE CHILDHOOD.'

AND I WAS LIKE: OHMYGOD. The DUPLICITY.

10 p.m. update

OK FINE THEN! THE NICE LIST! Because EVEN WORSE than being BLANKED by Johnny, he is NO LONGER BLANKING ME. Because THAT'S HOW NICE HE IS.

So the whole Secret Santa thing – I didn't FORGET to buy him a present. I MADE HIM a present. That involved S. Dodge.

And you're like, OH NO – she sheared/has shorn his beloved pet lamb and knitted him a sweater from the wool. And probably embroidered her name on the back. This is some Silence-Of-The-Lambs &&&&. And it IS. In its own way.

But it is NOT a sweater.

It's a PERFORMANCE PIECE.

I knowww. You're like BRING BACK THE BALD LAMB IDEA.

Which is WHY – before I do a THING – I need to ASSESS THE **WISDOM OF THIS WHOLE ENTERPRISE** by using the part of my brain that deals with WISDOM: Megser. We do this in the Walk-in Wardrobe where I'm hoping we can channel the erstwhile energy of Without Incidence.

I explain to Megser that the performance piece is in honour of Johnny saving S. Dodge's life.

'You couldn't have just got him a box of HEROES,' says Megser.

And I'm ignoring that by explaining that the PROBLEM on Secret Santa day that caused the **LAST-MINUTE ABANDONMENT** of it, was that one of the lines refers to Johnny as a HANDSOME SILENT FARMER . . . which was FINE because no reasonable person could DENY that. BUT in between WRITING that and PERFORMING IT IN PUBLIC, I discovered he LIKED me and realised I like HIM, so it took on a CREEPY quality. And I didn't think I could pull it off without blushing in front of the whole class.

'The WHOLE THING sounds TAPPED,' says Megser. 'But GO FOR IT.'

And I'm like, Whutttt?

'And why were you defining someone by their LOOKS?' says Megser. 'AND their silence? Instead of their SKILLS.'

And I'm like I knowww. But also: 'WHAT ELSE HAS THE SAME NUMBER OF SYLLABLES as HANDSOME SILENT FARMER?'

And then I CRACK IT.

Which makes me decide to GO FOR IT. So I enlist Megser to help me rearrange the sofas so that everyone can see . . . ME . . .

which is the first of my regrets. The REST is the rest of my regrets.

I explain that due to a technical error on Friday (I was technically a chicken), Johnny did not receive his Secret Santa gift.

'So, Johnny,' I say while **LOOKING HIM IN THE EYE,** 'I am so sorry about that. But tonight I hope we can put all that behind us.'

And then I explain that his gift is not IN a wrapper. It IS a rapper. ELLERY A.M. Performing her latest/only rap: STAY GAMBOLLING, feat. S. Dodge and Twister (inspired by S. Dodge and Johnny).

The Ferals LEAVE THE ROOM.

NOTE: Obviously I delivered this rap in my one hundred per cent American accent, dressed in my normal clothes. Like, I'm not wearing a BASEBALL CAP BACKWARDS or loads of GOLD JOORY.

The Ferals return to the room. Wearing BASEBALL CAPS BACKWARDS and loads of GOLD JOORY (Susan's), and they're all CAN WE RAP? CAN WE DO SOME? So I take them into the hall and I give them the Feat. bits.

And I can hear Mrs Daly saying, 'ANYTHING to keep them quiet.'

And Megser saying, 'It's literally the EXACT OPPOSITE of keeping them quiet.'

I stick my head into the room and Johnny is TOTALLY looking

like how I pictured him AGED SEVEN before Mom rescued him from a humiliating ordeal.

And in Too Late Now News ...

I knowwww ... I'm stalling. Okay. This is IT.

Or I could do a SKIP THIS IF ...

But NO! It took AGES.

Have a bit of RESPECT. As Mrs Daly would say.

STAY GAMBOLLING
BY ELLERY A.M.

(feat. S. Dodge as played by the Younger Feral
and Twister as played by the Elder Feral)

ELLERY A.M.

I'm the daughter of an author

You're a lamb who dodged the slaughter

Living inside in the shed

When you really should be dead

He's your knight in shining armour

He's a * FOOTBALL-PLAYING * farmer!

Saw you trembling, held you tightly

Fed you daily, fed you nightly.

(FEAT. S.DODGE)

It was a woolly situation

An adjacent emigration

My mama's not around?

She in the next field down.

I couldn't stop her from travelling

Leaving blessings unravelling

My mama knows I can't save her

Knitting patterns of behaviour

Serving up agricultural drama

Saying she bald from the trauma

You ask her 'Got any wool?'

She'll give you three bags full.

ELLERY A.M.

Johnny keeping you for keeps

He's yo personal Bo-Peep

But respecting his profession

Never making a confession

'Oh, I lost my sheep but Imma leave 'em alone

Now lemme pick up my cheque, I'll make my own way home.'

(FEAT. S.DODGE)

Everywhere S. Dodge goes

S. Dodge be stealing the show

My tail be wagging behind me

My past won't ever define me

I won't let life defeat me

Let meat-eaters mistreat me

Or roast me so they can eat me

Use microwaves to reheat me

No, I won't mince my words
And you won't mince my body
I won't be mixing with herbs
When I come up to yo party
I'm the gambolling lamb
And I'll be mixing the grooves
And I'll be hitting the floor
With my dancing hooves.

(FEAT. TWISTER)

I got my watchful eye
And I never blink
I serve my little lamb
But not the way you think
I'm her close protection
Her slaughter firewall
Her life after rejection
The catcher when she fall
So any lambs in da house
You think you can touch her?
Know every speed dial I got
is set to call the butcher.

(FEAT. S.DODGE)

This LAMB's NOT done.

MIC. CHOP.

Anyone find my copy of *Gauging Audience Reaction for Dummies*?

All I know is that there was zero hurt in Johnny's eyes at the end.

Especially when Dan said to me: 'That must have taken you AGES!' and Lola said: 'WEEKS.'

11.30 p.m. update

Lola and Grandpa and Auntie Elaine were leaving, and I was supposed to go with them, but I wanted to stay with Megser, so Dan said he'd drop me home instead, so they took Johnny to save his dad the trip to town.

And I was SO glad to get an extra hour with Megser. And also: or WAS I?

Because: just when you think that nothing could possibly top a rap about a lamb . . .

On the **STROKE OF MIDNIGHT . . .**

MISTLETOEMYGOD!

I honestly can't really explain how this all happened. But it involves me and Megser accidentally being out of sight in the gap between the TV unit and the wall in the living room because: playing with GLOW-IN-THE-DARK ARROWS.

NEXT THING: Susan comes in to get some more Prosecco from the refrigerator.

AND NEXT THING: Dan comes in asking if he could grab another water, and thanking her for inviting him, and Susan's saying NOT A BOTHER IT WAS A PLEASURE AND SHE'S DELIGHTED HOW EVERYTHING WORKED OUT AND SHE CAN'T THANK HIM ENOUGH FOR THE GREAT JOB HE DID ON THE HOUSE.

And Dan's like IT WAS AN ABSOLUTE PLEASURE. IT WAS SOME CRAIC WITH THE LADS AND—

NEXT THING: it goes REALLY QUIET.

For a WHILE.

And Megser and I are looking at each other like, Whutttt?

AND NEXT THING: we LOOK.

And Susan and Dan are standing in front of each other **UNDER THE MISTLETOE.**

And I can FEEL that Megser is doing this thing she does: where she's like a JACK-IN-THE-BOX about to BLOW, and I'm like,

439

WE NEED TO KEEP THE LID ON THIS THING but also I don't want to be NEAR the thing because of the THREAT TO HUMAN LIFE. Like I genuinely think if I touch her the IMPACT would be like an AIRBAG going off.

Meanwhile, Susan and Dan are just sort of HOVERING there like aircraft waiting for permission to land.

And then I glance at Megser and her eyes are like KEEP CIRCLING UNTIL YOU RUN OUT OF FUEL.

Susan and Dan DO NOT keep circling until they run out of fuel. They HAVE FUEL.

And I can see Megser out of the corner of my eye and her hand is CLAMPED over her mouth and her eyes are *TERRIFYING ME.*

And seriously, I thought that one of the perks of being older was **NO MORE AWKWARD KISSES.** I was COMPLETELY RELYING on that.

So after Susan and Dan SPRING APART and stumble separately out of the room, me and Mesger could come out of hiding.

Megser, wasting not a SINGLE SECOND, turns to me and says: 'If HE THINKS he can just WALTZ in here like that, and sweep Mam off her feet, he is sorely mistaken.'

'CLEARLY,' I say, 'your mam was HAPPILY MISTLETAKEN.'

Meg is ALARMED. 'He just COMES IN to OUR HOUSE and

takes advantage of Mam's HOSPITALITY [he ate, like, three olives he was so nervous], and that's NOT ON, and—'

'Heyyyyy!' I say. 'That's my DAD you're talking about.'

And then we look at each other, and we scream: 'OH. MY. GOD! OH. MY GOD! OH. MY. GOD!'

And then Susan walks back in and I'm thinking OH. MY. GOD – you'll be MY STEPMOM! I LOVE YOU! OH. MY. GOD!

Then the Ferals come bouncing in topless – WHO GOES AROUND TOPLESS AT CHRISTMAS? – and I'm thinking NOOOO!

Then Mrs Daly walks in and I'm like, REEEALLY?

Then I look at Meg, and I'm back to *OHMYGOD! OHMYGOD! OHMYGOD! OHMYGOD!*

And then Dan walks in all SHEEPISH. 'Well, goodnight, so, girls . . . and boys.' And then he nods at me like I'm a completely different species and then he remembers that he's DRIVING ME HOME but I know he's so flustered that that's okay and I nod at him as if we're not actually in some **ALTERNATE UNIVERSE** because this is SERIOUSLY the picture of what's going on around us: two topless Ferals wearing antlers and taking turns to put each other in a headlock; Mrs Daly holding the MAIN CUSTARD BOWL that was definitely actively licked clean, saying: 'Is there any more of that custard?'; Susan who can't bear to get eye contact with ANY OF HER CHILDREN because she has BETRAYED THEM ALL; Megs, the freaky JACK-IN-THE-BOX; Dan, the PREDATOR; and ME, up on the stoppers of my roller-skates, but then having to bend down to pick up the plastic elf ear that just fell off randomly. I stand back up and then, just when I think we had reached MAXIMUM DISCOMFORT, I see Meg standing there, NOW CLUTCHING A FRAMED PHOTO OF HER FATHER AND MOTHER, facing out towards Dan like it's a crucifix.

LUCKILY the recessed kitchen lighting is hitting the glass at a weird angle, kind of bleaching her father out in an angelic way. If you were religiously inclined, you might think that it was a SIGN from her father: like Dan is a good man, I'll always be here, but I'm going to leave space. **WEIRDLY** I think Susan felt the same way. She was just staring at the photo. And I could see her eyes. At the same time I managed to grab Meg's elbow, even though RIGOR MORTIS HAD SET IN. But I needed to pull her to her senses, if I could manage to locate them. LUCKILY Dan missed ALL OF THIS because there's a Feral on his back, so he's distracted.

I PRISE the photo out of Meg's grip, and, staying on that subject, HISS AT HER to GET A GRIP. Then I politely excuse us both, and we go out into the back hallway.

'What is WRONG with you?' I say. 'Your POOR MOM. What do

you expect her to do for the rest of her life? Be on her own? My mom had no boyfriend or no husband when she died—'

'Because she was CLEVER!' says Megser.

And I'm laughing but I'm also, 'But she might have liked to have someone who loved her, and who/whom she loved right back, and who/whom looked on me as the **AMAZING BONUS** I would clearly be to the whole thing. SURE: my mom had me and Lola and Grandpa and Auntie Elaine and guest, but maybe she would have LIKED someone else.'

And Megser has **TOTALLY DOUBT IT EYES.**

'BUT imagine if I said to you in a few years: "But, Meg! Why would YOU need a boyfriend? You're FINE – you have your mom, and your brothers – why would you need anyone else?"

We glance in the window at the Ferals. One of them is smelling his own armpit. And the other one is smelling the armpit that the other one isn't smelling.

Meg **LOCKS EYES** with me. Then goes: 'I won't EVER NEED A BOYFRIEND. No one should NEED ANYONE to make them happy.'

TERRRUE but I don't like it. 'I need YOU,' I say.

'Not to be HAPPY,' she says.

And I can't agree because I've only ever been MISERABLE

without Megser, but I know she doesn't want to hear that so instead, I address a concern I think she MIGHT have.

'*Have you learned* ANYTHING *about love?*'

I say. 'Do you GET that it's like AIR? That it doesn't run out? That you can love, and love, and keep loving, and add more things and people to love, and—'

She's just **DEAD IN THE EYE** now.

'Okay,' I say. 'Have you ever loved anyone—'

'No!' she says.

'Okay – shut up. Me neither,' I say. 'But just ... okay ... when you got your first *fairy* door ... what colour was it?'

'Red.'

'Okay ... and then you got the pink one.'

'Yes.'

'And then the green one.'

She's just smiling at me now. 'I can't believe you remember the order I got my *fairy* doors in.'

'*That's because I love you!*'

Then we look at each other. 'HOW DID WE NOT REALISE UNTIL JUST NOW THAT WE *LOVE* EACH OTHER?' I say.

'I don't know, but get to the point.'

'What I'm saying is: do you love your red fairy door any less than the green one?'

'No.'

'Is it – POSSIBLY – even more special than the green one because you had it first?'

'Maybe . . .'

'HAVE YOU RUN OUT OF LOVE FOR ANY OF YOUR TWENTY-SIX FAIRY DOORS?'

'What? No way!' she says.

'Exactly,' I say. 'NOW do you get it?'

She just SHRUGS! And I'm thinking I'm ON FIRE!

'Okay!' I say. 'Tell me – use your words – what do you think is going to happen if your mom falls in love with a man?'

OHMYGOD LOVE! STOP! she says.

'Hold on!' I say – 'YOU'RE the one who told me to write about my feelings, but I'm not allowed to ask about yours?'

'I didn't ASK you about your feelings,' says Meg. 'I sent you away OUT OF MY FACE to write them down.'

'GIRLS! Are you fighting?' shouts Susan.

'We don't fight!' we shout back.

And Susan's nice enough not to point out that VERY RECENTLY that became a lie.

'Well, do you write YOUR feelings down, then?' I say.

'I DO actually,' she says.

And I'm looking at her: 'HOW have we never spoken about YOUR diary?'

'Because . . . yours is more important.'

'Whyyy?'

'Because your mom DIED!'

And I don't want to mention her DAD so I just say, 'But your mom's ALIVE. And shouldn't she MAKE IT HER BUSINESS TO MAKE HER LIFE COMPLETE?'

'That's a weird sentence, first of all,' says Megser. And then: 'And her life IS complete.'

'How do YOU know? Do you think the world revolves around you guys?'

'Maybe . . .' says Meg.

We glance through the window again, and the Elder Feral is literally pouring a GIANT BAG OF SKITTLES into the open mouth of the Younger Feral until Dan notices, and grabs him and turns him upside down and shakes him. And the Skittles are all over

446

the floor, and Susan is ROARING at Mrs Daly NOT TO MOVE or she'll BREAK HER NECK.

I turn to Meg. 'I think it's time for you to accept, Megsers, that even though YOU'RE perfectly happy NEVER TO HAVE A ROMANTIC LIFE, maybe it's something your mom might like. Or . . . need.' DESPERATELY.

And poor Meg goes: 'But . . . what if . . . she . . . has more kids?'

'THEN,' I say, 'you might actually get some DECENT SIBLINGS.'

It was **THE RISKIEST THING I'VE EVER SAID TO MEG IN MY WHOLE LIFE.**

But it made her laugh.

🌲 25 December (SATURDAY) 🌲

I called in to Dan on Christmas Day to give him his present that was only small and I wasn't even expecting one back because SURPRISE DAUGHTER and also YOUNG WOMAN, but OHMYGOD.

He goes, 'Right! Walk!' and I'm thinking WORST PRESENT EVER but then we do walk . . . down to the pier, and it's obvious we're going to the inside information spot, and he guides me ahead of him. And there's this BENCH overlooking the sea. And Dan MADE

IT. And it's got a panel on the back with THREE LITTLE FLAMES carved into it. And he points to them and goes, 'One for your mom, one for you, and . . . one for me. If that's okay.' And I'm like OHMYGOD OF COURSE IT'S OK. And we have this HUG. And we're both crying, and I'm sitting on the bench thinking I can't BELIEVE that THIS is what I get, and I give him the secondhand book: **HOW NOT TO SCREW UP YOUR CHILDREN.**

28 December (TUESDAY)

Lola and Grandpa have invited Dan and the (right) O'Sullivans over for drinks, and Dan gets here first, so we're in the living room and it's just the two of us, and I go: 'Did you . . . love my mom?'

And he looks at me and I can see he's probably thinking do I have to answer these kinds of personal questions now that I'm a dad? And PROBABLY then BACKTRACK, BACKTRACK on being a dad.

But he smiles and says: 'I could write a book about it.'

And THAT'S ENOUGH FOR ME. Because: HIS EYES.

And then he starts saying something else. And he STOPS. But I'm thinking JUST SAY IT, ASK IT, because I think I know what it is.

'Did your mom . . . ever . . . fall in *love* again?' he says.

And at least he says AGAIN because that means he knows she was in love with him.

And I go: 'I've found NO EVIDENCE of that.'

And he laughs.

'I've only found evidence of FRACTIOUS relationships,' I say. And then I go: 'Do you know ANOTHER THING that made you so special to Mom? Like apart from the ME element? You did something that NO OTHER MAN ever did for her.'

And he looks at me with the **BRIGHT EYES.**

And I point to the shelves. 'You SUPPORTED HER WORK.'

And he LAUGHS. 'I suppose I did,' he said.

And then he's looking at them nodding and then we both have tears in our eyes. Because I think we're both thinking SIXTEEN YEARS. SIXTEEN YEARS of COULD-HAVE-BEEN-TOGETHER-but-WEREN'T.

'I'm so sorry Mom didn't tell you about me,' I said. 'And that she didn't tell me about you. But I don't think we should take it personally.'

And Dan laughs out loud and I only laugh because he does. And then I'm **EMBARRASSED.**

'Just . . . I meant . . . it wasn't in ANY MEAN WAY,' I say. 'She

449

really thought she was doing the right thing.'

And he looks SO SAD.

'I think authors think they know how everything is going to turn out in real life,' I say. 'Because the rest of the time . . . they get to DECIDE.'

29 December (WEDNESDAY)

I honestly think Mom has spent the first year of her heavenly life moving us all around in these PUFFS OF SMOKE. Like: Lola is thrown together with Dan because of a linen closet, then thrown into a ditch so she's thrown together with him again so she gets to realise what a GOOD GUY he is. Johnny is thrown together with a REJECTED LAMB so that when I'm thrown together with him inside in the shed I can see HOW ADORABLE he is. Then I'm thrown together with Leon Adler, and Jay Evans, and Jean-Luc Catastroph(e), and Quentin Schaeffer (okay . . . whyyy?) And Susan is thrown together with Dan. The Ferals **THROW THEMSELVES TOGETHER REPEATEDLY,** so I don't think Mom had anything to do with that. But stiiill.

30 December (THURSDAY)

And THEN because it's the end of the year and they were probably reminded I was the weirdest part of theirs, I'm getting all these messages! So UPDATES! On:

● LEON ADLER

Leon Adler won that French literary prize! He is now writing his first thriller: *Gone Girl II: Skates of Fury*. Okay, no he's not. But what he IS doing is tweeting way less about anxiety because he realised it was keeping his focus off . . . guess WHAT?

JOY!

And I decided to look up:

● QUENTIN SCHAEFFER

Quentin Schaeffer was STRANGLED IN HIS SLEEP in a fit of JEALOUS RAGE by Valentina from Venezuela.

Kidding.

He's at an UNKNOWN LOCATION being treated for 'EXHAUSTION' (quotes by everyone).

VALENTINA from VENEZUELA

Is pregnant. SERIOUSLY.

ID DEAN

Texted me a hand-drawn sign for the nail bar he plans to open in Bantry some time in the new year. It's called: CRIMINAILS (!) with a line underneath: Meeting *ALL* Your Fake Needs.

NEPOTERN WILL

Nepotern Will has not yet shaken the title of NEPOTERN and it's kind of my fault. Because, after the book awards, I told Lola about her and she had a word with a theatre contact in London, and now Will is happily spending her days in high-end utilitarian-chic jumpsuits, surprising everyone around her by painting INCREDIBLE scenery as part of her unpaid internship at St Martin's Theatre. ('Who's looking for coins down the back of the sofa now?' Nep Will! xoxo)

JAY EVANS

SADNESS: a JAYSTALKER broke into one of Jay Evans' coastal homes (sub-sadness: the one I had mentally selected as the location for my twenty-first birthday party) but luckily he wasn't in the building at the time, because, apparently, when the police raided the Jaystalker's home they discovered a 'DISTURBING GALLERY' of images of Jay Evans and his coastal homes, along with detailed accounts of all his upcoming public engagements. **NON-SADNESS:** NO ONE raided Megser's house where they would have found WAY MORE.

JEAN-LUC CATASTROPH(E)

SENT ME A CHRISTMAS CARD!!! It turns out that he was a HUGE FAN of my mom's! He said borderline nothing on the night of the book awards (clearly because he was cent pour cent convinced I was a pathological liar) but since then, he must have got his hands on EVERYTHING ANYONE COULD POSSIBLY NEED to confirm someone's identity and anyway, I emailed him to say thank you for the card and he asked if we could talk, and we did, and he told me all kinds of cool stories about Mom and . . .

SERIOUSLY. I made friends with **CATASTROPH(E).**

31 December (FRIDAY)

NEW YEAR'S EVE

Every year there are fireworks on the bridge in Eyeries. When I was about nine Mom told me that her first New Year here she didn't go – she just watched from her window. She was all alone and I thought that was SO SAD. And she said, 'But I didn't really know anyone here yet.'

And I couldn't understand how you would just GO SOMEWHERE you had NO FRIENDS and I said, 'You must have been REALLY LONELY.'

And she said: 'I am never lonely. Because, wherever I go, I always have words. Words will always be my friends.'

And I looked at her, and said, 'You are SUCH A WEIRDO.'

And now here I am: her BELOVED – OBVIOUSLY – WEIRDO DAUGHTER standing on the same bridge. But I am NOT ALONE. I'm with Grandpa and Lola and Auntie Elaine, and MY DAD! Who I am calling DAN to his face but probably my DAD sometimes to you only, NFJ. And then Megser and Susan arrive and Johnny shows up with his family and sometimes The Ferals behave PERFECTLY because when they started a child brawl, it gave two people the chance to go for a terrifying walk marked by long silences and . . .

MYSTERY, remember! The disappearance of mystery!

KIDDING. Because come ONNN:

JOHNNY KISSED ME!

That is literally the LAST THING any girl would ACTIVELY allow to be an UNSOLVED MYSTERY. And DEFINITELY NOT ME when it comes to you, NJF.

I'm NOT SURE, though, where you draw the line between INFORMATION and TOO MUCH INFORMATION, so how about THIS?

If I were to give Johnny a STAR RATING as a KISSER, it would be . . . a MYSTERY . . . to all but ONE LUCKY GIRL and the FARMER WHO STOLE HER HEART.

THE ONE SHE CALLED: MILLION-STAR JOHNNY.

And if you think that was the end of the night's stardom - NO! Because sweeping into the New Year with a BANG is LOLA DEL MONACO. 'The Resurrection,' she announces, arms in the air, fireworks exploding overhead. It turns out Lola was NOT visiting a sick friend when she flew to LA in the summer; she was going for an audition that she TOTALLY NAILED. And in Things You Couldn't Make Up: the show that LOLA has been cast in is *TERRORS*!

And the BEST PART IS the part. Lola will be playing the role of: HUNTER THREAT'S GRANDMOTHER!

WHO IS A VAGRANT!

She will be spending the first few episodes PUSHING A SHOPPING CART AROUND THE STREETS and HURLING ABUSE at RANDOMERS. NO MAKE-UP. NO GLAMOUR. VASELINE IN HER HAIR. And . . . she LOVES IT! She says it will be LIBERATING.

But we ALL KNOW that by the season finale she'll undergo a MAKEOVER and show up at a BLACK-TIE EVENT involving someone running for political office [no idea] and WE, as the audience, will be expected to FORGET that she was PUSHING-A-SHOPPING-CART/SHOUTING-AT-RANDOMERS-LEVEL UNHINGED in episode one. But we WILL forget because: MAKEOVER.

NON-SADNESS: I AM RELATED TO HUNTER THREAT! QUICKER than I EVER IMAGINED!

SADNESS: I IMAGINED it would be THROUGH MARRIAGE.

Grandpa is processing the return of Lola Del Monaco with the support of a dry stone wall. Then he pats it and goes, 'This has probably seen greater battles for independence,' and Lola ASSURES him he will be coming to LA with her, and Grandpa's got HAVE YOU MET ME EYES and then Lola opens her arms and sashays towards him, Del Monaco-style, and you can SEE Grandpa's SO proud of his girl.

Onlooker Auntie Elaine has drained her glass. And in a BOLD MOVE she flicks at it with her nail to draw our attention her away. Lola is TORN.

'I too have an announcement,' says Auntie Elaine. 'Mother, stop looking at me like all of my announcements will bring shame to the family. This is about Laurie and Ellery. I just got an email from the Winbornes. Apparently Ellery showed them her picture book at the book awards and told them that she loved that there was only one copy of it in the whole world but—'

And I'm like, 'That I'd love it EVEN MORE if there were **MILLIONS OF COPIES!'**

And Auntie Elaine nods and says, 'Ellery Brown, your WISH is their command. Because *Who I Am* by Laurie Brown, with a few tweaks to make it less ELLERY-SPECIFIC, is going to be published NEXT YEAR! Royalties going to your chosen charity!' And then she turns away and adds, 'Oh and I'm back with Gabe.'

I think this whole night was Mom's magic and kind people thinking about calendars attacking and doing whatever they can on the big days and the big nights to add something into the empty space Mom left behind. Like throwing a coin in a wishing well.

And do you want to know what my chosen charity is, NJF? Remember the lovely woman from the plane? Who wanted to pay for my tea and my Kit Kats and gave me tissues? And told me I was doing great? And pretended her hotel was near mine so she could make sure I got there safely? And was head of a children's charity? YES! I tracked her down like the NON-FADED detective I am. Her name is Pia and and the charity is called LITERARY GENIES and it's made up of all kinds of writers – novelists, and poets, and songwriters, and screenwriters, and librettists [no idea] – who donate their time, or their money, or their talent in lots of creative ways, but whatever they decide to do, the end result is that it will help children **ALL OVER THE WORLD**.

Which is *AWESOME*.

Which makes sense.

BECAUSE: Mom, Who You Are is AWESOME. XX

i love my book. and i love you.
For EVER and EVER and EVER.

XXXXX

Mother's Day: LET'S DO THIS

•••••▶ (PART IV)

I Can Do This (Now)

WHO I AM BY LAURIE BROWN

I'm the single star when the sky turns pink

I'm the bubbles that pop in your favourite drink

I'm the brilliant white in your eyeshadow palette

I'm the horse that runs free when you try to corral it

I'm the red on the soles of your favourite shoes

I'm the oranges, yellows, the greens and the blues

I'm the glow from the screen when you're watching TV

And the shine of the sun on your fairy-door key

I'm none of the things that I know you don't like

I'm none of the hills that I know you won't hike

I'm not the burrito that falls on the floor

I'm not the loose knob on your underwear drawer

I'm not the first pancake, I'm not your last chance

I'm not the slow song when you just want to dance

I'm all that you look on that fills up your heart

The all that I know is just really a start

Because life will not stop laying gifts at your feet

So make it your business to make it complete

Make your own magic

Make words your friend:

a story unfolding is never The End.

OMG, NJF! I know I'm supposed to wait until you move into your new home with your fresh sheets but I REALISED: It's NEW YEAR'S DAY. And do you know what that means?

It's OUR ANNIVERSARY, Non-Judgemental Friend.

And I just want to say **THANK YOU FOR ALWAYS BEING THERE FOR ME.**

I get it now. Mom.
Words. I get it.

Acknowledgements

I Acknowledge HarperCollins and All Its Works

Thank you, Charlie Redmayne, Ann-Janine Murtagh, Nick Lake, Rachel Denwood, Samantha Stewart, Hannah Marshall, Megan Reid, Tony Purdue, Ciara Swift and everyone in HarperCollins Children's Books who loved and cared for Ellery Brown from the moment they met her. What a beautiful gift you gave me.

I Acknowledge Eve White Literary Agency and All Its Works

Thank you, Eve White, Ludo Cinelli and Steven Evans who look after my books and the author thereof, with such great care.

I Acknowledge Non-Judgemental Friendship and All Its Works

Thank you, Sue Booth-Forbes, Aideen Brennan, David Browne, Jane Casey, Eoin Colfer, Joe Duffy, David Geraghty, Majella Geraghty, Mary Harrington Causkey, Damian Healy, Ger Holland, Paula Kavanagh, Derek Landy, Jackie Lynam, PJ Lynch, Aoife Marley, Deirdre Miller, Richard McCullough, Eoin McHugh, Jenny Murphy, Liz Nugent, David O'Callaghan, John O'Donnell, Marie O'Halloran, Vanessa O'Loughlin, Sue Swansborough, Julie Sheridan, Ronan Sheridan, Ryan Tubridy, Brian Williams.

I Acknowledge Family and All Its Works

Thank you, Mom, Dad, Ciaran, Melanie, Ronan, Gráinne, Lorraine and Damien.

I Acknowledge the Amazing Children in My Life and All Their Works

To Lily, Abby, Sophie, Emily, Michael, Lucy, Harry, Will, Ben, Max, Emma, Phoebe, Oghie, Eve and Cordy – I've TRIED! But I GIVE UP! I COULD NOT LOVE YOU MORE.

If you were drawn to this title because you've lost someone, or your heart is broken, I know that Ellery would want you to know that writing about it can help, and talking about it to caring people can help, and hugs from caring people can help, and you are definitely not alone.